PRAISE FOR

THE ICE CREAM QUEEN
OF ORCHARD STREET

Finalist for the 2014 National Jewish Book Award,
Outstanding Debut Fiction

"An outstanding fiction debut... Gilman's numerous strengths are showcased, such as character-driven narrative, a ready sense of wit, and a rich historical canvas."

— *Publishers Weekly* (starred review)

"[A] smart, darkly comic story, which is perfect for a summer weekend read... Gilman understands the great sweep of the 20th century, from life in a tenement on Orchard Street, to Italian Communists, Joe McCarthy, McDonald's franchises, suburbanization, and, of course, the history of ice cream in America. She blends it in a delicious swirl, and adds a topical spin."

— Elizabeth Taylor, *Chicago Tribune* (Editor's Choice)

"With a picaresque tone and first person narration reminiscent of Charles Dickens, Gilman's novel is a delightful chronicle of New York history as seen through the eyes of the kind of person who built it and turned it into what it eventually became."

— Popmatters.com

"Polished yet pointed, deceptively cheery but shaded in the sinister—an upside-down, funhouse treat... You'll lick it up."

— *USA Today*

"THE ICE CREAM QUEEN OF ORCHARD STREET is a wonderful read, by turns poignant and wickedly funny. This is the immigrant story updated, with a brazenly re-imagined American anti-hero, and delicious all along the way."
—Kevin Baker, author of *The Big Crowd* and *Paradise Alley*

"Magnificent...[A] fascinating ride through history."
—Bookbrowse.com

"The daughter of Russian Jewish immigrants, raised by Italians on New York's Lower East Side, Lillian Dunkle is the archetypical American heroine, and THE ICE CREAM QUEEN OF ORCHARD STREET is the story of America itself. Brash, brassy, and larger than life, it is a scintillating romp of a book."
—Joshua Henkin, author of *The World Without You*

"With its vivid depictions of old New York City tenement life and its tale of the American ice cream business set against the backdrop of the major events of the 20th century, this rags-to-riches saga will appeal greatly to readers of American historical novels."
—*Library Journal*

"This shrewd and lively novel tells us about those chasms between public success and private truths that make up so much of American life. The energetic narrator, the ice cream queen, is a confidence-woman, and her darkly comic story about life in the big city and in the media spotlight will give readers chills."
—Charles Baxter, author of *The Soul Thief*

"This page-turner of a book is a tart alternative to the usual sweet summer refreshment...The author's research is meticulous.

Gilman's Dickensian description of the Lower East Side of the early-20th century conjures up the intensity of such classics as *The Rise of David Levinsky* or *Call it Sleep*... The historical references are seamlessly woven into the story and add an extra topping to an already delightful tale."

—*The Jewish Week*

"An epic novel about a tough, determined immigrant girl who suffers more than her fair share of licks—but who grows to become the greatest ice cream maker in America."

—*The Missourian*

"A compelling, haunting story of an immigrant... So well written, so rich in detail and such an honest story... Like an ice cream sundae in that it begs to be enjoyed slowly and appreciated for each new taste and texture."

—*Deseret News*

"Gilman mixes two of the world's best creations, ice cream and New York City, with brains, irreverence, panoramic historical research, and a huge heart. Set aside a chunk of time when you scoop this wonderful novel up, because you won't be able to put it back down."

—Anne Korkeakivi, author of *An Unexpected Guest*

"An ambitious and lavish immigrant rags-to-riches-to-rags first novel rife with humor and moxie."

—*Booklist*

"Take an unforgettable female protagonist, the classic immigrant story of the 20th century and a whole lot of ice cream, and you have the perfect summer novel... Lillian is part Tom Carvel, part

Bob McAllister and part Leona Helmsley, and all attitude. This is a very entertaining story and a character you will not soon forget."

—*Montpelier Bridge* (VT)

"Picture a scrappy young immigrant who amasses fame and fortune through bone-grinding labor, canny speculation, and the gift of gab, only to wind up a paranoid alcoholic mired in the trappings of luxury, in trouble with the Feds for tax fraud. You pictured a man, right? Gotcha! This is the genius of THE ICE CREAM QUEEN OF ORCHARD STREET: in a novel that condenses the innocence, the calculation, the hope, and the delusions of twentieth-century America into one figure, Susan Jane Gilman taps a heroine to do the heavy lifting. The scope is broad, the writing is sumptuous, and Lillian Dunkle née Malka Treynovsky leaves Kane and Gatsby in the dust: She's a full-steam-ahead geyser tapped into the American life force itself."

—Ellis Avery, author of *The Teahouse Fire*

The Ice Cream Queen
of Orchard Street

ALSO BY SUSAN JANE GILMAN

The Ice Cream Queen of Orchard Street

A Novel

SUSAN JANE GILMAN

GRAND CENTRAL
PUBLISHING

NEW YORK   BOSTON

Copyright © 2014 by Susan Jane Gilman
Reading Group Guide © 2014 by Hachette Book Group, Inc.

Grand Central Publishing
Hachette Book Group
1290 Avenue of the Americas
New York, NY 10104

www.HachetteBookGroup.com

Printed in the United States of America

RRD-C

Originally published in hardcover by Hachette Book Group.

First trade edition: June 2015

10 9 8 7 6 5 4 3 2

Grand Central Publishing is a division of Hachette Book Group, Inc.
The Grand Central Publishing name and logo are trademarks of Hachette Book Group, Inc.

The Hachette Speakers Bureau provides a wide range of authors for speaking events. To find out more, go to www.hachettespeakersbureau.com or call (866) 376-6591.

The publisher is not responsible for websites (or their content) that are not owned by the publisher.

Library of Congress Cataloging-in-Publication Data

Gilman, Susan Jane.
  The Ice Cream Queen of Orchard Street : a novel / Susan Jane Gilman. — First edition.
      pages cm
  ISBN 978-0-446-57893-6 (hardcover) — ISBN 978-1-61969-652-5 (audio download)—ISBN 978-1-4555-5545-1 (ebook) 1. Celebrities—Fiction.
2. Reminiscing in old age—Fiction. I. Title.
  PS3607.I45214I24 2014
  813'.6—dc23
                                    2013030543

ISBN 978-0-446-69694-4 (pbk.)

for

Steve Blumenthal
&
Frank McCourt

PART ONE

Chapter 1

WE'D BEEN IN AMERICA just three months when the horse ran over me. I don't know exactly how old I was. Six perhaps? When I was born, they didn't keep records. All I remember was running down Hester Street, looking for Papa. Overhead, a bleached sky was flanked by rooftops, iron fire escapes. Pigeons circled, street peddlers shouted, chickens squawked; there was the strange, rickety calliope of the organ-grinder. Great upheavals of dust swirled around the pushcarts, making the shop signs swing back and forth like flags. I heard a clop, then I was tumbling. There was a split-second flash of hoof, then a white-hot bolt of pain. Then: nothing.

The horse that trampled me was pulling a penny-ices cart. What a peculiar twist of fate that turned out to be, no? If I'd been crippled by, say, a rag man or a coal vendor, I would never have become Lillian Dunkle, as the world knows her today. Certainly, I would never have become a legend at all.

The public, however, always assumes that my fortunes are due solely to my husband. Oh, how the media hates its queens. How it begrudges us! That horrible photograph the newspapers keep running now—the one that makes me look like Joan Crawford getting an enema—is all the proof you need. So quick they are to judge!

But let me tell you, darlings: the Wonder Tundra, with chocolate chips, rainbow sprinkles, M&M's, or chopped peanuts mixed in to order. Our signature novelty cake, the Nilla Rilla, molded into the shape of our trademark cartoon monkey, coated in shaved coconut with the secret cookie-crunch layer inside. We'd first marketed this for birthdays and Father's Day, but do you realize how many of you ordered versions of this for your weddings? We did one custom cake for a reception out in Syosset that fed 215 people. It would've made the Guinness Book of World Records if Bert had remembered the goddamn camera.

The Tower of Sprinkles. The Mint Everest. The Fudgie Puppie. All of these—*all of these*, millions sold every year—were my concoctions, my ideas. In our heyday we had 302 stores nationwide. We revolutionized production, franchising, marketing. You think this was an accident? President Dwight D. Eisenhower himself once christened me "The Ice Cream Queen of America." I have the signed photograph of us (with Mamie, of course—all pearls and bad teeth) shaking hands in the Rose Garden. I'm wearing my first-ever Chanel suit, too, very nearly the color of strawberry ice cream. (And this was years before Jackie Kennedy, thank you!) Today I have no fewer than three dozen engraved plaques, trophies, ribbons. A cut-glass bowl. Even a ghastly pewter commemorative ashtray—how I'd love to give it away, except what do you do with something with your name on it from the Children's Association for Diabetes Research, for God's sake? Plus an entire wall of certificates—from the North Carolina Chamber of Commerce. The American Dairy Association. Dow Chemical. Even the Institute of the Maharishi Mahesh Yogi in Rishikesh, India. Yogis love ice cream, apparently. Who knew?

Yet when people hear my name now, all they think of are sordid headlines. A single incident on live television. Claims of tax evasion and an arrest—wrongful, too, need I remind you? Unfunny jokes on Johnny Carson, that *schlemiel*. You want funny? Please. I know from funny.

Just yesterday my grandson informed me that I'm even an answer in the latest edition of Trivial Pursuit. "Wow, Grandma, how awesome is that?" he said. Live long enough, I suppose, you see everything. But it's a witch-hunt. WPIX was only a local station, for God's sake. And we aired at 7:00 A.M. on a Sunday—a Sunday! And maybe I *had* had a few drinks. But darlings, *you* try hosting a kiddie show for thirteen goddamn years.

But, oh. I'm getting ahead of myself.

Let me start back at the beginning, before satellite trucks were parked across the street, blocking my driveway. Before our "Sundaes on Saturdays" campaign, the Mocktail Milkshakes, and Spreckles the Clown. I'll begin on the sweltering Lower East Side of Manhattan, with the peddler with the horse-drawn cart: A rotund, sweating man. Salvatore Dinello. His last name was stenciled on the side of his wagon in flaking red and gold paint. DINELLO'S ICES. He was the last of his kind, really. Most other vendors had already started working for wholesalers by then. Mr. Dinello wore a slouch cap and a brown canvas smock. Instead of shouting like the other hawkers, he sang. "I-SEES, I-SEES." Like an aria. Oh, it was marvelous. I could hear his baritone all the way down Hester Street, above the incredible din.

Dinello's Ices came in lemon and sometimes cherry. They had the consistency of snow. Once, when Flora and I were supposed to be fetching dinner, I bought a scoop for us instead. We devoured it—cherry, I remember—and our mouths turned lurid, candy red. It was delicious. It was a delirium. But immediately afterward—oh, such guilt we felt! That two cents was supposed to go for a potato. From then on, I tried to keep my distance.

But whenever we were on Hester Street, I'd watch longingly as Mr. Dinello scooped a small, glittering mound into his tiny glass cup for a customer. The customer licked the cup clean, then handed it back to Mr. Dinello, who rinsed it out in a zinc pail dangling from the back of his wagon. He used the same cup for each person. That's just how it was back then.

Our family didn't have a penny when we stepped off the boat. But whose did? The people who arrived in America with money, their stories aren't interesting. So your eldest brother, Lord Such-and-Such, inherited the family estate, and you, Poor Thing, had to make your fortune in the New World instead? Please. Don't even bother me with that.

At the time of my accident, we were living in a tenement on Orchard Street, on the fourth floor in the back. We paid a tailor named Mr. Lefkowitz two dollars a week to let us sleep in his parlor. Mama took cushions from the settee and spread them across a pair of creaky wooden crates. During the day she worked for Mr. Lefkowitz cutting patterns with two other women in the front room in a cloud of airborne fibers.

When he wasn't in the streets himself, Papa worked for Mr. Lefkowitz, too. He pressed shirts with a heavy iron heated up on the stove in the kitchen. When the hot metal hissed against the cotton, it smelled like burnt vanilla. I loved that smell. Years later I tried to re-create it in our laboratory.

My parents worked within seven feet of each other. And yet, they weren't speaking.

Their plan, you see, hadn't been to go to America at all.

The night we fled our little village of Vishnev, my mother stitched two hundred rubles into the lining of my coat. Some of it she'd saved herself; the rest had been sent by her brother, my Uncle

Hyram, from South Africa. A little secret pocket Mama fashioned, just below my armpit. She jabbed herself with the needle twice, her hands shook so. Too many stories we had heard, of families transported in a wagon, only to be robbed, dumped at a roadside, left for the Cossacks. The week before our departure, Mama refused to have my sisters and me wash either, lest we look too enticing. My gray, boiled-wool overcoat had been Bella's first, then Rose's, then Flora's. (Only Samuel, when he was alive, apparently got new clothes.) The wool was so thin it was a coat more in theory than in practice. "Who would give such rags a second look?" my mother reasoned. "Who would frisk a tiny child with a *punim* like yours?"

I was the baby of the family, the youngest child in our entire shtetl. I was born after the mobs had retreated, after the ransacked houses had been boarded up, after the shards of bubbled, broken glass had been swept away and the bloodstains scrubbed from floorboards with vinegar. While others moved about Vishnev in a ghostly state of shock, I disrupted the silence as only a happy, oblivious child can.

I pirouetted and hollered and laughed, forgetting to cover my mouth the way Mama instructed. As I wandered about our yard, I sang meandering little songs to myself that I made up. Notes rose in my mouth like carbonation: "The Frog in the Well" and "I Love Chicken" are two I remember. I simply had to sing. It was like swinging my legs when I sat on a stool.

And so sue me: I was curious.

"Mama, why is our barn burned?" I'd ask in a clear voice. "Why is Sol missing an arm?" "How come Etta doesn't have any parents?"

My mother was a buxom woman with a hawkish, ravaged face. Much of her hair had turned gray years before its time. "This is from you," she'd say, pointing to each strand. Her hands were rawboned and enormous. They pounded out dough for kreplach and yanked the bloody feathers off unyielding chickens. They hauled basins of water from the well and scrubbed first my sisters and me, then our clothes, then our linens, into a vicious state of purity every Friday afternoon.

Within a second these hands reached over and gave me such a wallop as I had ever known. Soon, it seemed, almost every time I opened my mouth, they were arriving in a clop on my ear or with a *thwuck!* on my backside, accompanied by, "I said, 'That's enough,' Malka." Or "Don't be such a wisenheimer, Malka." Or simply, "Oy! You!" At synagogue on Fridays, Mama frowned to the other women. "The *mouth* on that one," she clucked, motioning in my direction. "It's going to cause us nothing but *tsuris.*"

Of our journey out of Russia I remember very little, except lying beneath a pile of cabbages in a wagon. Mama had packed me into the sad gray wool coat as if it were a suit of armor. "Anybody lays a hand on your pocket, I want you to give such a *geschrei* as they have never heard, *bubeleh.* Don't let anyone near this coat, not even Papa, you understand?"

I nodded. My mother rarely called me *bubeleh.* I felt inordinately special, but a moment later, when she had finished adjusting my collar, she frowned. "With a face like yours, no one may ever marry you," she said. "But at least you can put that big mouth to some use."

Men with lanterns at checkpoints ordered us around in furious whispers. Robbers and Cossacks were waiting at every turn to leap out from the woods, I imagined, and I clutched my coat tightly around me all day, while in my head I practiced giving such a *geschrei* as the world had ever heard. But with our family's entire meager fortune tucked beneath my armpit, the truth was, I didn't dare sing or hum or even speak out loud at all.

When we finally arrived in Hamburg—days, perhaps weeks later—we waited on benches at the Hilfsverein's processing center. I have a vague memory of dormitories, of endless, dismal corridors. Penned-in chaos. Anxiety. And oh, the human stink! Everyone acting like beggars and handled as such. Let me tell you: I know some dairy cows in Vermont these days who receive better treatment. Don't get me started.

One afternoon my father returned to the bench with a piece of paper that had been stamped many times. "Come," my mother ordered. Marching me into the privy, she latched the door. The stench was unbearable. "Arms out." As she peeled me out of my scratchy, dust-caked coat, she felt around. The rubles were no longer there. Someone had robbed me in my sleep.

But Mama reached deeper into the lining and finally dug out the damp, creased bills. As she counted and recounted them, I exhaled proudly.

"What?" She shot me a look. "You want I should applaud the sun each day for rising?"

She unlocked the door and motioned in toward the courtyard. Other children's shrieks of laughter could be heard. "Go." She sighed. "Raise all the ruckus you want now."

Our plan was to sail to Cape Town. Uncle Hyram ran a dry-goods store in the Transvaal with some cousins from Vilnius. He was apparently a very religious man, Uncle Hyram. Before the pogroms he'd been studying to become a rabbi. I'd never met him, but Bella said he smelled like boiled onions and Rose said he had a tic by his left eye that made you think he was winking at you all the time. Papa didn't seem to care for him much. He referred to him as "that *shmendrik*." But Uncle Hyram wrote letters and dutifully sent money. *"Come to South Africa. G-d willing, we can employ you as a bookkeeper, Tillie as a clerk. There's opportunity enough."*

Cape Town, Cape Town—the name played in my head. Today you have atlases and televisions and libraries. But when I was small, nobody in our shtetl had a globe or a map. None of my sisters had schoolbooks. Where was this "South Africa"? No one knew. When my family went to the shipping office with our paperwork and our life savings—our precious rubles and rands exchanged at exorbitant rates for German marks—those Prussian *gonifs*, Mama swore—a man on line took us over to a giant, faded map tacked to the wall. This was my first glimpse of the bigger world: an arrangement of squiggles and blobs, grubby with the fingerprints of thousands of salesclerks and immigrants. Pale blue was an "ocean," light pink was "land." "Nations" were outlined in lime green. The man pointed to a faded red star smack in the center of the map. "That's Hamburg," he explained. Then he swung his finger down to a tiny black bull's-eye way at the very bottom. "And there's your Cape Town."

"Is that where you're going?" Papa asked.

The man seemed taken aback. "Oh, no. I'm going to America," he said with a tinge of pride. He pointed to a dot that appeared to be even farther away than South Africa but on a par with Hamburg. "Milwaukee."

America: *Milwaukee. New York. Pittsburgh. Chicago.* From the moment we'd arrived at the processing center, we'd been hearing these names spoken with a religious reverence. *Ah-MEH-rih-kah.* "The *goldene medina,*" some Jews called it, nattering on rapturously about twenty-four-karat paving stones, its rivers of milk and honey. The steamship companies themselves put up great advertisements showing lavish parties on board their ships carrying passengers toward an American flag unfurling above a waterfall of gold coins. Leaflets were circulated. Everyone but us, it seemed, was going to this *Ah-MEH-rih-kah*. "They give you free land," someone said. "My sister writes me that there are trees that rain apples," said another. "She lives in a place called Connecticut."

"You step off the boat and they hire you on the spot," another informed us. "One year and you're rich."

My mother, however, dismissed this all as just so much nonsense and wishful thinking. "These *meshuggenehs*, what do they know?" she clucked. "Since when does anybody not have to work? They are like idiots in love."

Six tickets for Cape Town were purchased, folded, and carefully tucked back into the secret little pocket in the lining of my coat. I had become our family's wallet.

Cape Town, Cape Town.

Three days before we were to sail, my sister Rose woke up crying. Rose, in my esteem, was a kvetch. Pale and trembling, she was always moaning about her nervous stomach, her sun rashes, her delicate constitution. She was older than me and pretty like a china cup: I didn't understand why she couldn't just stop hogging all the attention all the time. "Mama," she sobbed, twisting her head around in a panic. "I can't see. It's all blurry."

Within hours Bella, Flora, and my mother couldn't open their eyes either. They tried to hide it by pretending they were cold and pulling their shawls down low over their foreheads, but their pink, runny eyelids were oozing with glittery crust. They squinted and stumbled about miserably. Rose moaned. Flora wept. Other émigrés at the center quickly moved away from us on the benches, giving us a wide berth. Perhaps somebody tattled; I wouldn't put it past them. Immigration officials appeared. In an instant my mother and sisters were whisked away into quarantine. "Conjunctivitis," the doctor explained. Our names were stricken from the ship's manifest. "All peoples with contagious illnesses are barred from boarding," the clerk informed my father. "You should know better."

My father stared at him. "But what are we supposed to do?" he said. "Six fares. They cost us all that we had."

"As soon as your family is better, you can exchange your tickets, Mr. Treynovsky. Other ships sail for Cape Town later in the season. Until then"—the clerk pointed back toward the crowded benches—"you wait."

"How long?" my father asked desperately.

The man shrugged.

Papa could only find a little place for us on the floor by the wall. We each sat down heavily in the grime, my father and I. He chewed on his bottom lip and stared straight ahead. I knew for a fact we had only a few marks left, barely enough for a week's worth of food. It was there in my little pocket, along with our tickets.

"Papa," I asked, "how long till Mama gets better?"

He gave a start. Whenever I called him "Papa," he looked surprised. With four girls in his house, he often seemed to have trouble placing me. In Vishnev, from what I understood, Papa had been a peddler of sorts—a trader, a junk man, always bartering goods from one town to another. There was never the same thing in his cart: One week he'd have kettles, then perhaps cucumbers, then fleece. Often he was gone for weeks at a time. He'd been absent for my birth. He had also been away during the pogrom. This no doubt saved his life. However, during their many arguments, my mother was always quick to shout, her voice palsied with recrimination and fury: Had he been home, he might've saved my grandfather. Had he been there to defend us, perhaps our barn wouldn't have been burned to the ground. How was she supposed to protect a family all by herself? she wanted to know. In fact, she often insisted, as her hysteria mounted, if my father stayed home a bit more, perhaps she'd have had another son instead of four useless daughters. "Look around you—nothing but four mouths to feed and marry off," she'd cried. "But what do you expect, with you hardly here? How could a boy baby possibly take root?"

Since the day she was married, apparently, my mother had been harvesting grievances; it was like a dowry in reverse. Hearing her litanies of woe, my father just threw up his hands and sighed. "What do you want me to do, Tillie? Do I look like God?"

Now, as I sat beside my father at the detention center, he was like a work of art to me. I'd never seen him in broad daylight before, quite so close up. Throughout the Russian Pale, Papa had been known as an extremely handsome man. The bones of his face, I saw, were strong and pleasingly symmetrical, his eyelashes as long as petals. As I studied him, he seemed to breathe with his whole body. The solid, muscular presence of him in his dark jacket, with his thick, ginger hair curling out from beneath his hat, awed me. My papa. I had never had him all to myself.

I tugged on his coat. "Papa? Will Mama and Rose go blind? Will Flora and Bella?"

Sighing, he shook his head.

"What's it like to be blind, Papa?" I asked, the words warming in my mouth. "If a person is blind, can they still eat? With a spoon, or only with their hands? Are they allowed to have soup?"

He gave a mirthless little laugh, then unfolded himself and stood up. His dark, storm-gray eyes darted about. Papa was too restless for his own good, Mama often complained. Even at the Sabbath table he jiggled his leg, drummed his fingers on the table-top. While other fathers could remain hunched over the Torah for hours, Papa studied for only a few minutes before abandoning it and heading out, looking for something to fix, something to trade. Unlike most of the men from Vishnev, he wore his beard clipped close to his face, his hat pushed back rakishly.

Now, stretching, he surveyed the chaos of the detention

center—with its crying babies and scolding women—and let out
a long, low whistle.

"*Kindeleh*," he said, not to me but to the air above my head,
"what do you say you and I, we take a walk?"

He held out his hand. Its calluses were smooth, like peeled almonds. "Let's go explore, yes?" To my great delight, he winked.

We set out together, my father and I: he in his black coat
and the dark saucer of his hat, I tiny beside him, a small child
dressed the way all children dressed in those days—like miniature
adults—in a long frayed skirt, a little hand-crocheted shawl, my
horrid gray coat.

Together we stepped into the leafy streets of what was then a
jewel of the German Empire, the third-largest port in the world.

Hamburg was laced with canals and ornate lakeside cafés. Its
delicate spires pierced the sky like hatpins. Half-timbered houses
stood four stories high, crimson geraniums cascading from their
rippled windows. Oh, what a beautiful waste!

We happened upon a square, a garden fenced with wrought-
iron lace, a fountain bedecked with angels, arcaded buildings. Of
course I had never, ever seen anything remotely like this before.
For all his travels, neither had Papa. Until we arrived in Hamburg, no one in our family had so much as seen an indoor toilet,
a streetcar, an electric light. Even the synagogue back in our shtetl
had been lit only with candles and lanterns.

Papa and I stood in the middle of Hamburg's Neustadt quarter.
"That's something, eh?" he said, staring up at the tower of the
Rathaus.

Using the tower as a sort of compass needle, he led us from
Strasse to *Strasse*. "Papa, look." We marveled before the windows
of the *Konditorei* and *Bäckerei*; at shops selling fabrics, soaps, ointments; at shelves of porcelain dishes filled with peppermints and
glazed fruits. My world, suddenly, had gone to color. On a wide

boulevard stood a magnificent entranceway. Bright pictures hung on either side. Papa stopped and pushed his hat back on his head.

"Who builds a thing like this?" he wondered. Of course, we could not understand the signs or the language above the marquee. But Papa and I, we grasped their enticement, the visual invitation, the temptation they presented. It was late in the afternoon. A windowed booth stood stationed beneath the marquee, yet it was unmanned. Beside it, a door was propped open with a bit of brick. "Can I?" I whispered.

Guiding me by the shoulders, Papa pushed me inside.

We found ourselves in a grand red velvet foyer. From behind a tall curtain came music. There was an implicit hush. I took a tentative step through the slice of velvet. We were at the back of a hall as dark as a tunnel, filled with lazy white curlicues of smoke. On the wall opposite, two people were dancing in jiggly, lint-flecked black and white; they were alive but not alive—the culmination of a long, bright beam of dust. I was just old enough to know that what I was seeing was a picture but not a picture. It was wholly animated with light and velocity. I squeezed Papa's hand. A vast new world within a world flickered before us. I stood in astonishment as two strangers in the most dazzling, unusual clothes waltzed through drawing rooms full of armchairs with antimacassars, curvaceous electric lamps, a voluptuous grand piano. A sylphlike lady with dark lips and a glittering gown swooned on a couch. Instantly, I wanted to be her.

A strange, heavy palm landed on my shoulder just then, and a man began whispering to Papa in a hiss of anger. Whatever he was saying needed no translation. "Pfft!" My father laughed dismissively. But he grabbed my hand and pulled me quickly back out onto the street. "Dirty *scheygitz*," he swore, tossing the end of his cigarette into the gutter. Until that moment, I hadn't known that my father smoked. "Ah, but so what?" As he ground out the

butt with his foot, he winked at me with a delicious look of con-
spiracy. "We got to see plenty, didn't we, *kindeleh?*"

Back at the immigration hostel, Papa described what we'd seen
to the other men. Since I was too little to be left on my own,
he'd smuggled me into the men's dormitory. He placed me on his
mat in the corner, where everyone promptly forgot about me. It
was a bit like being in synagogue. Most of the men in the room
kept their hats and yarmulkes on and bowed over prayer books.
Some sat propped against the wall with their eyes shut. But Papa
had a coterie of friends who seemed to have carved out a special
club for themselves in the back. Their hats and jackets lay flung
about. Pale tobacco smoke filled the air. Men were dealing cards
and passing around a flask. Papa sat on a stool with his legs splayed
out, his collar unbuttoned, his shirtsleeves rolled up. He was far
livelier than he ever was at home—commanding, jovial—sitting
in the center of the men like a little czar, slapping some of them
on the back, doling out cigarettes, kibitzing with all of them.

"What you saw today, that was a 'moving picture,'" a heavyset
man said. He had pockmarked cheeks, and every time he slapped
one of his cards down on a stool, the flesh of his jowls shook.
The air around him smelled of wet wool, smoke, rotting onions.
"These moving pictures, they come from America."

"Keep watching them, Herschel," a scrawny man said, patting
my father on the back. "In three weeks' time, I'll be in one of
them."

Papa hooted.

"What?" The scrawny man insisted, "You think I'm going to
America to keep being a tailor? You can be anything you want
there."

"Not a lot of moving pictures in Africa, from what I hear,

Hersch." The pockmarked man grinned. "What kind of Jew goes from Russia to Africa, I'd like to know. It's not enough we spent forty years wandering in the desert already? You want you should go back for forty more?"

"The Cossacks aren't enough for you, Hersch?" teased another man in a torn brown coat.

My father leaped up, kicked aside his chair, and motioned to him. "Okay, Yossi, you big *macher*." Papa rolled up his sleeves and stood in a pose with his hands cocked, beckoning. "Friends." He grinned magnanimously. "Who wants to bet?"

The men laughed nonchalantly. My father lunged forward and began pummeling Yossi. There was a violent explosion of shouting, cheering. Stools fell over. I saw Papa wallop someone in the head, then the man in the brown coat lock his elbow around Papa's neck.

"Papa!" I shrieked.

The men stopped and turned to me.

"Stop! Don't hurt my papa!"

All of them, including Papa, burst out laughing. I started to cry.

"Oy, you've scared the child," someone said. "Very nice, you two."

The man in the torn brown coat released Papa and took a step back. "Saved by your little girl, Hersch. Lucky schmuck."

Papa looked at me. "We're just playing, *kindeleh*."

Tears were running down my face. "Papa," I wailed. "I don't want you to die!"

He gave a little incredulous laugh. "No one's dying."

When I wouldn't stop crying, he shook his head. "Ach. Come here." I was reluctant to approach him in the midst of all the big, ungainly men, but Papa held out his arms. He knelt down and rumpled my hair. His embrace felt marvelous.

Motioning for the flask, he took a swig, then wiped his mouth on the back of his wrist. He grabbed my right hand firmly in his. "Make a fist," he ordered.

Somebody laughed. The men were in a semicircle around us. A few of them had rotting teeth, breath like sour cabbage. I tried to ignore their gaze.

"Tighter," Papa instructed. "Like a rock. Okay. Good. Now the other one, too. Very good. Now hold them like this." Reaching out, he adjusted me in a pose, with my fists held up close to my chest.

"Take a step out with that leg, so that your weight is more balanced." Papa held up his palm. "Now, when I count to three, punch my hand with your right. As hard as you can, okay? Thrust from the shoulder, not your wrist, you see?" He demonstrated with his own fist. "Like this."

I looked at him dubiously, then down at my fist, curled, snail-like. "It won't hurt?"

My father grinned, shook his head. "As hard as you can." The man in the brown coat chuckled. I tried to envision my fist going hard into Papa's palm. I tried to remember to thrust from the shoulder. I prayed it wouldn't hurt. "One. Two. Three," Papa said.

I punched his hand as hard as I could. It made a tiny clapping sound. "*Ai!*" someone said, though the punch didn't seem to have any effect on my father at all.

"Again," Papa commanded. "Harder."

"What are you doing, Hersch?"

"Shush," Papa said. "Why shouldn't she know? Again," he ordered.

I punched again.

"Harder."

Papa held up his other hand. "Now punch with your left." I punched with my left.

"Now your right."

I punched with my right. I did as I was told. Each time I swung, the sound of the blow grew a little louder.

Soon a couple of men were chanting along with Papa—"Right! Left! Right! Left! Right!"—and I was punching Papa's palm as fast and as hard as I could. My face grew hot, and I burned inside my coat, but I kept swinging. I felt strong. I felt bigger, as if my arms and fists themselves were swelling into little hammers. With each punch my father beamed, as if my blows were infusing him with oxygen, making his internal light burn brighter. "That's a girl," he laughed. His attention, it felt like liquid love, like apples and honey pouring down on me. The man with the pockmarked face put his fingers in his mouth and whistled. Some of the men sat back heavily, watching, passing around the flask.

"Quite a spiel, enh? Herschel's got himself a little fighting *maideleh*."

"Hersch, she's a natural."

"Not like her father!"

"Give her a few years," Papa chortled. "She'll have all of you schmucks on the ropes!" But as he said this, he turned to grin at the men. For just a moment, he forgot to keep his palm up. My punch landed right on the side of his jaw with a *thwock!*

"Ouch!" he cried. Oh, I was mortified. But the men chuckled. Papa staggered up and raised my little fist in the air. "Okay. Enough." He took a swallow from the flask. "Who wants to place a bet?" He squeezed me tightly. His breath smelled sweet and smoky. "Who wants to go up against her next?"

He swung me over his shoulder. The room spun with color and noise.

"Take her to America, Hersch," someone said. "Put her in those moving pictures you saw."

"Nah, if you're going to Africa, keep her for yourself. You're going to need her, Hersch. For protection."

The next morning, however, Papa was oddly quiet. In the dining hall, all the émigrés sat at a table. For breakfast we were given a chunk of bread. If you were a child like me, you also got half a cup of warm milk. Papa and I squeezed in along the wobbling bench.

"Oh, the streets in America," someone was saying excitedly. "My brother-in-law writes that they are like you have never seen, with shining gold towers that reach into the sky, as ornate as To-rah scrolls!"

"They say that in the squares there are fountains that you can drink from—not just water but milk!"

"Every day, people in America, they eat big pots of beef stewed with carrots and dill swimming in broth!"

Neither Papa nor I said anything. As I chewed, I kept thinking about the woman in the dark, glittering dress I'd seen dancing on the wall—imagining that I was her. I thought of the shops we'd passed filled with porcelain and silks, the apothecaries with their glistening jars of peppermints and hair pomades, the red vel-vet theater with its filigreed balustrades and gilt doorway. Then I thought about Mama and Papa and me and my three sisters, wan-dering in the desert for forty years.

Papa barely paid me any mind. He kept drumming his fingers on the table and glancing around distractedly. As soon as I was done with my milk, he took the tin cup from my hand and set it brusquely on the table. "Stay here and behave yourself," he or-dered. "Papa will be back shortly."

"Be back shortly" turned into three hours, then four. I played games with some of the other children in the courtyard until their mothers realized that I was the little girl whose family was in quarantine. Then I sat on a bench and sang to myself. I made up a song called "Waiting on the Bench." When Papa finally returned, it was nearly dinnertime.

This happened the next day, and the next. I grew restless. Cranky.

Finally Papa said to me after breakfast, "Today, you come with me on another walk. Yes? I have some special business."

As we stepped back into the majestic streets of Hamburg, he walked so quickly it was as if he'd forgotten I was beside him. I had to struggle to keep up. A few times I stumbled in my worn, ill-fitting shoes. As we hurried, Papa kept scanning the storefronts, checking a little piece of paper clutched in his hand. I barely had time to look at the chemist's, the butcher's, the bakery. When we passed the shop with the windows full of peppermints, I pleaded with him to stop.

"We don't have time," he snapped. Yet then he seemed to reconsider. Pivoting around, he knelt down and looked me straight in the eye. "Malka. How would you like a little sweet for the mouth?"

The prospect was so tantalizing, I could only gulp in a mouthful of air.

We entered the shop the way we would enter a temple. The air was fragrant with a baked, buttery sweetness that made me lightheaded with deliciousness. An ornate glass case ran the length of the store. Heaps of chocolaty gems were displayed inside on silver trays. Some had walnuts nestled in them, some were molded into decorative cameos, ovals, and glistening, beveled squares. Quivering half-moons of brilliant red, green, and orange jelly sparkled with sugar beside little frosted pink and brown cakes layered with jam. I was transfixed. The woman behind the counter eyed us narrowly.

"What would you like, *kindeleh*?" my father said.

I looked from the display case to Papa. "I can have anything?"

The counterwoman sniffed audibly, her mouth bracketing with disapproval.

"Anything." Pointedly, Papa ignored the woman. "You choose."

The decision was delicious agony. My fingers skated from one confection to another. Finally, nearly dizzy with possibilities—and sensing Papa's growing impatience—I settled on the biggest piece I could find, a dark brown, braided block. Papa held up his finger and nodded at the woman.

Reaching in with a pair of silver tongs, she lifted the bar out of the case and wrapped it crisply in filmy white paper. Only then, as she walked over to an ornate machine at the end of the counter, pushed several keys, and announced *"Funf"* did it occur to me that we needed to pay.

Before I could ask Papa what we should do, he knelt down, pulled off his tattered shoe, and removed a damp bill from its insole. He handed the money to the woman as if this were the most natural thing in the world. In return she gave him the little bar and a handful of coins though her eyes, fixed on him, were like bullets.

"Come, *kindeleh*," Papa said quickly.

As he hustled me out of the shop, I said, "Papa, you found more money?"

"Your papa always finds more money," he said pridefully. "As long as there's cards." Unwrapping the chocolate bar, he handed it to me. "Now, eat."

The coating was thin, and when I bit into it, the shell cracked. Sweet red jam oozed through, sticking to the roof of my mouth. I had no idea what I was eating, but it was miraculous. And I was so hungry.

For a moment, Papa watched me indulgently. Then he cleared

his throat. "So you and I, Malka, we have a few secrets now, enh?" He grinned.

My mouth was full, but I nodded vigorously. It was not lost on me that only I had been allowed to walk through the streets of Hamburg with him. Only I had been allowed to sleep in the men's dorm wrapped in his coat. Only I had been taught to throw a punch and been given a sweet to eat—none of my sisters. And the money in Papa's shoe: I sensed that this, too, was a secret. I felt anointed.

But then I recalled my mother scolding Bella and Rose for whispering at the dinner table.

"Mama says secrets are bad," I informed him. "She says that if you can't say something to everybody, you probably have no business saying it at all."

Papa frowned. "True," he said carefully, "but sometimes, *kindeleh,* doesn't Mama also tell you that *some* things are best kept to yourself? That good little girls should *keep quiet* when they're asked?"

I considered this. Slowly, I nodded. How I wanted to agree with him, to preserve my sense of being prized. "She says I'm not very quiet. She says the mouth on me is going to cause nothing but *tsuris.*"

My father threw his head back and laughed. "Okay, then. Can we agree then, that with me, your papa, you are going to be a very good little girl? That you're going to make a special effort and keep all of our secrets?"

He squeezed my hand. I had finished my chocolate, and the end of it was a sort of grief. But in the beam of his attention, oh, I felt like blossoms. "Yes, Papa," I said.

We walked past warehouses toward the port. Suddenly, Papa stopped and squinted out across the harbor. "Do you know what a *shmendrik* is, Malka?"

Yet he did not wait for my response. "Sometimes," he exhaled, "a person has to think for himself."

Inside a drafty hall by the pier, men sat behind little barred windows and stabbed squares of paper onto spindles. The great room was far larger than the detention center, yet nearly as chaotic. One wall was plastered with pictures of ships with different-colored flags spread behind them. Papa looked at the paper in his hand, then steered us over to a long line. "I have some important business," he said. "You stay close."

We waited. And waited. I was getting very good at this. "Important business" in those days was the concern of grown men only, and it held no interest. I sang to myself and imagined myself waltzing in a glittering dress. When that little fantasy was exhausted, I made up a game in which I picked out patterns in the floor tiles and tapped on them with my toes. Finally, when we were almost at the front of the line, my father knelt down. His dark gray eyes were exactly level with mine.

"Now, *kindeleh*, I need you to do me a big favor." Gingerly, he began to unbutton my coat. He ran his hand along my sleeve and felt for my hidden pocket.

I gave a little cry.

Papa smiled at me intensely. "Why the noise, *kindeleh*?" he said softly. "Didn't we agree that you were going to be a good girl?"

He smiled at me so hard it seemed as if his face would crack.

"But Mama—"

"It's okay." He glanced around the hall. "Mama is sick, right? She is in quarantine, yes? Well, I have to replace our tickets. The ones for South Africa are no good anymore. So I want us to do this as our secret. As a surprise. To help make her feel better."

"A surprise?"

Papa nodded rigorously and cupped my face firmly between his hands, as if to steady me, and gave me a violent kiss on my forehead. Then he quickly resumed fumbling with my coat buttons.

My lips started to tremble. "Papa, no!" I cried, taking a step back. "No! Stop! I don't want to! Don't make me!"

He glared at me. "Shush, shush!" he fairly spit, his face growing livid. "Listen to me, Malka!"

But I couldn't help it. I stomped my feet and flailed and wriggled and cried, "I don't want to wander forty years in the desert! I don't want to go to the bottom of the map!" I wailed, "I don't want to go to Africa! I want to go to America! I want to be with the moving pictures!"

My father froze. For a moment I was sure he was going to give me such a wallop as I had never felt. But instead he regarded me slowly, with a sort of delighted amazement.

"Do you, now, *kindeleh*?" he said. "Well, then." Exhaling, he reached out, rumpled my hair, and drew me toward him. He gave me another loud, wet kiss on the forehead. "Then it just so happens," he said, "that this is exactly what you and I are going to do."

For days, the new tickets burned like six little coals in the secret pocket of my coat. Oh, how I wanted to tell Mama! The minute she and my sisters were released from quarantine, it became agony. Every night I lay beside my sisters, imagining Mama's delight when we finally boarded the ship and Papa and I announced that we were going to America instead. I tingled with the thrill of it— it would be like Purim! I didn't think I could keep quiet, but anytime I looked at Papa, he gave me his special wink and brought a finger to his lips. Even if I so much as hinted, he warned me, it would ruin the surprise utterly.

And so I continued to wear my gray coat all day long and to

bed at night. But it was my silence that raised suspicion, not my words. "What's wrong with you? You're too quiet," Mama said with a frown one night, touching the back of her palm to my forehead. "Don't tell me you're getting sick now. That's all that we need."

When Mama asked Papa if they shouldn't exchange the old tickets to Cape Town for the next steamer to Africa, Papa informed her that he'd already gone ahead and done just that. For one heart-stopping moment, Mama looked at him darkly.

"Oh," she said tightly. "And how much did that cost you? I suppose you had to go ahead and spend the rest of the money as well?"

Papa gave her a severe, wounded look. "What? You don't trust your own husband to make a simple exchange? Steerage on one ship costs the same as another, Tillie."

He hadn't spent any of the remaining marks, he insisted, beyond what we'd needed for food, of course. And if she didn't believe him, so help him God, she could see for herself. "Malka," Papa called out, motioning me over. "Please. Take off your coat. Show Mama the money we have left."

When he said this, my father appeared perfectly at ease—so at ease, in fact, that I wondered for a moment if he'd forgotten about the new tickets altogether. My heart beat furiously. But before I could undo the first button of my coat, Mama waved me away.

"Fine, okay, I believe you," she said wearily.

But I needn't have worried. You see, my mother could do and survive many things: She'd had seven children, ripped from her loins on a burlap mattress beneath the spastic flame of a kerosene lamp—two of the babies stillborn—and the last one, me, nearly bleeding her to death.... She could till the potato fields that remained hard as a fist and yielded little all year.... She could pay bribes to keep my brother, Samuel, out of the Russian army for another year, only to have him die of influenza.... She could give birth to me after the pogrom that my father insisted would never happen—in which she saw her own father beaten to death, blood and teeth spraying from his mouth like water as two soldiers batted at him with the butts of their rifles while he writhed on the floor—the crowd outside torching our forlorn barn and cheering as she hid with my siblings, petrified, in a neighbor's chicken coop.... She could help my father arrange for counterfeit papers, and she could endure the nighttime ride across checkpoints hidden in a cart beneath piles of rotting cabbages with her hand clamped over my little mouth.... She could look piously, then flirtatiously, then pleadingly, at the smug officials at the immigration office as they yawned and cracked their knuckles and cleaned their fingernails with pocketknives while she and a hundred other immigrants accumulated beseechingly in a line before them, hour after hour. After finally—finally!—getting all the necessary forms and stamps and signatures and approvals, she could nurse herself and three daughters through conjunctivitis in a cold infirmary in a foreign city that was understaffed and overextended and utterly indifferent. She could even calculate on the side of a paper bag how much the money changers had cheated us in exchanging our precious rubles and rands for German marks. She could do a multitude of things, my mother, and bravely so. But she could not tell the simple difference between a boat ticket for South Africa and one to the United States. Because my mother, of course, could not read.

Chapter 2

IN THE MANY INTERVIEWS I've given over the years, I've often recounted what it was like to see the Statue of Liberty for the first time. As a starving little Russian girl, I'd stood in the crush of people on deck, forlorn and shivering, utterly wretched. And then, suddenly, the statue appeared before us like a mint green goddess arising from the sea, a modern-day Venus on the half shell. Always, I describe how I'd felt a bolt of elation at this moment—how I'd pointed and jumped up and down, crying, "Mama, Papa—it's *her*!" From the way she'd stood sentry in New York Harbor, I'd thought Lady Liberty was some sort of American angel. For months after our arrival in New York, I've confessed to reporters, I actually prayed to the Statue of Liberty each night.

And the media, oh, how they loved this story! Even today, they still quote it occasionally.

Our customers loved it, too—especially when I told them how it was the inspiration behind our first national logo: the Statue of Liberty holding a red-white-and-blue ice cream cone in place of her torch. We'd developed this just before the war, crediting my childhood experience, of course. Nowadays, everybody copies it. I can't tell you how many goddamn times I've had to go to court over trademark infringements.

Yet—I might as well say it now, darlings—what else do I have to lose?

The truth is, I actually don't remember seeing the Statue of Liberty at all. Of course, we must have passed it. But I was upset at the time. And I was so little. The only details I recall from our arrival were a man beside me weeping uncontrollably—embarrassingly—and that in the commotion Flora lost her hat.

But my legendary first glimpse of the Statue of Liberty?

So sue me: I made it up.

∞

Today my grandson, Jason, calls 1913 "the olden days." But the year our family arrived in America, New York City already had its first skyscrapers, its first rickety cars, its first subway lines—the Interborough Rapid Transit—running beneath Broadway. Bridges were garlanded with electric lights. Already it was a great, throbbing, concrete heart.

That same year, 1913, was also when the Sixteenth Amendment to the U.S. Constitution was passed, establishing the income tax. Of course, there was no way I could've known that seventy years later this very piece of legislation would be used to persecute me—*unduly*, may I remind you. It was also the year Henry Ford perfected his assembly line. And I suppose it must be said, too, that it was the year Al Smith, governor of New York, pushed through a slew of labor laws. While these probably saved Flora and me from the most dangerous factory work as children, they proved to be a major pain in my ass later on. Please: You're telling me a teenager can't serve a milk shake?

But most significant of all, in 1913 the first continuous freezing process was patented. This meant that ice cream could soon be manufactured in bulk, on an industrial scale. It arrived in New York at almost the very same moment that I did.

Already, you see, darlings, the fates were converging.

By 1913, numerous services had also been established to help immigrants landing in New York. Each ethnic group seemed to have its own sort of welcome wagon, a small legion of interpreters, advocates, and social workers who met know-nothings like us right on Ellis Island. When my family staggered off our ship, the Hebrew Immigrant Aid Society was already waiting. Women in skirts, in these voluminous blouses with navy bows at their necks. Mustachioed men in tweed jackets and derbies, with clipboards—all looking so modern, so wealthy and clean! These were Jews?

They stood in the disembarkation area holding signs in Yiddish, then whisked us before a phalanx of doctors. I was tugged at, my shirt was lifted. A man pressed a frigid metal disk to my chest. My eyelids were pulled back with a buttonhook to determine if I had trachoma. Officials went through the lines putting chalk marks on some people's jackets. I wondered if this was a good thing, a lucky thing, until I heard the women shrieking, wailing, pleading.

In a cold, forbidding room, officials asked our parents: Did they have jobs awaiting them, relatives, marketable skills? My mother shot my father a vicious look. The Jewish representatives in their fancy American clothes swept in. Their association would be lending us the twenty-five-dollar debarkation fee, they announced. Surely two people with skills such as my parents' could find work quickly enough. Why, they could provide us with references. One of the social workers hoisted Flora up in her arms and gave her a soft pinch on the cheek. "The children, all four of them, are healthy and robust."

Remarkably, our parents' silent treatment of each other went unnoticed. Most immigrants seemed to be struck dumb when they arrived. When anyone spoke to them, they just nodded and nodded. It almost didn't matter that they had a translator. A couple would stand before a health official, nodding as he spoke. Then, as soon as they were released, the woman would turn to her husband. "What did he say, Yankel?" And the husband would look at her, alarmed. "I have no idea, Bessie. I thought you knew."

After our family had been thoroughly inspected, examined, and given the stamp of approval like so much kosher meat, we were "deloused" with violent sprays of powder from a can. The Hebrew Immigrant Aid workers then pulled my mother, Bella, and Rose behind a curtain.

Today, everyone wears the same *schmattes*: the blue jeans, the T-shirts, those terrible tracksuits. My grandson, Jason—his idea of fashion is to rip up his T-shirts, then pin them back together with safety pins. "You know, you could save yourself a lot of time," I tell him, "by not tearing them up in the first place." I know, I know: It's a "look." He tells me he's making a "statement." But back then in Europe, we all had a look. We all made a statement—whether we wanted to or not. People's clothes were like identity cards. You could instantly tell if someone was from Bavaria or Silesia or Galicia just by the embroidery on a bodice or the cut of a topcoat. Different villages had their own styles. Certainly, you could tell the Jews from the gentiles.

Before our family was even permitted to set foot in America, my mother and older sisters were given modern haircuts. Their tattered, filthy clothes from the old country were disposed of and replaced with secondhand "American" dresses. Flora, perhaps because she was the prettiest, was given a small straw hat with felt violets on the brim. And, finally, a sweet-smelling woman in a striped blouse attempted to remove my gray coat.

"Let me take that, *kindeleh*," she said gently, trying to unbutton
it. "It's springtime here, and very warm already. We've got better
for you now."

"No!" I hollered, as loud as I could. It was the *geschrei* I had
been practicing since Vishnev, a *geschrei* designed to scare away
the Cossacks. It bounced off the walls of the arrivals station and
echoed through the tiled vaults of the enormous Registry Room.

My mother glared at me furiously. "Oh, so *now* you scream?
Now you finally listen to me?"

These words were the first that she'd spoken to me in eighteen
days. For you see, darlings—and I suppose this comes as a surprise
to no one—Mama was not happy in the least when she discovered
the change in our plans.

The way I'd imagined it, Mama wouldn't learn that we'd
switched the tickets until long *after* we'd set sail. We'd be
out on the open seas, dining in one of the great salons that
the shipping companies had illustrated in their brochures. Papa
would say to Mama, "Malka has a wonderful surprise for us."
And then I would announce that we were sailing not to Cape
Town but to America. And then Papa and I would describe
all that awaited us—everything that we'd seen in the moving
pictures and on the streets of Hamburg. We'd tell Mama and
Bella and Flora and Rose that in America we'd all be dancing in a grand parlor with armchairs and electric lights—all of
us clothed as richly as Queen Esther—and we'd ride streetcars
and eat magnificent chocolates while Papa grew rich with gold.
Upon hearing this, Mama, I was certain, would be overjoyed.
She'd be beside herself with gratitude and relief. I had imagined this scenario in my head so many times I could practically
act it out—all the parts—right down to my sisters' rapturous
applause at the end.

Yet what Papa hadn't realized was that the ship we were sailing on to New York was named the SS *Amerika*. When our family arrived at the pier the morning of our departure, crewmen shouted at us through megaphones, "All passengers for the *Amerika*, form your lines here!" Around us, people strained against the barriers waving little American flags, cheering. A brass band played "Yankee Doodle" and "Hail Columbia." My mother was not a stupid woman. "Herschel," she cried, "we're in the wrong line!"

She reeled about frantically, looking for some official to rectify the situation. My father busied himself with our bundles, pretending not to hear.

"Herschel!" she cried.

That's when I could contain myself no further. "No, Mama! This is the right line! This is the right line, Mama! We're going to America!" I jumped up and down. "Papa and I, we switched the tickets!"

Mama froze. She stared at us with the shocked, devastated look of someone who's just realized they've been shot. Reflexively, she gripped her breast. Beside her my sister Flora tugged anxiously at the hem of her skirt. Mama brushed her away.

"What?" she cried. "Herschel, is this true?"

My father continued rearranging our sacks. Without looking at her, he grabbed three by their necks, twisted them violently, and slung them over his shoulder. "America is a better bet, Tillie. Hyram is a *schlemiel*."

My mother let out a horrific cry.

"What?" said Bella. "We're not going to Cape Town?"

"We're going to America instead?" said Rose. "But they gave us quinine at the infirmary!"

"We saw the moving pictures! We saw the moving pictures!" I yelled, bouncing ecstatically. "There are women in gowns! And cream cakes! And fancy lights! And—"

"*Oy! Vey iz mir!*" my mother cried.

"You think I'd last a week in the desert with that *shmendrik?*" said my father.

"And fountains of milk! And walls of bread! And gold buildings!" I shouted. "I'm going to dance in the pictures! Mama, it's a surprise!"

Uniformed men on the dock were motioning at us fiercely, barking, "Move up! Move up!" Crowds were surging behind us, pressing in at all sides with their bundles of rags; their rope-tied suitcases; their lone framed wedding photos; their ornately carved, chipped jewelry boxes containing every sad, woeful, pawed-over keepsake; their chunky brass candlesticks and heirloom lace tablecloths. Some, having heard about a dearth of kosher food on board, were loaded down with tins of sardines, herring wrapped in newspaper, loaves of hard brown bread that the rats and mold would soon get at.

Swept up in the desperate pandemonium, my mother continued to glare at my father and me with furious disbelief. Then Papa reached out and grabbed her about the waist. My mother screamed. For a moment I thought Papa was going to sling her over his shoulder like one of his bundles. But before he could, she elbowed him low in the ribs and shrieked, and he set her down.

"Fine, you don't want to go, don't go!" he shouted. I'd never seen Papa so angry before, and it was terrifying. Grabbing me, he reached into my coat, yanked out some of the tickets, and thrust them at my mother. "You want to go to Cape Town, go live in the desert with that *shmegegge* brother of yours, listening to his kvetching, letting him tell you to go this way and that? I'm off to America. Who's with me? Malka? Anybody else? Bella? Rose?"

I started to wail. All my sisters were crying.

My mother looked first at Papa, then at me, as if she wanted to strangle us both. She tore at her own hair, rent her skirt. "You *mamzer*!" she cried. "And you! You little *gonif*!"

The crowds pushed in around us. People were shouting. Baggage was spilling open, hats were being whipped off in the wind. I didn't know which way to go, what to do. Papa seized my hand furiously and pulled me toward the gangway. "Mama, please! Don't be angry!" I wailed. My mother swore and raised her fist at Papa, but the surge of the crowd was overwhelming, and she grabbed my sisters and pushed in behind us, carried helplessly toward the enormous maw of the ship. Papa dragged me up the gangway, into the crush that was suspended precariously over a dark slice of water rainbowed with oil. Then we all spilled onto the deck. My sisters were crying. Mama redfaced. A man with a great clipboard pushed through the crowds, shouting for tickets over the sonic belch of a horn. "What's your name?" He scribbled frantically on his pad. "Where are you from?" A deafening cheer erupted around us. Hats flew into the air. Confetti of torn newspaper—gray, black, and ivory—rained down into the water.

And that was it. We were off.

But my mother gripped the railing. Her hands shook. Slowly, she turned toward my father.

"So help you God, Herschel," she whispered venomously, "I will never, ever forgive you."

My sisters experienced the hardships of the voyage across the Atlantic in physical terms. The maggoty bread, the meager soup with bits of gristle and cabbage floating in it like refuse. The scratchy blankets, thin as old felt, which offered us no warmth; we had to sleep in all our filthy clothes, mildewed with perspiration or stiff with dried salt. The smell of wet wool, fermenting vegetables, and sour milk that emanated from 530 bedraggled passengers in steerage who hadn't a place to bathe.

The berths were claustrophobic, damp, and heaving; it was like being in the interior of a tubercular lung. Men and women were separated. Mama and my sisters and I lay moaning on our bunk or keeled over in the corridor, sweating and vomiting profusely in a great mass of choking, sobbing misery, which only grew worse as the toilets clogged and the rancid-cheese stench of excrement and bile filled the deck. Around us women cried and prayed in Yiddish and Hebrew, in Hungarian, Polish, Russian, and German, some of them saying the Shema, their voices often drowned out by the thundering of the ship's engine. I remember a mixture of seawater and vomit sloshing beneath us on the floor and awakening in the middle of the night, sandwiched between Bella and Flora, terrified of the darkness and the violent pitching of the ship.

There was typhoid and consumption, too; the coughing went on all night.

Yet my own misery had little to do with the conditions. For the entire voyage, my mother refused to say a single word to either Papa or me. She refused to even look at us. Each time she turned her back to me, it felt like an incision.

I tried to win her back. I gave her bits of soap I'd found in one of the lavatories. I composed little songs: "How Beautiful Is My Mama" and "I Love You More Than Flowers."

But no sooner did I begin to sing than Mama held up her hand. "Rose," she'd instruct my sister, "tell Malka I don't want to hear it. Not one word."

She shot a look in my father's direction. "And, Bella, please tell your papa that to get into America I hear there is a test. Tell him he might have considered this before switching the tickets."

"Papa," Bella said dutifully, "Mama wants to know if you know—"

"I hear you, Tillie," my father said wearily. "What? You think I don't have ears?"

"Rose, please tell your papa that of course I know he has ears. I also know that this little *meeskite* sister of yours, Malka, has a mouth. Now, please ask them both, if they know so much, what is their plan for America? Do they know who is this President Taft we should all know about? Do they know what is this Declaration of Independence? And do they know, pray tell, where are we going to live? How we are going to eat?"

Papa sat stonily sipping his tea and gazing at the horizon, at the unchanging, unyielding sea. "Stop, Tillie," he said finally.

"President Taft?" I couldn't help asking. "Who's that?"

"*Who's that?*" my mother mimicked contemptuously. "Bella, tell that little sister of yours that she's a fool and a criminal, just like her father."

Planting her hands on her wide hips, Mama marched over and stood before me. "Tell Malka that I asked her to do one thing, just one thing: Don't let anybody touch that coat! Not even Papa! But did she listen?" Her voice was so loud it carried over the relentless chug of the engine. Bella glared at me. So did Rose. Flora began to weep. Other passengers regarded us nervously.

Mama stood there, breathless. "Did she?" she cried again.

"Tillie, leave the child alone," my father said. "She only did what her papa asked her to do."

My mother glared from me to him. "Oh. *You* she listens to," she spit.

For seventeen days, my mother ignored me. Even when the boat stopped pitching and I was no longer seasick, I still couldn't eat. Nor could I sing. All I wanted was for her not to hate me anymore.

And then, on the eighteenth morning, Papa appeared in the doorway to the women's berths. "Bella, tell your mother," he panted, "there's land."

When the people at Ellis Island finished readying Mama and Papa for America, my parents were almost unrecognizable. Mama had her hair shortened and arranged in a loose bun. Her dress had a faint waist and a collar with a button. Dressed in a different coat and a derby, my father looked like the men from the Hebrew Immigrant Aid Society themselves. His beard was closely shaven and his hair slicked back. When Flora first saw them, she started to cry. "Where's Mama? Where's Papa?" In their new American clothing, both our parents were suddenly stiff and tentative, moving as if they were afraid of breaking something. They smiled shyly, like strangers. Framed by their new hats and haircuts, the lines of their faces seemed to have been redrawn.

Since I refused to relinquish my coat, I received only some navy blue hair ribbons and a new pair of wool stockings. But after this, we were fed. At a long wooden table with other Jewish immigrants. Fresh challah and rich noodle kugel and bowls of broth with pillowy kreplach floating in it.

We ate and we ate, as we had never eaten before. The food and the new clothes felt celebratory. From across the table, my father couldn't help grinning at my mother triumphantly. "See," he said proudly as he slurped his soup. "Malka, tell your mother: We are not even living in America, yet already so much to eat!"

Like most factory owners, Yacob Lefkowitz ran his business out of his tenement apartment. During the day his tiny parlor doubled as the cutting and sewing "floor," while his small kitchen served as the pressing area, with an ironing board set up next to the stove. In a mere two years since his arrival from Lodz, Mr. Lefkowitz had gone from being a peddler to a tailor to a sweatshop owner, producing winter coats and "car dusters" for Valentine's, Wanamaker's, and Gimbels uptown.

He made enough money so that he and his wife, Clara, didn't have to take in boarders the way most of their neighbors did.

But then Clara died in childbirth—along with their newborn girl. When the shiva—the mourning period—was officially over, the seamstress, cutters, and presser employed by Mr. Lefkowitz arrived on the fourth floor on Orchard Street at 7:00 A.M. to find themselves with nothing to do: No cloth had been purchased, no new orders commissioned. Unfinished coats lay untouched on the floor and strewn across the couch like casualties of war. Mr. Lefkowitz sat in his kitchen with his hands sandwiched between his knees, rocking back and forth, eyes fixed in the middle distance, murmuring the Shema. It was heartbreaking to be sure, but the workers took quick stock of the situation, saw the train of destitution rumbling toward them, and scrambled to secure work elsewhere.

After receiving an eviction notice, Mr. Lefkowitz drank himself to near blindness at the saloon downstairs, then came home and stumbled around his apartment, cursing his one God. By the end of the night, there wasn't a single neighbor in the tenement who hadn't heard his *tsuris* and grievances documented loudly and in great detail through the air shaft. He contemplated killing himself. Death was the only way to rejoin Clara, to see their stillborn daughter, he yelled—death and then the Messiah, of course. It could be a very long process. Why didn't Jews make anything easy? But then, he discovered, he didn't own a sharp enough knife. He didn't own any pills.

As the purple-black sky started to bleed into a sad, filmy morning, Mr. Lefkowitz sank into a chair and shouted, "Look at me, God! I'm too poor to even commit suicide properly!"

To win back his contracts with the department stores, he'd have to produce coats again—more cheaply than ever. As he did the math the next morning, he saw the necessity of taking in boarders, too—if boarders could be found who wouldn't drink, run off in the middle of the night with his valuables (such as they were), or steal his sewing machine.

Two days later, when my weary father knocked on his door with a referral from the Hebrew Immigrant Aid Society, Mr. Lefkowitz ushered us into his kitchen like six answered prayers.

He was a twitchy, spindly man, Mr. Lefkowitz, gone prematurely bald. Behind his glasses his eyes were red-rimmed and startled. He led the six of us into his apartment with a nervous hiccup. "In this room you can sleep," he said, motioning to a tiny parlor filled with old newspapers and rags. Bolts of charcoal-colored fabric were propped against the walls and piled haphazardly atop the furnishings. By the window was a sewing machine with a wrought-iron pedal. Mr. Lefkowitz pointed to the settee in front of the fireplace. "The children can sleep on the cushions. One on the frame, maybe—"

Most immigrant families came to America piecemeal—first a father and a daughter, perhaps, would arrive and get jobs. A year or two later, they'd send for the mother, the brothers. Lots of new arrivals were barely more than teenagers. But our family had arrived in New York intact—we were half a dozen, yet utterly alone. Six was a lot. There was barely enough space in the parlor for all of us to stand. The walls, papered with faded green and mustard cabbage roses, seemed to perspire and ripple with the heat. From the alley beneath the windows, I could hear chickens squawking, then their unearthly, strangulated cries as a butcher broke their necks with a single twist of his hands and a grunt. I ran to take a look. "Look, that butcher isn't kosher!" I shouted, leaning over the windowsill and pointing. I felt rather proud that I could discern this.

My mother shot my father another vicious look.

"Mama," said Flora, tugging at her skirt, "where's the toilet?"

"Ask your father," my mother said. "And ask him, too, if you please: Is he fool enough to believe that this is better than Africa?"

Come nightfall, the sound of chickens being slaughtered was replaced by the noise from the saloon downstairs: beer steins pounding on tabletops, stomping, singing, bullying, drunken love songs performed a cappella to the fire escapes. Bellowing men staggered into the courtyard to urinate by the chicken coop. It was even louder than Papa's friends had been at the detention center in Hamburg. When the commotion died down late into the night, we could still hear muffled weeping coming from Mr. Lefkowitz's tiny bedroom on the other side of the kitchen.

Crammed together on the old velvet cushions, which buckled and grew damp with our sweat, surrounded by bolts of wool, tickled by fleas and cockroaches, my sisters and I flailed and tore at our nightdresses in the airless room until we were teary with frustration. Papa shushed us, then finally stood up. "Tell your mother I'll be on the stoop." Pulling on his pants, he grabbed his shoes and maneuvered his way over the detritus of us toward the door. Rose started to cry. "Papa, where are you going?" It was the middle of the night. This made Flora and me start weeping, too. *Papa! Papa!* Our sobs only seemed to fuel Mr. Lefkowitz's staccato cries in the back room, which grew ever louder. Our father's footsteps rang down the staircase.

"Stop it," my mother hissed. "All of you."

Walking over to the window, she stared down at the noisy, garbage-strewn courtyard and began twisting the frayed ends of her hem around her knuckles. "Again he leaves?" she spit. "On our very first night? That *mamzer*."

Sitting up on my cushion on the floor, I wiped my nose on the back of my wrist and coughed. My throat hurt; my arms and shoulders itched. I couldn't for the life of me understand: Why weren't we there yet? Perhaps there was still another ferry boat to take, or a streetcar. Perhaps we just hadn't walked far enough into the city. "Mama? Maybe tomorrow," I suggested, "we can go to America."

My mother turned and glared at me, her stare ossifying into something cold and hard, like agate. Then she gave a vicious little laugh. "Oh, you think so, *bubeleh*?"

The next morning my sisters and I awoke to the sound of scissors snipping. In the anemic yellow light of the gas jets, we saw Mama's back bobbing over a bolt of fabric. Her back bobbed at sunrise, at midday, well into the darkness of evening. As she bent over the patterns, she muttered in Yiddish. In the kitchen Papa stood over the ironing board. As soon as one garment was finished and Mr. Lefkowitz handed him another, Papa heaved the heavy iron off the stove top with a grunt and smoothed it, hissing, over the fabric. He paced about constantly in between jobs, but in the tiny kitchen there was almost nowhere to move. Several times, Papa excused himself and headed out into the streets for a "break." These were almost unheard of in those days, but Mr. Lefkowitz didn't seem to notice. Seated at the sewing machine, he stared out the window in a sort of trance while my mother's piecework piled up on the floor before him, waiting to be stitched. When he finally remembered to pick up a piece and begin, he often forgot that his foot was on the pedal, and he'd let the needle run clear over the edge of the fabric so that he'd have to redo the seam entirely. We could see why he needed the help. By the end of the week, two more women from Lodz had been hired and installed in the tiny parlor as well. All of them labored in silence. Not knowing what else to do, my sisters and I headed downstairs to the streets.

The dawn of the twentieth century had seen, among other things, the inventions of structural steel and electric elevators. Nothing at the Hilfsverein's detention center or Ellis Island had prepared us for this. On the ferry to Manhattan the day of our arrival, we'd gazed upon a skyline rising above the harbor like a colossus of stalagmites. The afternoon sun lacquered it in brilliant gold light. As the ferry churned closer and closer and the city bore in, Flora, Bella, Rose, and I stood beside our parents, bedazzled and stunned. My father and the Jews back in Hamburg—they had been exactly right: Buildings soared to the sky covered in gold and crystal, as ornate as Torah scrolls! Papa was smiling. His cheeks were wet. Mama's, too. Everyone around us was gasping, weeping, applauding. The scale of it! The unspeakable beauty!

Straining against the railing, my sisters and I squealed and shouted and pointed up at the spires, their filigreed façades, their diamante windows. My God! They went to the clouds! Who'd ever seen such a thing?

"How do the people get in there?" said Rose.

"How do they not fall down?" said Bella.

"Is this where we are going to live?"

"Let's live way up on the very top!" I shouted, twirling. "Above everything!"

Now, however, blinking into the dusty morning light, my sisters and I found ourselves on cramped, crowded, low-lying Orchard Street. It sounded more like Vishnev than America. Yiddish everywhere. Pushcarts, hawkers, shoppers, horses, and gangs of children clogged the sidewalks. The noise was incredible. There was nothing left of the Manhattan skyline. It had vanished behind us as quickly as it had appeared, like a mirage. All we had now was *this*.

The immigrant experience on the Lower East Side—oh, how people go on about it! Such nostalgia. The pickle men, the peddlers' wagons, the children playing marbles on the stoops.... Now, apparently, there are even "cultural walking tours" for tourists: Some schmuck with an umbrella points out a knish store to a bunch of Japanese.

Well, let me tell you, darlings: immigrant, schmimmigrant. The streets were cobblestone and asphalt, the buildings masonry. The stoops and fire escapes were iron, the rooftops tar, the ceilings pressed tin. There were no trees, no breezes from the river, no respite from the sun. Can you imagine? We roasted. My sisters and I—four little Russian girls—we had never experienced such heat in our lives. As we linked arms, the four of us, and stepped carefully off into the gutter, the crooks of our elbows and the backs of our necks instantly became wet.

And the stench!

Manure, hay, chicken shit, urine, beer, frying grease, chalk dust, coke, coal—even decomposing animal carcasses. Crossing Forsyth Street, we had to step over a dead horse lying in the gutter, infested with maggots. All of these odors hung noxiously in the air, mixing with the pierce of kerosene, camphor, and turpentine from the cobblers and the tanneries. Fumes of queasy-sweet gasoline billowed from new cars rattling noisily up the avenues. And since none of the tenements had bathtubs, these odors, in turn, mixed with the gamy smell of thousands of strains of human perspiration. Yeasty, fungal skin. Rose water. Decaying teeth. Dirty diapers. Sharp, vinegary hair tonic. The *New York Post* recently made a ruckus about how I spray Shalimar in my bathrooms, my trash cans, even Petunia's doghouse. The "Spritz Witch," they called me in a headline. But since when is it a crime to deodorize? *You* grow up in a tenement, darlings, then tell me what *you'd* do.

As we wandered through the neighborhood that first morning, Bella pinched her nostrils and rasped, "So, Malka, this is the promised land? Did anyone ever tell you and Papa how horrible it would smell?"

As the week wore on, we found we were eating scarcely better than we had back in Vishnev. We had a piece of bread for breakfast, a piece of bread for lunch with a boiled egg shared between the four of us, and a piece of bread for dinner with soup that Mama made from carrots and onions.

To keep from getting too faint with hunger, I pooled my saliva in my mouth, then swallowed it and chewed the insides of my cheeks. Sometimes I'd pluck at the air and say to my sisters, "Let's pretend we're eating roast lamb." Bella and Rose ignored me, but Flora was willing to play. She and I would pretend to chew nothing—but we chewed it with relish. Or I'd divide a piece of bread crust between us and say, "Let's pretend this is honey cake with apples," and we'd chew luxuriantly and rub our bellies with exaggerated motions and say, "Mmm. Isn't this the most marvelous cake you've ever eaten?" We did all of this reflexively, the same way we got used to relaying messages between our parents.

For our first Sabbath in America, Mama made soup with chicken necks for all of us, Mr. Lefkowitz included. After she lit the candles and said the prayers, she made an announcement: "Next week you're all going to have to go to work." She pointed at me and each of my sisters individually, so as to make no mistake. "All of you. Anyone who doesn't earn doesn't eat. It's as simple as that. You don't like it? Then you can thank your papa."

Bella found work as a day maid. Rose got hired as a baster in a dress factory; she awoke before dawn and returned only at dinnertime.

But for Flora and me, it wasn't so easy. Just two years earlier, the Triangle Shirtwaist Fire had killed 146 young immigrant girls. New York had become swept up in a fever of labor reforms. Sweatshop owners, factory foremen—suddenly they refused to hire children as little as Flora and myself. "Look at them." The foreman frowned when Rose brought us to her factory. "They can't be older than five. I can't have that kind of trouble here now."

But for Mama this was no excuse. "Out," she said, hustling Flora and me through the door. "Don't come back until you have something. Either you work or you starve."

Flora and I stood out on the landing. "Malka," she said, her eyes filling with tears, "what are we going to do?"

Flora was a year or two older than me, but just as small. She had a lovely, milk-white face, sad blue eyes, and a high forehead, which gave her a bleached, sleepy look. Her lower lip always trembled as if she were about to cry.

I shrugged. "We have to find work."

I looked down the dim, narrow hallway of the tenement. It seemed to me that a door was the place you were supposed to start. But for the life of me, I couldn't think of what I was supposed to say or do. Did I just knock? Was there a place where children went to learn what to do? What could I offer anyone? I hadn't yet learned how to cook or to sew like my older sisters. Back in Vishnev, Flora and I had gone to the well sometimes with Mama. We had helped sweep and dust and hang out the washing and peel onions and set the table. But what could anyone pay us for? We were going to starve, Flora and I, and I realized it was all my fault, for letting Papa change the tickets.

Slowly, we made our way down the stairs, one grim step at a time. Flora was sniffling; I tried not to cry myself. When we reached the next floor, I thought of what Mama had said to me back in Vishnev: *At least you can put that big mouth of yours to some use.*

I walked over to one of the doors and knocked on it. "Hello!"
I shouted. "Does anybody in there want to hear a song?"

There was no answer.

I walked to the next door.

I pulled Flora down another flight of stairs and knocked again.
And again. One woman opened her door and yelled at us in a
strange language. Another shooed us away. I knocked on another
door, then another. We were getting hungry now and starting to
panic. People shook their heads. My pounding went unanswered.

Finally an elderly man opened his door. "Who's making such
a ruckus?" he said. He had eyeglasses perched halfway down his
nose. Flora lingered behind me.

I took a deep breath. "Do you want to hear a song? It costs a
penny."

The man crossed his arms. "You don't say," he declared.

"Mama says that if we don't come home with something to eat,
we don't come home at all."

"Oh," said the man, frowning. "Well. That sounds serious."
He reached into his pocket and took out a penny. "Do you both
sing?"

I shook my head. "Only me." I added quickly, "Flora dances,
though."

"Malka!" Flora whispered.

"Just twirl," I whispered back. "For another penny," I told the
man.

The sides of his mouth twitched faintly. "Well," he said, leaning
against the doorframe. "One penny for the singer and one penny
for the twirler. So okay, then. Let's see."

Standing there in the narrow, urine-scented corridor, I was utterly at a loss. I hadn't thought beyond knocking on the door; I
hadn't imagined we would actually get a reply. But then one of
the little songs I'd invented back in Vishnev came to me. As loudly

as I could, I belted out "Why I Love Chicken." It went some-thing like "I love chicken...chicken hearts and chicken soup....I love chicken, the way it jiggles on the spoon...." For a moment Flora just stood there, staring incredulously as I sang. I glared at her. Belatedly, she started to twirl.

The man at the door began to clap along but quickly gave up, as my song had no consistent rhythm. My voice went higher and higher; it warbled with a life of its own. A moment later he halted me in midnote, Flora in midtwirl. "Why don't we do this?" he said with a sigh. "I've paid you a penny to sing and a penny to twirl. Now I'll pay each of you a penny to stop."

We had four cents. Flora and I had earned our first meal in America.

Slowly, my sister and I became known as the Little Singing, Cleaning Bialystoker Sisters. For while we were boarding the ship to America, it seems, our family name had been changed. In all the hubbub, the steward checking our tickets had asked us where we were from. Since most villages in the Russian Pale were so small, they weren't even on a map, Papa had been coached to answer simply "Bialystok," the biggest, best-known city in the re-gion. Confused and harried, the clerk simply wrote "Bialystoker" after Papa's name. Now we were no longer the Treynovskys. I was Malka Bialystoker.

For a penny here, a nickel there, Flora and I did errands for our elderly neighbors while singing little songs. Most of these I made up myself, about the very people we were working for: "Mrs. Nachmann Has Pretty China Dishes" was one. "Helping Make the Challah" was another. So sue me: They were not Greatest Hits. Still, word got out around the tenements: You could pay us to sing or you could pay us to be quiet. I suppose we were a novelty act, a charming little joke. With so much sadness and hardship around, the adults liked the cheap entertainment, the innocence of two little girls.

For a nickel Flora and I scrubbed Mrs. Nachmann's dishes. For two pennies we climbed out the Sokolovs' window onto the fire escape to hang their laundry on the line running across the courtyard. For two pennies we carried the Levines' settee cushions up onto the roof—it took a couple of trips—and beat the dust and fleas out of them in the broiling sun with our fists. For a nickel we swept Mr. Abromovitz's kitchen, stomped on the cockroaches, kept the rat holes stuffed with rags soaked in lye, and dusted as best we could. We hauled the scraps from Mr. Lefkowitz's floor downstairs to the rag man. We helped Mr. Tomashevski—an infirm old man from the Ukraine who lived on the second floor next door—by heating up water for him to soak his bunions in.

Per Mama's orders we made ourselves useful. In nickels and pennies, we earned our keep. If we could just bring home enough, I thought, maybe Mama wouldn't be so angry all the time. Maybe she and Papa would start talking again. Maybe she would forgive me.

Flora and I would try to find as many odd jobs as possible until the late afternoon. Then, per Mama's order, we did the shopping. It was better to go late. Although the produce was well picked over, we were more likely to get a bargain. I quickly learned which peddlers charged a penny less here, a half cent less there—and how to haggle.

"When I pinch you," I instructed Flora, "cry. Not loudly. Then say, 'Oh, Malka, I'm so hungry.' Okay?"

I made her practice. Then I approached a vegetable cart. "Excuse me, sir. How much are the potatoes?"

"Two cents each, three for five."

"Oh, dear." I frowned in what I imagined was an extremely

grown-up, exaggerated fashion. I held out my palm with three dull pennies in it. "Mama needs two. But this is all we have."

The peddler shook his head. "Tell Mama the potato peddler's got to eat, too," he said.

"What about a small one and a big one for three?"

The peddler frowned. "There are no small potatoes."

"Please, sir?" I pleaded, opening my eyes extra wide. "I've got three more sisters and Papa. Mama won't let me come home with only one potato." Then, discreetly, I pinched Flora on the arm. She started crying, just as I'd coached. "Oh, Malka, I'm so hungry," she wailed. And then, although I hadn't planned to, I found that I was crying myself. It was surprisingly easy, given that I was truly hungry and could envision Mama, the wallop she'd give me. "Please, Mama, don't be angry with me!" I wailed. Flora looked genuinely distressed. The peddler looked exasperated. Rolling his eyes, he made a surrendering gesture at the three coins in my palm. "Okay, okay. Two for three."

"Oh, thank you!" I sang. Flora gave a little twirl.

They say that whenever you have a sister who is prettier than you, you have a tragedy. Vicious neighbors back in the shtetl used to whisper that Flora had the blood of the Cossacks coursing through her. How else to explain the blue eyes and blond hair? The delicate, *goyishe* features? The dairymaid skin?

The Lower East Side was teeming with shivering, wolf-eyed children. Its merchants were barely getting by themselves. Flora's beauty—combined with the fact that she did and said absolutely everything I told her to—earned us an extra scoop of rice thrown in the sack, a discounted parsnip. And we were no dummies, my sister and I. We played it right up. We became marvelous performers. Oh, you should have seen us. Not like the other kids, mewling and begging so pathetically. We really figured how to work it. On the streets of Lower Manhattan, I got my first great education in marketing. Be shameless. Be different. And appeal to the emotions—never the head.

I picked up English quickly. I even picked up a little Italian. Words everywhere, they were like musical notes. Yet being on the noisy streets—that never, ever stopped being noisy—with their peddlers shouting, "Carrots, fresh carrots!" "Pickles! Half sours!" "I-SEES! I-SEES!"—and the dizzying smells—of fresh-baked bread, of pungent garlic, of potatoes frying somewhere in butter—all this was its own particular type of torture.

And so one afternoon I bought those cherry ices from Mr. Dinello. Oh, they were a revelation: Flora and I, we'd never eaten anything so sweet and so cold before. The iciness, laced with the sugar and the tartness of the cherries—it blossomed, then dissolved on our tongues. It was like eating magic.

Another time I bought us half a baked sweet potato. Oh, heaven, too! And a kasha knish. I made sure to take Flora a few blocks away from Orchard Street so as not to be seen. Then she and I devoured our bounty, scalding and doused with sweet mustard, while hiding beneath a stoop.

Later that evening Mama demanded an accounting of everything we'd bought—"I know what things cost. I'd like to know where those extra two pennies are."

Flora panicked. "Malka bought a knish," she said.

I stood there blinking. Mama backhanded me across the face. "Stupid, stupid!" she cried. "You want that all of us should starve to death from your selfishness?"

I started to cry. I looked around the kitchen for Papa, but he was gone. He seemed to be at Mr. Lefkowitz's less and less in the evenings. Sometimes Flora and I spotted him in the streets in broad daylight, smoking and joking with groups of men gathered around various storefronts with stairs leading down into basements. A few evenings, as we made our way home, I thought

I'd even seen Papa in the tavern downstairs, though I couldn't be sure. When I managed to catch his eye at the dinner table once, he winked at me. I kept hoping he might ask me to take another walk with him, or to practice punching. I kept hoping that he might give some indication of when we might leave Orchard Street for a place more like the one we'd seen together in the moving pictures. But he never did. When I tugged on his sleeve and said, "Papa?" he sometimes looked at me blankly for a moment, as if he'd forgotten which daughter I was.

Occasionally, late at night, I could hear him and my mother whispering fiercely—"You spent *all* of it?" "I told you, Tillie. It pays five to one!" This meant that they were speaking again, which gave me some relief. But mostly I just saw Papa's back, bent over the ironing board, or the top of his head disappearing down the stairway, or his figure, in the distance, a blur in the shadows of men.

"I'm sorry, Mama!" I cried when she slapped me. "I was just so hungry."

"Oh, you were, were you? Then go eat some of that gold off the pavements. Go drink from those fountains of milk you were talking so much about."

One night Papa didn't come home at all. "He's out drunk somewhere, is where he is," said Mama. She had made egg noodles for dinner; my sisters and I were allowed to share his portion. He was home by breakfast, however, so we didn't get to have his bread.

Two nights later he was gone again. This time my three sisters and I shared his boiled egg.

At dawn, Bella left for her job on Chrystie Street, Rose left for the factory. By the time Flora and I finished our breakfast of bread and milk, Papa still hadn't returned. It was Friday. "It's not enough he gets drunk and gambles away all his earnings?" Mama cried. "Now he should show up late for his job and get himself fired as well?

"Go," she ordered me and Flora. "Work as much as you can today so we won't all of us be out on the street."

When Flora and I returned that afternoon, we found our mother furiously hacking away at a piece of fabric with her scissors. She hacked it entirely to bits, then snatched up another and started in. Little patches were flying everywhere, spraying around her, falling at her feet. The girls from Lodz sat with their piecework untouched, staring at her in horror. Mr. Lefkowitz himself was standing behind Mama, trying to stay her wrist without getting clipped himself.

"Tillie, please," he said. "Leave it be. Go look for him."

My mother continued clipping away violently. "He wants to play games? Let him play games."

Mr. Lefkowitz pulled two pennies from his pocket and hurried over to my sister. "Flora," he said with exaggerated care. He knelt down and looked her straight in the eyes, as if she were a book he was reading. "I think your mother could use some parsley for the Sabbath. Why don't you and Malka go to buy some? And on your way, look in the saloons, and the barber's, and anyplace else you might think of where your papa might be."

Suddenly Mama threw down her scissors and stomped over to me. Grabbing me by the arm, she twisted me around and gave me a hard thwack on my backside. I howled.

"This is all your fault! Why didn't you listen?" she shouted. "The one thing I asked you to do! The one thing! 'Don't let anybody touch your coat—'"

"Tillie!" Mr. Lefkowitz cried.

With a great sob, I turned and dashed down the stairs and out into the street. I had to find Papa, I knew. It was the only way to set things right.

The saloon downstairs was long and dark inside. Behind the counter a lone man stood twisting a rag around the inside of a thick glass. "You lost?"

"I'm looking for my papa," I panted. "I have to find him. I have to bring him home."

He shrugged.

I looked inside the nonkosher butcher's, in the shoemaker's. I ran to a little gambling parlor set down off the street in a basement. I thought that perhaps this was where I'd seen Papa before, smoking outside. I asked a man to go in and look for me. He seemed to be gone awhile. When he finally came out, he said "Sorry, *kindeleh*." Just in case, I went in the synagogue next door and one farther up the street—perhaps Papa had had a change of heart?—but they were empty. The tailor's, the bakery, the barber's: all closing.

"Malka, wait!"

I turned and saw Flora running down the street after me. "Do you see him?" she said.

I shook my head.

"Mama, she is going crazy," Flora said.

Together, we ran along Hester Street, looking in all the doorways, all the little alleys. It was late afternoon. Peddlers were starting to pack up. Markets were shuttering. I had to find Papa. A terrible feeling mushroomed inside me. If I hadn't given him the tickets. If I hadn't begged to go to America instead of South Africa. If I hadn't kept the secrets. I led Flora down one block, then another, at a frantic pace. I ran into another tavern, a cigar shop, then across toward a settlement house.

And I would've kept going, too, if I hadn't stopped paying attention to where I was running and dashed blindly off a curb and not listened when Flora shrieked, "Malka!" and, in one terrible, vicious instant, collided with the right front hoof of Mr. Dinello's horse.

The horse. Ah, yes, darlings. We're finally back to that.

Chapter 3

I AWOKE SOMEPLACE GREENISH, DIM. Dusty light, rippling. The pain was excruciating, radiating from my calf, ankle, knee.

Mama? The taste of mud and hay lingered in the back of my throat. My right leg throbbed terribly. *Papa?*

"Ach, ach. Don't shout. You'll wake the others." A voice came: Yiddish, but unfamiliar.

A broad face hovered over me, bald and wide like the moon. Her jowls jiggled like chicken fat. I screamed. "Shush, *kindeleh*," the voice said. *Where was Mama?* A hand, big and raw, like a slice of corned beef, reached in and pressed itself to the back of my forehead. Cold, stony knuckles. "No fever. That is good." She wasn't bald. It was a white kerchief, I realized, tied tight around her head, with no hair showing at all.

"Where's Mama?" I asked again. My chest felt trussed.

"Shush." The frowning face vanished. My chin was wet. My nose was running.

When I touched my leg, my palm knocked up against something hard. Where was my leg? *Mama!* My voice boomeranged. Beside me was another bed. Something stirred beneath a blanket, gave an animal groan. I screamed. The moon reappeared

with its meaty hand curved around a glass of water. "*Kindeleh.*
Drink this."

Today Beth Israel is a big, fancy-schmancy medical center
that—up until recently—constantly solicited me for money. Up
until recently, they loved me at Beth Israel, even though I usually couldn't be bothered to attend their functions and had no
problem letting them know that I thought their fund-raiser was
a putz. But back then Beth Israel was simply a "dispensary"—a
small clinic run by Orthodox Jews to serve the poorest of us
poor on the Lower East Side. Mount Sinai, the nicer Jewish
hospital uptown, had been founded by German Jews, you see.
Oh, what a bunch of *machers*. Such aristocrats. They looked
down on those of us from Eastern Europe. At one time they'd
even formed a society to keep us "cruder" Jews from im-
migrating. They believed we'd make them look bad. Ha, I
always say. Peel back any "superior" culture, and all you see is
brutality.

Nowadays it's standard procedure to rush an accident victim to
a hospital. Back then, however, hospitals were regarded the way
public bathhouses and toilets are today—they spoke of charity,
humiliation—to be avoided at all costs. For immigrants, hospitals
were where people simply went to die.

If there was a medical problem on the Lower East Side, families
usually sent for one of the roving nurses from the Henry Street
Settlement House. She'd climb the treacherous stairs to the apartment (or even step nimbly from rooftop to rooftop) to minister
to you there. You could have cholera, diphtheria, tuberculosis.
Health officials might be called in to quarantine your entire
family—a mark or a decree would be placed on your front
door—and a dozen of you could be confined there for

months—until all of you were either healthy or dead. But you cared for one another at home.

Poultices, ointments, boiled onions wrapped in cheesecloth, camphor, vinegar mixtures, brandy, tonics, chicken soup of course—these were the standard medicines of the day.

Yet even back then, when a tiny girl was knocked unconscious in the street, her right leg twisted out from her body like a paper clip with her broken fibula poking through her skin, people knew enough to know that she needed a type of medical attention that went beyond anything that Henry Street or a nurse could carry up the steps in a worn leather satchel. And so someone—Mr. Dinello himself, it turns out—put me in his wagon and rushed me to the Beth Israel Dispensary.

I have no memory of my arrival, nor of being X-rayed by a brand-new mechanical contraption that was the pride of the hospital. What I will see and remember later, groggily, is my mother. She materializes with her back to me, standing beneath the high, frosted window across from my bed. I am now propped up with pillows but slack-jawed and atrophied with pain. A doctor beside her holds dark panes up to the light. The eerie, translucent rectangles are mapped with bands, wisps, and knobs. One, he explains to my mother, is my leg.

Though she has no working knowledge of science or anatomy, the visual makes it obvious: My tibia has a compound fracture, and my fibula has cleanly snapped in two like a branch. My right foot is broken. My pelvis is also fractured. Another film shows the graduated tines of my rib cage. Three of my ribs are cracked.

"She is young, so her bones are soft. They will heal, Mrs. Bialystoker," the doctor says. "Now?" He raises his eyebrows and shrugs exaggeratedly. "Whether she will walk again or walk with a limp? Or a cane? That we will have to see."

"*Oy. Vey iz mir!*" my mother cries.

The doctor looks at her, not unsympathetically. "She's very lucky, Mrs. Bialystoker," he says softly. "She easily could've died."

My mother stares at me, immobilized and swollen, then at the doctor. After a moment she wails, "Oh, that she should have!"

With a look of distress, she points accusingly toward my bed. "Bad enough she is one of four girls. Bad enough she is ugly. But now you're telling me she is also a cripple? Tell me, please, Doctor. What am I supposed to do with a daughter like this?"

Picking up her basket, she sobs, "Keep her, for all I care. She is useless." Turning, she hurries out.

Once, a few years ago, I mentioned this to Sunny, my domestic. She set down the silver polish and stared at me. "Oh, Missus Dunkle," she said, shaking her head sadly.

"Please," I said. "Spare me the tears."

Parents just didn't coddle their children back then. They needed you to walk? You got up and walked. If you didn't, they left you sitting. What if the Cossacks came? You had better be able to run.

Nowadays? Don't get me started. People name their offspring Tiffany, Brittany, Courtney—all this baby royalty. Everyone pretends their kids are little aristocrats. I want to say to them, What did America fight the War of Independence for? Or, worse yet, the hippies. Lotus. Crocus. Who the hell knows where they get these *farkakte* names for their kids. One of Rita's friends named her son Bodhisattva. Bodhisattva Rosenblatt. Can you imagine? Rita always says, "It's no big deal. They call him 'Bodi,' is all." Please. And the newspapers say *I'm* abusive to children?

Besides, nobody ever loves you the way you want.

For days—weeks—I lay in that dispensary. *Mama, Mama,* I wept. But she never came back. My voice bounced unheeded off the ugly waxed floors, the bare walls. Other patients complained. The nurses tried shushing me. *Please, Mama,* I sobbed. *I promise I'll be good. I promise not to eat any food. I promise to be quiet. Please, Mama,* I wailed. *I'll find Papa.* I cried the way only a child can, feverishly, hysterically, until I hyperventilated, my lungs and throat scorched from sobbing. *Please, Mama, I'm sorry.*

Please, Mama. I'll be useful.

Nurses glided in and out, regarding me sadly. As they changed my bandages and put a salve on my heat rash, they tsk-tsked and tenderly touched the backs of their hands to my brow. I slapped them away.

A rabbi who smelled of pipe tobacco and fried potatoes appeared. He was enormous. I screamed until he left. *I want Mama!* Probably there was a social worker, someone from a settlement house. I seem to recall a white blouse, a braided gold pin on a collar. *Mama!* I howled. It was hard to throw a tantrum with a broken leg and a bandaged chest, but I managed. *I want Mama!*

Finally I lost my voice.

The days grew hotter and hotter until the heat was its own animal. It hung over the beds in the infirmary, stalking and tormenting us like a predator. Even with the transoms and the windows cranked open, patients around me moaned. Sweat pooled beneath my bandages. Everything felt peed in. I itched, tore at my damp sheets. The smell of bedpans and ointments turned rancid.

Eventually the doctor sawed off my heavy cast and exchanged it for a lighter one and a brace made of metal, leather, and wood. "Where's Mama?" I rasped. Each morning a nurse hoisted me out of bed by my armpits and held me upright until my contorted, throbbing foot grazed the floor and my heels sat atop her own feet. Moving slowly, she tried to coax me to walk in tandem with her, her feet guiding my own. Pain shot up my hip; my ankle seemed to buckle. The weight of the brace was almost unmanageable. I balked. When one of them tried to bully me into taking a few steps, I bit her.

After that, no one seemed inclined to continue my physical therapy.

The family has nothing. They're fresh off the ship.... Come over here expecting charity, did they? Oh, the worst of the worst. They give all of us Jews a bad name.... But she's only a child... Nu? Did you see those teeth marks she left? Not so much a child as a dybbuk... The place for the cripples? She has to have been here a year to qualify.... Gouverneur's full up.... But what are we supposed to do? Send her to beg on the streets? Well, if that leg of hers doesn't heal properly, there's always the sideshow at Coney Island.... Oh! Gertie! (Laughing) You're terrible!

Leaning languidly in the doorway, fanning themselves with folded ladies' magazines and copies of the Yiddish *Forward*, the nurses didn't even attempt to whisper.

Slowly, a thought began to dawn in me: The reason my mother wasn't coming back was because she was off looking for Papa. She'd left Mr. Lefkowitz's apartment on Orchard Street to search for him. And my sisters had gone along to help, of course. Perhaps Papa had found the place in America with the gold and the beautiful furniture. Or changed his mind and sailed to South Africa to make amends with Uncle Hyram. Africa was a very big place, perhaps as big as New York. I pictured my family, crammed back into steerage berths, rocking in time with the heaving sea. I imagined my father in Uncle Hyram's dry-goods store deep in the desert, miserable, missing all of us terribly, wishing he could come back. Then, suddenly, my mother appears—surprise!

My father's face explodes with happiness. Right away he says, "Where's Malka?" My mother tells him, "Oh, Herschel, she had a terrible accident. We have to go get her."

And that will be it—what convinces him to return to America immediately and what convinces my mother and him to stop fighting. Me, in the hospital. Soon they will all sail back to America together, this time with plenty of gold and bread in their pockets. Soon they'll be arriving. They'll go straight from the pier to the dispensary to carry me home.

My voice was ruined from all the crying and wailing. It was like paper. I could barely speak above a whisper. But it didn't matter. I wanted to remain quiet, for when my parents returned. I had to show Mama that my big mouth wouldn't cause her any more *tsuris*.

A doctor came in to examine my leg, hips, and ribs. The pain was unbearable, but I had no voice left to cry out with. A nurse asked if I needed to use the toilet. I simply nodded. When the enormous rabbi returned, I stared at the transom over his head the entire time. I noticed floaters in my vision, those little translucent bugs of cells; I followed them up and down. It helped me to stay quiet, to keep still. Only once could I manage to speak. Accompanied by a doctor, the worried-looking young woman in the white blouse leaned over my bed and stared directly into my eyes. "Malka, *kindeleh*," she said softly, clutching my arm. "Can you hear me? Do you know where you are? Do you understand what has happened to you?"

I stared right back at her. "Mama and Papa are in Africa," I whispered hoarsely, "getting some gold."

The nurses began regarding me oddly. Another doctor examined my leg and manipulated it methodically. I thought he'd be impressed by my ability not to cry out, but when he left the room, he just shook his head.

The next morning Gertie came in. For some reason, since I had gone mute, people began talking to me extremely loudly and slowly, as if I were deaf as well. Whipping off my top sheet, Gertie bellowed, "YOU'RE MOVING, MALKA. TO THE ASYLUM UPTOWN."

"Oh, Gertie," another nurse scolded from across the room. "Don't scare the child."

Gertie glanced at her—then at me—with irritation. "WE CAN'T TAKE CARE OF YOU HERE ANYMORE, MALKA. WE NEED THE BED FOR OTHER PATIENTS WHO ARE MORE RESPONSIVE."

I didn't understand this. I had tried to be quiet, to be good. Certainly I wasn't singing or being a wisenheimer or keeping secrets. I wondered how Mama and Papa would be able to find me once I was moved. "Promise?" I whispered feebly. "You'll tell Mama where I am?"

Gertie frowned and eyed me with a sort of pity. "Oh, your mama knows, *kindeleh*. Who do you think is sending you? The orphan asylum is where all the women put children they can't care for any longer."

Yet just then, in the corridor outside my ward, the staff seemed to be arguing. Several languages collided at once. *Mi dispiace. . . . Oh, Mr. Aaronson, please. Let the child . . . kindeleh . . . Per favore. È per il bambino. Devo aiutare. . . . He can't be serious. . . . Do you have a better suggestion?* Gertie appeared in the doorway and pointed to my metal bed, frowning. A stooped man entered the ward. His face was fleshy and sad, though his gleaming mustache was twirled up hopefully at the ends. He moved heavily. When he reached my bedside, he gave me a wan smile.

"I sorry," he said. "I no speak the English so good. No Hebrew."

Hearing his voice, I sat up as best I could. I studied his face, the grandfatherly folds of it.

"You remember me?" he asked.

Without his apron and his cap, he looked smaller somehow, older.

Slowly, I nodded. "The ices man?"

Mr. Dinello smiled sheepishly. "How you are feeling? Your leg? Is she no good?"

"My foot is better." My voice was shattered again, barely above a whisper. I was so happy to see him, though, to have a visitor— someone I vaguely knew—that I tried to be on my best possible behavior. Pulling aside the sheet, I showed him my unbandaged foot, bright pink and inverted slightly. "My sides are better. My leg still hurts." I showed him my brace. "Look." I knocked against it. The hollow sound appealed to me. I'd taken to amusing myself by beating out little tunes on it and seeing how long it took to annoy people.

"Have you seen my mama?" I asked.

Mr. Dinello got an uncomfortable look on his face. He glanced around the ward. In the bed nearest mine, a little girl sang in a small, plaintive voice, "Turn Off Your Light, Mr. Moon Man." Another lay facing the wall, sniffling. Perspiration soaked into Mr. Dinello's collar where it rubbed against his neck. He put his hands on his knees, drew in a deep breath, and arranged his face into a smile.

He said, "You come with me, *ninella*, yes?"

◯

My son, he brings me a new television, a Sony Trinitron thirty-four-inch color, along with one of those brand-new gadgets they have now that can record any show you want on a large cassette.

"It's called a VCR, Ma," he says. He tells me I can tape *Dynasty* and *Dallas* and watch them whenever I want with this VCR. But I don't care for it. It has a separate remote control that has nothing to do with the controls for the television, and to program it you need an adviser from NASA. "For this you paid good money?" I say.

Yet now that I'm often confined to my house in Bedford, I do find myself sitting in Bert's antique wing chair—the one I had reupholstered in lilac last year—in front of the big new Sony. *This*, I like. At four o'clock every afternoon, I order my domestic to bring me a little something sweet for the mouth—a gin and tonic, a bowl of our premium Rocky Road and vanilla fudge—plus the cold sliced sirloin for Petunia. Then Petunia and I settle in together to watch *Donahue*. Such a handsome man! His show is quite the theater. All these confessions—forbidden love affairs, children secretly put up for adoption, grown men telling their mothers they're *feygelehs* on national TV. Surely it can't be worse than anything I ever did. But what strikes me most is that it's clearly entertainment for people who have grown up with privacy.

The day I arrived on Mulberry Street, everybody already knew. Mrs. DiPietro, the widow with the orthopedic shoes and a different-colored rosary for every day of the week. Mrs. Ferrendino, who never stopped perspiring and whose enormous forearms flapped as she fanned herself in her housedress. Mrs. Salucci, the cadaverous, slit-eyed lacemaker who offered vicious opinions on everything whether you asked for them or not. Every neighborhood has its yentas. They arranged themselves around the front stoop like the three Furies, watching as Mr. Dinello carried me up the stairs as if I were a tiny bride, my arms clutching his neck, my right leg jutting out in its brace. I had never been stared at so in my life. Their faces pressed in so close to me I could see their enormous pores, their errant eyebrows, their stained, dilapidated teeth. *"Ai, ai, ai!"* they exclaimed, running their hands over the wood of my crutches as we passed them.

The whole neighborhood had heard about the accident, of course. Some of them had even witnessed my mother stomping down the street afterward on her way home from the dispensary. They claimed she had actually *kicked* Mr. Dinello's horse in revenge, then shrieked at Mr. Dinello that he'd ruined her baby, that her child was now lame, that he was responsible. What was she supposed to do now—with three other mouths to feed and no husband in sight? Did he suppose she could just carry me up and down four flights of steps every day? How on earth was she supposed to make a living with an invalid child? They'd seen my mother make a V with her fingers and spit through them at Mr. Dinello. He'd apparently stood there miserably, saying nothing.

Most likely they'd also seen the name Herschel Bialystoker plastered on lampposts and store windows. Every month posters in Yiddish, Italian, and English papered the neighborhood with names and short descriptions of all the men who had deserted their families or gone missing: LOST. SEEKING. LAST SEEN. It was epidemic. In all those ridiculous fairy tales about immigrant life, poor-but-happy families pull together to launch a rag business—that turns into a tailor's shop—that turns into Ralph Lauren. Please. You half expect butterflies to be fluttering, elves whistling on the fire escapes, and everyone to burst into song. I have no use for that sort of nonsense. On the Lower East Side, families shattered like glass bottles. Men up and left all the time.

If you went to the schoolyard on Ludlow Street that September, you'd have seen another list, too. The obliterating summer heat turned the Lower East Side into an enormous petri dish

of bacteria and infection. July and August were polio season.
Diphtheria, cholera, typhoid, rheumatic fever. Every fall, children
returned to school to find names written in chalk on the schoolyard wall of all their classmates who'd died over the summer.
Esther Lezack. Marta Horvath. Saul Pinsker. You didn't need Phil
Donahue. You didn't need tabloids. You didn't need reporters
poking around your driveway and reprinting unflattering photos
of you looking like Joan Crawford.

That September of 1913, everyone in the neighborhood
would've seen another name from my family publicly on display
as well. Chalked on the bloodred wall of P.S. 42 in shaky white
letters: ROSE BIALYSTOKER—TYPHUS.

As Mr. Dinello carried me past his neighbors toward the
wrought-iron steps, I didn't know that my family and Mr. Lefkowitz had been in quarantine for most of the summer or
that my sister Rose had died. I didn't even know where Mulberry Street was in relation to Orchard Street. It could have
been miles away. The streets, to me, were like oceans of iron-
work and brick. I knew only that Mama had vanished—gone
off somewhere—in search of Papa, perhaps? And these new
neighborhood women were different from the ones on Orchard
Street, with their heavy floral perfume and the cut of their
dresses and their smells of hair oil, rosemary, coffee, and camphor. The inky sheen of their hair, the fat wattles beneath their
chins. I could feel their eyes studying me as if I were a speci-
men. They didn't bother to whisper.

"Look at that leg. No wonder her mother gave her up."

"Generosa is furious. As if they don't have enough trouble?"

"He claims it's only temporary. Apparently a tailor over on Orchard is helping to pay for her upkeep. Until she can climb stairs,
he says."

"Ha! She can climb stairs the day I can fly."

"Salvatore's too good. He thinks he's doing penance."

"So go to confession, then—don't take in a little *Ammazza Christi!*"

The Dinellos had three grown sons, Vincenzo, Luigi, and Silvio. They were all burly, muscled men in overalls and heavy boots; when they clomped up and down the stairs, the whole tenement shook.

I would learn later that the sons were sandhogs, employed to help dig the tunnels for the new Lexington Avenue subway extending north of Forty-Second Street. Each day they dug down, down into the bowels of the city—with their metal lunch pails and their dented shovels and their St. Anthony medals hanging around their necks—to face off against the bedrock and crumbly earth, the network of sewers and train lines already in place, the potential tsunami of muck and debris. Every evening they returned to the Mulberry Street tenement like heavy phantoms covered in fine gray dust, their overalls caked in mud. Before they even set foot in the kitchen, Mrs. Dinello yelled "*Ai, ai, ai!*" and made them remove their boots. But even as she pointed to the tracks they left in the front hallway—sloppy kisses of dirt, manure, and cement—she touched herself quickly: first on the forehead, then the heart, then on each shoulder. "*Grazie,*" she mouthed to the ceiling.

Silvio and Vincenzo had yet to be married. Brides had already been arranged for them, however. Back in Napoli families who knew the Dinellos were preparing to send their daughters to America, to build a bridge of a different sort. It was simply a matter of money, of time. Yet Luigi, the oldest, was already married to Annunziata, a shrill, industrious woman who'd given birth to four shrill, pummeling boys. The oldest, a skulking teenager named Vittorio, spent most of his time on the streets. A set of twins, Pasquale and Pietro, ignored me. But the youngest, Rocco, did not. He was about my age, perhaps six or seven, wiry and knock-kneed. His eyes were calculating black slots, and he had a cowlick that never stayed down no matter how much pomade his mother put on his head. The animosity between Rocco and me was instantaneous. He seemed to go out of his way to stick his tongue out at me or make a hateful "Bah-ha" sound whenever he saw me. He gave me the nickname "*Ragazza del Cavallo.*" Horse Girl. Although Mr. Dinello slapped him in the back of the head when he heard this, the name quickly stuck. I overheard the other boys calling me this very matter-of-factly as they clambered down the stairs on their way to school each morning. They weren't intending to be cruel. They were merely unquestioning and indifferent, which is another type of cruelty altogether.

If Rocco ever got close enough to me, I decided I'd punch him.

The Dinellos also had a niece, Beatrice, unmarried, who worked making lace for Mrs. Salucci on the fourth floor. The whole Dinello family lived on the second floor of the Mulberry Street tenement in three of the four apartments. But there was so much activity and movement and noise back and forth it felt more like one big town house. They had the run of the place, and their voices rang through the air shafts, windows, and hallways, filling the building with arguments and laughter.

They talked not just with their voices but with their whole bodies. When they spoke, they pinched the air, they shrugged at the ceiling, they pointed to themselves, they raised their arms beseechingly to the heavens, they conducted vast invisible symphonies with their arms, they held up their palms in mock supplication.

Even though I didn't speak much Italian, I could always glean what they were saying simply by watching them. It was like living in a house full of mimes.

The day I arrived, Generosa Dinello took one look at me—with my little twisted leg and my brace and my crutches—and started right in on her husband.

"How many times did I tell you? Don't buy a horse from the Hungarian—he is crazy in the head!"

"It wasn't the horse. I told you. It was the chicken!" Mr. Dinello roared. "The crazy chicken, running loose in the street. She scare the horse. The horse, she was good price."

"So this is how you save us money? You bring home a cripple to feed?"

"What do you want me to do, Generosa? I should leave her in the orphan asylum? Send her away to be locked with the crazy people?"

"Since when is she our problem?"

"Since she is. What if it were Beatrice? Look at her, Generosa." Mr. Dinello waved his arm toward me, as if toward a display. "A helpless little girl."

Their word for "little girl" was "ninella." I'd learned this on the streets. Hearing it now, I sensed my opportunity. Drawing upon the skills I had honed with Flora, I burst into voluptuous tears. I didn't much like the look of Mrs. Dinello, with her dark, arched brows and grim, frowning lips, but I sensed that her kitchen was far preferable to the place called the asylum. "Please, Mrs. Dinello!" I wailed. "Please don't send me away. I promise I'll be good. I promise I won't eat very much."

Mrs. Dinello regarded me. A comma of shiny black hair fell into her eyes. A small gold cross glinted in the crepe gully of her throat. With a deflated sigh, she shook her head. "Fine. You want to take care of a crippled little *Ammazza Christi*," she said to Mr.

Dinello, "we'll take care of a crippled little *Ammazza Christi.*"
Pointing at me, she made an eating motion with her hands, then
a shoveling motion. "But I don't care how crippled she is. If she's
going to stay, she's going to work."

∞

Not long ago, before refrigeration, ice was more precious than
gold. Nothing else could do what ice did, and in most parts
of the world it simply didn't exist. And where it did, it was
nearly impossible to harvest, transport, or store. It was the
one commodity that could literally vanish in your hand. Not
many people consider this today. If I weren't in my line of
business, I suppose I wouldn't, either. Yet for much of human
history, ice was a phenomenon. Ice was elitist. Rare. Powerful.
Ephemeral.

As early as the fifth century B.C., the Greeks apparently sold
snow in the markets of Athens. Roman emperors had ice hauled
down from the mountains; Egyptian royalty had snow shipped
from Lebanon. Yet for all these centuries, the precious commodity of ice could be used only to cool liquids—never to freeze
them.

That is, until Giambattista della Porta comes along in the sixteenth century.

He's a noble autodidact, this one, and as ambitious as his
name. Born to an aristocratic family outside Naples, della Porta
is a narrow-faced gentleman, as elegant as a calla lily. He wears
frocks of the finest embroidered silk with a ruff like one of those
paper frills on a crown roast. As the Italians say, he cuts *una bella
figura.*

Intellectually, the man is an octopus. Not only is he a play-
wright but a philosopher, a cryptographer, and a scientist. Me-

teorology, physiognomy, horticulture, astronomy, physics—everything in the natural world fascinates him.

Some put della Porta in the same league as Kepler and Galileo. Others, perhaps, categorize him more as a privileged oddball who's licentious with science, combining bona fide experiments with supernatural dabblings. This is due to della Porta's most famous book, published in 1558. *Natural Magic* is a voluminous, illustrated hodgepodge of occult practices, fantastical theories, and genuine scientific experiments. There are formulas for facial rouge and increased fertility. Instructions on how to produce "beautiful" pitted peaches. Descriptions of flying dragons.

And among its illustrations, theorems, and supernatural claims, there is a recipe for wine that is not merely chilled but *frozen*. To achieve this, della Porta instructs, one has to immerse and agitate a vial of wine inside a wooden bucket filled with snow and saltpeter.

Saltpeter: potassium nitrate. Or even simple salt: sodium chloride.

Salt, you see, makes ice melt faster. When the ice in della Porta's wooden bucket melts, the heat is transferred away from the contents of the vial. The wine inside the vial grows increasingly colder, until it freezes, while the ice around it grows increasingly warmer, until it melts. Solid becomes liquid, liquid becomes solid. A perfect ballet, a conversion of energy; matter is neither created nor destroyed, merely changing form. Ice to water, wine to ice. Fundamental science.

Della Porta's recipe for frozen wine is a hit at lavish banquets throughout Naples. The method for manufacturing ice cream is born.

And three centuries later, one Mr. Salvatore Dinello faithfully employs this method every morning, six days a week, in a cramped storefront tenement on New York City's Mulberry Street on the Lower East Side.

Dinello's Ices was one of the few small ices manufacturers still operating at that time. Ice cream—or "gelato" as he called it—was Mr. Dinello's true passion. As I'd soon discover, he made it for the Dinello family on special occasions, rhapsodizing about it as he did the opera. *Oh! Fragola! Crema!* But for commercial purposes, Mr. Dinello just made Italian ices. These were far cheaper and easier to produce than ice cream, and easier to sell because they contained no dairy. He could move his wagon down Hester Street from the Italian section to the Jewish section of the neighborhood without having to worry about kosher laws impeding his business.

His production plant, on the ground floor of his building, wasn't any bigger than Mr. Lefkowitz's factory, except that the space consisted of a big kitchen and a small office alcove in the back. What I did not fully comprehend then was that Mr. Dinello was a small *padrone*, an overseer of sorts—a miniature version of the wholesalers who would soon take over the industry. Manufacturing ices and ice cream in tenement apartments had been made illegal back in 1906. And so Mr. Dinello had established a separate little commercial kitchen in the ground-floor storefront and gone through the rigmarole of procuring not only a production license but peddlers' licenses as well. He rented these out, along with three wagons, for a dollar a day to three other men he'd known back in Napoli. The men paid him an additional dollar and a half per day for the lemon ices he made and supplied to them, which they then sold along designated routes on Canal Street, Wall Street, and over by Broome. Anything they earned above what they paid him, they kept. Mr. Dinello, I would learn, was a generous and honest *padrone*; the men peddling for him usually took home about a dollar and a half a day after expenses—fifty cents more than most others earned. Today, of course, all of this buys you nothing.

It was there, in the little office alcove behind the Dinello's Ices production kitchen, that the Dinellos installed me. Mr. Dinello placed a bench against the back wall. Mrs. Dinello covered it with some wine-colored cushions that she brought down from her parlor. In the courtyard was the privy. "Down here you no have to climb steps," Mr. Dinello said, lowering me onto the bench.

Children tell me all the time how they dream of living in an ice cream factory. Well. Good luck to them.

The storefront's high ceilings were made of pressed tin, and the big window looked directly onto Mulberry Street, the pushcarts and peddlers and horse carts all clamoring by. Delivery boys, suppliers, neighbors, men from the church brotherhood tromped in and out all day, gesticulating in Italian and Napolese and English and raising a ruckus. At night, finally empty, the cold kitchen crept with eerie purple shadows filtering in through cracks in the shutters. I could hear the scratching of vermin. Occasionally, a dark slink of rats scuttled toward me from a crevice in the corner, their teeth and tails gleaming in the residual light, and I jabbed at them viciously with a broom. The bench itself was narrow and rickety. I had never slept alone before. I missed my sisters terribly.

On the office wall high above me hung a wooden crucifix with a knotted figure on it, which scared me: I believed it to be some sort of weapon. Beside it, though, was a gilt-framed picture of a bearded father in lush brown robes hugging a rosy infant. Radiant gold rings encircled their heads. Looking at it made me feel sad and forsaken and hopeful all at once. Perhaps, I thought, it was a sign.

At daybreak I was awoken by the jangle of a horse and an oxlike man trundling up the steps from the street and pounding on the door. Mr. Dinello came hurrying down the stairs in his boots and his smock.

"Gennaro!" he cried, ushering the panting man into the storefront. *"Prego."*

Gennaro wore a thick leather apron knotted over his coat. A pair of tongs, shaped like calipers, dangled ominously from his belt. He balanced an enormous burlap-covered block on his shoulder. *Angling* his way into the kitchen, he slammed the block down on the tabletop so hard that the whole room seemed to shake. When he unwrapped the block, he revealed a glistening chunk of ice. Drawing a pick from his belt, he stabbed it expertly through its translucent heart. Like a diamond cutter or a surgeon, he seemed to know exactly where to aim the chisel to create a wholesale seizure of fractures. The ice cracked and cleaved with a sound like breaking tree branches. He jabbed at the ice again and again with staccato movements, turning it to crystalline shrapnel. It was both violent and beautiful to watch.

While Gennaro cut up one block of ice, then another, Mr. Dinello milled some of the ice in a pewter grinder until it was fine as snow, then scooped it into a large metal canister. Mrs. Dinello and Beatrice hoisted a pot from the stove and poured a cloudy, pale yellow liquid into the canister as well. The room filled with the scent of lemons. The canister was then placed in a large barrel with a crank. Mr. Dinello packed chunks of ice all around it and showered them with rock salt.

Before they were permitted to leave for school, Rocco and his brothers were enlisted to help wind the crank attached to the enormous barrel. They took turns, shoving and slapping each other in between.

That first morning, as I lay on the bench at the back of the kitchen, I kept hoping that at some point Mrs. Dinello would notice me and help me to the toilet. But she never did. I felt more immobilized and alone than I ever had at the dispensary. There, I'd had a feeling of being in somebody's care, enveloped, accounted for. But propped up in the rear office of Dinello's Ices, trying to hold my urine and pallid with hunger, I was almost a ghost, a silent witness to a hive of activity in which a strange family loved and worked and laughed and argued in a foreign language with their backs to me.

The boys took turns winding the crank over and over with a spine-slicing creak, rotating the canister of ingredients around and around inside its bath of ice and salt, the liquid sloshing and slapping, until it grew quiet. They worked quickly. Most commercial establishments by this time used motorized churns and barrels. But the Dinellos still cranked their large ice cream maker by hand.

When all the batches of ices were done, they scraped them into frosted metal pails with heavy lids and wrapped them in burlap, then helped Mr. Dinello carry these down to the four wagons.

After the grandsons had left for school, the other vendors had paid Mrs. Dinello their daily fees, and Mr. Dinello himself had commenced clopping down Mulberry Street with his skittish, Hungarian-bred horse, singing "I-SEES, I-SEES," the kitchen lay in ruins. Pails, melted ice, sopping burlap, ladles, lemon rinds, a huge sack of granulated sugar... Mrs. Dinello stood surveying the wreckage like a war nurse. She was a sturdy, violin-shaped woman, but her eyes were like black pebbles tossed into the pond of her face, the soft flesh hanging in rings beneath them.

Sighing, she wiped her hands on her apron and said aloud, "*Tutto questo.*" All this. Picking up a ladle as if it were a dead mouse, she released it above a zinc pail with a disdainful clatter. I drew in my breath. Only then did she seem to realize I was there.

"Oh," she said, frowning. "*La ninella.* Okay, you." She flicked her thumb toward the ceiling. "Up.

"Up, up, up!" She clapped. I struggled to stand. The hem of my nightdress was caught in my brace.

"Please," I said as I untangled myself and wrestled with my crutches. "The toilet?"

Mrs. Dinello shook her head and motioned between me and the door. It became clear that she expected me to make my way on my own. "*Uno, due,*" she counted, clapping out my steps. The problem wasn't only my leg but my arms. I was just too small and too weak to hold myself up on the crutches for very long. I barely made it to her before I collapsed.

"*Di nuovo,*" she said. "Again."

She pointed to the courtyard. As I struggled to the privy, Mrs. Dinello stood behind me and held the doors open. However, I had to figure out how to maneuver into the little stall by myself. My right leg was still rigid in its brace; I hopped on my left leg as I hoisted up my nightdress. I was terrified of falling in or not making it in time. *Horse Girl*: I could imagine the nicknames I'd be called if I soiled myself.

After I did my business, Mrs. Dinello made me walk back through the narrow front hallway, then across the storefront unassisted. I did not understand why she pushed me so; it seemed she derived some sort of cruel pleasure from watching me struggle. The rubber nibs of my crutches sometimes caught in the floorboards. I yanked and flailed until I was nearly in tears. And somehow, when I did, I thought of Mama and Bella and Rose and Flora—perhaps hundreds, perhaps thousands of miles away by now—gone somewhere, I imagined, still looking for Papa. The details of what had happened were puzzle pieces, shards of something big and broken that I could not assemble. *When would someone explain what was happening to me?*

I couldn't help sniffling. But only when I had completed my trip across the kitchen did Mrs. Dinello help me back onto the bench and stuff extra cushions beneath my leg to keep it elevated. Only then did she feed me: a slice of dry bread bathed in a mixture of coffee and warm milk. Oh, how luxurious it seemed! I ate wolfishly, gratefully. I was ashamed of how hungry I was, of how animal and helpless I felt. While I chewed, Mrs. Dinello restacked the pails and put a kettle on the stove. Once the water was scalding, she poured it liberally over the large enamel tabletop and all the utensils in a baptism of steam. "*Ai, ai, ai,*" she muttered. Bandaging her hand in a thick towel, she picked up the spoons and spatulas and whisked them around in a soapy pail.

When I finished my breakfast, she lifted the cup from my hands. As she did, for a moment we caught each other's eyes, my face tilted up toward hers, a timid flower, I suppose, fragile, brown-eyed, trembling. Something in Mrs. Dinello's face softened then. Her eyes seemed to thaw. She suddenly regarded me not with resentment but with something woeful and disbelieving—something akin to pity.

Her fingertips were like raisins. Gently, she touched them to the base of my chin. "You are so tiny," she whispered, shaking her head. "Who does this to a child?"

Then she drew back and assessed me. "Tomorrow," she announced, gesturing to the mess behind her, "you help."

Chapter 4

M Y PROBLEMS BACK THEN. Who could imagine the ones I have now?

This morning, a car snakes up my driveway. A slick black sedan with tinted windows. Inside? One pain in my ass after another. Lawyers from Beecham, Mather & Greene. Biggest guns in the business. They've already gotten the assault charges against me dropped, but the parents, it seems, are still filing a civil suit: One ten-second mishap and they think I should subsidize their daughter for the rest of her life? Please. It's not as if a horse kick left her crippled forever. Why, there wasn't even much of a bruise! And as anyone could see, I was doing her a favor!

I am also suing NBC for breach of contract. As I see it, they had simply been looking for any excuse to fire me all along. These new lawyers, they're counseling against it. But so what? What do they really know from fighting? Patrician faces they have, all of them. Expensive, feathered haircuts. Pink shirts. Ties tossed over their shoulders. They write on legal pads with tortoiseshell pens. Such a new breed—nobody tells jokes anymore. I can't distinguish one from another, except for Miss Slocum, the girl. A tiny thing, no taller than me. A pinched, serious face. Hair yellow and stiff as straw. She's attractive, I suppose, in a plain, frontier-woman sort of way—in another era you could picture her in a gingham bonnet, driving a buggy with a whip. She wears blouses with oversize bows at the throat. When I asked her what these were for, she informed me they're called "power bows." I told her they reminded me of our mascot, Spreckles the Clown.

The other lawyers insist, however, that it's better to have me represented in court by a woman. This will "soften" me in the eyes of the jury, they claim. I don't know who they think they're kidding. One look at this Miss Slocum, and you know she's a little viper.

I'd wanted to use the same lawyer we've always had, but Isaac wouldn't hear of it. "Edgar helped get you into this mess in the first place, Ma," he said.

Okay, so we fell a little behind in some paperwork. We improvised a few invoices when my records got muddled. I suppose the fact that Edgar is under indictment himself right now, it does not help matters. And so sue me: I once boasted, "Taxes are for *pishers*. Taxes are for the little people to pay." For God's sake, I was kidding. I was being a wisenheimer! How the hell was I supposed to know that the woman seated beside me at Trader Vic's was a reporter for Page Six?

So now we've got the tax-evasion charges along with the civil suit. One little slipup and people start digging through everything. It becomes a free-for-all, an open house for every disgruntled and slanderous nobody you've ever met in your life.

The first time my new lawyers came here, I had Sunny serve them ice cream. Mocha chip, vanilla bourbon. Our old-fashioned style. Still our best. The *gonifs*, they sat there telling me how delicious it was—then billed me for the fifteen minutes they spent in my parlor eating it. So I sent them a bill in return—for exactly the same amount—charging them for the ice cream they consumed. Now whenever they come here, it's strictly business. Which is too bad. Back when Edgar was our lawyer, Bert and I kept a tub of his favorite flavor on hand—black cherry—and we'd all sit around the pool afterward, washing it down with martinis.

The only person I can stand to see nowadays? Jason. He's home from college for the summer, so every Thursday he comes. I have my driver pick him up at the train station.

Sunny helps me into my red silk kimono. She styles my hair for me. Fixes my face. Settles me into the lilac wing chair in the conservatory.

"Turn up the air-conditioning," I say. "And spray some Shalimar around here."

"I open the drapes for you, too, yes, Mrs. Dunkle?" she says, bowing in that little way she has. Filipinos. Nicest people on the planet. All these years and Sunny's the only one who never talked to the press.

She pulls a cord and unleashes the view: Beyond the lawn and the pool, I can see clear to the lake, to the jade hills rising gently from the opposite shore, scalloping the horizon. It is marvelous. But otherwise I don't care for this house much. It was Bert's taste, Bert's dream. Bert used the tennis courts. Sure, the pool was nice when Jason was little. But now the upkeep is nothing but a pain in my ass. "Lil, you should use it," Rita nags. "The exercise will help your leg."

I don't want to help my leg. I've helped it enough. I'm tired. I'm done. I'm counting the days until I can return to Park Avenue. Give me New York any day. All these fancy bedroom communities, all these estates, they're like aspic. Trust me, darlings: A big city is where you want to grow old. Concert halls and picture houses everywhere. Bakeries and liquor stores just around the corner. You can cling to your shopping cart so you don't need your cane. People of all ages are outside: On any park bench, any crosstown bus, you've got yourself some vaudeville.

But after the incident on my television show, some schmucks

from the *New York Post* began camping out in front of my building, harassing the doormen. Photographers, gossip columnists. Geraldo Rivera showed up. The co-op board got all up in arms. Those shysters. Wall Street types, media moguls, all of them. They earn about $16 million apiece; you should see the preening that goes on in the damn elevator: the seven-hundred-dollar oxblood briefcases, the Armani suits, the cars these people drive. They'd sell their own daughters for a mention in *Women's Wear Daily* or *Town & Country*. But suddenly *I'm* attracting "unwanted attention"? Please.

Still, I had the staff close up the apartment—the way they used to every winter—and I came to Bedford. The lawyers thought it was best I "lie low" for a while. Tell that to the satellite trucks, I say.

The gardener, the butler, the pool boy—they tiptoe around me here. Maybe it's because they're new employees, but even Sunny kowtows. "You scare them, Ma," Isaac says.

Why? Because I made them all sign confidentiality agreements? Because I speak my mind and know exactly what I want? Why should I pretend people are doing me a favor when I'm paying them? I have no use for that sort of nonsense.

Once you reach a certain age, oh, the world assumes you're stupid and deaf and irrelevant. Other women my age—darlings, they would make marvelous spies. They could slip in and out of the Soviet Union without anyone giving them a second glance.

Not me, though. I make sure of it.

"Sunny!" I yell into the intercom when I spot the Cadillac pull in to the driveway. "More gin!"

My glass is empty already. From the side window, I can see my Cadillac turning and crunching to a halt. Hector comes around, opens the door, and my grandson unfurls himself.

Jason.

As he steps out onto the gravel, he yawns and stretches; he's gangly, pantherlike, proud and new in his muscles, the way teenage boys so often are. For a moment he can't resist pausing to glance at his reflection in the tinted windows. I watch him tilt his head and touch his jaw appraisingly. The top of his hair looks like a chrysanthemum, though it's oddly long in back, clipped into a chevron. Who styles their hair like that? Half girl, half boy, as if the barber couldn't make up his mind. He's still got that *farkakte* safety pin stuck through his earlobe, too, and that ugly spiked dog collar he insists on wearing (Petunia's is more elegant!). Also, one of those T-shirts he destroys himself. Its sleeves are ripped off, and the front looks clawed. Such a handsome boy, but *this* he has to do? The last time he paid me a visit, he even wore black eye makeup. His girlfriend put it on him, he said.

"You're sure you're not just a *feygeleh*?" I said.

He's trying to look tough, I suppose, but a baby face is a baby face. Good luck disguising it. No matter. My grandson's "look" rankles his mother even more than me, which I suspect is the whole point. Earlier this year Jason changed his major from economics to theater, too. Isaac practically had a heart attack and called me in a panic, but what do I care, really? The kid still has more business sense than his father. Let Isaac sweat it a little.

Jason fiddles with a pair of sunglasses and drops them into the shopping bag he's carrying. He lets out a long breath, as if bracing himself. Then he lopes across the gravel to my front door.

"Hey, uh. How's it going?" I hear him say to my butler, his voice echoing through the foyer. "Grandma's upstairs?"

He bounds up the marble staircase and is standing in the doorway in no time. Ah, youth! "Hey, Grams, what's up?" he says. Slinging his shopping bag on top of the piano with a *thunk!*, he comes over to the chair, leans down, and gives me a quick, dry kiss on the cheek. He smells of baby powder and french fries. "Everything copacetic?"

"Come closer." I smile. "Let me get a look at you."

He makes a face but obliges. I put my hand to his cheek. I feel the downiness of his young skin. The boy is an Adonis—and he knows it. Deep-set green eyes, just like his grandfather. Fierce cheekbones. That mass of curls atop his head as dark as strong coffee. "Oh," I say, "such a *punim*. Such a heartbreaker. Turn around."

"Grams," he groans. But he does—with a tinge of bravado no less. He thinks I don't see him flexing his biceps and straightening his shoulders, but I do. Young men are never so beautiful as when they are on the brink of nineteen.

"Such a *tuches*!" I laugh, slapping him playfully on the backside. "Oy. What are those pants made out of?"

"Leather."

"Leather? It's eighty degrees outside. Who the hell wears leather in August? What's 'Sandinista'?" I motion to his shredded T-shirt.

"An album by the Clash," he says, staring down at his shirt as if he's only just realized what he's wearing. "I played it for you last week? Sandinistas are the socialist party in Nicaragua."

"Oh?" I adjust my eyeglasses. "So you're a socialist now?"

He sighs. "I've always been a socialist, Grams."

"Of course you are, *tateleh*." I smile, patting his hand. "After all, I'm the one paying your tuition.

"Sit," I order.

Jason pulls up a chair. One of the Hepplewhites, upholstered in peach silk, where Petunia likes to curl up. My grandson sprawls in it, his legs splayed. He's like his great-grandfather; he can't really sit still. His foot jiggles, he fidgets with that safety pin in his ear. He glances about. "I've only got like a couple of hours," he says, eyeing the swimming pool. "I gotta catch the 2:54 back for re-hearsal." Jason is in a performance-art troupe called Alarm Clock. His father, however, refers to it as "the Future Unemployment Line of America." I saw one of their shows in an abandoned ware-house off First Avenue last year. Jason made a big fuss over my coming, which I certainly appreciated—and of course, I *kvelled* over him. Yet I can't say I cared for it much. It was all very loud, and the seating was terrible. Jason read a series of haikus I did not understand, then played an electric guitar while a couple of girls in greasepaint and sheets writhed around on the floor curs-ing Ronald Reagan. There was one poet, one girl in a tutu, one ukulele player, one unicyclist, one "interpretive dancer"—but no script. Everyone seemed angry about something. It was like vaudeville for the disgruntled.

"We're working on a new piece for Alarm Clock," Jason says. "Thatcher, U.S. involvement in El Salvador, Bill Bennett—they're all going in it. It's going to be awesome."

Sunny knocks, the silver tray balanced awkwardly between her hip and the doorframe. "Mrs. Dunkle?"

"Here." I point to the coffee table. Supposedly it's an original from France—Louis the Someteenth. "Just leave the bottle, the ice, everything. We don't want to be disturbed."

"A new show. Really? Good for you," I say. "Close the door!" I shout to Sunny.

"Happy hour?" Jason says. "It's barely noon, Grams."

"Oh, shush, you. You'll have some, yes?"

"Well"—he smiles slyly and wiggles his eyebrows—"if you in-sist." Every time, it's the same thing. Leaning in, he rubs his hands together expectantly. The drinking age in New York State was raised last year, so technically, I suppose, this is still illegal for my grandson. But we Jews didn't spend forty years wandering the desert so that I could forfeit a gin and tonic with my progeny. As

Jason reaches for the ice tongs, however, I slap his hand. "Not so fast. What did you bring me?"

"Oh. Some truly awesome tunes," he says, leaping up. He goes to the piano, pulls an album out of the bag. "You'll either love them or hate them." He holds up an ugly shocking pink record sleeve slashed with fluorescent green. "Classic punk." He holds up another record, packaged in a blue paper sleeve. "And some new stuff, too. The Butthole Surfers. Some Aztec Camera. Grandmaster Flash."

"Okay, then." I drop three ice cubes into my tumbler, then three into his. They sound like marbles hitting. "You know where the hi-fi is."

"Awesome." He pulls out the bright pink square. Now he's happy. Now he's fully engaged. "We'll start with this one first, definitely. The Sex Pistols."

I snap my fingers and point. "Bring it here. Let me see."

"Johnny Rotten, the singer, has had another band for a while now, called PiL. But it's not nearly as good." Jason hands the album over to me proudly. I adjust my eyeglasses and study it.

The cover looks like a hostage note.

"Johnny Rotten?" I scowl. "His parents named him that?"

"Nuh-uh. His real name is John Lydon. He changed it."

"Lydon/Rotten. Not much difference." I shrug. "Now, if he changed it to Grossberger, that would be something."

While Jason sets up the record, I pour us both generous gin and tonics. In an instant the conservatory pulsates with violence. I hear a singer, if you can call him that, shrieking that he's an Antichrist. That he wants to *be* anarchy. *Sure he does*, I think. *Until he needs a fire department or the postal service.* Petunia, who's been sleeping on her pillow, leaps up in a seizure of panic and scampers under the sofa. "Okay. Enough with that one," I say.

Jason snatches the needle off the record with a zipping sound. "I wondered how long you'd last," he says with a laugh.

"If I wanted to listen to people yelling at me, I could just invite your parents for dinner."

"Affirmative. Okay, let's try this, then." He slides another record out of its sleeve and guides it gently onto the turntable.

"Oh, hey," he says as he settles back in. "Speaking of parents, Mom and Dad say hi, and...you know, they're sorry they haven't been up to visit, and *blah-blah-blah*." He rolls his eyes at me.

"Oh, do they now?" I say archly.

Jason shrugs. "Hey, I hardly see them myself...." His voice trails off.

For a few minutes, we sip our gin and tonics and just listen. The music is a stuttering sort of computerized beat; it's like music for robots. Finally a voice begins speaking about how he's "close to the edge" and how he is trying not to lose his head, followed by a bitter sort of laugh. It is not altogether unpleasant at all. Certainly it's original.

After a moment I say, "He's not really singing, is he?"

"It's called rapping, Grandma."

"Rapping? Where I come from, it's called kvetching." Jason looks at me dryly. I can't help smiling. He knows I'm being a wisenheimer.

"Maybe I should rap, too," I chuckle, stirring my gin and tonic with my finger. "If you believe the papers."

"Yeah, I know." Jason frowns. "Like, what's up with that?"

"*Meshuggenehs.*" I shrug, reaching for the bottle. "As if I'm the first business owner ever to have a little workplace incident? Or get audited? Please. More gin, *tateleh?*"

Jason smiles: flawless, orthodontiaed, all-American teeth, eggshell white and shining. His hair glistens. I study the perfect, childish face of my grandson as he dutifully toasts me with his second double gin and tonic. Together, Petunia and I listen to the music that enraptures him, sharing his abandon, his angry pleasure in it.

People think teenagers are a pain in the ass. Well, they are, of course. But not if you tap into what they're passionate about. People also think that if you're old, you can't appreciate anything new. Or if you do, it's adorable. Put this in an advertisement, they say: Granny on a motorcycle—isn't that funny? Show Granny rock-'n'-rolling around the kitchen with her Mop & Glo—isn't that a hoot? Please. Don't patronize me with such nonsense. The first time I heard Salvatore Dinello performing opera in his kitchen? Or Enrico Caruso and Sophie Tucker on the Victrola? Louis Armstrong? Billie Holiday? Benny Goodman? Judy Garland? Edith Piaf? Oh, each time it was like sparklers going off!

Sinatra, him I never cared for much, because he sounded too much like the guys in my neighborhood. But Henry Mancini? Wonderful. Sarah Vaughan? Gene Kelly, as far as I'm concerned, was as good a singer as he was a dancer: like velvet. Johnny Mathis. Oh, and Harry Belafonte! Elvis, the Beatles, the Supremes—I liked them all, too, when they came out. My children couldn't believe it. But if you've got to come up with a different flavor of ice cream each month, you had better be open to new ideas, darlings. You've got to stay fresh, innovative. Plus, we had guest stars perform live on our *Sundae Morning Funhouse* all the time. The "Dance-O-Rama" segment of the show was hugely popular. Some critic once accused us of ripping off *American Bandstand*, but it was a contest, for God's sake, and just one song. That's all that young children have the patience for! We got some big names in our studio, too, I'll have you know. Dusty Springfield sang one week. Neil Sedaka. Frankie Valli. Ohio Express performed that hit of theirs, "Yummy Yummy

Yummy," which the children positively loved. In the seventies Bobby Sherman came on and agreed to dub himself "Bobby Sherbet."

Of course, my favorite singer of all time is Johnny Cash. That baritone of his is like hot fudge just brought to a boil. We never got him to sing on the *Sundae Morning Funhouse*, though. But I used to play his records at home so often, Bert would get jealous.

Jason lifts his glass to the light and frowns.

"Oh, dear. Empty," I say. "Would you like another?"

He shakes his head and winks mischievously. Digging down deep into the pocket of his leather pants—it's a wonder he can get his hand in, that leather looks so tight—he pulls out a slim little twist of paper. "Ta-da." He grins. "Time to pump up the volume, eh, Grams?"

"Oh, you horrible child!" I swat him on the knee. "Tempting me like this. The ashtray's over there"—I point—"by the piano. The matches are in the box."

My grandson scrambles up, retrieves all the paraphernalia, then lights up. He takes several deep drags, then passes it to me carefully pinched between his thumb and forefinger.

This is always our favorite part of the visit.

"Wow," he says, grinning as he exhales. He coughs a bit. "You know, if the 'rents ever saw us doing this, they'd have a total shit fit."

"So let them," I say. "What else are grandmothers for, *tateleh*?" I struggle to keep the smoke deep in my lungs, just as Jason has taught me. I begin coughing, too, and try to turn it into a chuckle. The taste I don't care for much, but the effect is extremely pleasant.

I motion to him to refill our tumblers. "So tell me everything," I say. "The girl, your ghastly parents, the summer job, the Alarm Clock—"

"Okay," he says dreamily, glancing around the room. "Hey, you don't by any chance, like, have some ice cream?"

I giggle. "Oh, you little *schnorrer*. Mmm. Let me think. There's Rocky Road. Maple walnut. Strawberry. Coffee. I think there's also some vanilla fudge left—"

"Oooh." He smiles lasciviously. "They all sound so, so good."

"Don't they, now!" I clasp my hands together. "Maple walnut. Oh, my."

"Oh, man," he moans to the ceiling. "I am so baked."

I press the button on the intercom.

"Yes, Mrs. Dunkle?" Sunny's disembodied voice. I have never noticed this until now: Intercoms are astonishing. A human voice, right out of a little speaker! Right out of thin air, really! Words from a box! All of it: electricity, magnets, plastic. It's a tiny miracle! Who actually invented the intercom? I wonder. Certainly, I will have to look it up.

"We need spoons." I hiccup. "And a few ice cream scoops." I'm having trouble, I realize, fully moving my jaw. The room around me suddenly looks a bit like film caught in a projector. "The vanilla fudge, the Rocky— Oh, hell. Bring up everything in the Frigidaire."

"Everything, Mrs. Dunkle?"

"Yes! No! Just the ice cream."

That voice in the box—it disappears.

Then I realize I've forgotten something. I press the button on the intercom again.

"Yes, Mrs. Dunkle?"

"You're a mensch, Sunny, you know that?"

"Um, yes, thank you, Mrs. Dunkle."

Then it disappears again, and I remember something else and push the button.

"Yes, Mrs. Dunkle?"

"My grandson," I whisper loudly. "Is he not an Adonis? Have you ever seen anything more beautiful in this world than my grandson?"

"Uh, your grandson, he is a very nice young man, Mrs. Dunkle."

"And such a *tuches* on him! Did you see? Just like his grandfather—"

"Grandma!" Jason groans.

There is a pause over the intercom. "Um, his grandfather was a very lovely man, too, yes, Mrs. Dunkle."

"My grandson, Sunny? You think he loves me?" I say loudly into the intercom. "Or is he just paying me all this attention because he's after my money?"

Jason sits up suddenly. His face reddens. "Grandma!"

From over the intercom, I can hear Sunny take a deep breath. "Oh, Mrs. Dunkle. Your grandson is a very sweet boy. I come with the ice cream now, yes?"

I look at Jason, his face arranged into a dramatic, wounded look of incredulity. "Grandma, c'mon. Do you actually, like, really believe—"

"Oh, shush, you," I say. "Don't even try. You think I don't know why some college kid would go out of his way every week to visit his damn grandmother? Why you'd schlep all the way up to a dreary mansion in Bedford when you could be out at the beach all summer?"

Jason stares at me. He's utterly at a loss for what to say. Youth: They always think they're cleverer and cannier than they ever really are.

"So what?" I say. "So I let you drink and smoke marijuana? You think I don't know that you could be doing the same things with your friends?"

"You think, like, I'm partying with you just to, like, get in good with you?" Jason says slowly.

"Well, it's more fun than being with your horrible parents," I concede. "But of course you're hustling me, *tateleh*! And why shouldn't you? At least one person in this family besides me ought to have some brains, a little naked ambition. You think I give a damn?"

He stares at me. After a moment he says carefully, "Uh, I'm not sure what I'm supposed to say."

"Please," I tell him. "Just keep visiting whenever you're back from school, and I'll take good care of you, *tateleh*. You understand? Just don't bullshit me."

Sunny arrives with the ice cream, five quarts crammed onto a tray with two of my little cut-glass dishes and the utensils. She sets it down on the Louis-the-Something table next to the gin.

"Take the lids off the quarts," I say. "I can't do it with my arthritis."

Jason leans forward to assist her.

"It needs to thaw," I tell him. "It's too hard."

"Nuh-uh. I got it," he says quietly. With the scoop he gouges into the first fresh quart—strawberry—and spoons a heap of glistening pink into one of the little crystal bowls. He reaches for the Rocky Road next, his muscles flexing, his face grave. "You like all of these, right, Grandma?"

From the hi-fi the singer who talks instead of sings is describing the street noise and the bad stench of the ghetto. "It's like a jungle sometimes," he says.

I reach over and take my dish of ice cream from my grandson. He looks stricken. And suddenly, for some reason, I'm overcome by sadness, a wallop of grief. Is this what it has all come to? How did it turn out like this? I can feel it in my eyes, swelling. "Oh," I say with surprise. I grip the padded armrest of my chair.

Jason stops in the middle of scooping. "Grandma? You okay?"

I shake my head and wave him off. I cough, pound myself on the breastbone.

"This singer," I remark, blinking behind my eyeglasses and pointing to the hi-fi. "So much complaining. Please. That neighborhood of his sounds no worse than mine was, growing up."

Chapter 5

P EOPLE NEVER SUFFICIENTLY appreciate their saviors. Look at France, for God's sake. Or Japan. After the war, we rebuilt their economy—and what thanks do we get? They're taking over the world again with their cars and electronics.

Myself, I was no exception. In 1913 there were floods of immigrants and a polio epidemic in New York. Hospitals, charities, social services were stretched to breaking. I was nobody's priority. I was falling through the cracks. But the Dinellos, they caught me.

On the food they fed me, I grew less feeble. My shattered bones began to mend thanks to dandelion greens sautéed in lemon and garlic, to broccoli rabe and soft cheese, to lenticchie and pasta e fagioli that Mrs. Dinello simmered every day in a cast-iron pot.

The Dinellos insisted I earn my keep, too—which was a gift in itself, darlings.

Each morning, as soon as the ingredients for the lemon ices were assembled, Mrs. Dinello clamped my hands onto the handle of the beastly ice cream maker and forced me to crank it in tandem with her. *Up, forward, and over. Up, forward, and over.* The ice chunks put up a lot of resistance; the crunching sound was hideous. Pain shot down my side where my ribs had been broken. But Mrs. Dinello kept her hands on mine. "Only your legs are

crippled, not your arms," she said, flexing her biceps and pointing. "This make you strong, you understand? *Capisce?*"

Up, forward, and over. Up, forward, and over. The barrel creaked,
gears squealed. When we finally finished, Mrs. Dinello's housedress gave off a musky stench; her damp bosom stuck against the
back of my neck. My arms trembled. Mr. Dinello himself had to
unscrew the barrel top and pull out the dasher. And yet after just
a week of such torture, I found that I could in fact hoist myself up
on my crutches with greater ease. My arms had grown sturdier.

Beatrice taught me to hem lace as well, so I could do piecework for Mrs. Salucci upstairs. It was painstaking, tedious work,
done under the anemic light of one small gas lamp in the office,
but it was a job I could do sitting in the storefront. With my
child's tiny fingers, I proved to be unusually adept at working the
fine thread around the most delicate bobbins. For the very first
order I completed, Mrs. Salucci paid the Dinellos twenty cents.
That was a lot of money in those days, trust me.

"*Molto buono,*" Mrs. Dinello said. Taking a mason jar from the
shelf, she popped a single penny into it and pointed at me. "This
we save for the moving pictures."

Mrs. Dinello, I quickly learned, was obsessed with two activ-
ities besides earning money: attending church and going to the
movies. That is, until one evening when the front door banged
open and Luigi and Vincenzo staggered into the storefront carrying a polished wooden box the size of a small trunk. Behind
them came Silvio, clutching a stack of flat squares to his chest and
singing at the top of his lungs.

That evening everyone in the Mulberry Street tenement
crowded eagerly into the storefront. For many of us, it was the
first time we'd ever heard a gramophone. It was a small, honey-
colored box with a small brass crank, designed by the Victor
Company for listeners of modest means; indeed, Luigi had won

it from another sandhog in a card game. A horn was tucked on the underside of the little tabletop cabinet, and it needed to be rewound after every two songs. The records themselves—oh, they were like dinner plates.

Yet the amazement! How did the sound rise off of those flat black disks? Where were the instruments coming from? Six records had been won with the deal, and after Mrs. Dinello finished admonishing her sons for gambling, the Dinello brothers played them over and over again. "I Want A Girl Just Like The Girl That Married Dear Old Dad." "Alexander's Ragtime Band." And then a trembling tenor filled the ices factory. Enrico Caruso. He sang "Addio Mia Bella Napoli," "Canta Pe' Me," and "Ave Maria"—all in Italian, of course. Gathered by the Victrola, Silvio and Mrs. Dinello openly wept. Beatrice and Mr. Dinello waltzed. All the grandsons were strangely quiet, almost not daring to breathe. Mrs. Ferrendino closed her eyes rapturously. Mrs. Salucci frowned with disapproval. A few neighbors sang along; someone ran upstairs and returned with a bottle of grappa. Immigrants, all of us, and every one of us astonished.

Today everybody's such a wisenheimer, a know-it-all. Everyone's a critic. Nothing surprises us anymore. Even the moon landing: We'd been hearing about it for years before Neil Armstrong finally took his first step. But to hear a Victrola for the very first time? Darlings, it was miraculous. It was like falling in love.

Afterward the Dinello boys carried their prize upstairs, where it was given a place of honor in the Dinellos' parlor beside the mantelpiece flanked by the two grim portraits of Mrs. Dinello's parents that she'd carried all the way over from Napoli. From then on, with the door propped open and the cabinet angled toward the air shaft, Mrs. Dinello made sure that the entire tenement could listen to "Canta Pe' Me" or "When You and I Were Young, Maggie," as we worked.

Yet not for a moment did I stop thinking about my family, picturing them all reunited happily somewhere in South Africa without me. My yearning and shame throbbed like a heartbeat. Why had nobody sent for me? Why was I still being punished?

Every Sunday morning the Dinellos went out—the men in derbies, the women's heads draped in veils, the boys freshly scrubbed. All of Mulberry Street was still, except for the bonging of church bells. The carillons seemed to reverberate off the empty fire escapes and shuttered storefronts. I sat alone in the kitchen and listened sullenly. As soon as I was sure they were gone, I hobbled over to the Dinellos' desk and pulled open the drawers. I riffled through the ledger books and piles of receipts tucked inside. I pried open a tin of violet candy to find that it contained not candy at all but a thin loop of wooden beads with an X dangling from it—a copy of so many I'd seen around, threaded through women's trembling fingers like lace. This one, though, I put on over my pinafore like a necklace. I pawed through letters in fragile onionskin envelopes, holding them to the light even though I could not read. Sometimes I played with Mrs. Dinello's precious pen, pretending to dip it into the inkwell and write numbers in columns, as she did. I fingered the lozenges of her small abacus. I pretended to be a shopkeeper in Hamburg, impressing my mother with my industriousness. *How clever Malka is*, I imagined Mama saying as she walked in awe through my shop. *Look at her making so much money for us selling pencils and necklaces!* I made sure to put everything back before the Dinellos returned. Yet I particularly liked the wooden necklace, and once I forgot to remove it. I discovered it hours later still dangling against my pinafore. Yet no one had paid me any mind. The whole family clambered directly upstairs when they returned. I could hear boisterousness, the clatter of pots, tables being set. I could smell tomato sauce simmering, that delirious scent of garlic and sweetness and frying meat. I could hear Mrs. Dinello reciting a string of prayers over her children and grandchildren and, later, the entire family assembling for their dinner without me.

One Sunday after the family meal, Mr. Dinello lumbered down to the storefront carrying a small bottle with a stopper.

"*Salute*, Ninella. You help me today, *si?*" he said. "We make the special *dolce*."

I tried to scowl and appear indifferent. But the truth was, anything to do with food interested me. Taking bottles of milk and cream from the icebox, Mr. Dinello measured their contents into a large porcelain bowl, cracked a few eggs with a theatrical flutter, and whisked in generous scoops of sugar. He added several drops of pearly brown liquid from his vial. "*Mm, buono, si?*" he said, running it under my nose to sniff. I had to admit: It smelled marvelous.

Ice chips were still in the icebox from Saturday. After Mr. Dinello loaded them into the barrel and sprinkled them with rock salt, he had me crank the ices maker with him all over again.

"*O Mimì, tu più non torni,*" he sang gently. "Now you."

"*O Mimì, tu più non torni,*" I parroted.

"*Di nouvo.*" He sang another line and waited for me to copy. Together, in fits and starts, we sang—strange, beautiful arias in Italian.

Mr. Dinello winked. "The singing, she is the secret ingredient."

Finally he unscrewed the barrel top. Usually when we made Italian ices, the dasher came out dripping with translucent chunks. Yet now it was coated in thick gobs of what looked like sloppy butter. Scraping off a great quantity with a spoon, Mr. Dinello handed it to me. "Mm. You like, *si?*"

The white gooeyness was peculiar; the wisps of frosty steam rising from the container made it look almost dangerous. But Mr.

Dinello rubbed his stomach with exaggerated motions: *Gelato. Delizioso.*

Slowly, I closed my eyes and touched the spoon lightly to the tip of my tongue.

Unctuous, milky sweetness spread through my mouth like cold fire. Silky and impossible, it dissolved into a flavor I'd never known—vanilla—then slid down my throat like a salve. I supposed that my eyes must have widened with astonishment. And I could not help it. I smiled. It was a cataclysm of deliciousness "Ahahaha, *si?*" Mr. Dinello said with pleasure.

Gelato, he called it. *Gel-La-Toe.* The word itself was like music. And the ingredients Mr. Dinello used were unknown to me then. Who'd ever seen pistachios in Vishnev? Or tasted cinnamon? There were no artificial colorings in his ice cream—no garish, dead-giveaway yellows, browns, or pinks. So each time we made a new batch of gelato together—as became our habit—it was a fresh revelation. One Sunday I put the spoon in my mouth and tasted *fragola*—strawberry—for the first time. Then *cioccolato!*

Each time I did, Mr. Dinello watched me intently, with pleasure. I couldn't hide my delight. I slurped and licked. I grinned. It was the best food I had ever eaten. My fate, it had been set in motion.

It was hard for me to be mean to Mr. Dinello when we made ice cream together. And yet, except for the singing, I remained silent as we worked. Even when I wanted to speak, the words simply refused to come. Sometimes the ice cream itself seemed to stick at the back of my mouth like a web, and an ache grew in my throat.

Of course, I always tell the public that I fell in love with ice cream as soon as I first ate it—that it was my one great pleasure as a poor little immigrant girl on the Lower East Side. For decades I marketed Dunkle's as a confection of pure joy—as a distillation of childhood, sprinkles, rainbows, and magic. Some of our advertisements even promoted it subliminally as—dare I say?—a source of redemption. In the 1960s, after I did my famous "Please Come to Dunkle's" campaign, we ran a series of television commercials that depicted a family having a very bad day. Mary loses the spelling bee, Willie strikes out at baseball, Dad gets yelled at by his boss, Mom burns the roast beef—even the dog gets a burr in his paw and trots into the kitchen whimpering. But after dinner the family opens a carton of Dunkle's ice cream together—or piles into the car and goes to Dunkle's for Happy Cones and Mint Everest sundaes—and presto! Suddenly their world turns Technicolor again and all is well. "Dunkle's," Spreckles the Clown, our mascot, says, waving into the camera, "for happy endings always."

Yet the truth is, darlings, that ice cream, for me, was not a food of happiness at all. Oh, yes, of course: Whenever I first put it in my mouth, I experienced an explosion of delight. But there was no chewing ice cream, no way to let it linger to trick my hunger. As soon as I began to lick the spoon, the ice cream inevitably started to turn to liquid. By the time Mr. Dinello disappeared back upstairs, leaving me alone in the kitchen with the debris—the sweetness on my tongue was already becoming a memory. It was like love: No sooner had I finished it than a devastating sense of loss always set in. Sitting alone in the drafty storefront, staring down at the dirty spoon in my hand, I wondered why everything I adored disappeared so quickly. Clearly it was my fault. Filling with guilt, with shame, I thought about my family—and of what I had done to them to drive them away. Ice cream? All it did was intensify my grief.

Mama, I always thought. *What would she say if she could see me in the little ices factory?*

"Why you eat but never smile?" Mr. Dinello asked me sadly. "You no like anymore? You try another flavor?"

He could have flavored it with gold, I suppose. He could have flavored it with diamonds.

I had to run away. I had to escape the ice cream factory on Mulberry Street, I decided, and somehow find my way back to my family in South Africa and show them how worthy I had become.

Instead of performing my duties grudgingly, I began to crank the handle of the ices maker each morning with the determination of an athlete, until my biceps cramped and Mrs. Dinello herself had to say, "*Ninella. Basta.*" Enough. Later, when Mrs. Dinello went to "*messe,*" I practiced walking back and forth across the storefront on my crutches. Four times I walked across the drafty room, then five. Soon, not only could I cross the storefront with ease, but hop across the floorboards using just one crutch to support me.

By then, however, afternoon light slanted across the storefronts on Mulberry Street in slices of deep, autumn gold. Mr. Dinello mounted a blackened grill onto the back of his wagon and replaced its sign with a new one reading, CASTAGNE CALDE. HOT CHESTNUTS. 5 CENTS.

The season for ices was over.

One afternoon he arrived in the office panting. "Ninella," he said. Behind him followed a man with a tweed cap and a drooping mustache.

"This is Mr. Fabricante, from L'Ordine Figli d'Italia," Mr. Dinello said. "He bring a gift."

The stranger held out a wooden hook. A cane, a tiny one, meant for a child. "My son, he had the polio. Maybe you can use this now," Mr. Fabricante said quietly.

Hesitantly, I shed my crutches and leaned on the cane. Mr. Fabricante gingerly held my elbow. I took a trembling, jerky step.

I wobbled and flailed a little. A ribbon of pain shot up my right leg, but only for an instant. Then I found I could balance, and slowly I hobbled forward. Once, then again. Then again. Then again.

Walking with my cane was very much like turning the crank of the ice cream maker. The more I did it, the more I endured and the more I could do. My left leg grew stronger, and though my right leg jutted inward—still in its brace—and pain sizzled in my calf on occasion, I found I could put more and more weight on it.

The first frost came. The sidewalks of Mulberry Street glistened with ice. Though I pleaded to go out, Mrs. Dinello insisted I remain indoors. "You should not trip on the sidewalk with your cane and break the other leg." She frowned. "That is the last thing we need."

And so every morning I climbed up and down the tenement stairs instead.

One labored step after another I took, dragging my right leg up behind me. Tenants let me limp about the building and in and out of their homes, paying me no mind. It could be like that back then. Trying to maintain privacy was often more trouble than it was worth, especially when everyone could hear you doing your business in the toilets on the landings, and your sneezes rang through the air shafts, and your arguments over love and money and family, no matter how hotly whispered, became common knowledge as soon as they began.

On each floor I hobbled through the Dinello family's living quarters, then their neighbors'. Each apartment was covered in its own sadly hopeful wallpaper, the cheap patterns of roses and paisleys streaked with a thin film of soot. Paint peeled on the doorframes, soups simmered on blackened stoves, tiny statues and a few treasured keepsakes from the old country sat displayed proudly on warped breakfronts and rigorously polished mantels. My right leg was often tender and throbbing, but each step brought me closer to the pier on Whitehall Street, to the ticket booth at the shipping office.

Mrs. Salucci was so busy nattering away and snubbing me as we worked that I found it surprisingly easy to steal from her. A spool of blue thread. A pair of tassels from her curtain stays. A card of straight pins. Downstairs in the storefront, I managed to pry loose a floorboard in the office with the tip of my cane and hollow out a little space beneath it. A tin teaspoon, I put in it. A hairpin from Mrs. Ferrendino's nightstand. A cake of brown soap from the Piccolo family on the third floor. And so sue me: a rubber ball from a drawer in the room where Rocco and his brothers slept. I also took the violet-candy tin with the necklace of wooden beads inside it from Mrs. Dinello's desk. With my brace it was easy to slip things beneath my skirt and clutch them against my bad leg with one hand. People in the tenement were so used to seeing me limp like that that they stopped seeing me altogether—if, in fact, they had ever seen me at all. Everybody looks away when a cripple enters a room, and certainly no one expects her to steal. Who filches things when they can't run?

Although I sometimes felt a stab of guilt when I slipped a shoehorn or a glass marble into my stash, my heart raced with the inexplicable thrill of it. And as soon as I stole the items, I truly believed they'd been mine all along. My treasures. Alone at night, I would sometimes examine them, turning them over lovingly in my hands—lifting the wooden necklace on over my head, squinting through the clear glass marble shot through with wisps of blue like smoke.

Oh, I adored the novelty of them, the delight of having little things of my very own—things that would stay put and be there for me to play with. Yet I was aware, of course, that every week a junk man came around to the tenement. (In retrospect it seems he was often more akin to a pawnbroker. People bought and sold things that they dearly needed, that weren't junk at all. Once I'd seen the Sciottos sell a fancy coverlet they'd brought over from Reggio. It was so they could pay their rent that week and not get evicted, Mrs. Salucci reported smugly.) If I could bear to part with my treasures, I hoped, the junk man would give me money, too.

It was Christmas, it was something called New Year's, it was the winter of 1914. Far beyond Mulberry Street, great gears of history were turning. Half a world away, in a chilly, abandoned farm on a Bosnian hillside, a young man named Gavrilo Princip was being trained in marksmanship. Come late spring, in a plot hatched by a group of secret Serbian revolutionaries called "the Black Hand," Gavrilo would assassinate the Austrian Archduke Ferdinand and his wife, Princess Sophie. At age nineteen, Princip would inadvertently set off a world war that would claim the lives of over 8.5 million soldiers—including three from America named Silvio, Vincenzo, and Luigi Dinello. Between Gavrilo Princip and the Spanish flu, the Dinello family would be decimated by the end of the decade.

Also of significance, in that same winter of 1914, two Russian-Jewish immigrants, Dora and Daniel Salk, were conceiving their first child in an East Harlem tenement just a few miles north of the Dinellos. Born late that October, their son would be named Jonas. Forty years later, he would go on to create one of the most important vaccines in history—and inadvertently help catapult me to fortune and fame as well.

But who could know all this back then? Of the winter of 1914, I have little memory. Eventually the gutters pooled with grayish sludge as the snow melted and the sewers backed up. Parades appeared in the street; Italian men singing and carrying gilded statues balanced on their shoulders garlanded with paper flowers. They tossed candy to children watching from the curbs. Oh, how I longed to go out!

And then, I was in a thin brown coat, a size too big. The air was chill, my breath vaporous. Mr. Dinello was holding my elbow. Carefully, I was maneuvering down one metal stair, then another. They were corrugated, with slits cut into them like the top of a pie. A doctor appeared, red-faced, nodding. My brace was unbuckled, discarded, my leg discolored and throbbing, Mrs. Dinello kneading it like bread dough as I sat lengthwise on a settee.

Soon my gait was improving. Yet I sensed that no one quite knew what was to be done with me.

One night I heard the Dinellos' whispers tumbling down through the air shaft.

"But we can't. I made a promise—"

"Ha! To who? A ghost? That tailor, he's only come around once. Not one letter, not one nickel he's sent."

"But it's not right, Generosa."

"Oh? What if something happens to her? If she is going to continue to live in this house—"

"What you tell Father Antonucci? Her people, they would never agree—"

"Her people? She has no people, Salvatore!"

Silence.

Then Mr. Dinello sighing. "*Allora*, she will just go with us and sit."

The next Sunday, Mrs. Dinello announced that I was to accompany the family to the Most Precious Blood Church. Its white marble façade rose among the tenements on Baxter Street like a beautiful piece of lace, as magnificent as any building I had seen in Hamburg. About "church" I understood very little, except I suppose I had gleaned that it was where Italians went to synagogue. Directed into one of the long, polished benches beside Rocco, I forgot to be mean to him. On the far wall, extending up toward a dome in the heavens, winged babies alighted from clouds above figures with gold rings radiating from their heads. A large, pale statue of a man rose before us. He was absolutely naked except for his midsection, which appeared to be wrapped in a tallis, and he was suspended by his wrists from a pair of crossbeams. Streams of blood were clearly visible on his hands and also dripping down the sides of his head, encircled in a ring of vicious thorns. "Mrs. Dinello, Mrs. Dinello!" I cried, tugging at her sleeve and pointing. "Why is that man nailed up there like that? What happened to his clothes? Why is he bleeding? Is he supposed to be dead?"

My voice pierced the din; everyone inside Most Precious Blood Church seemed to pause. Rocco and his brothers began snickering. "That's Jesus, you numbskull." Rocco elbowed me in the ribs. Mrs. Dinello looked appalled. Reaching over, she gave Rocco a wallop, then grabbed me by the wrists. "You do not speak in the church. You do not say anything, *capisce?*" she whispered fiercely.

I nodded. I teared up, but I refused to cry in front of Rocco. "That's Father Antonucci," she said more gently, gesturing to a sad-eyed man wearing a white robe with an olive green tallis draped over his shoulders. "Our priest." Father Antonucci began speaking in a strange language. He turned his back to the congregation, however, as if he were angry with us. It was odd to see him speaking to the wall. At one point the audience stood up, then sat down. Then they stood up again. Then people were kneeling.

Mostly women, I noticed. At first it was disquieting. Then frustrating. Then, just like at synagogue in Vishnev, tedious.

It was hard to keep from swinging my legs or humming. I kept trying to avoid looking at the terrifying statue overhead. I kept waiting for the Torah to come out, but it didn't. Instead a large basket was passed around. When the basket arrived before me, Mrs. Dinello drew out a few coins from a little pouch pinned inside her bosom. She handed me a penny and made it clear I was to put it in the basket. I did, then watched hungrily as it was spirited away. Rocco watched the basket move among the congregation, too. "Where does the money go?" I whispered.

"To Jesus." With his sharp little chin, he motioned to the statue of the man hanging from the cross in agony.

"What does he buy with it?"

"He answers prayers. When you die, if you're good, he sends you to heaven."

Finally Father Antonucci held up a big silver kiddush cup and chanted something. Everyone in front of us began to file out of the benches and form a line. When it was our turn to go up, Mrs. Dinello stayed my arm. I watched Rocco and his brothers and their mother and Beatrice slide out of the pew. "Can't I go, too?" I said.

Mrs. Dinello shook her head. "The Communion, she is for the Catholics only," she whispered, glancing fiercely at her husband. "You must be baptized first. Then make the first confession. How old are you, Ninella?"

"Generosa!" Mr. Dinello said.

Mrs. Dinello frowned at him and slid out of the pew.

Watching her join the line, Mr. Dinello shook his head and patted me on the knee. "Ninella, you do not do anything you do not want, *capisce?*" he said softly. "You do not get baptized unless your people say *si, si?*"

I nodded, though I did not comprehend him at all. My eyes were fixed on the basket of money sitting on a little podium to the side of the altar.

∞

A grand society wedding was taking place uptown that spring. The bride required an ocean of lace. For weeks Mrs. Dinello, Beatrice, and I stayed up far into the night in Mrs. Salucci's factory, meticulously weaving and stitching beneath the glow of a single gas lamp, our backs bent, our fingers growing bubbled with blisters, our necks drooping with fatigue. The day when the order was finally completed and delivered, Mrs. Salucci plucked a roll of damp bills from the sweating gap in her bosom. The pay was more money than Mr. Dinello had earned that whole month selling roasted chestnuts. To celebrate, Mrs. Dinello announced, she would take Rocco, Pasquale, Pietro, Vittorio, and even me to one of the new moving pictures uptown that she had been hearing so much about from Mrs. Ferrendino.

We took the trolley all the way up to Herald Square. Rocco insisted on showing off by reading all the signs aloud: THE SARNOFF $2 HAT SHOP. SHOESHINES. SCHLITZ BEER. The marquee of Weber's Theatre was jeweled with lights. "'D. W. Griffith's *The Battle of the Sexes*,'" Rocco announced proudly. "'Starring Donald Crisp and Lillian Gish.'" He smiled so smugly I wanted to box his ears.

In the lobby a blond woman in a filmy blue dress stood holding a tray of cigarettes for sale. For a moment I recalled standing with Papa inside the picture house in Hamburg. It made me unbearably sad.

The Battle of the Sexes was a melodrama. It was hard to tell precisely what was going on. Since Mrs. Dinello and I could not read, Rocco and his brothers kept having to read the titles aloud, then translate them for their grandmother, while the people seated beside us grew increasingly annoyed and told them to shush. But I was entranced. For there, on the screen, was the same glamorous young woman who had bedazzled me back in Hamburg. She had long ringlets of hair, an angelic mouth, and a radiant litheness that was so graceful and captivating, I was utterly beside myself. Seeing her, I was infatuated all over again, swollen with longing and ambition. For the first time since my accident, perhaps, I felt something akin to hope.

When we stepped out onto the dusty sidewalk afterward, however, blinking and disoriented in the afternoon light, Mrs. Dinello sniffed, "You should not have to read at the pictures. They are supposed to be like the opera." As we walked to the streetcar, she appeared increasingly irritated. Yet, I tagged behind the Dinellos as though in a dream. It felt as if roses were blooming inside me. As I hobbled along with my cane, my right leg jerking and dragging over the pavement, in my mind's eye I was waltzing. I was twirling. I was the beautiful young daughter in the moving picture, resplendent, dancing high above the city.

That evening Mrs. Dinello herself brought my supper plate down to the storefront.

"Tomorrow we take you to school," she announced, setting down a bowl of soup. "You sew for Mrs. Salucci afterward, when you get home."

The school's attendance office smelled like brown soap. A beefy administrator with a monocle and his arm in a sling gave us forms printed in Italian, Yiddish, and English. When it became clear that Mrs. Dinello could not read them, a secretary was summoned to translate. A prim woman named Graziana entered. Mrs. Dinello gave a cry of glee. It turned out that Graziana had grown up in Avellino, right outside Napoli, just one village over from Mrs. Dinello.

After much commotion and gossip, Graziana dipped her pen into a little jar of blue ink and prepared to write.

"Family name?" she asked.

Mrs. Dinello looked at me quizzically. In all my time in her house, she had not known. And neither, really, did I. Was it "Bi-alystoker" or "Treynovsky"? I said them both.

"Excuse me?"

I repeated, "Bialystoker? Treynovsky?"

The secretary looked at Mrs. Dinello with exasperation. "Bialy, I think," Mrs. Dinello said finally, pointing to the form.

"B-I-A-L-L-I?" the secretary spelled aloud as she wrote. She showed it to Mrs. Dinello. Mrs. Dinello shrugged.

"Given name?" said Graziana.

"Malka," Mrs. Dinello said.

"Age?"

"Rocco, he just turned eight," Mrs. Dinello said. "She is maybe six?"

The secretary regarded me dubiously. "She looks very small."

"Six is the age for school, yes?" said Mrs. Dinello. "It is the age for reading?"

"You do not know her birthday?"

Mrs. Dinello looked at me.

"My mama, she said I was born when it was very cold," I volunteered.

"January," Mrs. Dinello said. "She was born January twelfth. Write that." She pointed to the form. "*Compleanno di mio padre.* It can be hers, too."

"I will put 1907 as the birth year," Graziana offered. "That makes her seven instead of six. Seven is better because she is so small. This way no one will question her."

By the time my son, Isaac, was enrolling in school, of course, I was required to provide his birth certificate. And by the time

Rita applied to private elementary schools for Jason, oh, the rig-marole she had to go through! *Tax returns*, those shysters wanted, and even a psychological evaluation. "What will they ask for next?" I said. "A blood sample? The kid is six, for God's sake." Today, if one of our franchises wants to hire a sixteen-year-old to scoop ice cream for a summer, the management is required to provide more information than my entire family was asked to supply at Ellis Island: Social Security numbers, education history, past employers, health-insurance forms, character references, lia-bility waivers.

But back then? Public schools were designed to be great "civ-ilizing" factories for the onslaught of us "heathen" immigrants. Administrators were used to families showing up with nothing at all. And because a school secretary happened to have come from the same part of Italy as Mrs. Dinello and had grown weary of walking uncomprehending immigrants through the registration process again and again and again that year, she just wrote down whatever caused her the least amount of hassle, and that was that. Nobody doubled-checked those things. In an instant it was de-cided that I was born on January 12, 1907—a full year before I had, in all likelihood, ever existed.

In 1914 it was not uncommon to see children who were hideously deformed. Faces were still pitted from smallpox. Eyes were milky and blinded from scarlet fever, limbs gnarled and shriveled from polio, necks paralyzed at disturbing angles from diphtheria. Flesh was sometimes puckered and scarred from when small children, as babies, crawled too close to an open fire. Fingers, even hands, went missing from factory accidents. Otherwise-healthy children had rotting teeth. Beauty was harder to come by, darlings. Life infected you early.

Yet children themselves were no less cruel.

The day I limped into the schoolyard with my cane, bathed and neatly dressed in my good, secondhand navy church dress, a gang of children I had glimpsed on Mulberry Street surrounded me. The tallest one, a hatchet-faced girl with inky slits for eyes, planted herself in front of me, blocking my way farther into the yard.

"What's your name?" she demanded.

I looked at her plainly. "Malka," I said. "What's yours?"

"Malka?" The girl gave a contemptuous laugh. "What kind of name is Malka?"

Two boys standing behind her, wearing tweed caps and knickers but barely taller than me, gave a little hoot. "Malka!" they shouted, as if it were the most preposterous word they had ever heard.

The tall girl crossed her arms across her brown coat. It was ill-fitting, too tight on her. It looked as if her entire body were erupting from the miniature garment limb by limb. "Rocco says you're some little *Ammazza Christi* who ran under his grandfather's horse," she said.

I did not know what to say to this. "It was an accident." I glanced around the schoolyard for Rocco or the twins.

"*Ammazza Christi*—Christ killer!" said one of the boys. Lunging forward, he swiped my cane. I tottered and almost fell, but not quite. The other children gave a vicious laugh as I stood on one leg like a stork, trying to maintain my balance. The boy danced around with the cane, doing a sort of jig.

"Hey!" I cried. I tried to put my full weight on my right leg, but a dull, burning pain ran up it. I looked around frantically. I realized I was too far from any wall or railing I could grab onto. "That's my cane! Give it back!"

"Give it back!" the boy mimicked gleefully. "My name's

Malka!" With that he began limping about grotesquely with the cane. "I'm Malka the gimp Jew!" The other children laughed. "I'm Maaall-kah," he taunted, drawing out the syllables of my name with the exaggerated drag of his right leg. "Maaall-kah. I'm an *Ammazza Christi*! I killed Jesus. I'm going to helllllll."

"Maaall-kah, Maaall-kah, *Ammazza Christi*!" the other boy and another girl with long, tight braids began chanting. "You're going to he-elll!"

I had no idea, of course, what they were talking about. "I'm not going to hell!" I shouted. "I'm going to South Africa!"

I did not know what had possessed me to say this, or why. The sheer strangeness of my response seemed to stop the children in their tracks.

"What?" said the tall girl in the shabby coat, squinting at me. "What did you say?"

"I'm going to South Africa. To join my parents. Give me back my cane!"

For a moment the tall girl regarded me with incredulous fascination. Then her face scrunched into a look of malicious delight. "Your parents are not in Africa, stupid!" she cried. "Everybody on the whole block knows your papa ran off and your mama's in the lunatic asylum!"

"What?"

"The crazy house," said the boy mildly, looking not at me but up at my cane, which he was now attempting to balance upended on his open palm. He danced about, seeming to chase after it. "The sanitarium. Where they put all the insane, dirty Jews."

"That's not true!" I shouted. "You're lying!"

"It is true," said the girl. "Your mama is *pazza*."

"The police, they took her away," sneered the boy. "Mrs. Salucci said so. She said even some Jew tailor said so—"

At that instant I was suddenly not aware of my throbbing leg or my difficulty standing. I raced forward and punched the boy right in the face as Papa had taught me. "Liar!" I hollered. My leg buckled then, but he staggered back startled, one hand on his jaw, his eyes filling with tears. "Give me my cane!" I shrieked. Throwing it down with disgust, he turned and ran. I snatched it up. I was suddenly aware that I was crying, but I whirled around with my fist still clenched in time to see the tall girl and the two other children slowly back away from me.

"She is crazy like her mama," the tall girl murmured. "You are crazy like your mama," she repeated to me directly, tauntingly, though her voice was leached of power.

"Come on, Angela," said the second boy, pulling at her arm.

"We don't play with crazy, dirty Jews," she announced. "Maaall-kah." She turned away.

I stood blinking tearily at the three of them, then looked down at my cane. I brushed the dust from it and from my blue dress and my brown coat and tried to straighten myself up as best I could. I was crying so hard my nose was running. "Maaall-kah!" I heard a voice call. From above me on the landing, the smaller girl with the braids stuck her tongue out at me one last time before the heavy red school door swung shut behind her.

Of my first day in class, I remember nothing: not the lessons, the teacher, the alphabet written on ruled lines across the blackboard. All I could think about was Mama. What the children in the schoolyard had told me—was it true?

After dismissal I did not wait outside for Rocco and the twins as instructed. When I asked a peddler how to get to Orchard Street, I was surprised to learn that it was just a few blocks away. All this time it had been so near! As I crossed Chrystie, then Forsyth Streets, I noticed the signs suddenly began appearing in Yiddish again. Yet Orchard was on the other side of Allen Street, a broad boulevard cleaving the neighborhood; it was so wide it might as well have been a great river. I fought the impulse to shut my eyes as I stepped off the curb and limped as fast as I could through the traffic. Perhaps there was a streetlight or a traffic warden. There must have been. Yet I recall weaving amid rattling cars, the horse-drawn coaches whisking by me in a furious blur, the oncoming streetcars clanging ominously as they drew closer, the Elevated roaring overhead. Once I was safely on the opposite corner, I saw a Star of David adorning a brick-faced building. Orchard, the peddler had told me, would be down the block, on the right. I was approaching from an unfamiliar direction. Carts jiggled by. Harried women pushed past in their shawls. But by then, I had a dawning sense of knowing again where I was. Peddlers called out, "Four cents a bissel." My heart beat as I turned onto my old block.

The noise was horrific, even greater than on Mulberry Street, the market going full force. Amid the ruckus I almost missed the saloon and the butcher's; more signs had gone up in my absence. But there they were. I stared up at the Orchard Street tenement, hoping, for one impossible moment, that Mama and Papa might be at the window, looking down. In an instant they'd see me, call out my name joyously, wave me upstairs. It would all have been some horrible misunderstanding, they would explain, just a terrible dream. But the façade of the building loomed before me indifferently. I looked around, hoping to see someone from the neighborhood who could come to my aid. My right leg throbbed. My foot felt numb. I'd walked more than I ever had since my accident.

The front entrance was set off the street by a flight of eight metal stairs. Two women I didn't recognize were sitting on them with their knees spread wide beneath their skirts and toddlers balancing in the robed space between their legs. Whispering to each other, they laughed grimly. When I asked them if Mr. Lefkowitz was there, they looked at me blankly without bothering to shift aside, so I had to navigate around them with my cane. Inside, the vestibule was humid with the stench of boiled cabbage, urine, chalky plaster. The corridor rang with a cacophony of voices. I couldn't pick out a single one. The dark, narrow stairs rose steeply; they seemed far more daunting than the ones at Mulberry Street.

When I finally reached the top floor, I steadied myself, swallowed, and listened for a moment. Slowly, I knocked on Mr. Lefkowitz's door. A woman I had never seen before answered. Her hair was pulled back in an unraveling bun, and the delicate skin around her nose and eyes was raw pink. As she frowned at me, I noticed her belly pressing out insistently beneath her dark muslin dress. A small, sticky-faced child with matted hair clung to her skirts.

"Yes? What do you want?" she said sharply in Yiddish.

"Is Mr. Lefkowitz here?"

"We have no work available," she said. "I keep telling you children. Go look elsewhere."

"I'm just looking for Mr. Lefkowitz," I pleaded. "I don't need work."

She crossed her arms. "My husband is out."

A man pushed past her then and tromped out into the hallway, carrying a tin lunch box. He pulled his hat down over his eyes and grunted as he hurried down the stairs.

"We're full up for boarders, too," the woman said curtly. I heard a baby start to cry. The woman's face developed a drowning look. "Try across the street," she said, moving quickly to shut the door.

"I'm looking for my mama," I said, gripping the knob. My voice was suddenly palsied with tears. "Please. Does Mr. Lefkowitz know where she is? Or my papa? He went away, but maybe he's come back here?"

The woman glanced back toward the bedroom, where the baby's cries were growing. "I'm sorry. I don't know anything about a missing family."

"My sisters? Bella and Rose and Flora?"

At this she grimaced. "Flora," she said flatly. "Flora is your sister?"

"Yes. Do you know her? Do you know where she is?"

The woman looked me up and down, taking in my secondhand coat and navy blue dress with its white collar that Mrs. Dinello had carefully mended, now covered in dust from the streets and the schoolyard, and my hair frizzing out in filaments from my disheveled braids. I saw her swollen eyes quickly flutter over my cane, my worn black shoe on my crippled right foot, twisting inward.

"Flora is out," she said quickly. "But you can't stay here. You have to be gone. We have too many mouths to feed already."

"Flora is here?"

"Your father has not come back. Your mother—I'm sorry." She shook her head violently, as if trying to banish a terrible thought. "You have to go. Flora, I told her to get some onions. Some celery. Maybe you can find her at the markets downstairs. We are managing as best we can, you understand? But you cannot come back here."

Mama-Papa, Mama-Papa—the rhythm in my head beat furiously as I hobbled down the filthy stairs. Which peddler might Flora have gone to? Where was everybody else? Outside, Orchard Street swam before me in my distress, all the crowds and peddlers blurring together. Yet then, as if a beam of light had been angled down upon her from the heavens, I saw a little blond head bobbing amid the sea of dark hats, tweed caps, and kerchiefed heads filling the streets. "Flora!" I shouted. "Flora!"

When she saw me, her mouth grew as round as an apple. She

nearly dropped her basket and raced toward me. In an instant her arms were wrapped around me. She had no coat, only a shawl of gnarled wool draped across her tiny shoulders. Her hair was lank. Her once dairy-fresh face looked strangely shrunken. I could see a bluish vein streaking down from her left temple like a scar.

"Malka, you're alive! You can walk!" she cried. "They said you were lame!"

"I learned! I only need a cane now!"

"Where have you been? Oh, Malka!" Flora jiggled before me on the balls of her feet as the words tumbled out of her. "I'm so glad you've come back! Oh, Malka! Rose is dead. She had the fever. We all did. We were in quarantine. They put a big sign on our door, and tape, and one of the nurses, she climbed up on the roof and sent down food for us in a basket on a rope. And we had medicine—"

"Rose is dead?" I said. "Where? Forever?"

"Because we were in quarantine, we couldn't even go to the funeral or sit shiva. We were all crying, and Mr. Lefkowitz covered the mirror with the fabric for the coat linings. Mama was crying so hard she started to choke. First she was calling, 'Rose, Rose,' but then she started wailing for Zeyde, too, saying over and over, 'The Cossacks, they killed him,' and then she was shouting, 'Samuelah, Samuel!' and saying again and again how you were as good as dead, too, because all your bones were broken—and then she started screaming horrible things, just terrible things that made no sense at all, and then she started to hit herself on her head with the wall, and there was blood, and the rabbi had to come—"

"Flora, where is she?"

"And then she started destroying the parlor. Oh, Malka. She was hitting the rabbi and smashing things with the fire poker. And the rabbi, he fell on the floor! And she threw the iron out the window! Out the window, Malka! It hit the chicken coop in the yard and made a hole in the roof! And she was ripping up fabric with her hands and throwing the scissors, and she kept shouting, and she wouldn't listen to us when we begged her to stop. Mr. Lefkowitz's sewing machine, she tipped it over. Mr. Lefkowitz, he made Bella and me hide in the bedroom, but we could still hear! Everything was crashing, and the neighbors were shouting and banging on the doors. And then, Malka, the police came! And even though Mama was supposed to be in quarantine, the police, they took her to a hospital. A special hospital, they said. Very far away. And she is not allowed to come out. Mama is like a dybbuk, Mr. Lefkowitz says."

When Flora finished, she breathed in huge gulps of air. We sat down heavily on the stoop. She grabbed my arm and clutched it.

"But you can walk, and you came back!" she said, her eyes shining. She propped her head on my shoulder. "I am so happy to see you."

For a moment I sat there. Orchard Street seemed to carousel around me.

"Mama's gone?" I whispered, trying to envision it.

Flora nodded solemnly. Her lower lip trembled.

"The woman upstairs," I said slowly. "She says I can't come in the house."

Flora glanced at me darkly. "She's Mr. Lefkowitz's new wife. She came from Lodz to marry him after Mama went to the hospital."

"She seems mean."

Flora shrugged. "She cries a lot because she has another baby coming and there's no food." Flora looked at me. "Except soup, with celery and onions. And sometimes I make eggs."

Her blue eyes suddenly appeared fathomless.

"I miss our game," she said softly. She mimed eating with a fork and chewing. "Mmm. My, isn't this chicken delicious?"

"Oh, and the potatoes," I said, rubbing my stomach, "with parsley?" I pretended to pass her a plate. "Here. Won't you have some more?"

"Oh," said Flora. "Don't mind if I do."

"The Dinellos have a lot of bread," I said. "Maybe I can bring some for you. But just for you. Not anyone else."

"Who are the Dinellos?"

"Do you remember the ices man? With the horse? They let me live with them now. I work for them. We make ices and lace. Today I went to school, too."

Flora looked down.

"The kids there," I said. "They called me a dirty Jew. But Mrs. Dinello, she bathes me every week, just like Mama."

"Mr. Lefkowitz, after Mama went away, he let me live with him, too," Flora said softly, picking at a bit of gum on the step. "He told that lady with the blouse that he lost one little girl and that was enough. He promised to take care of me. But I have to work so we can eat. Mrs. Lefkowitz, she is not happy to have me. But I once heard Mr. Lefkowitz tell her that I bring more money into the house than her own children do and that he did not ask for them either."

"Do you go to school?"

Flora shook her head. "Mama, when she was being a dybbuk, she broke Mr. Lefkowitz's sewing machine. And he had to pay the butcher for the roof of the chicken coop and the chickens that got killed, too. So he has no business and no money left. I make gloves with him at Mr. Metusowich's factory. I shop, too, because Mrs. Lefkowitz's condition is too delicate, she says. It's no fun without you, though. I sing or twirl sometimes, but..." Her voice trailed off. She suddenly looked as if she would cry.

"I wish Mama and Papa would come back," I whispered.

"Me, too," Flora said.

"Do you think they will?"

Flora shrugged, stared out at the street. "These men come in and out all night. They even sleep on the kitchen floor," she said.

"Where's Bella?"

"She got a job living with a family as a maid. But just before the High Holy Days, they moved to a place called the Bronx, so she went with them."

A peddler trundled by, hauling a wooden cart behind him laden with small, knobby apples, the remains of the day, picked over and fermenting. The wheels made a kissing sound in the mud, and a cloud of flies trailed after it. Flora and I watched, hoping an apple or two would roll off the cart without him noticing. The sky was darkening to the color of a bruise, but the streetlamps had not yet been lit.

"Mr. Dinello makes gelato," I said. "Ice cream. It's the best food in the world, Flora. When we make it next time, I can try to bring you some."

Flora nodded dolefully, her eyes fixed on her shoes, which, I saw only then, were held together with string.

"I thought you were in South Africa," I said. "That you and Mama and Papa and Bella and Rose had all gone back without me to be with Uncle Hyram."

"I wish we were all there!" Flora said with sudden distress. "Why did you switch the tickets? Why did you make us come here?"

I bit my lip and looked down and twisted the hem of my dress around my index finger.

"It's all your fault, Malka!" she cried, turning to me reproachfully.

"It is not! Don't say that!" I gripped my cane.

"It is too! Mama even said!"

"She did not!"

"Did too!"

"Did not!"

"How do you know?"

We were both standing now, panting, our faces wild and red with fury.

"You're stupid!" I said.

"*You're* stupid!" Flora shouted.

"*You're* stupid!" I shouted. "You're not even going to school."

"I am not stupid," Flora sobbed. "You're ugly! And lame!"

"You're a dirty little Jew!" I said.

"You and your big mouth cause nothing but *tsuris*!"

I whirled around and tried to limp off. Yet my legs were sore and trembling, and my right knee buckled. I dropped halfway to the ground. Then I felt Flora upon me, wrapping her arms tightly around my thin coat, sobbing. "Oh, Malka, I'm sorry. I am so, so sorry. Please, Malka, don't go."

And I was crying, too, loudly, baldly—"Oh, Flora!"—and clutching her equally hard, so hard, in fact, that it felt like our bones, our muscles, our very heartbeats were fusing.

We arranged a plan to meet every Friday after school, when Flora's sweatshop closed early for the Sabbath. We picked a spot on the southeast corner of Allen Street under a Yiddish sign for a defunct funeral home, where we were certain no one would see.

I do not recall exactly why we felt that our meetings needed to be clandestine. Perhaps it was because we were children, and children like to be sneaky. It makes them feel smarter and more powerful than the adults around them. Yet mostly, I suppose, we were afraid. If either the Dinellos or the Lefkowitzes discovered we were meeting, we imagined, they would think we did not need them anymore—or that we would *both* want to live with them—and cast us out as a burden. Indeed, the Dinellos must have known that Flora existed somewhere, and yet I was convinced that telling them about her would amount to a form of betrayal or ingratitude. Which it was, I suppose, in that Flora and I were plotting to run away together.

At Metusowich's sweatshop Flora had overheard the older workers talking about places called "Vaudeville" and "the Jewish Rialto," a string of Yiddish theaters on Second Avenue. A singer named Sophie Tucker apparently earned more than a thousand dollars a week performing there. "A thousand dollars a week! Not bad for a good Jewish girl from Tulchyn, no?" Mr. Metusowich had said, chuckling. "And such a *meeskite*, too. Not pretty at all!"

As soon as my leg was fully healed, Flora and I decided, we would perform together at the Jewish Rialto, too. Flora would dance, and I would be the singing *meeskite*. If we earned a thousand dollars a week ourselves, perhaps Mama would feel better and not have to stay in the sanitarium. Bella would no longer have to work as a maid, and we could find an apartment for all of us in the Bronx.

The first day when Flora and I stood huddled in the doorway of the abandoned funeral parlor, I taught her to sing "Addio." I had tried making up more little songs of my own as well, but after hearing the music on the Victrola, tunes like "Why I Love Chicken" no longer held much interest. Flora, oh, she had such a pretty voice! Like Mama's. As we sang, "*Addio mia bella Napoli. Addio, addio,*" she managed to pronounce the Italian beautifully— far better than I could, in fact. But when I said we should make up a little dance for her to go with it, she smiled weakly. "I'm too cold today, Malka." She pulled her shawl around her. "Do you think maybe we can find something to eat?"

Indeed, though she had been born first, I was now slightly

taller, my shoulders wider. I could feel her ribs whenever she hugged me.

All week long I endured my lessons and my sewing by thinking of her. Each morning the schoolyard awaited me like a Roman arena. Children ringed it, hooting, "Maaall-kah, Maaall-kah," while someone—usually Angela and the boy I had punched, Tommaso—played keep-away with my cane and mimicked my limp. Occasionally I hauled off and punched one of them, but they quickly grew wise and nimbly danced out of my way as I swung, which only increased the jeering. My teacher, Mrs. Trafficante, was scarcely kinder. So sue me: I had trouble remembering to raise my hand before speaking. The lessons excited me, sparked my curiosity. One could chew on numbers and English, gulping them down like a food. "That spells 'hat,' Mrs. Trafficante! H-A-T, hat!" "The president of the United States of America is Woodrow Wilson, Mrs. Trafficante! I know this! And before him it was President Taft! They told us on the boat!"

"Do you talk like that at home?" she cried, thwacking me across my left palm with her ruler. "Are you so rude as that to your own parents?"

But back at the Dinellos', I was becoming more agreeable. Like a prisoner on the brink of parole or a worker who secretly knows he will soon be leaving his position for a more lucrative job at a better company, I grew more forgiving, more profligate with my affections. I said *"per favore"* and *"grazie."* When Mr. Dinello wiggled his bushy white eyebrows in time to "Alexander's Ragtime Band," I allowed myself to laugh out loud. I accompanied the Dinellos to church each Sunday without dawdling or sighing aloud too often.

"Ninella," Mr. Dinello said one afternoon as I helped him add the sugar to the gelato and mix it. "Your leg, she is not so bad anymore, *si?*"

When I nodded, he reached over and tousled my hair.

Yet all the while, I was stealing from him. And his neighbors. I had stolen so much that I'd had to loosen another floorboard in the office. It didn't come up as easily as the first, and the plank stuck out a little when I put it back, but with all the men tromping in and out the whole day—delivering goods, demanding money, bringing over receipts, smelling of cigars, smelling of hair tonic, speaking mellifluously in Italian—I could not imagine how anyone would notice.

Mrs. Dinello had stitched for me a little school satchel made from a sugar sack, just as she had made for Rocco, Pietro, and Pasquale. On Friday mornings before school, I'd quickly loosen one of the floorboards and stuff as many items as I could bear to part with into the sack, along with the apple she gave me for lunch and the tablet and pencil provided to me by the school. As soon as my lessons were over, I made my way to the Hungarian junk man on the corner of Elizabeth and Hester Streets, where he parked between his rounds. For the brown shoelaces he gave me a nickel, for the rubber ball three cents. The wooden comb earned me a nickel as well. When I handed him the tin of mustache wax, he turned it over in his hands. "Where did you get this?" he asked, eyeing me. "It is brand-new."

I quickly thought of Luigi and the Victrola. "I won it," I told him. "In a card game."

Each week I took whatever he paid me—perhaps seven cents or a dime in total—and brought it to Flora.

"Oh, Malka," she wheezed. She always seemed to be panting, my sister, hungry for air. "Let's go. Before all the peddlers leave."

As fast as we could, we walked to Hester Street before the markets shut down for the Sabbath. Spicy chickpeas scooped into folded squares of newspaper were one of our favorites. So were baked sweet potatoes and boiled eggs, served straight from chipped enameled pots boiling above tiny grills on carts. These filled you up most. Whenever I could, I let Flora have the extra few chickpeas or the bigger half of the potato. I kept intending to let her have it all for herself, but often I was just too hungry. Still, I always let her alone have an apple or a pickle, and I watched her devour it with a mixture of longing and pride. "Flora, I promise," I told her, gripping her hands. "Next time I'll bring more."

One Friday, when I sold the cache of Mrs. Salucci's sewing notions that I had accumulated over the course of the winter—two spools of white thread, a wooden thimble, and two dozen straight pins—for fifteen cents, Flora and I managed to buy a half dozen potatoes and a chicken carcass for her to bring home to the Lefkowitzes on top of everything we'd eaten ourselves. Oh, the feeling of that! The bounty!

"Malka," Flora rasped, hugging me tightly when it was time to go. "I'm so happy you're here. Promise next week you'll come back, too?"

"Cross my heart and hope to die. Stick a needle in my eye." I'd learned this phrase in the schoolyard. "You promise me *you'll* come back?" I squeezed her hand.

"Cross my heart and hope to die. Stick a needle in *my* eye," she wheezed. And then, because neither of us could stand to watch the other walk away, we counted to three in unison, then shouted, "On your mark, get set, go!" At which point we were both supposed to hurry off in opposite directions down Hester Street as fast as we could without looking back.

"Whoever looks back will be cursed, so don't do it," Flora said, wrapping her shawl around herself and sniffling with a little laugh. She tossed her golden head and bobbed away. She was so good and careful. She walked slowly—almost as reluctantly as I did—but she never turned around.

Yet I, of course, always did.

Springtime was approaching. Mr. and Mrs. Dinello spent more time in the kitchen, readying it for another season of penny-ices production. However, they had been put on warning by the local health department: Using the same little glass cup for each customer to lick clean was not hygienic. In fact, it was illegal. Penny-ices carts were quickly becoming extinct; more and more peddlers were selling ice cream manufactured in big commercial plants—sometimes in the form of ice cream bricks, served in paper-wrapped slices for a nickel—for an even smaller fraction of the profit. More and more, candy stores were opening up around the neighborhood, too, selling ice cream. Beyond the Lower East Side, drugstore soda fountains were flourishing. It was rumored that there were even more soda fountains in New York City than saloons.

For a while the Dinellos engaged in a great debate over what to do. Did they shut down production and begin purchasing from a larger company? Should they expand the flavors and products they made? Invest, perhaps, in a motorized ice cream maker?

"We already have equipment. She works good enough. We make good ices. Everybody likes them," said Mr. Dinello.

"But how are we serving them?" said Mrs. Dinello. "What do we do? Pass around a spoon?"

"We sell the cones. Like everybody else."

Eleven years earlier, right there on the Lower East Side of Manhattan, another Italian immigrant, Italo Marchiony, had filed a patent for a mold he had invented to make little edible ice cream cups out of waffle mix. For a while, in fact, these cups had made him one of the most popular ices men in the neighborhood. At one point, just a year before the Dinellos themselves arrived in New York, Marchiony had upward of forty vendors working for him in the Wall Street district, selling his ices in his wafer cups. He believed he had invented the ice cream cone.

Yet what he had patented was actually a flat-bottomed cup. Soon after, no fewer than five other vendors each claimed to have invented the "real" ice cream cone during the 1904 World's Fair in St. Louis.

An immigrant pastry maker named Ernest Hamwi claimed he'd invented the ice cream cone from crisp wafers he baked called "zalabia." A Syrian immigrant, Abe Doumar, claimed that one evening at the fair he suggested that a waffle vendor turn his penny waffle into a ten-cent cone by adding ice cream from a neighboring stall. He himself then began selling these "Syrian ice cream sandwiches." Still another Syrian immigrant, Nick Kabbaz, claimed that he and his brother Albert created the first ice cream cone at the fair when they decided to fold flat little cakes into cones. (Kabbaz went on to become president of the St. Louis Ice Cream Cone Company.) A Turkish immigrant, David Avayou, said that no, it was actually he who had introduced ice cream cones. He had first seen ice cream served in paper or metal cones in France, he claimed, and thought it would be better if such cones were edible. "I spent three weeks and used hundreds of pounds of flour and eggs before I got it right," he insisted. And finally there were Charles Robert Menches and his brother Frank, of St. Louis. Their family claims that the two invented the ice cream cone at the world's fair when they saw a lady roll a waffle around a scoop so that it was daintier to eat.

Whether the Dinellos were aware of the debate raging around ice cream cones remains a mystery. Their own debate revolved around whether to use them at all.

Mr. Dinello was partial to the cones. "I try one. She is delicious. The children, everybody, they can eat the ices, the gelato, and the cone, too. The idea, she is a good one."

But Mrs. Dinello, who, like my own illiterate mother, could add three-digit numbers in her head, insisted that it was not cost-effective. "The cones? They are too expensive to buy. We don't have that kind of money."

"So? We have a kitchen. We make them ourselves!"

"With what, Salvatore? The molds, they cost. And the ingredients?"

"So we get another loan from Carlo, from the brotherhood. We buy a mold. We take the flour. We take the eggs. We add *di latte*—"

"Oh, flour, eggs, and milk. You think these grow on trees, Salvatore?"

"I talk to Giovanni the grocer. He make us a deal—"

"Giovanni the grocer, he is a lowlife. He is like a Sicilian. He is crazy in the head. We are not getting milk and flour from Giovanni—"

"So we ask Vito the baker, or Savio—"

"*Ai, ai, ai!* For their prices you should just make cones out of paper dollars and serve ices in those!"

Mr. Dinello's hands froze in midair. He stared at her and moved his mouth in such a way that his white mustache seemed to tilt from side to side. "Generosa," he said, "that is not a terrible idea."

Which is how the Dinellos came up with the idea of serving their Italian ices in little paper cones. They experimented first with newsprint, which got too soggy and bled, then parchment and simple white tablet paper, which was too hard to manipulate and, Mrs. Dinello calculated, far too expensive. Brown wrapping paper used for packages came apart when it got wet. Finally they settled on using the same paper as the butcher down the street did. Thin but lightly waxed, it was supple, strong, and cheap. Mr. Dinello could purchase it in bulk on a roll, then cut it into squares and twist them into little cones himself for each serving.

Somebody else, of course, eventually patented the waxed-paper ices cone and the Dixie cup and the machines invented for mass-producing them. Somebody else, as it so often goes, got all the money and the credit. But trust me, darlings, it was the Dinellos who invented it first. I know this: I watched them do it myself.

And with the new inspiration for the cones, Mr. Dinello, he began to dream a bit more. Why not make strawberry ices as well? Or chocolate? Or grape? Why not sell gelato, too, and expand what Dinello's Ices had to offer, particularly in light of the new candy shop that had opened on Mott Street selling ice cream cones?

Each night he began to experiment in the kitchen, with Mrs. Dinello and the grandsons and me as his assistants, helping to concoct and boil down syrups, mixing, taste-testing. Each flavor gave the confections a different consistency. Each flavor had to be blended differently, with greater delicacy or speed. Some ingredients made the mixture thicken faster or separate too easily or crystallize. One day Mr. Dinello added gelatin to the gelato, which he had heard would make it bind more smoothly. He added cocoa. Chestnut puree. Chopped cherries. Peaches. Marsala wine.

It was hard to remain petulant in his kitchen: I tasted everything.

Flora, in the meantime, was growing thinner. With each passing week, I noticed violet smudges deepening beneath my sister's eyes. Her body trembling. A papery cough emanating from her throat. One week when I arrived on Allen Street, I found her sitting in the doorway of the funeral parlor instead of standing, her arms wrapped tightly around her knees. "Oh, Malka," she said when she saw me, smiling wanly. "I just feel so dizzy."

The next Friday, after selling a curtain pull and a box of paper clips to the Hungarian junk man, I didn't wait. Springtime made the cooking smells in the Italian street markets intensify like perfume. I purchased a bag of *arancini* from a vendor right on the corner of Hester and Elizabeth. I bought a cube of hard, dry cheese and a piece of salami as I had seen Beatrice do. Any inkling I had about kosher laws was gone, and if Flora realized she was eating milk with meat, she didn't seem to care. She fell upon the Italian food in a disturbing frenzy, biting off a piece of the salami, then pinching off a piece of the rice balls with her fingers and stuffing it into her mouth while she was still chewing the meat, then reaching for the cheese. I stood over her, watching, not daring to join her.

"I'll bring you more next time," I said, kneeling down and touching the back of my hand to her damp, bluish forehead. "I promise."

She blinked up at me, nearly unseeing, and nodded.

In the pit of my stomach, I sensed something terrible, something urgent. She was so sad, my sister, so wan with misery and hunger. Nothing I brought her could cheer her up for long. Meat and potatoes, she needed. Good food every day, for weeks. Food, somehow, like pasta and pickled herring—a whole barrel's worth—that might last. I needed something big to sell, something far greater than the bric-a-brac I stole, which fetched a few pennies at a time. What was worth at least a quarter, or a fifty-cent piece—a dollar, even?

Sidling through the apartments on Mulberry Street, I tried to act casual as I inventoried the neighbors' belongings. Each apartment had its one precious china figurine, its statues of saints, its single pair of pewter wine cups or brass candlesticks from the old country. In the Dinellos' parlor, my gaze fell upon the stack of records enshrined on the tiny credenza. But these, too, I knew, would be too difficult to take. Records back then were weighty and thick and packaged in flat cardboard boxes. They were nothing I could slip beneath my skirt unnoticed or even hold with just one hand.

Mrs. Dinello and Beatrice were downstairs working in the storefront as I hobbled in; their presence was dismaying, though they seemed to take no notice of me. I went back into the little office and sat down despairingly on my bench. I glanced around. From the adjoining kitchen, I could hear the clatter of pots and the rhythmic thwacking of Mrs. Dinello's knife against the cutting board as she sliced lemon after lemon, chatting all the while to Beatrice.

Glancing around the office, I spied a row of instruments arranged neatly on a piece of oilcloth spread out atop the desk: a stunted spoon with a polished wooden handle, two small ladles, and what looked like a trowel. Ice cream utensils. Mrs. Dinello had no doubt purchased these for her husband to scoop ices and gelato quickly and neatly. The implements looked brand-new; certainly I had never seen them before, and the metal was shiny and mirrorlike. Perhaps, I thought, they were made of silver. Silver could sell for dollars, I imagined. And there were four of them. Perhaps, the Dinellos wouldn't notice if only one went missing.

The floorboards overhead squeaked as Luigi and Vincenzo tromped around upstairs, preparing for their evening shift in the tunnel. Rocco and his brothers were out in the street causing a ruckus, though they could dash in at any minute. Mr. Dinello was not yet back with his wagon, though he would be returning imminently. In the kitchen Beatrice was standing with her back to me, chattering away to Mrs. Dinello, their heads bowed over their cutting boards, thoroughly absorbed in their conversation. The opportunity was there, but for only an instant.

Swiftly, I grabbed the utensil closest to me—one of the ice cream scoops—and jammed it beneath the blanket on my bench. I was surprised by how heavy it was.

"Ninella," Mrs. Dinello called out.

I froze, certain she'd seen me. There was no door, after all, between the office alcove and the kitchen.

"*Si,* Senora Dinello?" I said, stepping out from the shadows.

"As soon as Vittorio comes in, tell him to bring a pail of water from the pump, *si?*" Mrs. Dinello said, barely glancing up from the cutting board, pointing the tip of her knife in the direction of the sink. "The faucet, she is broken again."

It seemed to take forever for her and Beatrice to finish slicing up the lemons and vacate the kitchen, leaving it for me to clean up. And it wasn't until everyone had gone to bed that night that I was certain I was alone. My fingers, my whole body trembled. Removing the floorboard beside my bench, I realized that the ice cream scoop was too big to hide in that little space. For a moment I panicked, wondering what to do. I decided to sleep with it under my pillow, where it jutted into my cheek.

Slipping the scoop into my little school satchel, I prayed that the Dinellos would not go into the office before I left nor notice entirely that one of their utensils was missing. All day long, I kept peeking into my school bag to make sure the ice cream scoop was still there, my heart pounding furiously with its secret. I kept speculating how much money I could get for it. After school, I knew, I had to hurry. As quickly as I could, I limped through the schoolyard, down Baxter onto Hester Street, and searched for the junk man. When I finally found him, I was nearly beside myself with excitement. "Look," I said proudly, unsheathing the ice cream scoop from its burlap. "How much?"

The Hungarian picked it up carefully and studied it.

"It's silver!" I said. "It must be worth fifty or a hundred dollars!"

The Hungarian turned it over and frowned. "It is not silver," he said. "It is maybe tin."

"But it is brand-new," I said.

"Yes, I see," said the Hungarian noncommittally. "Where you get this?"

Before I could answer, he nodded wryly. "Yes, yes, I know. You won it at cards." He bent down to look me squarely in the eyes. "You know, *kislány*, you might want to tell your papa if he comes here himself, he may get better price."

I shifted a little on my good leg. "So how much?" I said evenly.

He tilted his head. "I give you twenty cents."

"Twenty cents? But it's brand-new!"

"It won't be when I sell it."

I suppose he could see my desperation, my eyes filling with tears, because he said, "All right. A quarter."

"No, I need more. I need a dollar!"

The man laughed. His teeth, I noticed, were covered in grime. "Brand-new this is not a dollar."

"I need food!" I cried. "It's for my sister." And for the first time in my life, I was not pretending to weep before a peddler. "There's no food, and they put Mama in the hospital, and it's my fault—"

The junk man looked exasperated. "I run a business, not a charity," he said.

Yet when I would not stop weeping, he exhaled. "*Gyermek*, brand-new this cost fifty cents, maybe fifty-five. I give you forty. If I am lucky, I can sell it for that. But no more. Best I can do."

Wiping my nose on my sleeve, I nodded. The junk man dug

into his pockets and counted out a quarter, a dime, and a nickel into my hand. "Go feed your sister," he said irritably.

Forty cents! Forty cents! For Flora that was more than a full day's wages at Metusowich's factory! I wished I could run; I wished I could fly across Allen Street. Imagining Flora's face when I presented her with the three coins, picturing her elation and relief, and how we would buy pickles and knishes and rice balls—barrels of herring and garlands of salamis—sacks of flour and oats and rice to eat for weeks. Perhaps even American chocolate candy bars wrapped in paper. The three coins—silver-colored coins, no less—not copper! I held them so tightly in my left fist that the edges embossed little crescents in my palm, and the streetcars and carriages and shoppers and vendors all whisked past me in a smear of color and ecstatic velocity.

Flora wasn't there yet when I arrived at the doorway of the funeral parlor. I watched the streetcars rumble by, their bells chiming, and the wagon wheels turning on the carriages. I counted the different colors of the horses and watched the sea of hats bobbing up and down beneath the grimy steel lattice-work of the Elevated. I looked up at the rooftops. I made myself count to twenty in my head—the highest I had learned to go in English, then to thirty in Italian. A tinge of lavender bled into the sky. Stores along Allen Street began rolling down their grates and locking their doors.

Still Flora did not come.

It was Friday, wasn't it? I stopped and asked a passerby; she nodded at me strangely. Perhaps Flora had forgotten? Finally I headed down Grand Street. On Orchard Street the last of the peddlers were packing up. A small crowd in black was gathering before the synagogue at the end of the block. A few men milled about outside the saloon, but otherwise most of the stoops had cleared.

I struggled up the staircase. Mrs. Lefkowitz would be furious to have me appear before her door again. But I couldn't help it. I knocked once, then more vehemently. From behind the door, finally, I heard an urgent exchange of whispers in Yiddish, then silence.

I banged again.

"Please, Mrs. Lefkowitz. It's Malka," I said.

Someone murmured. There were footsteps. Slowly, the door creaked open. A small man I had never seen before stood facing me. He was balding, with a waxy, sallow face and thick black beard, wearing a mottled overcoat two sizes too big. Behind him, in the kitchen, a petite, fearful-looking woman eyed me, clad in a gray dress and a moth-eaten shawl. Two little girls, dressed in miniature versions of her own threadbare clothes, cowered behind her. An older boy in a cap stood with his legs spread and his arms crossed defiantly amid a pile of bundles. Except for the pale yellow curtain on the window overlooking the air shaft, the kitchen was completely empty. Only one light burned, and the stove was cold. A small pan sat on it.

"Yes, please. Can I help you?" the man said nervously in Yiddish.

"Where's Mr. Lefkowitz?" I said. "Is Flora here?"

The man looked at me helplessly. "I am sorry?"

Behind him I noticed a pair of empty candlesticks and a small loaf of challah arranged atop an old steamer trunk.

"Where are the Lefkowitzes?"

The man shook his head uncomprehendingly.

"This is their house. Mrs. Lefkowitz and the babies. Flora—"

The man shrugged. "We arrive only yesterday. The apartment, it is empty."

"But where is my sister?" I cried.

The man began to say something, but I turned and stumbled down the stairs. I banged on one door, then the other, yelling, "Flora! Flora, where are you?"

"*Ai, ai, ai!*" somebody shouted. "Don't interrupt! We're saying the *berakhot!*"

"Flora!"

I knocked and knocked, one floor, then the next. Finally a door opened. It was Mr. Tomashevski—the old Ukrainian man whom Flora and I used to help with his bunions for a nickel. "Yes?" he said shakily. He looked past me to the hallway, his blue eyes milky and unfocused.

"Mr. Tomashevski, it's me, Malka," I said.

"Yes?"

"Mr. Tomashevski, do you know where Flora is, and the Lefkowitzes?"

"Yes?"

"Do you realize it's the Sabbath? You should not be disturbing people," said a plump woman in a soup-stained apron, stepping up behind him. Lines extended from the corners of her mouth to her chin. "Go back inside, Baba," she said to Mr. Tomashevski. "What are you doing here at this hour?" she said to me.

"I'm looking for my sister," I said. "Flora. And the Lefkowitzes."

The woman frowned. "Gone," she said. "Evicted Monday. Hadn't paid their rent in two weeks and too many boarders."

"Do you know where they went?"

The woman shook her head.

"What about Flora? Do you know if she went with them?"

The woman shrugged. "The little blond girl? I assume so. I guess so. Why wouldn't she? I'm sorry." She sighed. "They were nice enough people." As she moved to close the door, she paused.

"Do you have someplace to go, *kindeleh*?" she said. "It's the Sabbath, you know."

But already I was struggling down the stairs.

I sat on a stoop, I recall, staring down at the coins in my hand, then up at the inky, impossible New York sky, the vast blue-black sea of it, illuminated by bursts of orange fumes from the tanneries and forges near the waterfront and the electric lights blazing from the skyscrapers and bridges farther downtown, the greater city roaring all around me indifferently, even during the hush of the Sabbath. My leg hurt, my stomach hurt; I wiped my nose on the sleeve of my coat. "*Mama!*" I sobbed aloud. "*Flora!*"

A gang of boys appeared at the end of the block. I could see their silhouettes in the lamplight. They seemed to be picking bits of debris out of the gutter and hurling them at street signs, cheering every time they hit their target and the metallic *sproing* of the strike echoed down the block. I grabbed my cane and moved away as quickly as I could. I hobbled up one street, then another, avoiding the rats and the garbage, not really seeing where I was going at all. It was like chanting, but with my feet—the good and the damaged one together. A rhythm took over; I became a part of it, breathing into it, moving without thinking. I suddenly found myself back on Grand Street, then Chrystie. I had no idea how late it was. I stood there for a while, frightened to cross. But eventually I suppose I did, because I found myself again on the Italian side of the avenue. Slowly, in a fog of devastation and fatigue, I made my way back to the Dinellos. I realized I had nowhere else to go.

When I arrived at the storefront, all the lights were blazing, which was unusual, and both Mr. and Mrs. Dinello were sitting in the kitchen, which surprised me. Then I saw that Mrs. Salucci and Mrs. DiPietro were there as well, speaking in low tones over in the corner by the window. As soon as I hobbled in, Mrs. DiPietro touched her hand to her forehead and chest, then to each of her shoulders: "See, I told you, Generosa." Mrs. Salucci shot me a vicious look. With a little harrumph, she and Mrs. DiPietro swept past me and mounted the stairs. "How many times do I tell them?" she said loudly.

"Ninella," Mr. Dinello said. He leaned back in his chair with his arms crossed, regarding me with horrible resignation. His look was not cruel, or even angry, but one of such terrible disappointment I felt as if I had been kicked. He fixed his eyes on mine for a long, heavy moment, then glanced sadly toward the countertop.

There, like the damning pieces of evidence they were, were the remaining three items I had hidden beneath the floorboards.

I realized instantly that I was in a great deal of trouble.

"Now you come back?" Mrs. Dinello shouted at me, leaping to her feet. "We feed you. We treat you like a daughter? And this—this is the thanks we get?"

"Generosa," Mr. Dinello said evenly, making a staying motion with his hand.

"You disappear. You steal our tools. You even steal our rosary?" She yanked open the candy tin and dangled the string of wooden beads before me. "What are you doing with this?"

I blinked back my tears. "I just like to wear it sometimes," I said barely audibly.

"You wear it? This is not jewelry. This is not a toy. This, she does not belong to you—"

"I was careful," I pleaded. "I didn't break it."

"*Ai!*" Mrs. Dinello cried. Throwing up her hands, she looked at Mr. Dinello with exasperation.

"The scoop, Ninella," said Mr. Dinello, "that you took this morning? Where is it?"

This I could not bear to answer. I looked down at the floorboards, my face flushing with shame.

"You did take it, *si?*" he said.

Slowly, almost imperceptibly, I nodded.

"So where is it?" Mrs. Dinello demanded.

Even with my head down, I could feel their gaze on me, waiting, and yet I could not find a voice. Finally I whispered, "I sold it."

"You sold it?"

I nodded. There was nothing left to lie for, of course. And then, carefully, I unfurled my palm. All this time I had been clutching the three coins. They were now embedded in my skin, sticking to it and turning it dark green. Unbending my fingers was painful.

Mrs. Dinello stared at my proffered palm. "Forty cents? You sold it for forty cents?"

Mr. Dinello gave her a look of mild, bitter surprise. "At least she make a profit."

I started to cry.

All the air seemed to go out of Mrs. Dinello then. "Why? Why you do all this? Ninella. Why you disrespect us so?"

This time the question was a statement not of anger, but despair. She genuinely seemed to want to know. I sniffled and choked on my sobs. All I longed to do, of course, was to drop to my knees and beg them not to put me out on the street or send me to the asylum. All I wanted to do was promise I'd be better, promise I'd be good. But I understood that this was no longer enough. The Dinellos were positioned before me like judge and jury. I had to make a compelling case for myself. Otherwise they were finished with me. They were exhausted. They were done.

I blinked up at the Dinellos—her with her black hair shot with its streak of silver and her weary eyes—him with his white hair and earnest face, almost pleading with me—the two of them standing before me in their shabby clothes, as the office alcove that I had come to know as home rose behind them, with its well-meaning bench, and its cross on the wall, and its picture of the bearded saint in robes lovingly clutching a child.

Children sense what adults want to hear; they have an instinct for what will endear them to the people who control their fate. As I stood there in the little ices factory, everything before me suddenly coalesced.

"I just wanted some money to put in the church basket," I said softly, "for Jesus, so he will make my leg better. I just want to be a good Catholic"—I started to weep—"like you."

It was, of course, a grand, marvelous lie. Yet no sooner had I said it than I half believed it was true. Perhaps it was. Perhaps I did feel a great longing to be like them, to belong. Certainly at that moment I believed in what I was saying the way a drowning man believes in a life raft.

I had only a vague idea of how the rosary bolstered my case. What it meant for a Jew to go to church or pray to Jesus—it did not really register: I was merely a child, after all. Yet who knows? Perhaps after months and months of living among the Dinellos and their countrymen, I really did want to be like them. Or perhaps I simply had nowhere else to turn. So sue me, darlings: I did what I had to.

As soon as they heard my preposterous explanation, the Dinellos seemed to melt. The childishness of my reasoning was enough to make it ring true. ("Imagine! She wants to be Catholic so badly she sleeps with a rosary!" I heard Mrs. Dinello tell Mrs. Ferrendino later, with a tinge of bemused pride.) Perhaps, like most people, the Dinellos were easily undone by flattery. Or perhaps they were simply too forgiving, too kind, too buffeted by life's hardships not to allow me to redeem myself.

Mrs. Dinello shook her head and looked at me, her eyes welling. "Oh, Ninella," she sighed. Cocking his head, Mr. Dinello motioned me over. I limped across the warped floorboards with my cane to him and surrendered.

The Dinellos moved me upstairs to sleep in a room with Beatrice. While I believed at the time that this was designed to help me feel "more Catholic" and more a part of the family, I now suspect it was done to keep a better eye on me. To my great disappointment, Mrs. Dinello announced that the pennies we saved in the jar from my lace-making would be given to the church basket each week instead of used for excursions to the movies. More and more, I was enlisted to help Mr. Dinello in the kitchen before school each morning. As I assembled the ingredients before him, he sang in Italian and winked.

A few weeks later, clad in a white dress that Mrs. Dinello and Mrs. Salucci had stitched together themselves—and feeling quite regal—the most regal, in fact, that I would feel for many years—I proceeded solemnly up to the font in the corner of the Most Precious Blood Church. Around me were Mr. and Mrs. Dinello, of course, as well as Silvio, Vincenzo, Luigi, Annunziata, and all four grandsons. Mrs. Ferrendino was there, too, and the Piccolos, and the DiPietros, and even a sour-looking Mrs. Salucci. Just as Father Antonucci had shown me he would, he bent me gently over the rim.

It had been suggested to me beforehand that I might like to take a "more Christian, more Italian" name for my baptism. "Perhaps Maria," Father Antonucci suggested. "Since it is close to Malka. You could be Malka-Maria."

"Maria, she is a beautiful name." Mrs. Dinello nodded. "My grandmother was Maria-Teresa."

"No," I said solemnly.

Mrs. Dinello and the priest exchanged an anxious look.

"I don't want to be Malka at all," I said.

Malka. *Maaall-kah*. It scraped across my brain like my cane against the sidewalk and dragged after me like the deadweight of my leg. It rang in my head like the mockery it had become in the schoolyard. It came to me in the voice of my mother, furiously announcing that "all this" was my fault. Malka was the "violent" and "insane" girl who almost got locked away. Malka was the bigmouth who caused nothing but *tsuris*. Malka was the *Ammazza Christi*, the hellbound, the dirty Jew. "Please," I begged Mrs. Dinello and Father Antonucci, "can I have a new name altogether? An American one—the same as the beautiful girl in the moving pictures."

Scarcely more than a year after I had arrived at Ellis Island with my family from Vishnev, Father Antonucci said a solemn prayer in Latin and eased my head down into the marble basin of sacred water. As he scooped it over me, it ran through my hair like fingers, bathing my neck and pooling in the little wells of my clavicle. As he righted me, it soaked into the lace of my collar, ran down my arms, and fell about my feet in tiny, sparkling molecules, a rain of liquid diamonds washing away everything, rinsing me clean. Everyone cheered, everyone clapped.

I had entered the church Malka Treynovsky Bialystoker. I emerged, however, Lillian Maria Dinello.

The legend of my American life had begun.

Chapter 6

JUST DAYS BEFORE THE CIVIL TRIAL, a man named Robin Leach telephones. He has refused to go through my publicist, my secretary, my army of lawyers. He insists on speaking to me personally, and he has the most extraordinary English accent. It is like a parody of Cockney. He bellows so loudly through the receiver, I assume he thinks that I am deaf. At first I'm convinced it's all a hideous prank. But no. Leach really is his last name. And he really is hosting a new television show called *Lifestyles of the Rich and Famous*, slated to air next year. He asks: Might I be willing to open up my home in Bedford to his cameras? The fact that I'm currently under indictment doesn't seem to bother him in the least.

"What we're looking for is 'champagne wishes and caviar dreams' as they translate into home furnishings, luv," he explains. "Viewers don't care a whit about scandals. In fact, scandals are good, providing they're the right sort. Here's what they do care about, though: mirrored walls, leopard-print furniture, satin bedsheets, crystal chandeliers, and indoor swimming pools. And the more gold plating on anything, the better. Your late husband, for example, did he happen to own any gold-plated golf clubs? Do your sinks have any gold-plated faucets? What about your loo? Any chance the handles are gold? It's extraordinary, the amount of interest people will have in a gold-plated toilet. Also, extra points for home movie theaters, circular water beds, wet bars, wine cellars, grand pianos in any color other than black, fur vaults, pinball machines, and Jacuzzis. And multicar garages, those are the real money shots here, if you forgive my saying so, luv. You wouldn't happen to own any DeLoreans or Lamborghinis, say, would you?"

"Lamborghini, what is that? Some sort of pasta?" I say. So sue me: I am being a wisenheimer. I know what a Lamborghini is, thank you very much. However, I always purchase American only.

"What about Cadillacs?" I say. "Do they still count for something?"

"That depends. We prefer gold, silver, or magenta."

My home in Bedford, I suspect, is not nearly as extravagant as Mr. Leach believes it to be. Our old spread in Palm Beach, with its Italianate fountains, tennis courts, and the rotunda—that would have been more to his taste. "Really," I tell him, "we have only two pools and a sauna now. Except for the bar and the ballroom, it's all rather sedate." This television concept seems completely *meshuggeneh* to me. *You want to go through my closets? Show viewers my crystal drawer pulls?* Yet this Mr. Leach is trafficking in the same experience, I realize, that I had as a tiny girl walking through the streets of Hamburg. We all want to press our faces up against the glass. Peel back a velvet curtain. Peek inside.

And why shouldn't I be proud?

Besides, this Robin Leach says, his producers will pay me handsomely to participate.

Well then. Every bit can help defray my legal costs. And if I'm being hounded by cameras anyway, why not use it to my advantage? Who turns down a paycheck?

"If we do this, however, a few rooms are off-limits," I tell him. Bert's old dressing room, for one. And my "souvenir parlor." Over the years it seems, I have crammed it full of those marvelous little individual jars of raspberry jam and marmalade they always serve me with breakfast over at the Waldorf. Washcloths acquired from the Hilton. Ashtrays from the Plaza. Butter knives and tea-spoons from Delta. TWA. Marvelous luggage tags and porcelain saltshakers from the Concorde. Matchbooks from the Sherry-Netherland. Assorted guest soaps. Plastic swizzle sticks. Coffee stirrers. Sugar cubes. Hundreds of ketchup, salt, and soy-sauce packets from restaurants. Paper napkins. They are often sitting there just for the taking! So sue me: You never know when you might need something like these in a pinch. Still. I suspect it's bet-ter only to show the public my Chagall.

"Send over the paperwork," I tell Robin Leach, "and the mon-etary offer in writing."

"No, absolutely not. You can't do it, Ma," Isaac declares over lunch.

"Says who?" I say. "Who asked you? Mr. Big here. You haven't even finished stealing my estate, yet already you're acting like my landlord."

"I'm not trying to steal your property, Ma. I'm trying to protect it. And your reputation."

"Mrs. Dunkle, I have to side with your son on this," says my lawyer, Mr. Beecham, squeezing a half-moon of lemon into his Perrier, cupping his hand around it so it doesn't spray across the tablecloth. All around us, I know, other diners are sneaking glances at me. It is only a matter of time, I suspect, before some paparazzi start gathering in the street outside. "Right now the last thing you want is for the entire world to see you showing off your mansion on television," Beecham says in a quiet voice. "We need people to be sympathetic."

"I don't want sympathy," I sniff. "I want them to fear and re-spect me."

"Ma, you think they're going to respect someone who paid eighty-five thousand dollars for a doghouse that's a replica of Versailles?" Isaac says.

"What country did you grow up in?" I look at him mawkishly. "Of course they will. This is America, for Chrissakes."

"Lillian, if I might weigh in here," Rita says gently, patting my son's tweedy cuff. She has not touched her poached salmon, though it is the most expensive dish on the menu. My daughter-in-law. Suddenly she is a paragon of concern again. It is she, I suspect, who has urged Isaac to return from their summer home to meet with me and my lawyers before the trials. Perhaps she has planted a spy among my staff.

"Look, we're in your corner, Lillian," she insists. Oh. When have I heard this before? Canny, sharp-eyed Rita, with her expensive feathered haircut, her glittering gold necklaces nestling in her clavicle, her fancy degree from UPenn. Who pushes food around on her plate and owns a Cuisinart when she never even cooks anymore.

After Bert died, Rita became my new best friend for a while. "Come on over on Thursday, Lil, and I'll make my famous lasagna for you. We'll get some girl time alone in the kitchen." She offered to take me shopping each week at Saks. Accompanied me to my internist, my pulmonary-cardiologist, my physical therapist. Scheduled weekly appointments for us together at my beauty parlor. "Now that Jason's a teenager, he doesn't need me anymore," she'd said helplessly. "Come have tea with me at the Plaza?" Stupidly, I had actually begun to entertain the possibility that Rita genuinely liked spending time with me. The pocketbooks I bought for her. And that expensive John Kloss underwear—sixteen dollars for a brassiere without any lace on it? "You're such a comfort to me," she had said once, squeezing my arm as we burrowed into the wind together on Fifty-Seventh Street.

Yet I should have known better. That conniver. She was just making sure I was indisposed. Out of the office.

Now she taps the last of her Tab into her glass and says with asperity, "Rich guys can own two hundred sports cars, Lillian, and everyone simply calls them 'collectors' or 'enthusiasts.' But if a woman has a hundred pairs of shoes, people are like, 'Who the hell does she think she is?'" Reaching across the table, she touches her fingertips to my forearm. "I just don't want you to give them any more opportunity to bad-mouth you."

Yanking my arm away, I glower. The problem with my daughter-in-law is that she is often right. Rita is far shrewder—and savvier—than my own son: pepper to Isaac's salt. But she's like a magpie, too, Rita. Wave anything shiny in front of her and that's all she fixates on. Ambition. Single-mindedness. Desire. Consumption. I recognize them all in her. I know them only too well myself.

"You just don't want me to embarrass you, is all," I say bitterly, setting my fork down with a clatter. "You're all in cahoots. You just don't want the feds to seize everything I own before you get your hot little mitts on it."

"Ma," Isaac says.

"I built this fortune, not you."

∽

My husband, Bert, had the jaw, cheekbones, and torso that one usually finds sculpted in marble inside a Greek temple. His long-lashed eyes were set deep in his face, a serif of hair curled over his forehead. He was so dashing, darlings, he might as well have worn a pilot's scarf draped permanently around his neck.

The day he crashed our ice cream truck into the fire hydrant off Merrick Road all anyone thought was that a movie star had careened into their midst. What a movie star would be doing driving a Dunkle's Frozen Custard truck through Bellmore, Long Island, never occurred to them. Nor did they seem to mind that in swerving up onto the curb, he'd blown out the tire. The truck was now stuck with its front wheels on the sidewalk and its back fishtailed out into the street, blocking all the traffic to the beach, the little music box we'd installed in it playing a tinny version of "The Blue Danube" over and over. The fire hydrant, crushed against the side of the truck, had been ripped from the pavement, so that the pipes beneath it shot water up into the air like a geyser. Yet no one seemed to pay this any mind either.

"Oh, my God, Hazel, look!" someone shouted. "It's Douglas Fairbanks Jr.!"

"Where?"

"There! In that truck!"

"Doris, no. You're mad."

"See? Look!"

"Oh, my word. That's not Douglas Fairbanks. That's Errol Flynn!"

They seemed to believe it was all a stunt for some movie being filmed with hidden cameras. Within minutes, perhaps a dozen people—mostly women—gathered around our truck, smiling and fanning themselves in the midday sun and pointing giddily and shouting, "Mr. Flynn, Mr. Flynn! Oh, my word! Errol!" One woman angled for his autograph.

I was thrown beneath the dashboard when we swerved. After we jerked to a stop, however, my main thought wasn't for myself—I felt no pain—but rather for the truck. *Please*, I thought, *let nothing too terrible have happened*. Bert leaped out of the cab. For a moment he stood paralyzed in the street in his white apron and little white cap, unsure whether to come around to my side, or to get back in behind the wheel, or to respond to the squealing, waving women.

"Bert!" I hollered. "Come help me down!"

The women in the street stepped back reverently to let him pass. "Where do you think the movie cameras are?" I heard one say.

"L-L-L-Lil, I'm so sorry—oh, here, let me help you," Bert said, opening the door. The spray from the hydrant had drenched him. His white shirt and apron were matted to the plates of his chest. Bert had been a stutterer as a child. Whenever he was nervous, his stammer returned. "Are y-you all r-right?"

My cane had fallen onto the floor beneath the dashboard. "H-here, d-doll," he said quickly, fishing it out. With my arms looped around his shoulder, he helped me down gallantly onto the running board, then onto the sidewalk. I was unhurt. His wet skin and hair sparkled in the sunshine. He appeared freshly dipped in bronze. "Oooh," a woman sighed rapturously.

For a moment Bert and I stood there in dismay, assessing the damage. The water fountaining up against the truck from the hydrant was like blood gushing; I had an overwhelming impulse to stanch it. The front right tire was rapidly deflating. The truck listed like a shipwreck.

Merrick Road was the main thoroughfare. Several cars were now stalled behind us. A few of them began to honk, horns bleating like sheep. It was the Fourth of July weekend, and the little thermometer Bert had pasted to the inside rim of the window read eighty-five degrees.

"For God's sake, Bert!" I cried.

"L-L-Lil, it's just a t-tire," he said. "It can be fixed."

"Oh, really? How?"

"Just g-give me a minute, will you?"

"Veer left, I told you. Left. Why didn't you listen?"

"I did turn left!"

"You call this left?" I motioned to the lopsided truck collapsing against the right side of the curb. "Every time I say left, you turn right. I say right, you go left. What the hell am I supposed to do? Say right when I want you to go left?"

Bert hung his head. "You can't just yell directions at me like that."

"I WASN'T YELLING!"

As we stood facing each other in the visceral heat, the small crowd of locals watched us expectantly, as if it were theater. "The Blue Danube" kept playing, but slower and slower as the music box wound down. Finally Bert leaned through the front window and snapped it off, which was a relief. The water from the fire hydrant diminished from a great spray to a constant burble, like a pulse.

I sighed and gestured at the truck. "What are the chances it can still run?"

By this point a couple of the drivers stuck behind us had turned off their ignitions and climbed out of their cars—a Hudson, I remember, and a canary yellow Nash roadster that looked like an overstuffed armchair—people drove purely for pleasure in those days—and they came over to have a look.

"Oh, jeez." One of them squatted beside the chassis in the bleaching sunlight and shook his head. "I think your axle may be busted."

"Are they actors, too?" I heard a woman ask.

"No one is an actor here, ladies," I said with irritation, fanning myself with my hand. My skirt and apron stays were plastered to my backside. "We're selling ice cream. And that's my husband. Not Errol Flynn."

The women looked at him incredulously, then me, then our truck—the big striped loaf of it. Ice cream trucks were not common in 1936. Ours was actually a secondhand Divco Twin Coach bakery truck that Bert had retrofitted with a small continuous-batch freezer and a couple of cold-storage cabinets. These were wired to a generator that ran off the engine. Provided you hunched over, there was just enough room inside for two people. Bert usually scooped from the freezer inside to the left, then handed the cones to me to pass to the customers through the door, which folded open like an accordion. We'd painted the outside with broad bands of pale pink, white, and beige to resemble Neapolitans—the chocolate-strawberry-and-vanilla ice cream bricks that were very popular back then and often sold by the slice. I'd written DUNKLE'S FROZEN CUSTARD over the windshield and on both sides of the truck in cherry red script above what was, I suppose, our first logo—a picture of an ice cream cone (a triad of circles over a V) inside the outline of a heart.

With its music box, its whimsical lettering, and its now-collapsed front tire, this truck, it was all that Bert and I had in the world. Most nights we even slept in it.

"I'm sorry, folks," said the man from the roadster, squinting up at us from beside the crushed tire, "but from what I can see, this isn't going anywhere."

Other drivers crouched with Bert in the dust. "The axle's bent," Bert said. The men debated what to do. Sun burned through the salted breeze. Seagulls circled overhead, cawing. Before the accident we had stopped just twice. The playgrounds and parks in Queens had been nearly empty that morning. Fifteen cents, we had made. Most of our inventory sat nestled in dry ice in the cold cabinet, waiting to be sold. Fourth of July afternoon was supposed to be our single busiest day of the year.

I squinted up at the white-hot noon sky. The noxious smell of tar rose from the road.

In the past we had cut the engine for fifteen, even twenty minutes without a problem. We needed to stop it—and the generator—in order to sell the ice cream. Otherwise, of course, it was too noisy and dangerous, and our customers would choke on exhaust fumes. We worked quickly, Bert and I. Bert, in fact, could scoop a cone to weight—exactly 3.5 ounces and not a penny more—in eight seconds. This is important, darlings. You lose a lot of money if you don't scoop ice cream properly. You have to scrape the scoop across the face of the ice cream, curling a ribbon over itself so that it forms a ball that's hollow in the center. You need to create the illusion of size and density yet make each scoop no greater than 3.5 ounces. Otherwise you lose your profit margin.

Bert had practiced over and over, with me timing him and weighing his efforts on a little scale. Since I could add and make change in my head, we got to where we could serve thirty customers in just under fourteen minutes. We'd never had the engine off for more than twenty-five.

Over by the front of the truck, I could see one of the men stand up and sigh. Another shook his head. Bert looked bereft. A terrible feeling came over me. It was Saturday, a national holiday. Even if there was a service station nearby, it would not open until Monday at the earliest. Eighteen gallons of Dunkle's "frozen custard," all that we had left in the world, were just sitting there, stranded with us in the heat.

∽

The spring after I was baptized, Mr. Dinello seemed to disappear. Had I not heard his boots squeaking on the stairs early in the mornings, when the smoky, violet-cloaked alleys had not yet come to life, and had I not heard his voice whispering excitedly late at night when only a single gas jet remained lit in the kitchen and Mrs. Dinello wearily set out a plate of manicotti for him, I would have thought he had vanished completely, just as Papa had.

During the day, in his absence, a lot of men tromped in and out to speak to Mrs. Dinello, though the storefront kitchen itself remained closed. Mrs. Salucci kept shaking her head and tsking. "Salvatore, he is too much of a dreamer. He is going to wind up in the poorhouse—or getting a visit from La Mano Nera—or worse."

Yet the Dinellos' apartments filled with an air of expectation, a gleeful secret, a collective holding of breath.

"Come," Mrs. Dinello said to me one Saturday morning after I'd finished washing the dishes. The boys were already out, and the tenement rang with a peculiar silence. She braided my hair and cleaned my cheeks with spit as she often did just before we left for church. Instead of turning right, however, toward Baxter Street, she put her hand on the small of my back and guided me north then west, onto a big thoroughfare crowded with storefronts and chiming with streetcars. Halfway down the block, Mr. Dinello stood waving excitedly. "She is *magnifico, si?*" he said, gesturing grandly. Behind him, on a large, freshly washed window, were the words DINELLO & SONS FANCY ITALIAN ICES & ICE CREAMS stenciled in burnished gold letters. Through the glass we could glimpse a long enamel counter. The grandsons were already inside stacking crates and mopping the floors.

The new Lafayette Street factory was easily three times the size of the Mulberry Street storefront. Dusty floorboards, rats, gas jets, the competing scents of garlic, tomatoes, and marjoram—all of this was now gone. White tiles ran halfway up the walls, like wainscoting, and the walls above were painted cream. More remarkably, there was electricity. Three elaborate globe lamps hung above the countertop like pearl earrings. And then, standing sentinel in the back corner, was the factory's crowning glory: a motorized, vertical continuous-batch freezer—a remarkable, cylindrical machine, gleaming with nickel plating and promise.

In the decade before my family and I arrived in America, a man named Burr Walker, oddly enough—Burr, darlings, could you make this up?—invented a "circulating brine freezer." Instead of employing ice and rock salt, this curious contraption froze ingredients inside a cylinder encased in brine, cooled with an ammonia compressor. In 1905 another man, named Emery Thompson, who ran a soda fountain in one of the grand New York City department stores, took the idea one step further. He invented what was called a "gravity-fed continuous-process freezer." Such a mouthful, I know.

This machine was upright, so that you could pour the ingredients in the top, start the motor, and have it all come out as ice cream into a pail at the bottom. Batch after batch you could make without ever stopping.

The state-of-the-art freezers that Bert designed for our New Jersey plant are based, in fact, on this early model—and oh, they are beautiful things, darlings. A thousand gallons an hour they can turn out for our supermarket division. Twice a week we give tours at the facility. I'm telling you, you should see them.

The small freezer that Mr. Dinello purchased was far more modest, of course. As I recall, it could turn out thirty, perhaps forty gallons an hour. Yet it was a magnificent investment. Suddenly none of us had to hand-crank an ice cream maker any longer.

"You see? You see?" Mr. Dinello demonstrated, climbing up on a stepladder and pouring a great quantity of creamy liquid into an aperture. Tightening a seal, he flicked a switch. Suddenly a great noise filled the room and the entire kitchen seemed to shake violently. When the machine jerked to a halt scarcely a minute later, he removed an enormous pail from beneath it and winked. We gathered around and gasped. Inside was a gallon of glistening vanilla ice cream.

In twenty minutes Mr. Dinello could make what used to take us hours of labor.

Business, of course, exploded. Gelato, gelato: Talk of it rang through the Mulberry Street tenement like music. The Dinellos' sons gave up their sandhog jobs to help run the operation. Five flavors of ice cream they made now every morning—chocolate, strawberry, vanilla, coffee, and pistachio—plus two kinds of ices. Lemon or cherry, grape or orange, depending on what was in season. In addition to two cold-storage cabinets in the storefront, a dank room in the basement had been converted into a "hardening room," where ice cream could be packed in ice and stored. Six vendors soon worked for Mr. Dinello, selling Dinello & Sons Fancy Italian Ices & Ice Creams in distinctive white-and-gold wagons that Mr. Dinello himself designed. Fanning out from Wall Street all the way north to Houston, their cries of "I-SEE CREMA," mimicked the same cadences of his own chocolaty baritone, rising over the squares and the tenements like flocks of birds.

Occasionally a man came to the Mulberry Street apartment dressed in a jacket with a silk lining and an expensive bowler hat, speaking Italian, winking jocularly; Mrs. Dinello handed him a thick envelope tied with string.

Watching him come and go, Mrs. Salucci scowled. "Well, of course, the first payments are always the easiest to make."

The new ice cream machine enthralled me. It was a giant continual magic trick. In went the liquid—and presto!—out came ice cream! When nobody was looking, I touched my fingertips lightly to the dials, fondled the knobs, and peeked inside the spout at the bottom, trying to figure out how it worked. Ice cream, the frozen confection itself, still left me feeling melancholy when I ate it. But ice cream making—the astonishing, abracadabra, transformative process of it—that I adored. That I could watch happily for hours.

So could the grandsons. That very first day, we stood shouting "Look! Look!" each time a new batch of ice cream blobbed into the pail. It seemed inconceivable to us that the same miracle could occur over and over again. Mr. Dinello demonstrated one flavor after another. First vanilla! Then strawberry!

Yet when I patted the shiny silver chassis, Mr. Dinello scolded, "*Ai, ai, ai,* do not touch her. These machines, they are not for little girls."

Only the sons and grandsons were allowed to operate the brand-new equipment. Only the sons and grandsons were now privy to the Dinellos' updated ice cream recipes. Only they were entrusted to sample each batch, and shovel the fresh ice cream rapidly into large metal drums wrapped in burlap, and load them onto the waiting wagons, and wash down the freezers, sinks, and countertops with bleach. Only the grandsons could help themselves to heaping dishes of chocolate ice cream after school without asking permission. Only the boys and men worked with Mr. Dinello, all singing opera together in the bright new kitchen as they worked.

Me, I had to continue to report upstairs to Mrs. Salucci every day after school. "Why are you frowning?" said Mrs. Dinello, frowning herself as she wiped her hands on a dishrag. "You make good money for us with the lace. In the shop you will just get in the way."

I had thought that once I was baptized, of course, I would be magically transformed. At school, despite being bullied, I excelled—in math and reading in particular. After dinner I sat at the table patiently teaching Mrs. Dinello every evening, guiding her puckered fingers over the block letters in my school primers. "'House. Mouse. Louse,'" she repeated after me.

"Good," I said. "Now try these, signora. 'Birth. Girth. Mirth.'"

I made attempts to smile—something that has never, I'm afraid, come naturally to me. Every Sunday I went to confession and prayed to Jesus (even as I avoided gazing up at him, writhing, denuded, and bloody as he was), arranging my face into a beatific look of piety as I joined the line for Communion.

Yet Beatrice and Annunziata continued to regard me as little more than a washbasin or an ironing board. When I said "*Buona sera, mio zios*" as they hurried through the doorway, the Dinellos' three grown sons grimaced. I never sat on anyone's knee, or had my hair rumpled regularly, or called the Dinellos "Nonno" and "Nonna"—or received an affectionate swat on the backside and a kiss on the forehead before bed. Everyone still called me Ninella, or simply *la ragazza*—"the girl"—never Lillian. Except for Rocco. He now called me "Horsey."

I could not understand why I could not compel anyone's love. Surely, with my new name, I had become a new and better person. What was I doing wrong? The problem, I finally decided, lay in my one persistent, secret infidelity.

Some days after school, instead of heading directly to Mrs. Salucci's apartment, I found myself hobbling back to Orchard Street. Certainly I knew better—yet the impulse, it was as relentless as an itch. I stood before my family's old tenement, staring up at the fire escapes, at the cheap curtains pinned over the windows and the laundry laced across the façade, crossing my fingers and willing Mama and Papa and my sisters to materialize. Sometimes I approached the tenants or peddlers stationed nearby. "Please, when my papa comes back, or if you ever see a little blond girl here named Flora, could you tell them that I am at the Dinellos'? Tell them to look for the ices man." As I said this, a fragile, impossible bubble of hope always swelled within me. Like most abandoned children, I told myself stories, that Papa was simply too busy doing great, magnificent things to return to me just yet. One day he would no doubt reappear in an automobile, dressed in splendid clothing, carrying a paper sack for me, full of chocolates filled with jam.

The strangers on Orchard Street, however, they regarded me quizzically (I was oblivious to the effect that the tiny silver crucifix Mrs. Dinello had given me for my First Communion, dangling on a slim chain around my neck, might have had). And the whole neighborhood grew increasingly alien in my eyes. I had not learned to read Hebrew letters, after all, only Roman ones. The Jews in their odd clothing from a different part of the Old World began to appear distinctly separate from me, blurry and strange, as if from a long-ago dream.

Yet somehow I became convinced that Mrs. Salucci knew my dirty secret, my hidden longings. If the Dinellos were ever going to fully accept me, I concluded, I would have to renounce Orchard Street entirely. Otherwise they would think I was disloyal; they would think I was still Malka the Jew. Perhaps I truly believed this and began avoiding the street out of penance. Or perhaps returning there just made me too unbearably sad. No matter: I willed myself to sidestep the Jewish quarter entirely.

Yet sometimes in the broiling summer, when the grandsons and I climbed upstairs with our thin sheets and cushions to sleep outside on the rooftop, I couldn't help glancing across the forest of water towers and chimneys several blocks toward the east, to where I thought Mr. Lefkowitz's old window must be.

Setting my pillow down on the hot, scratchy tar roof, I imagined Mama in the sanitarium. I imagined Bella scrubbing floors in a grand apartment overlooking a garden in that place called "the Bronx." Flora, however, I could not bear to imagine at all.

Still, I watched the faraway window steadily in the growing darkness, hoping against hope to see a familiar face silhouetted in the gritty panes. But no one ever appeared, and finally, as the night inevitably set in, the light in the distant window always blinked out.

History. It never seems to have any relevance, darlings, until it happens to you.

In 1917, because of the war, sugar prices escalated 83 percent. To conserve cane sugar for the troops—and perhaps even to save the ice cream industry—the USDA encouraged ice cream makers to replace up to 50 percent of the sugar they used with corn syrup. Other substitutes—such as powdered eggs and milk solids—were also sanctioned.

When he taste-tested the first batch of Dinello's strawberry made with corn syrup and dried egg whites, Mr. Dinello flung his spoon down on the counter with uncharacteristic disgust. "This!" he cried. "She not even tastes like the food!"

Yet what choice did he have?

Then, in the spring of 1918, Luigi and Silvio were conscripted into the army, their brides-in-waiting long lost to them in Italy amid the war. Not wanting to be separated from his brothers—and eager to prove his loyalty to the new nation that had brought his family such prosperity—Vincenzo signed up as well. Such a sense of responsibility people had back then! The piers of Lower Manhattan, once teeming with new arrivals, were now teeming with these very same immigrants, reoutfitted in fine olive uniforms by the United States War Department, heading back the opposite way.

Those in our neighborhood who couldn't serve found jobs with the metalworkers, shipbuilders, machinists, and longshoremen, with tool-and-die casters, in factories turning out boot soles, tin cans, pocketknives, belt buckles, rivets, and rope. Mr. Dinello suddenly found himself an aging man with a few humble ice cream wagons, astronomical bills, and no one to help him sell a new product he despised. "*Gelato americano,*" he called it derisively. For a few terrible weeks, he returned home early—his boots heavy on the stairs, his white mustache drooping sadly—and sat on the settee with his head in his hands. "Oh, Generosa," he whispered. "What have I done?"

So sue me: I sensed an opportunity. One night after Beatrice had dropped off to sleep, I tiptoed into the kitchen in my bedclothes.

"*Ai*, Ninella. It is late," Mr. Dinello said. "What is it?"

"Please," I said softly, looking first at him, then Mrs. Dinello. "I want to help you. With the ice cream."

Mr. Dinello laughed wearily. "*Ai.* At midnight?"

"At the shop. With the boys. I'm strong. I'm good. I can work hard."

"Go to sleep, Ninella," he said.

Casting around for a final argument, I seized upon what seemed to be an important thing to say, what I was hearing all around me on the stoops and in the schoolyard. "Please," I said. "I want to do my part for the war."

At this, Mr. Dinello gave a mirthless little laugh. Yet when I climbed back into my bed a few minutes later, to my great delight I heard him and Mrs. Dinello arguing.

"Beatrice and Annunziata are helping now, Salvo. Why not her, too?"

"She cannot move quickly. She cannot lift things. The machines, they are dangerous."

"What is she going to do? Fall into them? She can sit on a stool. Nobody is ordering the lace now. Last week only one dollar she brought in."

The next morning, Mr. Dinello said with resignation, "Come, Ninella." Gripping my hand, he helped me down the steps into the chilly, sooty dawn. A few horse-drawn wagons clattered by; the sky was streaked with colors of sherbet. To be alone with Mr. Dinello—to be included—made me exultant. Just as we arrived at the little factory, a dairy wagon pulled up.

"The milk"—Mr. Dinello motioned—"you smell it. Like the perfume."

Before he committed to purchasing a case that morning, Mr. Dinello unscrewed a cap right there in the street. Kneeling before me, he placed the bottle under my nose. The milk was like a little quivering moon ringed in glass. "Sniff," he motioned. Dairy products in those days were terribly inconsistent. One bottle of turned milk could ruin gallons of ice cream. My sense of smell, as you may have surmised by now, is extremely acute. I suppose the Dinellos had noticed this by the way I could always tell what our neighbors were having for Sunday dinner simply by leaning out the air shaft. Instantly, there on the curbside, I could discern that the first seven bottles of milk were fine yet the eighth had gone "off" with an acrid, cheeselike tang.

"Ah, see?" Mr. Dinello said when I detected the spoiled bottle. "She has the magic nose."

Once the sons and grandsons arrived to unload the deliveries, I was put to work in the back room shelling pistachios. The next day I sliced strawberries, then made stacks of waxed-paper cones.

It was tedious, uninspiring work that I soon tried to syncopate with the thrumming of the machines. Beatrice and Annunziata usually took over once I had left for school, though occasionally Rocco was ordered to help me finish before class. "Why do I have to do chores with her?" he protested.

"Horse Girl," he said under his breath.

"Nincompoop," I replied.

"You just want free ice cream."

"You just want a free punch in the face."

Sometimes we began poking each other. Or tickling. When our boredom fully trumped our animosity, we folded the waxed paper into fans and mustaches and bow ties and scrunched them under our noses and paraded around with them, talking in silly voices, until Mr. Dinello yelled at us to stop making a ruckus and get back to work. If we could not reuse the paper, he said, we were in for big trouble. "This is our livelihood, *capisce?* Each paper you play with is a penny we lose."

Giving me a pinch on my forearm, Rocco would head off to inflict himself on his brothers instead. The four boys in the factory together, they were like wolf cubs, mauling, walloping, and head-locking one another, calling one another names as they waited for the freezer to finish churning.

"*Ai, cazzo!*"

"*Ai, stronzo!*"

"*Va fa Napoli!*"

Mr. Dinello did not even bother to try to curb them. Sometimes, however, he broke into song as he worked, and they stopped pummeling one another long enough to sing along. I did, too—my voice the only thin, reedy soprano among the tenors and baritones. *Addio, addio mia bella Napoli!*

Every chance I could, I lingered by the freezer. When nobody was looking, I ran my hand against the cold, smooth, silver flank of it.

In the early autumn of 1918, I had just started fifth grade when signs began popping up in windows and on doors, on broadsheets plastered on streetlamps around the neighborhood. Suddenly big public gatherings were being discouraged; taverns, moving-picture houses, soda fountains—even churches—grew empty. Nobody knew what it was exactly, except that it started quickly, with a cough and a fever.

Il Progresso, our local newspaper, urged parents to heed the health commissioner: Children would be better looked after in their classrooms instead of staying home and running loose. Yet each day at school, more desks sat unoccupied after the bell and dead leaves swirled around the empty schoolyard. At home, Beatrice began coughing. Some health workers arrived at our tenement, covering their mouths with gauze. I remember Rocco crying, and the sensation of icy claws scraping down my spine, and my teeth chattering, and nets of mucus forming at the back of my throat that seemed to strangle me. When I coughed, it felt as if my ribs had been broken all over again. Someone taped a sign on the front door of our apartment. From my illness itself, only a single memory remains: of watching the flocked wallpaper in Beatrice's room melting like ice cream running down to the floor.

When I seemed to regain consciousness after many bleary, feverish days, Beatrice had vanished. Annunziata was gone, too. And Pietro. The Spanish flu, doctors were saying—it was leaving the weak but killing the strong. They had never seen anything like it; comparisons were being made to the plague. Mrs. Dinello's hair, which had been nearly jet-black just weeks before, was suddenly white as salt. "Why the young ones? Why a whole generation but not Salvatore and me?" she moaned, rocking back and forth on the settee.

And then, no sooner had the funerals been conducted and the bodies buried across the river in Holy Cross Cemetery, which Father Antonucci himself arranged, and the Masses attended, than three telegrams arrived. One right after the other, three nightmarish mornings in a row, each yellow rectangle like a full-body blow, like a percussive blast through the tenement. The third one Mrs. Dinello wouldn't even touch. She backed away from the doorway as if it were a red–hot poker, shrieking, "No, no, no!" Her wails echoed through the building; the constant, agonized crescendo of them was like the ocean crashing on jagged boulders. She took to her bed. She stopped going to Mass. "What kind of God lets a son die?" she sobbed.

The grandsons, the three remaining, were hastily consolidated into the Dinellos' modest triptych of rooms. Their peculiar odors, bulk, and unruly, adolescent hair filled the parlor, whereas I was relegated to the bench again in the upstairs kitchen.

All the neighbors invaded the apartment, of course. Mrs. Ferrendino's fleshy forearms jiggling as she set down a tin of sugar. Mrs. Salucci smelling of camphor and looking more tragic than the Dinellos themselves, flinging her brittle self into Mrs. Dinello's arms with an embarrassing wail: "Oh, Generosa!" Rosaries strung through calloused fingers, incantations whispered, men blearily drinking coffee, smoking tiny stinking cigars. Vittorio, Pasquale, and Rocco sat stonily all in a row on the settee in their starched Sunday clothes, allowing themselves to be kissed and pressed to the women's bosoms and petted forlornly by the parade of mourners. Tears glittered in their eyes, which they quickly wiped away on their sleeves before swallowing, hard. I sat on a stool in the corner. Most of the visitors hurried straight over to the boys without ever acknowledging me.

"Why are you crying?" Rocco said, shooting me an accusatory look across the room. "It's not your family who's dead."

"Leave her alone," Vittorio said softly.

"You act like everything here is yours, when it isn't," Rocco said.

"I do not," I choked.

"She has a right to be sad," said Pasquale quietly.

Rocco turned toward his older brothers. "She doesn't even like us."

"That's not true!" I cried.

Yet I wept, in fact, because I had not liked the dead very much at all, and because I felt guilty. I was jealous of all the attention the boys were receiving. All their losses only revived my own. Luigi and Annunziata were never coming back. Nor were my own parents. Nor were my sisters, I realized now. Everyone had been scattered to the wind like ashes. Vittorio, Pasquale, Rocco, and me—we were, all of us, orphans. I wept with them copiously. Yet Rocco was right: I wept not for them but for my own mama and papa and siblings—and for my own forsaken self.

Still, I refused to let him believe he was right.

"If you don't stop hating me," I whispered to him, "I'll box your ears."

"I'll box yours first," he said.

Later that night, however, and for a long time afterward, Rocco tiptoed into the kitchen. Pulling me onto the floor with him with his blankets and cushions, he curled up inside my arms. "Please," he whispered hoarsely. Locking my hands as tightly as he could around his waist, he pressed his fists into his eyes and sobbed, his little shoulders heaving like bellows while I anchored him.

The war ended; all around us was confetti and elation. The gleeful squeals from fire escapes: *Oh, Frankie, you're back!* Jazz was suddenly playing everywhere on Victrolas, trumpets and trombones slashing the jubilant air. "Tiger Rag." "Original Dixieland One-Step." Yet at the Dinellos' we moved through the days as if we were made of rice paper.

Everyone worked in a soggy, ghostly trance. From dawn until dinnertime. That's just what you did back then. There was no "grief counseling." There were no "support groups." You didn't bellyache. Perhaps you resumed going to church. Perhaps, inside the confessional, you whispered hoarsely to the priest through the quatrefoils that it was all your fault. Everyone around you always seemed to disappear. First your papa, then your mama, then all your sisters, and now the Dinellos. Perhaps you scrubbed the utensils in the ice cream factory to an obsessive sheen each morning, until your knuckles were raw with absolution. Yet that was it. Most of the time, you simply worked.

And there was plenty to do, darlings. Prohibition may have been lousy for the country, but it was a godsend to ice cream manufacturers. All those abandoned saloons and barrooms—what was to become of them? Proprietors converted them into even more ice cream parlors and soda fountains, that's what. Not everybody wanted to risk arrest at a speakeasy in order to have fun. Five places opened within a three-block radius of Lafayette Street alone.

By 1923, Dinello & Sons had stopped selling ice cream from wagons on the streets entirely. The wholesale market was not only more lucrative but safer. The streets of the Lower East Side were growing choked with automobiles and exhaust. And Mr. Dinello, his back hurt, his knees locked, his eyesight was failing. And his heart, of course, had been butchered.

He installed half a dozen little café tables in the front of Dinello & Sons, so that people from the neighborhood could come in for ice cream and buyers could sample the products. A wireless, shaped like a church window, appeared on a shelf behind the counter to "give it the atmosphere." Competition among ice cream manufacturers was fierce. A few parlors in Lower Manhattan were even buying from an outfit in Secaucus now. The biggest challenge, however, came from just a few blocks away on Canal Street, where a Sicilian family had opened Cannoletti's Ice Cream

Company. Mr. Dinello thought their product was junk—"They don't use the fresh ingredients. All you taste is the chemicals and the air." Yet the Cannolettis gave the Dinellos a run for their money, if only because they were so aggressive in their marketing. They sponsored little parades. They had banners. All day long one of their ferret-faced sons stood on the street wearing a sandwich board reading CANNOLETTI'S! THE #1 ICE CREAM IN AMERICA and ringing a bell.

Since ice cream had replaced cocktails, parlors everywhere began competing to see who could come up with the newest and most fabulous ice cream concoctions—sundaes glistening with pineapple and candied walnuts, strawberry phosphates crowned with raspberry sherbet. They named them things like "Hawaiian Paradise" and "Pink Ladies." Each week was something new.

One afternoon as I sang along to "Yes! We Have No Bananas" over the wireless, I sensed a great opportunity for myself.

"I have a suggestion, signore," I said the next morning. "Can you make a 'Yes, We *Have* Bananas' ice cream sundae? Perhaps with banana ice cream and walnuts? Everybody loves that song. Every time they hear it playing, they could start to think of Dinello's."

Mr. Dinello seemed to weigh the idea with his cheeks, then presented the idea to Mrs. Dinello.

"Bananas, they are not so expensive," she conceded, "especially when they are overripe. We might be able to get a lot of flavor for not too much money."

They experimented. For the first time ever, I was permitted to help with the production, mashing bananas in a large bowl with a metal spoon. Mr. Dinello made one gallon, then another. Mashed bananas were particularly viscous, it turned out, and their sweetness variable. Any brown spots created blotches and lumpiness.

Overall they lent themselves better to sherbet rather than to full-fat ice cream. Mr. Dinello had to keep adjusting the proportions until he finally got it just right. What he had, in the end, was a sort of hybrid. Yet it was delicious.

We had a few leftover bananas; he told me to peel and cut them lengthwise.

"Maybe we arrange the gelato between the bananas like this, *si?*" he said, placing them in a long dish so that they created a sort of boat. Then he spooned strawberry syrup over it and a dollop of whipped cream. When the final product was assembled, gleaming in its dish, Mr. Dinello stepped back to look at it with pride. "'Yes, We *Have* Bananas.' I think she is a very good idea," he proclaimed. "You make a sign, Ninella, for the window, *si?* I think she will sell."

Sell she did. The flavor I had suggested, darlings, it was a huge hit in the neighborhood, almost as big, in fact, as the song itself. Even without all the toppings, the sheer novelty of banana ice cream itself sparked a craze. Most of our buyers ordered at least one tub of it. Yet the greatest proof that we had done well came not from our sales. Ten days after we'd unveiled our sundae, Pasquale saw a sign outside Cannoletti's Ice Cream Company reading, YES, WE HAVE BANANAS ICE CREAM, TOO! AND FOR A PENNY LESS!

"Ninella," Mrs. Dinello asked me slyly, "what else can you dream up?"

From a school project I had to do about the League of Nations, I came up with the idea of making a brick of spumoni with pistachio, vanilla, and black cherry ice cream to replicate the Italian flag. That, too, was a hit. To my great delight, Mrs. Dinello even made a point of bringing a slice upstairs for Mrs. Salucci. All of Little Italy, oh, they went mad for it. We lured even more buyers away from Cannoletti's.

For Christmas, at my suggestion, the Dinellos made a peppermint ice cream.

"Maybe we could decorate cones to look like Santa Clauses," I suggested one afternoon, doodling in my schoolbook.

"Well," Rocco said, twisting a rag out over a bucket of bleach. "Aren't you a great mother of invention?"

I glanced at him.

"What?" He shrugged, turning his back to me, scrubbing the counter vigorously. "You're finally doing something worthwhile around here, Horsey."

Demand for their ice cream grew so high that the Dinellos could barely keep up. Their tiny ice cream parlor itself became so popular that they installed one of the neighborhood's first pay telephones. Families began to make an evening out of placing a phone call. Mothers would buy the children ice cream cones, and everyone would eat while they waited on line. A second vertical-batch freezer, the Dinellos bought. Peach ice cream, they began making. And walnut. And cinnamon. And cherry vanilla. Each week, one of the Cannolettis' ferret-faced sons stood on the sidewalk of Canal Street, bellicosely ringing a bell to announce their newest flavors. Yet more often than not, the Dinellos noted with satisfaction, these new flavors were just cheaper versions of our own.

The wintry evening of my sixteenth *compleanno*, Mrs. Dinello fried up fat meatballs to go in the sauce and arranged golden sfogliatelli on a platter for dessert. Vittorio was engaged to a girl named Carmella by then, and Pasquale was courting as well, so there were eight of us at the table. Ever since the war, the dinner service of twelve plates had largely sat unused above the sink. Abandoned caps still hung on hooks by the doorways, because

Mrs. Dinello could not bear to part with them. Religious medals, statues of St. Joseph, St. Anthony, the Virgin Mary, gilt-framed portraits of still more saints had accumulated on every surface of the parlor and kitchen around sepia photographs of Luigi, Vincenzo, and Silvio, transforming the apartment into a progression of shrines. Yet that snowy night, the kitchen felt festive. As we sat down, Rocco grinned at me across the table.

"After tomorrow you'll be free, eh, Horsey?" he said, filching a meatball from the plate by the stove.

"*Ai!*" Mrs. Dinello slapped his hand. Rocco laughed and popped it steaming into his mouth. "No more school," he exulted. "You get to join the rest of us now. Sit on that stool of yours. Sniff the milk every morning. Dream up ice cream sundaes all day."

"Yes, more school." Mrs. Dinello frowned, stirring her pot. "She keeps going."

"What?" said Rocco. "Why?"

"Because she's lame, you idiot," Pasquale said under his breath.

"Girls shouldn't go to school," Carmella sniffed. She was a haughty gazelle of a girl whom I disliked instantly. "My papa says it's a waste."

"We see," Mr. Dinello said wearily, glaring at his wife. "Nobody decides anything yet."

Mrs. Dinello looked at him, then at me. After supper she ushered me into her bedroom and shut the door firmly. Her hair had thinned considerably, I noticed. Her face and neck were webbed with loose flesh. Putting a palsied hand beneath my chin, she whispered, "I tell my husband you do not quit school. I tell him we send you to college."

For a moment I almost could not dare to breathe, the news thrilled me so—and yet it also wounded.

"*Perché?*" I blinked. "Am I not good enough at the shop?"

"Oh, Ninella." Mrs. Dinello shook her head. Taking me by the shoulders, she pivoted me toward the oval mirror trimmed with gold braid. "Look at you." In the tempered glass stood a simple, woeful girl in a brown knotted blouse that seemed to drown her small frame. I had a sharp nose and thick eyebrows. My lips were a thin crease across my face. Overall there was nothing particularly wrong with me—yet there was something unappealing in the way these features assembled themselves. Beautiful girls, I had noticed, had luscious smiles, with lips like ribbons. Their marcelled hair was glossy, their faces like candy and ice cream. They had no dark rings beneath their eyes, no hollows in their cheeks. My chin was pointy and slightly upraised. No matter what I did, I had a vulpine, hungry look.

"You are plain, Ninella, like Beatrice was," Mrs. Dinello said, her eyes locking with mine in the mirror. "And Pasquale is right: You are lame. My grandsons, they will marry. Boys always do. But you? It is not like in the old country, where perhaps someone could make an arrangement."

Gently, she gathered my thick brown hair in her calloused hands, arranged it carefully over my shoulder, and smoothed it. I had been secretly hoping to bob it. Now I felt ashamed.

"You must get an education. You may not be *bellissima*, but you are smart." She tapped her index finger against the side of her temple. "They say this is not good for a girl. But if you are going to work your whole life, it is better to work with your head than your hands."

She squeezed my shoulder.

"You still help with the gelato after school. But you keep studying. There are things you can do that our boys—*ai!* They have no head for. As long as you learn, you will have a place with us, *capisce?*"

Hunter College for Women was up on East Sixty-Eighth Street. As it was public, girls from all over the city attended, many of them immigrants like me. "Most of our students here go on to become secretaries," the guidance counselor informed me. "That said, Miss Dinello, to be a secretary one needs to be obedient, quiet, and highly refined in her appearance. I daresay you would be better qualified for teaching, which comes more naturally to the garrulous Italian girls like yourself, I find, and the Jews. Best to leave the secretarial work to the Irish and the Protestants."

"I'm here to help my family with their business," I informed him. "I plan on taking chemistry and accounting, thank you."

Biology I also registered for. And literature. Oh, how I adored college! Though I often kept to myself, one girl offered to bob my hair; another taught me to smoke. "You may not be able to carry a tune," another said when I failed the auditions for the chorus, "but you certainly have pluck!" I was invited to join a playwriting group, the poetry discussion, the jazz lovers' society, the Young Socialists of America. There was a Victrola in the library, so girls who had records at home brought them in and we gathered to listen rapturously over lunch. Oh, we were mad for the music! Ethel Waters, Eddie Cantor, Bessie Smith—they were all big then. Al Jolson singing "California, Here I Come." Sometimes we cleared the tables away and girls practiced dancing together to "Tea for Two" and Paul Whiteman's "Charleston." Once they pulled me in from the sidelines. I managed as best I could with my cane.

Yet soon I found I needed more books and school fees. I was loath to ask the Dinellos for any more money, so I began to hire myself out as a tutor some evenings.

The Henry Street Settlement House sponsored a literacy program for new immigrants, and the Sons of Italy offered night classes for Italian war vets. I was younger than most tutors they cared to hire, but I spoke both Italian and still some Yiddish.

"We never see you anymore," Rocco said with a smirk whenever I came into the factory to help. "What? You're too smart for us now?"

I looked at him dryly. "I can't pay for textbooks with ice cream cones."

"Oh," he said, nudging his brothers, "she can't pay for books with ice cream cones? Did you know that? I didn't know that. I thought you could."

"Yeah, but you're just a *cazzo.*" Pasquale grinned, whacking him on the backside with a dish towel.

"Yeah," said Rocco, mashing his hand into Pasquale's face. "Not like Miss Smarty-Pants here."

Three evenings a week, after finishing at Hunter, I took the Second Avenue El downtown to the settlement houses. One evening at Henry Street, a tall, sallow Jewish man approached me after class. "Miss Dinello, do you have a moment?" he said. "A friend of mine needs help writing a letter, but the *nudnik* is too embarrassed to ask. Would you mind? I can pay for your time."

Pulling on my coat, I followed the thin man down the stairs. "I'm Mr. Shackter," he said affably. "I told him to wait in the foyer."

Lingering near the umbrella stand was a young man in a shabby felt coat. His long, slender hands held his hat nervously by the brim, and he leaned forward inquisitively, as if he were near-sighted. Indeed he was facing the wrong direction, away from the staircase, as we descended. When Mr. Shackter called to him, he blinked around, startled. A thick curl, dark as syrup, fell over his forehead. He smiled in relief; his deep green eyes turned lambent. With his strong cheekbones and cleft chin, he looked sculpted, almost magisterial. He was easily the handsomest man I had ever seen in my life.

"Get over here, you *shmendrik.*" Mr. Shackter chuckled, beckoning to him. "I found you a letter writer.

"Miss Dinello," Mr. Shackter said, presenting the young man to me with a flourish, "this is Albert Dunkle."

Now that it had become apparent that Errol Flynn had not, in fact, arrived in Bellmore, the small crowd that had gathered around our dying truck began to dissipate. It was clear to me we had to act quickly.

"Bert!" I hollered. "Toss me the keys." Hobbling around, I struggled back up into the front. I opened the cold-storage cabinet, set up the cones, and leaned out the doorway facing the road.

"ICE CREAM, FROZEN CUSTARD! HOMEMADE, DELICIOUS!" I shouted. My voice was surprisingly resonant. "ICE CREAM CONES! VANILLA! CHOCOLATE! AND STRAWBERRY!" I cried. "TRY THEM ALL AND SEE WHICH YOU LIKE BEST!"

One of the men who had stopped to examine our truck—the dapper one with the yellow roadster—sidled over, wiping his brow with a handkerchief.

"Make hay while the sun shines, eh?" he said, flicking his thumb up toward the sky. "Not a bad idea. Wait a minute. I'll go ask the missus." A woman in a red-and-white polka-dot dress had stepped out of the car and stood fanning herself in the tall sea grasses along the roadside. She sported pert red high heels, I noticed, and a matching red alligator pocketbook. "Ellie!" the man called out. "What flavor custard you want?"

The farmer whose roadside stand we had nearly run over shrugged. Beneath his overalls he was shirtless. "Why not? I'll take a vanilla," he said, digging into his pocket and sliding five warm pennies across the top of the cabinet.

A woman with two pigtailed girls approached. "One strawberry and one vanilla, please," she said, unsnapping her little purse. Her fingers trembled. "They're a nickel apiece, you say?"

I handed one cone to each wan little girl, both of whom gave an awkward sort of half-curtsy while saying, "Thank you, ma'am." As their mother led them away, I realized that all the other onlookers were returning to their cars and shops. A quarter in total was all I had just earned. Inside the cold cabinet, both the vanilla and the strawberry were beginning to melt around the edges. Even with the doors and windows open, the truck was heating up quickly.

"How about an ice cream for yourself, too, ma'am?" I called after the mother. "Fresh and delicious. Please? You'd really be helping me out here."

My words had a pleading quality, which I despised, and the moment they were out of my mouth, the woman's face became a rictus of embarrassment; a trapped look took hold of her. Only then did I notice that she was clad in a hand-sewn dress, the cotton worn so thin it was nearly translucent. That dime she had spent; it had been the last coin in her purse.

"It's on the house," I said quickly. "For every two cones you purchase, you get one free." I smiled and hoped I sounded genuine and magnanimous. I hated to give away any of our product—it triggered an actual physical reaction within me, an ache in my solar plexis—but my desperation and pushiness had shamed me, and now it seemed imperative to redeem myself. "A special. To commemorate the Fourth of July. Please, any flavor you like."

As one should always do when selling something, I did not wait for her response. I held a cone up grandly and proceeded to bend down into the freezer with my scoop. "Our strawberry is looking particularly good today. Does that suit you? Or would you prefer chocolate?"

"Oh, Mama, get chocolate," said one of her daughters excitedly. "So we can taste it, too?"

"Chocolate it is," I boomed, smiling intensely. "Excellent choice."

The woman shook her head. "Please. I can't."

"Sure you can. It's free," I said, holding the cone. "Buy two, get one free."

As she took the cone gingerly, she regarded me with a mixture of gratitude and distrust. Yet the man in the yellow roadster—who had already made quick work of his chocolate cone—called out, "Really? Why didn't you say so?"

His wife had already climbed back into the car and was in the process of tying a chiffon kerchief over her hair to keep it in place while he held her strawberry cone for her. "I bought two custards already." He waddled back toward me. "So I get an extra one, too, right?"

I shot him a vicious look and cocked my head promptingly in the direction of the young mother. Yet he paid me no mind. *You greedy* stronzo *bastard*, I wanted to say. *You little* gonif. Yet I thought about my big mouth and all the trouble it could cause. I glanced over at Bert, kneeling beside the front wheel of the truck.

"What will you have, sir?" I said tightly.

"Hmm, let's see." The man leaned back on his heels. My hand was clenched around the ice cream scoop. "You said the strawberry is good?"

As he headed back to his roadster, he held up his free ice cream cone like the spoils of war. "Ellie, three for the price of two!" he shouted.

A small traffic jam had formed behind our stalled truck, and his words were like a match igniting a long fuse on the road. Deals like this: No one had ever offered them before. Ice cream for free? Families and drivers who had stopped their engines in the heat now climbed out of their automobiles and hurried up to the truck.

"Is it true?" they said, their faces bright with incredulity and delight. "If I buy two, I get an extra one?"

Before I could protest, a line formed before me. One of the shop owners came out and leaned in her doorway, squinting at the spectacle in the chalky sunshine.

"Only because it's the Fourth of July," I insisted. I wiped my forehead with the back of my wrist and took a deep breath. "You, sir. What will it be?"

Six cones he wanted, three vanilla, a chocolate, and two strawberries. Twenty cents he counted out in corroding, greenish pennies. Barely enough to cover the cost of the ingredients. Chocolate, strawberry, vanilla—another dime in my apron, another two cents lost. A whole extended Irish family arrived in a jalopy. Word spread faster than I could work; with each order I bent deeper and deeper into the freezer, sweat blooming at the base of my back as I scooped. The ice cream was getting so soft it was difficult to curl it into a ball; it was filling up the four-ounce metal scoop without a bit of air and dripping down the sides of each cone as soon as I released it. It might as well have been dripping money. Our profits were evaporating before my eyes, yet I could not think of what else to do. The sun was making the pavement glisten and melt. Eventually, I suspected grimly, we would just end up having to simply give away all the remaining, half-melted ice cream anyway.

As I glopped the ice cream onto the cones, I glanced around Bellmore. It was not a town so much as a sprinkling of structures that loosely followed Merrick Road between the junction of the parkway and the new access road to the beach. On our right stood a row of small storefronts that seemed to have been constructed mainly out of driftwood—a souvenir shop, a farm stand, a general store with signs for Coca-Cola and "live bait." Two weather-beaten picnic tables sat in a clearing to one side under a lean-to made from a tattered sail. On the left side of the road, I could see a one-room white clapboard post office and a pharmacy with a Closed sign hanging in the door. Farther down, set back a ways, a few houses with front porches dotted lanes on either side. A church steeple rose in the distance, closer to the railroad, a good half a mile north. Yet that was it. Beyond Merrick to the south, the land quickly descended into a marshy plain giving way to dunes and sea grass and finally to a small marina and a bright finger of steel-blue bay glittering on the horizon.

The sound of a radio crackled from the souvenir store. Bing Crosby singing "Pennies from Heaven," his voice staccato with static. An American flag, bleached by the sun, jutted out above the window. The proprietor continued watching me from her doorway. She was tall and rawboned, her pale arms and legs dotted with angry red mosquito bites. A ribbon of dirty blond hair fell over one eye. As the latest batch of customers headed back to their cars, carefully maneuvering their mouths around their ice cream, her dull eyes trailed after them, then swung over to me. "Wow," she said flatly. "Quite a hustle you've got going there."

"Excuse me?"

"Buy two, get one free? Whoever heard of such a thing?"

I shrugged. "Without our generator, all this is going to melt soon. In an hour or two, it won't be worth anything."

"Smart." She nodded, squinting out at the line of cars rippling in the heat. "Wish I could draw a few customers in myself."

"It's tough times," I said.

"Don't I know it." Sighing, she shifted her weight from one hip to the other and glanced back into her store. "Not too many people looking to buy souvenirs these days. I told my husband, 'Donald, why are folks going to pay a dime for a seashell that they can find on the beach for free? You think they can't paint "Bell-more, Long Island" on it themselves if they want?' But he has ideas, Donald. Unfortunately, all these ideas, you can't sell them and you can't eat them."

I laughed. "Husbands," I said. "Mine just drove us into a fire hydrant."

The blond woman glanced at Bert slyly. "I saw," she said. "He's really your husband?" She brushed her hair from her eyes. "Gosh, he looks just like Errol Flynn."

Her surprise that Bert was my husband, it was like everybody else's surprise when they saw us together, yet still, it always stung. I thought to make a cutting retort. But something else occurred to me. "You've got a radio? You have electricity in there?"

The woman fanned herself with her hand and nodded.

I tilted my head at her. "I don't suppose you could let us run a line from your outlet to our generator here in the truck?"

She shrugged. "Donald's out back. Let me get him."

She disappeared, and another couple appeared before me. One chocolate cone and two vanillas, they wanted. Ten more cents.

Donald was a gaunt man with stubble on his face and sweat staining his old hat. He appraised me baldly, then the truck. The look on his face communicated to me that he did not think much of either.

"You're selling frozen custard, the wife says?"

"Yes, sir," I said, giving him my frankest smile.

"And you want to use my electricity?"

"For our generator. To keep it from melting. Only until we can get our truck fixed," I said. "And we'll pay for whatever power we consume, of course."

When I spoke, Donald looked not at me, but peered around the truck. "Let me talk to your husband."

I smiled. "It's all right," I said. "I can do the talking."

"Naw," he said. "I don't do business with women."

Swallowing hard, I sucked in my cheeks. "Bert," I called crisply. When he didn't respond, I struggled down from the truck with my cane.

"What you got there?" Donald gestured at my leg. "You sick? You got the polio?"

I frowned. "Bert?" I called again. He was under the truck. "Bert! Come here!"

When he wriggled out from beneath the chassis, Bert was covered in axle grease. He looked like a chimney sweep. "This man here, he has electricity in his store," I said. "He won't deal with me. Can you please see if we can hook up our generator?"

"Oh, that w-would be a lifesaver," said Bert, scrambling up. I untied my apron and he mopped himself off with it as best he could.

"B-Bert Dunkle," he said, extending his hand as he came around the back of the truck.

I could tell by the way Donald straightened up that he was surprised to see such a virile and good-looking man appear. His mouth hung open slightly as he stepped forward to meet Bert's grip. "Donald Corwin," he said slowly. "Dunkle. What kind of a name is that? You Irish?"

"Mr. C-Corwin. I cannot tell you how grateful we are."

"Well, hold on," said Donald.

Bert smiled his earnest, movie-star smile. Like sunlight hitting water. "I cannot tell you what a great, generous turn you're d-doing us. You are saving our business. We've got eighteen gallons back there, and w-with all this h-heat—"

"Well..." said Donald, "I don't normally—"

"Lil, isn't this marvelous?" said Bert. "Mr. Corwin, w-we cannot thank you enough. You and your l-lovely wife, Mrs. Corwin, over there." He motioned to the blond woman still standing in the

doorway. I hadn't realized that Bert had noticed her. Yet of course
he had. "Your s-sort of kindness we will never forget."

He grinned and rubbed his hands, as if it had all been settled.
Yet no one made a move. An uneasy silence bloomed. Mrs. Corwin glanced from Bert to her husband. Donald looked at Bert
expectantly, then finally at me.

"Bert." I nudged him.

"Oh, of course," Bert said, chuckling with embarrassment.
"H-how could I forget? As soon as we hook up the generator,
we've got three flavors today. Please, have as much ice cream as
you want. For as long as w-we're here. It's the l-least we can do.
Now, I guess I should get started right away. We don't want it
to melt."

With that, he leaped into the truck and hauled out the generator. He called to the other man who had been fiddling with the
tire, and the two of them rapidly began running cables from the
cold-storage cabinet out the back of the truck toward the front
door of the store.

"Um," Donald said to me after a moment, scratching the back
of his head, "I thought, in terms of compensation—"

Before I could answer, his wife came over and gave him a deliberate poke on his shoulder. "I thought you don't do business
with women," she said.

"Now, Doris," he said.

"All the ice cream we can eat. That's the deal you made with
her husband." She poked him again. "So that's the one we're
keeping." She looked at me. "Think you can salvage what you've
got in there?"

"I'm not sure," I said. "Once it turns at all soupy, it's ruined. I
need to move quickly."

She looked at my leg. "Well, Donald and I are just sitting here,"
she said gamely. "Put us to work." Yet as she said this, I noticed,

her gaze swept away from me and Donald and settled on Bert, kneeling before the generator in the sunshine.

⚭

Albert Jacob Dunkle was born the youngest son of a prosperous dry-goods merchant in Vienna. When his father, Heinrich Dunkle, wasn't traveling to Antwerp or Hamburg to haggle over linen and silk, he was pulling out his gold pocketwatch and timing his four sons as they performed calisthenics in the back garden in their underwear. Bert's mother had died when Bert was three. Every morning Bert's stepmother, Ida, yanked him out of bed to scrub his face and fingernails with ice water. She refused to let him go to the toilet until he had made his bed, dressed himself, and polished his shoes to her satisfaction. Fumbling and often terrified, little four-year-old Bert usually failed. He wet himself, and she beat him.

He began to stutter. At school, oh, how he yearned to understand! Squeezing his eyes shut, he would attempt to commit the alphabet to memory, yet the shapes somehow always differed on the pages from the way he'd conceived of them in his mind. Letters in books undulated and cleaved before his eyes, numbers do-si-do'd in their columns. All around him in the classroom, the other boys' hands shot up confidently. Everyone else seemed able to decode the hieroglyphics written on the chalkboard. Sometimes Bert tried to speak, yet phrases stuck and unraveled in his mouth. "P-p-p-p-p-p-p-leeease" was often all he could manage. His teachers assumed that he was simply not trying. Calling him lazy and stupid, they lashed his knuckles with their rulers. The headmaster decided that Bert's failings likely stemmed from his being "latently" left-handed. He ordered Bert's left hand to be tied behind his back throughout the school day, forcing him to do everything using only his right.

Heinrich Dunkle had no patience for his youngest son's constant stammering and befuddlement, for his failing grades, for his inability to read. There was a chronic glassiness in Bert's eyes—likely due to being uncomprehending, fearful, and ignored each day. Yet Heinrich mistook it for daydreaming. He had a business to run. A spoiled, careless child was nothing he had time for. Bert's extraordinary handsomeness likely did not help either. All across Vienna, women stopped in the streets to fuss over young Bert, touching their gloved hands adoringly to his florid cheeks and shaking their heads in blushing admiration. What a beautiful boy, they marveled in German. Such thick, honeyed curls. Such long eyelashes. Such a perfect face. Oh, what a heartbreaker this one will become.

Every father resents being upstaged by his son. "Look at you," Heinrich spit. "Utterly useless."

That a Jewish boy would forgo his bar mitzvah was inconceivable. Yet by age twelve Bert still could not get through a simple portion of the Torah. Hebrew, read right to left, was even more impossible to grasp than German. "Albert, he has a good heart," the rabbi told Heinrich sadly, "but it's likely the Messiah will arrive before this child ever learns Hebrew." Bert got through the ceremony only by chanting his parashah phonetically in tandem with the rabbi.

After the service, when friends and family returned to the Dunkles' town house on Fabergasse to celebrate with the customary sweet wine and cake, Heinrich Dunkle took Bert into the grand firelit library, locked the door with its elegant brass key, and backhanded him across the face. "What kind of a man are you?" he bellowed. "What kind of man is so lazy and insolent that he lets the rabbi be a bar mitzvah for him?

"You are an embarrassment," he said. "You cannot read, you cannot add. What do you think? You are too handsome to work?"

"B-b-b—" Bert stammered.

"Only a woman can get by on good looks, and then she is a prostitute. A Jewish man, he needs brains to survive. He needs chutzpah, he needs ingenuity. Otherwise he is finished in this world. Do you understand?"

"B-b-b—" Bert said again.

"What on earth is the matter with you?" Heinrich Dunkle hissed. "You can't even speak."

It had been assumed, of course, that, like his brothers, Bert would one day take up Heinrich's import business. Yet after the disastrous bar mitzvah, Heinrich decided that his youngest son should be sent to America instead. Manual labor in a new world full of ruffians, without any ladies patting his head and proffering him sweets from their purses; certainly, this was what the boy needed. This would teach him to focus and work. Heinrich had an old friend, Arnold Shackter, who had immigrated to New York, where he ran a haberdashery on Rivington Street. Arnold assured Heinrich that Bert could work as a stock boy for him. In the spring of 1914, just as Gavrilo Princip and the Black Hand were finalizing their plans in Serbia, Albert Jacob Dunkle was put aboard a train bound from Vienna to the port of Antwerp. He carried with him two sets of clothing, a new pair of leather suspenders, and, tucked into the Torah that he still could not read, a photograph of his parents on their wedding day. Forty American dollars were stitched into the lining of his coat, and his housekeeper had slipped him three butter cookies wrapped in a linen napkin. That was it. He was just thirteen years old.

Chapter 7

I EXPLAINED TO THE DINELLOS, of course, that Bert was merely one of several students I'd begun to tutor privately each week. As a source of extra income, nothing more. Yet his presence at their kitchen table—his earnest brow furrowed in concentration over his primer, the gold light playing off the mantels of his cheekbones—made me feel as if I were filled with whipped cream. When I earned enough extra pocket money, the first thing I did was purchase a new dress—ink-blue georgette with a dropped waist, I remember, and a silk rose appliquéd to the collar. Every time Bert came over for a lesson, I just happened to wear it.

Perhaps because he had a questioning, childlike quality that made him look younger than his twenty-five years. Perhaps because whenever he spoke, his careful enunciation made him sound thoughtful. Or perhaps because he was so inordinately masculine, so handsome—the Dinellos took to Bert. That he was a Jew, that he "had no people," might have ruffled them more in regard to me. However, what they saw developing was a friendship between Rocco and Bert. Nothing else.

The very first time Bert arrived in the doorway of our kitchen for his lesson, an instant camaraderie sprang up between him and Rocco. As two parentless young men, Rocco and Bert seemed to recognize something in each other's anxious eyes and preemptive bluster, in each other's eagerness to make a joke and have a good time and endear themselves to the world. They quickly teamed up as two young bachelors, talking of sports, eyeing the ladies, colluding about "deals." After I finished my tutoring sessions with Bert, I sat forlornly by the window, watching him and Rocco head off down the street together for their nights on the town.

Rocco was now twenty-one. His older brothers had both married and were sharing an apartment on Mott Street. On the streets of Little Italy, Rocco had developed a reputation as an enterprising young man. He had an easy, loose-limbed walk and a jaunty grin that seemed to split his narrow face in two. "*Ai, paesano,*" he greeted men he encountered, slapping them on the back. His laugh, like a machine gun—"Yah-ha-ha-ha-ha"—could be heard down the block. He was gangly, and his oil-black hair still never stayed in place, yet whenever he sauntered into a room, he managed to fill it.

Rocco loved to duck into speakeasies after work. He loved to buy a round of drinks and hold forth telling stories that grew more outrageous and bawdier as the evening wore on. Bert, always shy at first, was happy to laugh appreciatively and be shepherded into basements and card games by someone who could make the smoky crowds part before him and do the clever talking. His great looks always guaranteed that the women came flocking in a cloud of perfume. "He is like a flower to the bees," Rocco teased. "You should see him with the ladies, Horsey."

Every time Rocco called me this in front of Bert, it felt like the kick of a hoof.

"Bert, you stay for dinner, *si?*" Mrs. Dinello said whenever he came around. "You don't eat enough. A handsome young man like you needs his strength."

"Thank you, s-signora." The cuffs of his jacket were frayed, yet he never arrived without a small bag of dried apricots or a clutch of daisies for her. So good-looking and well mannered: Of course he really had to be Italian, Mrs. Salucci declared. As word got around, girls in the buildings suddenly found it incumbent upon themselves to drop by the Dinellos' unannounced whenever Bert was visiting, bearing plates of sfogliatelli that they just "happened" to have made that morning. Even though, as a Jew, Bert was forbidden fruit—or perhaps precisely because of this—they wanted a glimpse. One evening Lisa and Theresa Vitacello, two girls who had moved into one of the top-floor apartments across from Mrs. Salucci (and of whom she disapproved even more than me—*zoccola* she called them), dared to stop by on their way out to a nightclub. Dressed in a fringed, jet-beaded frock and clouds of marabou feathers, Lisa blithely perched on Bert's lap without a second thought, waving a long black cigarette holder and tossing her head like a Thoroughbred. "My, my," she said. "Who do we have here?"

I had never seen Mrs. Dinello pick up a broom and shoo someone out of her apartment before. Yet amid the melee of "Out, outs" and "Well, I nevers" and the clatter of cheap high heels on the metal stairs, Bert, I couldn't help noticing, looked delighted. Whenever women fluttered around him, his face lit up like Christmas.

Each time he and Rocco strode off together into the night after his lessons with me, I felt a horrible pang.

My other students, I taught them from my old school primers. But Bert's stammer, his inability to read—they belied the fact that he was at least as curious about the world as I was. "How does a continuous-batch freezer work?" he wanted to know. This Trotsky everyone was talking about, how did he differ from Engels? Could I explain Sigmund Freud to him? What about Nikola

Tesla? Why were the coloreds in the United States so reviled when they had done nothing wrong? The injustices of the world, he seemed to take them personally.

He loved the moving pictures, Bert. He loved all sorts of music. He loved baseball, Babe Ruth and the Yankees in particular. And Charles Lindbergh and that airplane of his. Bert loved quietly taking apart machines, seeing how they worked. If left to his own devices and allowed to focus solely on one task uninterrupted, he could dismantle and reassemble a bicycle, a clock, a coffee grinder. He only got into trouble if he was required to do more than one thing at a time, especially under pressure. Then he became, by his own admission, *fartootst*. Tangled up, malfunctioning. Though he still roomed at Mr. Shackter's, he now worked at one of the new garages that had opened on Houston Street. He could work there for hours beneath a car, unhurried, focused, learning in his own particular way.

To me he brought books he borrowed from the library and begged me to read them to him—Emma Goldman's *My Disillusionment in Russia*, a brand-new translation of Martin Buber's *I and Thou*, novels by John Dos Passos, Fitzgerald's *The Beautiful and Damned*. He brought me political pamphlets, playbills, sports pages, travel brochures for ocean liners—anything, really, that came across his path and intrigued him.

"Oh, L-Lil, you have a beautiful speaking voice," he said. "You understand so much. And you are s-so patient with me. Before this"—he motioned to the jumble of books and pamphlets arrayed across the table—"it—it felt like I was just living behind a th-thick wall of glass all the time."

Albert Dunkle. Albert Dunkle. His smell, like cut grass and fresh-baked bread. The muscular cords of his neck peeking through his loosened collar. Albert Dunkle. His name began to play in my mind like an aria. I heard his voice in the songs on the radio; I saw his face reflected in the freezers at the factory. As soon as I heard his knock on the Dinellos' door in the evenings, a frenzy shot through me. He'd walk in with a paper bag of toasted almonds held as gently as a dove in his solid, tapered left hand. The corners of his eyes crinkled as he smiled. The wingspan of his shoulders spread as he pulled off his overcoat. Oh, darlings, it was like having a seizure. Once I nearly dropped the kettle. I stood in the middle of the kitchen, trying to keep my legs from trembling as I wiped down the table. It took all my strength to inhale and say blithely, "Oh. Hello there, Albert. You're late."

So extravagant were the moods he set off in me—the incessant ache—that I believed I'd become possessed. I would've wriggled out of my skin and abandoned it in the street like a snake's if I could have. My hands would stray over my own body at night; I'd grip and twist my pillow in exquisite agony. Please. Don't be so shocked. Every new generation thinks they're the only ones in history ever to experience desire.

Albert Dunkle, Albert Dunkle. As soon as I slid into the polished pew on Sundays, I fell to my knees. Mrs. Dinello, she prayed beside me, of course, for her dead sons and niece and grandchild and daughter-in-law. But me? Instead of praying that I would find Mama and Papa and my sisters again one day, I now begged, simply, *Please, Lord. Make it stop.* Or: *Please, Lord. Make Albert Dunkle love me.* I could not decide which I craved more. And still I could not look up at the statue of Jesus. Yet now it was because his bare, writhing, muscular torso—I imagined it was Bert's.

After confession I could never say enough Hail Marys and Our Fathers.

I lied to my professor. I told him I needed to drop his poetry class so that I could work at my family's ice cream parlor in the afternoons. Then I lied to Bert. "The only time I can tutor you is after lunch," I said. For a moment I felt terribly guilty. Yet for two glorious hours a week, I managed to get him all to myself. No neighbors rapping on the door with baskets of rolls. No Rocco yah-ha-ha-ing. Just Bert and I, hunched over books, our heads bowed together as if in prayer. His voice as it tripped on the words. Our fingers running over the printed letters in tandem. Whenever I explained something to him, he blinked at me with such astonishment! My insides felt like an aviary.

Yet one week Bert arrived at the apartment breathless, carrying a stage script of all things. He'd met a showgirl from the Yiddish theater, he announced. "Oh, L-Lil, you should have s-seen her! Such a c-creature as I have never seen. She c-could make me fall to my kn-knees."

Her name was Frieda, he thought. "Oh, I am so *fartootst* with names," he said laughingly. But this Frieda, she had wrapped her smooth arms around him and whispered softly in his ear with her lipsticked mouth that he was so handsome, surely he should appear onstage with her. It was crazy, he confessed to me, but he wanted to try it. He had to! Oh, how he loved vaudeville! And this girl! Could I help him memorize a short monologue? Frieda had arranged for him to audition for a small production on Second Avenue of the play *Tevye the Milkman.*

What could I do? The idea of helping him win the heart of another woman, of him running off to join the theater, of course it was unbearable to me. Yet so was the thought of him being humiliated. Or heartbroken. Indeed, Bert's pain, to me, the prospect of it seemed worse than my own. And surely if I did not help him, Bert would find someone else who would.

I looked down. The scars on my leg were still visible through my pearl gray stockings. Angry red crosshatches.

"If you can't spit the lines out, why not try singing them," I suggested miserably.

"Like a song?"

"Mm-hm."

Slowly, I read him each line. Slowly, he sang them back to me. The words came out perfectly this way. "Lil!" he cried. "That's a miracle!" I tried to smile gamely, though I felt so utterly wretched, I thought my very sinews and bones would disintegrate.

Together we rehearsed like this, again and again, until he knew his lines by heart.

"You are a wonderful teacher," he said. "I c-cannot thank you enough."

The morning of his audition, as I took the subway up to Hunter, all I could think of was Bert kissing this Frieda, running his hand along the smooth, uninterrupted plain of her legs, the two of them starring in the Yiddish theater on Second Avenue, their names side by side on a marquee. My stomach hurt so badly that at one point, I believed I would faint.

Yet he did not pass the audition. The malicious jubilation I felt filled me with both guilt and relief. With all those onlookers in the drafty theater, shrouded in the darkness beyond the footlights, and Frieda observing him coolly beside her director, oh, Bert said somberly, as soon as he stood up before them, he just started to stutter and stutter. "F-finally I did manage to start singing the l-lines instead, just like you told me," he said. "And they all started to l-laugh, of course. I laughed with them, Lil. Wh-what else could I do? I t-told them, 'Look, I'm a terrible actor, but if you're ever c-casting for a musical comedy—'"

He smiled haplessly. "I tried, though, yes? And I'd have n-never believed that I could—"

Suddenly he turned to me. "Next Thursday evening. Some

p-people I know, from the neighborhood. They're having a political meeting. I'd like to s-speak at it, if I can. I never have before.
Do you think you could come with me, Lil?"

What little I knew about Communism I did not care for at all.
So sue me: I have never found the faceless masses terribly compelling. And the idea that the Dinellos could build their little ice
cream factory into a great success only to have it taken over by
"the proletariat"? This was repellant to me. I dreamed of being
rich myself one day, I informed Bert. What was America if not
the great promise of freedom and wealth? Certainly nobody I
knew had immigrated here to *share*. Nobody I knew was hoping
to hand over the fruits of their labors to every goddamn *nudnik* in
the tenement.

Besides, Communism had been invented by Russians. Those
drunken, murderous Cossacks who had beaten my grandfather to
death in his own kitchen. I had no use for any of them.

Bert, however, he saw it differently. "Only under Communism,
Lil," he insisted, "are the ideals of A-America truly lived. 'All men
are created equal,' they say. But look at how this country treats
women. And the coloreds. In Russia everyone is treated the same
n-now. Y-you can't have social equality without economic equality."

Disagree with him though I did, the look of conviction on his
face when he spoke—his deep-set eyes pained with compassion—
oh, it turned me to liquid, darlings. It made me nod as if hypno-
tized. *Yes. Of course. I'll accompany you.*

The gathering was in a basement on Delancey Street. Water
dripping from an overhead pipe into a metal pan. Everyone
shifting around on rickety benches in rain-soaked overcoats, trying to keep warm. The workers in attendance were mostly

young—and a passionate bunch, to be sure. A bespectacled young man named Jay greeted us, clutching a notebook. He looked scarcely older than I was, yet he turned out to be an editor of the *Daily Worker*.

"Please, do not be impressed. Social class and divisions of labor are merely artificial constructs." He looked me in the eye fiercely as he shook my hand, which few people did.

"Is he kidding?" I whispered.

"Jay is a bit of a character," Bert conceded, guiding me over to a bench. As soon as we settled in, a prepossessing woman with auburn hair and a swanlike neck sashayed over. "Well, hello there. Do you mind?" Without waiting for a reply, she lowered herself languorously into the other empty place beside Bert, gripping his arm to steady herself. "Oh, do excuse me." She smiled blazingly. I noticed, however, that she made no attempt to withdraw her hand from his sleeve. I felt my stomach knot.

Jay bounded to the front of the room. "Good evening, comrades." He seemed to be under the impression that he was addressing a vast proletarian army in Red Square. "Over a year ago today," he began, "Celestino Madeiros, already on trial for another murder, confessed. He said, 'Sacco and Vanzetti are innocent.' So why, comrades, I ask you tonight, why are they both still to be executed?"

Jay fixed his eyes on us the way that Father Antonucci sometimes did during a particularly portentous sermon at church. Sacco and Vanzetti. Two anarchists accused of murder in Boston. I had read newspaper articles about them to Bert. Debates about their innocence had flared up at Hunter College and even on Mulberry Street, since the accused were Italians and largely believed to be victims of prejudice. Nonetheless Mrs. Salucci had spit, "Sacco? Vanzetti? *Ai, ai!* They make an embarrassment out of all of us." Yet me, I had not followed the case closely.

"You and I know why they are being condemned to die, comrades," Jay declared. "You and I know the truth."

His pomposity quickly grated on me. I looked around. Beneath the one grimy window, I was surprised to see Rocco. He was leaning against the wall, fiddling with a bottle cap. When he saw me, he rolled his eyes and shot me a sly, conspiratorial look of boredom, then motioned for me to nudge Bert.

Bert, however, was transfixed. I was gratified to see, at least, that he had shaken off the redhead. He was leaning forward with his elbows on his knees, listening intently. I could smell the rain in his hair, the faint residue of his shaving cream. His broad back spread before me. The temptation to run my hands up and down the flank of him was excruciating.

"They are guilty of being immigrants. Italians. Radicals," Jay proclaimed, stabbing the air. "They are guilty of believing in the freedom of speech—"

So sue me: All I could concentrate on was how Bert and I were breathing the very same oxygen in that damp basement and how our knees, grazing each other in that cramped space, were nearly kissing.

When Jay finished, everyone began yakking at once. A petition was passed around in support of the doomed anarchists. When it arrived at our place, I saw Bert's panic. Grabbing the pencil, he practiced the motions in the air above the paper, rehearsing how to form each letter of his name just as I had taught him.

"You're doing fine," I murmured. "First an A. Then L."

The redhead next to Bert gave an incredulous little bark. "She's telling you how to write your own name? Who is this? Your own little schoolmarm?" Her eyes flashed at me with a sort of malicious triumph.

I could see Bert's face redden, the pencil slip from his fingers and roll under the bench. He opened his mouth to speak, but all that came out was "N-n-n-n-n-n-n-n—"

Leaning across his back, I hissed at the woman, "*Gai kaken oifen yam!*"

Go shit in the ocean.

I sat back heavily. Blood pounded in my ears. "You vulgar little *meeskite*," she spit. Huffily, she stood up and moved to a seat farther along on the bench. "Pathetic. Stupid. Crazy," she announced generally to the people around her.

Bert—I pointed quickly to the petition—*give it here*. Dejectedly, he surrendered it. His gaze remained fixed on the floor. I slipped the paper into my pocket. Sacco and Vanzetti would simply have to survive without it: I refused to give anyone any proof of Bert's shame.

"Come on. Let's get out of here," I said. It was a struggle to get to my feet, but to my relief, Bert helped me up and followed.

Back on Delancey Street, the two of us walked along doggedly, not saying anything, the way you sometimes do after fleeing a particularly dreadful movie or play.

"'Schoolmarm,'" I said finally, my shock giving way to the full brunt of our humiliation. "That little *puttana*. I should've boxed her ears."

"Oh, Lil, I am so, so sorry. I should have stepped up. I should have said something." Bert dug his hands deep into his pockets. "But what do you expect from me?" He shrugged miserably. "Me, who can't even speak. Who can't even write my own name."

Suddenly, he began to chuckle. "Though, you certainly said enough for both of us. 'Go shit in the ocean,' Lil?"

A yeast of embarrassment rose within me. That mouth of mine that caused nothing but *tsuris*. That redhead had been right. I was vulgar.

Yet Bert was gazing at me with a sort of enraptured astonishment.

"Well. Aren't we a pair?" He laughed. And suddenly, in his eyes, I saw a dawning, like the first flush of morning light creeping over the fields, turning everything to a blaze of gold. Reaching over, he slowly touched my cheek. He touched my cheek, darlings, with his rough mechanic's thumb, running it gently over the fine seam of my jaw, over to the corner of my lips. Our gazes fused, and it was clear: the two of us, like two sides of a mathematical equation, two halves of a broken coin.

Bert lifted my chin. He bent toward me. Footsteps came slapping along the pavement behind us. "Hey, what's the matter?" Rocco caught up, breathless. "The two of you don't speak English anymore? Half a block I've been calling." He pounded Bert amiably on the back. "Sorry, compadre, but that was just not my ball game. Glad you decided to skedaddle. The only appealing thing in that basement tonight was the ladies."

The rain had stopped. The milky smoke of our breaths trailed off in the frigid air. Bert's damp, glistening shoulder was lightly touching mine. We both grinned at Rocco, but we did not absorb him. Everything between us was frisson now, an unspoken language. Rocco, however, did not seem to notice.

"And Sacco and Vanzetti?" He shook his head, dancing a little two-step before us. "Those poor dumb bastards don't stand a chance."

That night when everyone was asleep back on Mulberry Street, I pulled the petition from my pocket. Sweat from Bert's hand had smeared across the bottom right corner of the page, puckering it. Even though he hadn't even signed it, it was now an artifact of him, and I smoothed it out lovingly, imagining that it was his hair I was stroking, and I relived the sensation of his thumb caressing my cheek and his hand pressing against the small of my back through the scratchy wool of my coat as he guided me out of that basement. Protectively. Proprietarily. We *were* quite a pair. He had said so himself! I tucked the petition into the little Bible that Mrs. Dinello had given me for my confirmation, beside a thin cotton handkerchief Bert had once lent me and a scrap of paper he had absentmindedly doodled on once during our lessons and a pressed dried daffodil left over from a bouquet he had brought over for Mrs. Dinello. Nothing Bert ever touched could I discard. Each item became a sacred keepsake. I knew it was childish, but from time to time, I took them out and ran my hands over them, imagining Bert's fingers merging with mine through them.

I did not dare tell the Dinellos, of course. I did not even tell Father Antonucci during confession that I often lied when I said I'd be spending my evenings tutoring at Henry Street. I was terrified that if I said it aloud—that Albert Dunkle had made me his girl—God would smite me and all my good fortune would vanish in a puff of smoke. Perhaps if it went unsaid, what I was doing was not really a sin. Sometimes as I watched the Dinellos in the mornings, struggling to help each other with their buttons and shoes, I felt such guilt, I thought I would split in two. Yet as soon as my thoughts returned to Bert, I was catapulted into happiness.

One morning, however, Mr. Dinello woke up and simply did not look right. His face had a messy quality to it; his eyes were unfocused. Soon one faculty after another began to shut down like a row of storefronts. He lost the feeling in his left arm. His breathing grew shallow. Most disturbingly, his sense of taste became damaged. Sometimes he'd sample a fresh batch of vanilla or coffee gelato and shake his head. *"Troppo aspro, troppo aspro."* Too sour.

His eyesight began to fail. The rest of us, discreetly we began double-checking the labels on the ice cream pails as he filled them, to make sure the flavors corresponded. We cleared mops and buckets out of his path as he shuffled to the storage room. Sometimes he became agitated, and Mrs. Dinello had trouble reasoning with him, even as she was becoming increasingly frail herself. One afternoon she summoned me.

"Ninella, come. Bring me the book." With her unsteady fingers, Mrs. Dinello pointed to each column in her ledgers—to words she had memorized but still could not read phonetically—then to numbers inked across from them on fine blue lines. There were entries for the egg man, I saw, the milkman, fruit and corn-syrup deliveries, bulk orders of gelatin, for the premade ice cream cones the Dinellos were now ordering from New Jersey, for garbage collectors, taxes, neighborhood security.

"The woman, she must always be in charge of the money, *capisce?*" she said. "But I am so tired lately, Ninella. And Carmella, she has birdseed for brains. This needs to be your job now."

I should have been elated, yet we were all working so hard now it often felt as though we were bailing out a sinking ocean liner with buckets. Cannoletti's Ice Cream Company, those Sicilian *mezza negri* with their "Cheap and Sweet" second-rate ice cream, they were luring away more and more of Dinello & Sons' regular customers. "Yes, yours is better," the drugstore owner on Mott Street told Vittorio. "But why I pay ten cents more a gallon? With all the toppings, nobody tastes the difference anyway."

The only upside was that in all the hubbub, no one noticed me and Bert.

He took me to the pictures. *College* with Buster Keaton, *Spring Fever* with Joan Crawford. *The Jazz Singer*, uptown at the great Warner's Theatre. Oh, to hear sound, Al Jolson actually speaking! We attended free art lectures at the Workmen's Circle. One unseasonably warm evening, Bert met me up at Hunter, and we rode one of the double-decker buses all the way down Fifth Avenue, sitting out on the top, looking at the fancy mansions and the Plaza Hotel and the grand New York Public Library, all lit up like jewelry boxes. Anything we did together—feeding the pigeons, watching the barges sliding by along the East River, listening to a wireless at the counter in a drugstore—felt exultant.

"I love your hair, how thick and shiny it is," Bert said one night, nuzzling my neck. "I love how you look like no other girl. So d-dramatic. So serious."

Yet one afternoon Rocco pulled me aside in the factory. "Horsey," he said, his grip firm on my arm. "You have to stop."

I gave him a withering look. "What in heaven are you talking about?"

"Don't play coy. I know you're stepping out with Bert Dunkle."

"You step out with girls all the time," I sniffed.

"That's different."

"You don't think I deserve a sweetheart?"

"Be serious." Rocco glanced around. "Come on. I'm like a brother to you, *si?*"

It was the first time he had ever said anything like this. The words hung significantly in the air between us like a heavy piece of fruit.

"I suppose," I said, camouflaging my pleasure, shifting my weight.

He gave me a prompting look. "It's a brother's job to look out for his family. Now, Bert may be one of my best buddies. And he's a good guy. I know that. But I don't forget for a minute either that he's a Jew and a Communist. For you to step out with him, after all that Nonno and Nonna have done for you? You will bring shame on them before the entire neighborhood."

"What? Why?" I said, though in my heart, of course I knew. Mrs. DiPietro's granddaughter had eloped with a longshoreman from Killarney—another Catholic, no less—scandalizing all of Mulberry Street. Now, no one but an uncle out in Brooklyn talked to her anymore. I knew how Mrs. Dinello felt about her. Even marrying a Sicilian was a disgrace. If the Dinellos learned I was seeing Bert, they'd be devastated.

"You don't think they'd perhaps be relieved?" I suggested, hoping against hope. "They're convinced no one will ever marry me."

"Oh. And you think Bert will?"

I jerked away. "Don't talk to me anymore, Rocco." I looked frantically around for something to clean, for utensils in the sink that could make a horrific clatter.

"You took our family's name," he pressed. "Maybe this suddenly doesn't mean anything to you, but it does to Nonno and Nonna. Don't you think they've had enough heartache already?"

"Get away from me." I hobbled as quickly as I could to the storage pantry. Once I was inside, I reeled around, scanning all the cases of Knox gelatin, the bottles of Durkee peppermint and vanilla extracts, as if a sudden exit might present itself.

Rocco pursued me. "You can't marry someone who's not a Catholic in the Church, you know. What are you going to do, Horsey? Just walk away? Is the Church just some sort of game to you that you pick up when you feel like it, then toss aside? Are all of us just a big joke to you?"

"No! Stop! I don't know! I don't know! Look at me, Rocco!" I gestured to my hideous right leg, twisted inward with its fishlike foot. I ran my hand in a circle around my unlovely face. "What am I supposed to do? Live alone for the rest of my life? Become a nun?"

"Well?" Though as soon as he said this, the absurdity of the notion became clear even to him, and he shook his head. "Bert will never convert. You know that. The guy doesn't even believe in religion."

"So I have to choose, Rocco, between God and love? Is that what you're saying?"

We regarded each other miserably, hemmed in by lurid jars of maraschino cherries, by crates of knobby, shriveled walnuts.

"Rocco?" His name caught in my throat like a burr. "Please. I didn't want to feel this way. I prayed not to, Rocco. I've lost so many people already. And for the first time—the only time probably in my entire life, some man..."

I looked at him imploringly. Rocco puffed up his cheeks and exhaled slowly. He began pacing the storage closet.

"There are far worse guys out there. I know that," he said finally. "And Nonno and Nonna, they don't have long for this world." His gaze pinned me to the wall. "I'm not saying it's right. It's not right at all. You be discreet, Horsey, do you understand?"

"Of course. What do you think I'm going to do? Tell Mrs. Salucci? Call *Il Progresso*?"

He snorted. "I'm serious. Not a word. You stay away from the neighborhood with him entirely. He doesn't set foot on Mulberry Street unless he's with me."

"You'll cover for us?"

His eyes were like hooks. "Three conditions. First." He gripped me by my shoulders as if I were a piece of furniture he was righting. "If I ever hear so much as a whisper that you're a *zoccola* I'll make sure you're out on the street in a second, you got that? You behave yourself."

"What's number two?"

"Second, I am going to have a little talk with Bert. If he's going to be stepping out with you, I want to make sure his intentions are honorable. Nobody disrespects the family. What? Why are you smiling?"

"I'm not," I said. "That's fine."

"Three. You stop with the college. Immediately. You work for us full-time now. You pick up the slack."

This last condition completely took me aback. "Excuse me?"

Rocco crossed his arms. "I don't want Nonno and Nonna spending any more money on you. If word does get around that you've been stepping out with an *Ammazza Christi* Commie, I don't want them feeling they've been taken advantage of any more than they have already."

"Even—"

"You know that Nonno can't see anymore. And Nonna is frail. But they won't quit working, and they won't let us hire anyone from outside either. Meanwhile, those *mezza negri* keep stealing our ideas and our clients. So what are we supposed to do, Horsey? You come back and work for us like you're supposed to. If you want to be with this family, then you be with us a hundred percent. *Capisce?*"

As far as Bert was concerned, I was amazed at how easily I was willing to give up the Church. Rocco, unfortunately, was right. I could slip off Catholicism like a borrowed coat; it was all ritual. Myths. An elaborate pageantry learned in childhood. But quitting college? That was nearly unthinkable.

"They won't think I'm being ungrateful by dropping out?" I proposed. "Your grandmother, you know, she wanted me to go."

"So you tell her it's temporary. You can always go back, can't you, if things don't work out with Bert?"

I allowed that I supposed that I could. "Yet what if things *do* work out with Bert? What then?"

Rocco stared at the concrete floor. "If Nonno and Nonna live to see that day"—he took a deep, unhappy breath—"I suppose we'll tell them that setting you up with Bert was *my* idea. That *I* thought you needed a husband—*any* husband. And since you'll have quit school to help with the business, maybe everyone will be more forgiving."

Grimly, he held out his hand. "That's the best I can do. You don't disgrace us, you be a good Catholic, and you work for us. In turn, I'll look out for you. *Capisce?*"

What choice did I have, darlings? Something inside me whispered, *This is all wrong.* Yet something else inside me exploded with gratitude and relief and secret, giddy glee. I could manage it. I could keep seeing Bert yet somehow still remain in the Dinellos' good graces. Rocco would help me. And I would help him—and everyone—as a *real* member of the family.

I slipped my hand into his. "Very well, then," I said.

A few weeks later, when it was time to reenroll at Hunter, I told Mrs. Dinello, "I think it's best if I skip this semester. The boys, they really need my help at the moment."

To my amazement, she didn't protest. "I suppose," she said vaguely, rubbing her leg, her gaze turning milky. "They have so much to do now."

Though nobody ever said it out loud, all of us knew: Mr. Dinello was dying. Like gold leaf flaking off a statue, like a cliff eroding into the sea. And then one Sunday morning that spring, as we were getting ready for church, he called to Mrs. Dinello from the bedroom. "Generosa? My tie, you have seen her?" Mrs. Dinello was in the kitchen with me, rinsing out the coffee press. A bemused, exasperated look—a look that wives everywhere get when their husbands cannot find an item that is clearly right in front of them—this look fluttered across her face. She nudged off the tap with her elbow and opened her mouth to reply. Before any sound came out of her, she went down.

People nowadays, they want all the horrible, lingering details, every rococo scene of somebody else's agony and pathos. So sue me: I'm not going to give them to you. Mrs. Dinello collapsed and died right there in her kitchen, leaving her half-coherent husband fumbling around in the bedroom, searching for his tie.

And I was the one who was with her and, in a moment, on the floor beside her, wailing.

And of course it was unspeakably terrible.

And that is all anybody needs to know.

After that, it was as if every remaining nerve and synapse inside Mr. Dinello disintegrated in grief. By late summer his left hand was convulsing uncontrollably and he was given to sudden fits of weeping like a child. In an odd twist, his left leg went lame, like a mirror image of my own. He stopped speaking entirely. By Thanksgiving he was refusing to eat. Lucia, Pasquale's wife, attempted to feed him the way she did their baby, with a bib and a tiny spoon.

In the end, he recognized none of us. His head and arms lolled like a rag doll's, his chin was shiny with spittle. A doctor, inexplicably, shaved off his mustache. To see him so infantilized was excruciating. When he finally died, three weeks before Christmas, we buried him beside his wife, his sons, his niece, and his grandchild at Holy Cross Cemetery out in Brooklyn, not back in Napoli as he and Mrs. Dinello had once dreamed.

And even now: I do not want to talk about that, either.

True to Mrs. Dinello's word, I received an unofficial inheritance of sorts—namely, all her old responsibilities. Even her apron. Nothing had been put in writing, yet by then it was a foregone conclusion. I was finally integral to Dinello & Sons. I continued keeping house for Rocco and myself on Mulberry Street and showing up for work as always in my scuffed shoes, my hair swaddled in a kerchief. When Rocco gave me a nod at the end of the evening, I slipped out and met Bert somewhere on Rivington Street or north by his garage.

Vittorio's wife, Carmella, began appearing at the factory more often, I noticed, looking petulant and bored, picking up utensils and setting them down mindlessly and asking what the different ingredients for ice cream were and offering inane suggestions. Sometimes Vittorio sat her down at a table and assigned her a task such as addressing envelopes or sorting napkins. Yet when the inventories needed to be recorded, the deliveries logged, and all the outlays and revenue entered into the ledger, he reflexively turned to me. "Can you take care of this?" he'd say, handing me a receipt for a delivery of vanilla extract.

The books, they needed a proper going-over. Studying them, I saw that Dinello & Sons Fancy Italian Ices & Ice Creams had been making steadily less profits since Mr. Dinello first had a stroke. The rent at Lafayette Street had increased, and many of the Dinellos' contracts had been poorly renegotiated over time, based more on friendship than on business savvy.

The good news, however, I told the grandsons, was that such problems could be easily solved.

"With a few changes in place, we can greatly increase our profit margin," I explained one evening.

After the machines were cleaned and shut down at the end of each day, Vittorio, Pasquale, and Rocco had gotten into the habit of lowering the shades and huddling around one of the café tables with a bottle. As the radio played late into the night, they talked quietly—or not at all—until the broadcasts stopped altogether and the three of them stumbled home. Sometimes when I came in early in the mornings to inspect the milk deliveries, I found the wireless still on, spitting static.

"Can I show you how we can save money?" I said, opening the ledger.

Vittorio put up his hand as if to signal, *Stop.*

"Is it legal?" he said, staring at the bottle in the center of the table.

"Of course." I laughed.

"Do I need to sign anything?"

"Perhaps later."

"Then just let me know if I do. Leave it for me on the desk."

I had never had such trust, such carte blanche before, darlings, and it made me feel buoyant. In the back office of the ice cream factory, I got to work. My early days on Orchard Street stood me well. I haggled mercilessly. I haggled with all the suppliers, the delivery boys, the milkmen, the egg men. I haggled with the garbage collectors, even the "security" insurers who stopped by every month. I imagined Mrs. Dinello perched over my shoulder, coaching me on. *You have a head for certain things that the boys don't, Ninella.* Had we not been good clients of theirs for twenty years? I asked our suppliers. Had we not been consistent and on time with our payments? We are buying in bulk now. Do right by us and we'll continue to do right by you, I told them. Otherwise we can go elsewhere.

"Look," I announced proudly one evening, waving a revised dairy contract for Vittorio to sign. "Another fifteen dollars a week saved."

"Good," he said, again without looking up. "Just leave it on the desk."

"Is there anything else I can do before I turn in for the evening?" I asked, removing my coat from the peg in the back.

"Nope. *Grazie.*"

Something in his tone sounded queer.

I stopped Rocco on the way out. "Is everything all right, Rocco?"

"Sure." He shrugged. "Why wouldn't it be?"

"Is there anything I should know about?"

"Of course not."

"Are you sure?"

"*Ai*, Horsey, what's with the twenty questions?"

"Something feels odd here," I said.

"It is odd here," he admitted, shaking his head. "It's all changing so quickly." Reaching into his pocket, he took out a few dollars and pressed them into my hand. "Go out with Bert tonight. Have a little fun. Somebody here should."

On March 19, 1929, Bert and I were finally married: a bright, chilly Tuesday with the trees just starting to bud and a brisk wind tearing in off the river. We met at City Hall on our lunch breaks. Only Rocco and Mr. Shackter served as witnesses. I wore a garnet-colored dress that Mr. Shackter had helped me purchase wholesale from a dressmaker he knew on Grand Street. Bert was in his work clothes—just shirtsleeves and suspenders, though Rocco had lent him his good Sunday jacket and Mr. Shackter gave him a tie from his shop. Wine red, like my dress, dotted with tiny gold fleurs-de-lis. Bert did not have enough money for a ring, so we used a cigar band instead.

Afterward, stepping out into the little park by the clerk's office, we were not quite sure what to do with ourselves. The sidewalk glittered under our feet. The sky domed over us like the vaults of a cathedral, bending the office buildings to its will. I suddenly felt we were so tiny, so little in the world. "Why not some lunch?" Mr. Shackter suggested. He steered us over to a delicatessen on

Broadway, where he ordered four lemonades and two kosher hot dogs apiece. "To love," he said gravely. As the glasses clinked, I felt a shiver of joy and sadness break through me at once. I looked at Bert, at the divine sculpture of him. He squeezed my hand. He was so shining and handsome. A flower of impossible hope and terror unfurled within me. I could never be too nice to him, I decided. Even when you were married—especially when you were married—you had to protect yourself. Love, kindness: Whenever Bert decided to withdraw them—and certainly one day he would—I sensed it would likely kill me.

Mr. Shackter insisted on paying for our wedding lunch, such as it was. "Save your pennies, newlyweds." He chuckled. After we ate, the four of us bowed into the wind and walked north to Canal Street, debris tumbling around our ankles. Bert gave me a quick, embarrassed peck on the cheek, and he and Mr. Shackter continued north on foot while Rocco and I headed west toward Lafayette Street. Not fifteen minutes later, I found myself back in my apron at Dinello & Sons, helping to mix a great vat of pistachio ice cream, a married lady now with a cigar band on her left hand, the damp imprint of Bert's lips still lingering on my jawline.

Bert had found us a room to rent up on Thompson Street with a little kitchenette and a light fixture overhead that you pulled on with a chain. In Greenwich Village nobody cared much if he was a Jewish Communist and I a lapsed Catholic.

That evening my new husband came to call for me at work. "H-h-hello." He smiled as he stepped politely into the shop, the little bell over the door tinkling tinnily. "Is the new Mrs. D-Dunkle here?"

Since our engagement, he had only come around to Dinello & Sons a few times. The other grandsons had learned our secret after the New Year. Yet they seemed more bemused than upset. "You don't say?" Vittorio had chuckled. "Rocco has been playing

Cupid? Finally that *cazzo* succeeds at something." Yet out of respect, Bert and I continued to avoid the neighborhood.

When Bert arrived that evening, the grandsons were in the process of pulling down the shades and setting the glasses on the table. "Come in, *amico*," Rocco said, motioning Bert toward the café table. "Horsey!" he called out. "Bring two more in, will you?"

Vittorio poured three fingers of bootleg whiskey for each of us. "To *amore*. To the newlyweds!" he bellowed. "Okay," he ordered. "Everyone drink."

We drank once, coughing and pounding on our chests. Then again.

"Okay, now," Vittorio said, setting his glass behind him on the counter. "The wedding gift."

I glanced at Bert, who looked at me with equal confusion.

"What?" Vittorio said. "You don't think we have any manners?"

He leaned back in his chair and knitted his fingers across his chest. He was past thirty now. Time had broadened him, and he was beginning to lose his hair. For the first time, I could see echoes of Mr. Dinello's avuncular face in his own, though Vittorio's eyes were smaller and perpetually bloodshot, and his jaw appeared peppered no matter how often he shaved. "You know from doing the books yourself," he said to me, "that we do not have much money to spare."

"And for obvious reasons, we could not throw you a wedding party," Rocco added quietly.

"But we can give you a little honeymoon," Vittorio said. "Rocco, he knows some people in Atlantic City. He made a few deals."

Both Bert and I looked at Rocco, stunned. His shiny black head bobbed; he seemed almost embarrassed. "Well, one of the bus drivers, he used to drive a Dinello's Ices wagon before the war—"

"And another guy we know, his sister-in-law in New Jersey, she runs a boardinghouse there," said Vittorio. "She can put you up for three nights, midweek. As a favor to us."

Bert and I glanced at each other incredulously again, then at the Dinello brothers. "She has a room for you starting next Wednesday," Rocco said. "Today, at the courthouse, I spoke to Mr. Shackter, Bert. He says he'll give you the time."

"It's early in the season," Pasquale said softly, "but it should be nice. Lucia herself has always wanted to go."

"I d-d-don't know how to thank you all," Bert stammered. This time it was pure emotion in his voice. Me, I was blinking back tears. *"Mio fratelli,"* I said. *"Molto grazie."*

"Let's all have another drink," said Rocco, reaching for the bottle.

A few years ago, there was an ice cream manufacturers' trade show out in Atlantic City. My God, darlings: The town looked like a place you would go only if you wanted to commit suicide. Buildings moldered like war ruins, awash with salt and crime and decay. Clock hands stuck at the hour they'd broken years before. The only people I saw were Negroes slumped in doorways like discarded packages. Even the boardwalk appeared to be disintegrating. For three days I mostly drank bourbon in my hotel suite. Isaac went crazy when he found out, but what else was I supposed to do? Besides, have you ever been to a convention of ice cream makers? Trust me, darlings—between the ridiculous balloon hats and the idiotic gimmicks and the competing xylophone jingles and the blinding bubblegum colors and all those cloyingly sunshiny salesmen with their murderous, bone-crushing handshakes—and some *shmendrik* they always hire to stand at the reception area dressed up like a cartoon ice cream man shrieking,

"I SCREAM, YOU SCREAM, WE ALL SCREAM FOR ICE CREAM!"—it's nothing you could ever possibly want to experience sober.

The day Bert and I arrived for our honeymoon, however, oh, Atlantic City was the most glamorous place on earth! Fancy motorcars in the streets. Women in furs. Baroque hotel palaces rising up out of the mist! Bert called it "Vienna on the sea." Even the long bus ride there was marvelous. I had traveled across the ocean, you see, but never across the Hudson.

"Oh, you are the Dinellos' girl! The newlyweds. Come in, come in!" exclaimed Mrs. Trevi, motioning us inside. Her boardinghouse was two blocks from the beach. She gave us her best room in the back, with a washstand and hand-crocheted doilies draped on all the furniture. A crucifix hung over the bed. Bert went to take it down, but I stayed his hand and told him that if he didn't believe in religion, what did it matter? Besides, perhaps it was placed there to exorcise us, two outlaws such as we were. He started laughing, then I did, and then neither of us could stop until he lowered me onto the bed.

Afterward we were like little children, fidgety. Eager to go out. We'd never had a day's vacation in our lives!

"Come, Lil, Let's see every sight there possibly is," Bert said, grabbing my hand.

The wind whipped in fiercely from the Atlantic. We huddled together and made our way along the boardwalk. The hotels rose above us majestically, heralded by gulls. Enormous signs advertised "spectacular" revues. A Dixieland band—its trombone player bundled in a raccoon coat—played atop a small bandstand. We stuck our faces through a pair of cutouts and had a novelty photo taken of ourselves. Bert was a muscleman in a striped bathing costume, me a sprightly acrobat in a tutu balanced on a unicycle beside him. Our first official portrait as man and wife! For the first time in our lives, we felt truly a part of America.

The next day Bert found a gambling house in a basement. "There's no n-need for you to come, Lil," he said as he pulled on his shirt after our "nap," as we called them. "I'll only be an hour, I promise. Y-you should rest."

I had never slept in the middle of the day before. Once Bert left, however, I tugged at the thin coverlet and pummeled the stale bed pillows until I finally gave up entirely and just lay there, blinking at the crucifix and the chipped ceiling rose. My thoughts suddenly strayed back to Mama and Papa, to a story Mama had once told me about her own wedding day, when Papa got drunk on plum wine and attempted to dance with Zeyde. What would they think of Bert? I wondered. What would they think of me now?

For years I used to try to recall their faces one by one just before I fell asleep—Mama, Papa, Bella, Rose, and Flora— inscribing them in my memory. Yet now I found that I could re- call Papa's close-clipped beard though not his nose, Mama's large, flat hands but not her arms. Rose's delicate complexion and her kvetching, but not her features. Of Bella I could picture her thick, dark hair and the fact that she was tall, and that her bony wrists seemed to pivot on their own accord whenever she spoke, but her face, it was a blur to me. Only Flora remained clear, and yet, I realized, my image of her was as an eight-year-old in a threadbare dress and shoes held together with string. It had been fifteen years since I'd seen her.

I limped over to the mirror above the washstand and studied myself. Certainly I was no great beauty, yet, as the magazines might have phrased it, I seemed to have developed a particular "look" that was "striking" if not quite attractive. At twenty-one I had grown into my features some. My nose no longer appeared so prominent, my cheekbones so severe. Yet as I stared at myself, I saw Mama.

In Vishnev I had once overheard a neighbor say that I looked most like my mother. I had her same dark, feverish eyes, set slightly too close together and deep in her face. Her thin, serious lips. Her austere brow and chin. Every time she looked at me, Mama must have seen her face reflected straight back at her, as I saw it mirrored at me right now.

Where was she? I wondered. Was it even possible she was still alive? Oh, Mama! I felt a sudden, overwhelming desire to scour the countryside to find her. How I longed to show her that—even with a *punim* like mine—someone had married me after all.

Washing myself, I put on my garnet-colored dress again, fixed my hair and face, and waited for this handsome new husband of mine.

And waited.

An hour went by.

Then two.

By the third hour, I was sick. My own naïveté, it stunned me. That merry glint in Bert's eyes whenever a woman swished by. The way he'd bloomed when those showgirls had planted themselves on his lap. Who had I been kidding? Even here in Atlantic City, people squinted at me and Bert when they saw us together, as if they were computing long division in their heads.

I had been such a fool! Sensing what was about to unfold, I stumbled across the room and yanked open the wardrobe. I grabbed my other dress from its hanger and scooped up my underthings. I was just pulling out the suitcase when Bert returned.

"Lil, look!" he cried, tossing a fistful of dollar bills in the air like confetti. "I did it!" Twenty-three dollars he'd won. More than a week's wages. "What's wrong, doll?" He stopped suddenly. "Why are you c-crying?"

I turned away, shaking. I could not bear to let him see my relief. "You *mamzer*. Already you're thinking of leaving me? On our honeymoon?"

"What? Oh, L-Lil. Oh, doll. No, no. Why would you even think that? Please. Come." He opened his arms.

"An hour! You said you'd be only an hour!"

"I am s-so s-sorry. I just got on a roll, is all." He touched my cheek with the back of his hand.

I slapped it away. "Don't you dare leave me waiting for you like that ever again."

"L-L-L-Lil. Oh, my love," he said woefully, drawing me toward him. Oddly, he never seemed more beholden to me, more adoring or close to me, than when I was yelling at him. A peculiar bolt of elation shot through me, coiled with the satisfaction of punishing him. Slowly, I gave in to his embrace.

"All the m-m-money, it's for us," Bert said, stroking my hair. "I thought we'd have a grand night on the town. Please, Lil. Will you forgive me?"

That evening he took me to a show. Ethel Waters, we saw! Oh, she was magnificent. And afterward Bert pulled out my chair for me in the first proper restaurant we'd ever eaten in, with white tablecloths and a waiter standing by with a pitcher of ice water. Tomato consommé. Boiled beef tips with noodles. Roasted chicken with lima beans and carrots. Cream pie for dessert. All the butter you could eat, pressed into the shape of roses on a little porcelain dish. "Oh, my," we marveled, over and over.

The next day when Bert went back to the gambling room, I went with him. Since women were not allowed inside, I sat in the vestibule quietly reading a penny novel. After an anxious hour, Bert added twelve dollars to our cache. Grabbing me around the waist, he lifted me into the air and spun me around. "I t-told you that you were my lucky charm," he declared. "Let's buy you a proper ring."

Mrs. Trevi said we'd get the best deal at a pawnshop on Pacific Avenue near the train station. Bert, he was willing to be extravagant, he was willing to spend everything we had. The salt air, the gambling—they'd gone to his head like champagne. Yet I said, "Let's save some money for a rainy day, eh? I'm certainly not going to wear a diamond ring while I scrub down a batch freezer."

I chose a modest white-gold band etched with designs like stalks of wheat. But then, looking at all those luxurious objects winking in their glass cases—the filigreed opera glasses, the mother-of-pearl cigarette case, the engraved pocketwatch hanging from its fob like a gold plum—and hearing the faint *fwip-fwip* of the dollar bills as Bert thumbed them out onto the countertop—I suppose the thrill of acquisition came over us like a fever. Surely, we agreed, we needed to buy the Dinellos and Mr. Shackter some tokens of our appreciation as well. Surely that was only fair. From shop to shop we went, almost giddy. For Vittorio we bought a brass cigar cutter, for Pasquale a bright green bottle of men's eau de cologne. For Carmella and Lucia identical cut-glass ashtrays with hand-painted pictures of the boardwalk. For Mr. Shackter a fancy letter opener with ATLANTIC CITY, NEW JERSEY 1929 embossed on the tip. And for Rocco, Bert purchased a crystal paperweight with a picture of the new Miss America embedded in it. We bought boxes of striped saltwater taffy, too. Raspberry. Lemon. With their juicy, marshmallowy zest—perhaps, I thought, we could adapt some of the different flavors for Dinello & Sons—a "Daffy Taffy" ice cream, even?

By the time we returned to the boardinghouse, we'd spent most of Bert's winnings. Dizzily, we set the treasures out on the bed and watched them gleam beneath the fringed, rose-colored light, feeling sated and rich and proud, as if the gifts were accomplishments, as if they were things we had wrought ourselves.

Once we arrived back in New York that Saturday afternoon, awash with love and effusiveness, I simply could not wait until work on Monday to distribute the presents. "Look at you, Lil." Bert chuckled. "You're bouncing around like a little girl. Go. Take them over today if you want." While he napped, I set off for the ice cream factory. Carrying our gifts through the streets of New York, while the city buzzed with all its magnificent traffic and construction and promise, my feet one pair in a sea of hundreds hurrying over the pavement—with my handsome new husband prone in our marital bed, my skin still flushed from his fingertips—I felt triumphant, darlings. Utterly jubilant. It was the best, perhaps, that I had ever felt in my life. I was nearly airborne: "*Addio Napoli!*" I sang aloud as I stepped into Houston Street. "*Addio! Addio!*"

At Dinello & Sons Fancy Italian Ices & Ice Creams, the door was propped open with a brick. I stepped inside. "*Buona sera,*" I sang.

The café tables and delicate wire chairs were gone. A boxy outline remained where the cash register had been. The two big, gleaming, gravity-fed continuous-batch freezers had vanished.

"Rocco? Vittorio? Pasquale?" I called.

I limped over to the pay telephone to dial the police. Yet all that remained of the phone were frayed copper wires spraying out of the holes in the plaster.

"Oh, it's you," a voice said mildly. Behind me, Carmella appeared holding a washrag. Her hair was tied back in a kerchief.

"What happened?" I said. "Where is everybody?"

"Canal Street." She shrugged. And she did not say anything

more. She just stood there squinting at me with her narrow, dark eyes. Her forearms were wet, I noticed, glinting with soap. "Oh," she said, as if she had only just remembered. "Did you have a nice honeymoon?"

"Carmella?" I gestured around. "Where did everything go?"

"We sold it." She said this as if it were the most natural response in the world. "Well, actually, we've joined forces."

"Excuse me?"

"With the Cannolettis." Noticing a line of dust on the tiled wainscoting, she frowned and wiped it off with her rag. "Two are better than one, Vito says."

I hobbled past her into the kitchen. A mop stood propped up in a bucket of soapy water in one corner. On the counter sat a pile of wet rags and a half-eaten sandwich on a chipped plate. Otherwise it was bare. The pantry door gaped open, all the inventory gone except for a jar with a few maraschino cherries bobbing at the bottom and a rusty mousetrap on the floor. In the little office in the back, there was just the lamp, unplugged, and a crate with papers dumped in it haphazardly. The desk was gone, the clock taken from the wall, even the crucifix removed. I snatched up the papers.

"I really don't think those are of any concern anymore," Carmella said, standing in the doorway.

Riffling through the piles of discarded receipts, lists, calendar pages, labels, and invoices, I saw the contracts I had renegotiated for Dinello & Sons Fancy Italian Ices & Ice Creams, securing better deals for milk, for gelatin, for flavorings, for garbage collection. Vittorio had never signed any of them.

When I reached Canal Street, I heard it before I saw it: the frantic sounds of hammering, the sickening splintering of wood coming from Cannoletti's Ice Cream Company. Inside, it appeared to be in the process of demolition, though a bright sign, forgotten on the sidewalk, still read #1 ICE CREAM IN AMERICA! 8 GREAT FLAVORS!

"What was supposed to happen?" I cried as Vittorio hustled me out onto the street to talk. "Was I just supposed to show up for work on Monday and find everyone gone?"

"What? No. Of course not," he said with irritation, as if I were being irrational. "We were going to pay you a visit tomorrow when we finished. Both shops have to be cleared out by the thirty-first or we get stuck with the leases for another month. Besides"—he frowned—"aren't you still on your honeymoon?"

"Where is everything?"

"Brooklyn." Looking over my head, back into the shop, he signaled to someone. "We got twice the space at half the price. We can triple our production."

"You sold us to the Cannolettis?"

Rocco emerged from the storefront. As soon as he saw me, he crossed his arms and stared at the ground.

"It's a partnership. We're renaming ourselves the 'Candie Ice Cream Company.' For Cannoletti and Dinello," Vittorio said.

"I thought they were the 'enemy.' The *mezza negri*!"

"Be reasonable. You know how it's been. We've been working ourselves to death. And so have the Cannolettis. And for what? To see who can sell ten gallons more banana ice cream? The big money is in volume. Places in New Jersey, now that they have refrigerated shipping, they're going to put us out of business if we don't—"

"But you didn't even try!" I cried. "I renegotiated all those contracts. We could have been making a much bigger profit if—"

"The Cannolettis have a lawyer. We're getting incorporated, we're setting up a payroll," Vittorio said. "No more nickel-and-dime stuff. No more scrambling around like crazy people sixteen hours a day."

"But, but—" And suddenly I felt like Bert, unable to get the words out. "But why didn't anyone ever say anything to me?"

Vittorio gave me a freighted look. "Because it's not your business. And the Cannolettis"—he looked at the ground—"they have a bookkeeper already. A professional. So I'm sorry."

A tremendous boom erupted from inside the storefront. A large shelf had fallen like a tree, sending up clouds of dust. Inside, men started yelling at each other in Italian.

"I have to get back to work." Vittorio hastened toward the doorstep.

I felt so queasy I could barely breathe, yet I planted myself before him, blocking his path. *Give such a* geschrei—I recalled Mama saying it—*as they have never heard.* And so I hollered.

"Please," Vittorio whispered fiercely.

"Your grandmother, she promised me— I've worked my whole life—"

He looked at me beseechingly. "Everything you've done for us, Lillian, we appreciate it. But you can't say you haven't gotten anything in return. My grandparents fed you, and clothed you, and housed you. Heck, they even sent you to college. And of course, as the Candie Company grows, if we ever find we have some money to hire you and you still want a job with us—"

When he saw I would not budge, he dug into his pocket, pulled out a roll of bills, and pressed them in my hand. I didn't want to take it, of course. I should have thrown it back in his face and spit at him. Yet I was simply in too much shock, I suppose.

"But where am I to work?" I said desperately. "I'm lame." As soon as these words were out of my mouth, I hated myself almost as much as I hated him. I never wanted to give anyone the satisfaction of hearing such words from my lips, to cast myself before them so pathetically. Yet I did.

Vittorio shifted uncomfortably. "You're a married lady now, yes? It's Bert's job to provide for you, not ours. Besides, look around." Vittorio swept his arm grandly across Canal Street. "We're in America. It's good times. You're smart. You'll land on your feet."

He walked swiftly back inside and was instantly enveloped by Italian workingmen, by chalky clouds of dust and plaster. I stared at the wad of money in my hand, then looked at Rocco, who stood there uneasily, unsure whether to slink back inside as well.

"Horsey. I'm sorry," he said.

"You sent me away! You sent me away on a honeymoon just to get rid of me!"

"No, it wasn't like that."

"I trusted you!" I cried. "I trusted you with everything!—and you cook up this scheme—"

"Horsey, I didn't intend it like that. I just— It was going to happen anyway. I wanted to make sure that at least, you and Bert, you had—"

"All three of you! You sat there and you looked us in the eye—'*To the newlyweds,*' you toasted. While all along, you knew!"

"I couldn't stop it, Horsey."

"I gave up college. We made a deal. And behind my back, you—"

"Horsey!" he shouted. "What did you expect me to do? They're my brothers. They're family."

In a flash I pulled out the crystal paperweight we'd bought for him and hurled it at his head. He ducked, and it smashed against the door. I threw the glass Atlantic City ashtray. It landed at his feet in an explosion of shards.

"*Ai, ai, ai!*" he said.

I hurled the bottle of aftershave as hard as I could, too. It hit the front window and cracked it, jagged fractures radiating out like a cobweb. All the men inside began hollering. Greenish, mentholated liquid slid down the glass.

"Crazy *puttana!*" someone shouted.

"Stop, Horsey, please." Grabbing me by the wrists, Rocco jerked me to him and pinned me. "Just stop." He stayed me fiercely.

I shouted and flailed.

"All right," Rocco breathed, clutching me. "It's all right." His grip loosened, and he took a step back. "It's all right," he said again. "We all have tempers."

I glared at him, panting.

"No hard feelings," he said carefully. "Just go. Okay?"

"Yes," I said viciously. "Yes, hard feelings."

"Horsey—"

"Let go of me!" I yanked my arm away from him. I wanted to whirl around and punch him hard in the stomach, hard in his weasel face. Right-left-right, just as Papa had taught me. Yet by then Vittorio was standing in the doorway furiously surveying the damage I'd caused, and one of the Cannolettis was behind him, eyeing me with the crowbar in his hands. They had all stopped what they were doing to regard me, the Cannolettis and the Dinellos, this small army of men with their tools. They did not appear alarmed, however, so much as bemused. In the cracked plate-glass window, I saw myself reflected back as they saw me: a crippled, craggy girl, hair awry, her mouth a smear of anger. Negligible. Unlovely. Shrewish. A white-hot spasm of pain shot down my leg.

I turned and hobbled away, trying to keep my gaze straight ahead, even as my jaw twitched. I could feel their stares boring into my back; I could imagine the hooting and wisecracks that would erupt as soon as I turned the corner.

Pivoting around, I hollered venomously, "You're all idiots! Idiots and cowards with no brains for business, you understand? You are nothing! You are worse than nothing! And your ice cream is garbage, you *pezzo di merda*."

From inside the store, someone shouted, "You owe us for the window you just broke, you crazy bitch!"

"I owe you nothing, *stronzo*!"

Rocco looked aghast.

"Oh, so now you're shocked? The little Horse Girl knows how to curse? *Vaffanculo*. All of you."

Whirling around, I hurried off as quickly as I could manage, dissolving into the crowds of Canal Street before they could hear my humiliated sobs, before they could see my leg buckle, before my true aloneness in this world hit me like a shock wave.

PART TWO

Chapter 8

APPARENTLY IT'S NOT ENOUGH that there are two separate trials pending against me—one federal, no less. While I am feeding Petunia bits of bacon from the breakfast table, my publicist, Sheila, calls. "Bad news," she says in her gritty, stuccoed voice. Two packs a day she smokes. If she can taste our ice cream at all, I'm Gina Lollobrigida.

"It looks like we may have another problem on our hands. Spreckles the Clown."

"Excuse me?"

"Harvey Ballentine."

"Harvey?" I say. "He's been off the show since 1980." The most recent actor to play Spreckles was hired by NBC directly. Some *nudnik* named Jared.

"Yeah, well, Harvey Ballentine hasn't left the limelight," Sheila says. "There's a Q&A with him in *New York* magazine this week."

I get a queasy feeling. Harvey Ballentine had been my sidekick for seventeen years. I'd hired him personally, in fact, right after the first Spreckles the Clown suffered a nervous breakdown. Harvey, he quickly proved to be a pain in the ass, too, yet in a whole new way. He was a germophobe, for starters. Had to wash his hands three times in a row before donning his puffy pink gloves. And he drove the producers crazy with his showbiz nonsense: What was his best camera angle? Was the lighting making his greasepaint melt? For a while, convinced he was gaining weight, he even refused to eat ice cream. He would lick his cone, then wipe his tongue off on a napkin as soon as we cut to a commercial.

"You're a goddamn ice cream clown in pink satin fat pants!" I once barked at him. "Eat your goddamn ice cream cone like everyone else!"

Oh, but the mouth on him! The wit! Harvey Ballentine could make me laugh like no one else. Darlings, do I even need to tell you how unfunny most clowns are? If I'd had my way, a bunny or even a goddamn donkey would've been Dunkle's trademark. But our admen at Promovox outvoted me. Clowns—*feh!* All that ghastly, forced gaiety, worse than New Year's Eve. And the moment they're out of their makeup: *If only you could've seen me perform* Waiting for Godot *in summer stock!* they moan. Please. Spare me the existential kvetching. Be a clown or be quiet. Harvey, when he wasn't fussing, he was marvelous, wicked fun.

Plus, he could hold his liquor. Trust me: This is a quality you want in a mascot.

"It seems he's capitalizing on his relationship with you now by trashing it, same as everyone else." Sheila sighs.

"Oh. Is he now?" My tone is haughty, though I feel my face growing hot. Harvey Ballentine and I drank and laughed and gossiped on the set together for seventeen years. He was one of the only employees I never fired, in fact. One morning when a little girl on the show vomited all over his floppy shoes, Harvey simply pulled off his rubber nose and threw it across the room as soon as the camera cut away. "That's it!" he cried. "Get me a bucket. Somebody please get me a bucket! Look at me. Look at this mess. I'm wrung out. I'm done. These little fuckers are killing me!"

Five months he had left on his contract. But did I sue? No, I did not. Severance I even gave him. Plus free dry cleaning! Certainly he, of all people, should not turn against me. Yet I can only imagine. Harvey. That tongue of his. He could slice people up like a chef at Benihana.

"Here's what he's saying, and I quote—" Over the line, I hear Sheila's cigarette lighter click, and she pauses to inhale. "'In my prior life, I worked with Lillian Dunkle, playing Spreckles the Clown on her *Sundae Morning Funhouse*. They call her the Ice Cream Queen, but she's more like the Ice Cream *Mussolini*. Talk about a dictator! All that woman is missing is a balcony and a pair of epaulets. After dealing with her and her insane demands for seventeen years, taking on Ed Koch and the Reagan administration for the GMHC should be a cakewalk."

The telephone receiver goes heavy in my hand. From the earpiece Sheila's voice continues to rasp across the velvety green lawn. *Harvey Ballentine.* I feel my eyes welling. *You of all people!*

"What's GMHC?" I swallow.

"The Gay Men's Health Crisis. Some group of fairies in the Village lobbying for better health care. Apparently Harvey Ballentine is their new spokesman, which is why he's getting all this attention now. Uh-oh," Sheila says suddenly. "Lillian, did you ever know Harvey was a homosexual?"

"Did I know? He was a man. In show business. You tell me."

"But when you hired him, you never asked?"

I pick up a crust of toast, then toss it back down on the china. *Harvey.* We used to drink Sazeracs together. The night Andy Warhol invited me to a party of his at Studio 54, it was Harvey whom I asked to accompany me. We sashayed through the velvet rope together and got our picture taken; for months afterward he yakked about it. And the morning his mother died, I gave him my car and my driver.

"Nobody asked back then, for Chrissakes, Sheila. It was 1963.

But of course I knew. We all knew. The man swanned around in his Spreckles the Clown costume like Carol Channing."

There is a silence.

"Lillian," Sheila says finally, "I think we could have a bigger PR problem on our hands than just a former employee bad-mouthing you."

"I should make a new line of ice cream flavors, you know," I say bitterly. "'Betrayal.' 'Ingratitude.'"

"Your former ice cream clown is presenting himself to the media as an open homosexual. Working for a group dedicated to fighting this crazy gay cancer. And all the while he's associating himself with *you*. Your ice cream. And your television show for *children*. Where for years he shook hands with the kids—"

Petunia whimpers up at me. For a moment I do not say anything.

"Oh, for Chrissakes. He was a clown, Sheila. Even his *nose* was encased in rubber."

"Look, all I'm saying is, nobody knows how it spreads. Right now it's just the Haitians, the homos, and the hemophiliacs. But this AIDS thing terrifies people. A teacher at my nephew's school was fired just because someone spotted him at a pride parade dressed as Zsa Zsa Gabor."

Suddenly I have the childish notion that maybe if I just shut my eyes, all of this will go away.

"What I'm saying is, you don't want this guy associating himself with Dunkle's Ice Cream right now, okay? Another boycott will likely kill your business. And with the IRS and everyone else going after you . . ."

I hold the telephone receiver away from my ear and nuzzle Petunia. As if I don't have enough breaking my heart. As if I'm not pacing the floorboards at night already. A shiver of misery runs through me. *The Mussolini of Ice Cream*. He'd really said that?

"Contact your lawyers, Lillian," Sheila says. "Protect your-self."

☁

In the spring of 1929, Bert and I, we were in the first blush of our marriage. It should have been delirious. I should have felt sylph-like, ecstatic. Bert Dunkle had married me! Yet as dawn filtered into our little room from the alley and Bert drew me toward him on the damp mattress, gliding his hands beneath my nightgown, my mind played over the images of the Dinello boys dismantling their shop behind our backs.

In the evenings after work, Bert and I climbed up onto the roof on Thompson Street to watch the sun set behind the water towers—the sky turning violet, the skyscrapers downtown il-luminating like an inverse sort of dawn. As Bert knitted his fingers through mine and kissed me hotly on the neck, however, I couldn't help it: My glance swung east toward Brooklyn, my thoughts careening into the traffic toward where I imagined the freezers being installed in the new Candie Ice Cream factory across the river.

Bert was now a full-time mechanic. Me, I had managed to get beadwork at a dress factory on Norfolk Street, in a large room crammed with girls, penned in by grubby, opaque windows. We had enough to get by, and our lives as newlyweds had a haiku-like poetry to them. Moving pictures at the Lyceum on Saturday nights. Cracker Jacks and orangeade by the carousel. Once a cus-tomer of Bert's gave us tickets for a Broadway show, *Grand Street Follies*. Me, stirring bean soup on the stove top in the evenings, reading aloud from the *Tribune* to Bert, a single bulb casting haunted, coppery light across the floorboards of our tiny apart-ment. I suppose it should have been enough.

Yet each time I passed a drugstore on Broadway with cardboard cutouts of banana splits and ice cream sodas taped to its front window, I could not resist ducking inside. "Excuse me," I would say, shuffling up to the counter. "But what brand of ice cream do you serve?"

Behind the spigots was invariably some boy with an insistent Adam's apple or an overbite. If he said Swankee's or Schrafft's or "someplace out in New Jersey, I think," a rocket of triumph ignited within me. But if he said, "It's Candie Ice Cream," my stomach dropped down into itself like it was falling through a trapdoor. "Oh, really," I'd say loudly, eyeing the customers seated within earshot, digging their spoons into their parfait glasses. "I hear that Candie Ice Cream has had trouble with spoilage lately. Rancid milk. Bugs in the ice cream. That sort of thing. Have you had any complaints here yet?"

The Candie Ice Cream Company had designed a little logo, their name spelled out with a red-and-white peppermint swirl in the center of the *C* in "Candie." Every time I saw it on a sign in a window, I arrived back home at Thompson Street in a vicious state, slamming the drawers in the kitchenette, raising a ruckus with the pots and pans as I cooked dinner.

"You mustn't go into the ice cream parlors anymore, Lil." Bert sighed, rubbing my leg. "Looking backward, it won't do any good."

The fact that my new husband did not share in my outrage only increased my fury.

That terrible afternoon when the Dinello boys discarded me, Bert had sat beside me on our bed, stroking my arm up and down with the back of his hand.

"Well," he said unhappily, "that's the corruption of capitalism for you."

"That's it?" I cried sharply. "That's your response?"

He fumbled, his face reddening. "I-I-I-I'm sorry. I don't know what else to do, Lil. I expected more from Rocco. I thought he was our friend. But people are sometimes like that."

He touched his hand to my cheek. "You're the smartest gal I've ever met. With you I don't worry. We'll manage."

Still. Every day, as I sewed bugle beads onto appliqués, I repeated a prayer in my head the way I had once recited my Hail Marys: *Please let the Dinello boys get what's coming to them. Please make them fail. Please unleash something monumental to destroy them.*

So sue me: My prayer was answered. The only problem, however, was that it nearly destroyed Bert and me as well, along with the rest of the nation.

By 1932, 1 million people in New York City were unemployed out of a workforce of 3.2 million. You do the math. And over the next couple of years, it only grew worse. People were starving, darlings. Not just us immigrants. The men in the breadlines along Broadway were dressed in the elegant ties and vests that my neighbors had stitched in sweatshops for Wanamaker's and Gimbels just a few years earlier.

And all those ice cream parlors that once concocted "Jubilee Sundaes" and "Lindy Cones" for Charles Lindbergh? One by one they soaped up their windows. Once Prohibition ended, it destroyed much of what was left of the ice cream industry. Soda fountains reverted back to taverns and bars. If people had an extra nickel in their pocket, they preferred to ease their troubles with a whiskey rather than an ice cream cone. I can't say I blamed them.

I stopped seeing the Candie Ice Cream logo around much at all. Three, four, five weeks passed without a single sighting. One day, passing one of the few ice cream parlors left on Sixth

Avenue, I could not help myself. Stepping inside, I asked the proprietor, "You don't happen to serve Candie Ice Cream here, do you?"

The man shook his head. "Nah," he said, twisting a rag out over the sink. "Schrafft's."

"Not Candie?" I said. "Their quality is no good?"

He shrugged. "No good? They're just not around anymore."

Given all the troubles in the world, darlings, you might think it was undignified to gloat. Yet that evening when Bert came home, he found a cup of Schrafft's chocolate ice cream waiting in the tiny icebox down the hall for the two of us to share.

"What is this for?" he said.

I grinned. "I just felt like something sweet tonight," I said.

With the Dinellos vanquished and Bert in my arms, I should have felt content. Yet by now we were simply too hungry. In the spring of 1934, Bert's garage shut down, and I was out of work myself. One wretched evening we dined on a small, greasy fish Bert caught in the East River using a fishing line I had shoplifted from a five-and-dime. "You know, doll," Bert said, dabbing one of the fine bones onto the side of his plate after he'd sucked off the last bit of flesh from it. "The landlord tells me there are apples growing upstate. Potatoes on Long Island. You think we should take to the road?"

From the garages and junkyards, he'd learned that a bakery was going bankrupt, selling off its trucks. And then, of course, it became inevitable. We would need something to sell, after all, as we moved from town to town.

By then, darlings, I fairly hated ice cream. I would have been happy never to see it again in my life. Yet it was portable. It was what I knew. And, frankly, the idea of making ice cream again when the Dinello boys had failed at it? It added a delicious, irresistible sting to the plan.

Ice cream shops were auctioning off their batch freezers, their old cases of gelatin and flavorings for nearly nothing. All Bert and I needed was seed money.

"We can sell my wedding ring," I said.

Bert "invested" this bit of cash the only way he knew how—at craps games underneath the Manhattan Bridge, in primeval cellars in Chinatown. Men. Even in the hardest of times, they will always find enough money for what I call "the three B's": betting, bosoms, and booze.

Bert doubled, then tripled our money.

"Do we really need a table?" he said laughingly one evening, glancing around our spartan little room—with its warped floorboards and leaky faucet—for something else to sell.

"No," I said. "We can be like the ancient Romans and eat on the bed."

The two chairs, a small vase, our books, our mirror—anything we hadn't sold for food already, he pawned.

One rainy night it was nearly dawn when Bert finally burst in. "Lil!" he cried. He no longer had his coat. A sense of foreboding broke over me. Yet he set a large leather case on the bed, then picked me up and spun me around.

"You won?" I cried. "How much did we get?"

"Not money. Something even better."

Unlatching the case, he revealed two luxurious rectangular trays striated with tiny disks. Wristwatches. Swiss made, on polished alligator bands with gold buckles, their casings gleaming gold and silver in the dim light from the window, their faces as white and fine as porcelain.

"We're going to make a fortune with these, Lil. They even told me the name of a big-time dealer on Rector Street who would take them!"

"Where on earth—"

"I was down, Lil, eighty, eighty-five dollars—I had to give up my coat at one point. Oh, doll, I didn't know how I was going to come home to you. But just when I thought I was going to lose it all, a guy shows up late to the game. His brother-in-law, he says, is a longshoreman down at the docks, and though he doesn't have enough cash to see us, he has a few of these cases that just happened, he says, to fall off a pallet while some cargo was being unloaded."

I looked down at the velvet trays before me. There were sixteen watches in total, each meticulously strapped to the lining by two little velvet strips with snaps on the ends. Carefully, I unfastened one. It was elegantly crafted, scarcely bigger than a half-dollar, the metal cool and weighty in my hand. A watch like this, I imagined, could sell for perhaps twenty or twenty-five dollars.

"Bert!" I cried as I wound it. I wanted to set every single one ticking at once in a chorus of victory. "Do you understand that we may have three or four hundred dollars here?"

"I know! I know, Lil! My hands were shaking so hard, but I just blew on the dice and rolled them!"

I held the watch to my ear. "Shush." I smiled, putting my finger to my lips. "I want to hear what money sounds like. Go stand in the corner," I ordered, laughing.

Fine watches, I'd been told, were like rich people themselves: You could barely discern them working. Yet even when I put the watch directly on my ear, I heard nothing.

Bert saw me frown. He picked up another watch to wind it, and the back fell off. And that's when we saw what he'd really won. Sixteen empty watch cases. Not so much as a gear or a spring inside them.

Every cent we had in the world was gone.

We looked at each other, then at the case full of junk. I should have been furious. I suppose I was. I recall the sensation of my legs buckling. But the world before me suddenly got very clear, like the mirrored face of a pond after all the ripples have subsided; I could see across and through to the bottom, to what needed to be done. It was not a terrible thing, really, just a passing on from hand to hand, being a go-between. Since the scam did not originate with us, I told myself, we could not truly be held responsible. We could always profess that we ourselves did not know.

"That's it," I told Bert. "We've done it your way. Now we're doing it mine."

As I knew from my days back on Orchard Street with Flora, it was always best to rehearse first.

Bert was miserable, opposed to the plan. "It's just not right, Lil," he kept saying.

"Do you know what is not right? That guy who took you for a chump with these watches. And that you didn't have the good sense to examine them first. We are not going to starve because he's a *gonif* and you're a *shmendrik*."

I sang him his lines. Dutifully, he sang them back. Over and over again.

Then, for the entire week, I refused to let him shave.

The man on Rector Street had an office in the back of a storefront. A handwritten card taped to the door read simply E. LAZARRE. PAWN/BUY/SELL/JEWELRY/CASH/IMPORTS. E. Lazarre, I realized, was known throughout the Lower East Side for his willingness to loan money to almost anyone, anytime, at exorbitant rates. He was not someone to be trifled with. Rumor had it, in fact, that he'd once amputated a man's thumbs with a cigar cutter. Yet, as we stood before his lair, what choice did we have?

Bert and I had arrived late on Friday afternoon, when I'd

hoped the pawnbroker would be tired and the light would be dim. I was right on both counts. The man in the dusty shop was slow-moving and wet-eyed, surrounded by mountains of relinquished heirlooms, musical instruments, rifles, even a silver tea service. The loot was stacked so high it appeared ready to topple over. Bert stepped timidly into the cramped office with all his charm and anxiety. "Are y-you Mr. Lazarre?" he said. The tremor in his voice lent him a marvelous air of unexpected innocence. We had recently arrived from Europe, Bert stammered to the man; his uncle back in Vienna had given him some watches to sell to help launch us in America. He had been told that "a Mr. E. Lazarre" could possibly help him get a good price?

I opened the heavy case, flashing the watches polished to a rich, oily sheen. Mr. Lazarre had the same initial reaction that we did. Dazzled by the contents and their luxurious packaging, he took out one of the watches and held it, reveling in the weight of it, the feel of it in his chubby hand. My pulse beat furiously.

"We are so sorry to disturb you with this," I added. "But we did not know where else to go, and a man on the street—"

I could see Lazarre's left eye twitch as he assessed us, concluded that we were bumpkins, and rapidly calculated how to best exploit this. Without even bothering to wind the watches, he announced, "These are not bad. But it's hard times here, you know." He shook his fleshy head. "I'm sorry. There is not a big market for wristwatches right now." He made a great point of sighing and tsking and putting the watch back down and arranging his face into a look of helplessness.

Bert, he gave Mr. Lazarre his best man-to-man hapless nod. "I-I understand, sir," he said. "We will try elsewhere."

Me, I let my eyes tear up on cue, just as I had all those years ago with the pushcarts.

"You can't help us at all?" I said woefully.

Lazarre's eyes glinted with both panic and greed as Bert reached for the case. "Look..." He sighed with exaggerated reluctance. "I hate to see newcomers in a predicament. I can pay fourteen, maybe fifteen dollars apiece. But no more. Purely as a favor to you, of course. A sort of welcome-to-America gift."

Bert looked at him with resignation. "I see. My uncle, he told me he b-believed they were worth twenty-five or thirty."

The man frowned, turned the watch over. All the air went out of the room. "Swiss," he said, reading the mark. "I'd like to help you if I can. But as I said..." He sighed again, with great, exaggerated effort. "Eighteen apiece, perhaps, if they're in good working order, of course."

Almost absentmindedly, his chubby fingers moved to the side of the watch to wind it.

That's when my leg buckled and I tumbled to the floor. "Oh, my! Oh, my!" I screamed in agony.

"Oh, n-n-n-ooo!" Bert exclaimed. "Oh, dear. Your leg. I'm sorry. We better go," he told the man. "My w-wife is in a—"

"No!" I groaned. "Please. I can't walk anymore today. Just take the money. Or not. Just—I need to lie down." I continued moaning most unpleasantly. Mr. Lazarre came around the counter. Together he and Bert helped me to my feet. "Thank you," I gasped. "Please. Can we go?"

Not wanting to see such a bargain hobble out the door, Mr. Lazarre said hurriedly, "Wait. I'll only be a minute." In his haste he took the wrong key for the safe and had to double back.

"D-d-doll, are you sure you're okay?" Bert said worriedly. "We don't have to do this now."

"Oooh," I moaned. "I think it's my calf. Can we find a taxi?"

"Here you go," Mr. Lazarre said quickly, huffing back to the counter. "Two hundred eighty-eight dollars." Each bill he counted out was like the pluck of a harp.

Bert snatched up the money as I collapsed against him. "Thank you so much," he said, grabbing me under the armpit and hustling me out the door.

Back in the street, he did in fact hail a taxi. For the entire ride back up to Thompson Street, as the world jiggled by, neither of us said a word. We just sat there, staring straight ahead, panting.

Now we really did need to leave New York—and quickly.

Yet our business, it was launched.

Yonkers, Tarrytown, Peekskill. Bert drove while my fingers smudged the Sears map, our preposterous truck rattling through towns as we surveyed the landscape, looking for children, for playgrounds, for country clubs—anyplace with picnic tables where people might have a nickel to spare for an ice cream cone. The evenings when we could, we rented a room in a boardinghouse. Yet mostly we slept on the floor of the truck in a bedroll, the doors flung open, or on a blanket on the hard ground outside, mosquitoes and fireflies hovering about us in the viscous summer air. Our necks and backs crimped, our muscles felt like tourniquets from hoisting cases of milk, hauling tubs of ice cream to the little window at the side of the Divco truck, scooping and standing and scrubbing from morning until sunset.

Chappaqua, Katonah, Brewster. From town to town we lurched, playing our tinny music box, the two of us bellowing, "Ice cream! Ice cream! Homemade ice cream! Sweet and cold! Delicious and nutritious!" out the windows like opera, like the traveling circus we had become, our cheeriness masking our desperation. In each county we had to suss out where local dairies and suppliers were—and how to purchase just enough milk and cream and sugar and eggs to last us from day to day with little left over or spoilage. Often we survived by eating whatever remained of our inventory at the end of the day.

"At least no one ever has to c-cook," Bert said, chuckling wearily as we sat on the running board with our shoes off and our feet splayed in the dry grass, scraping the dregs from the pails with our spoons. Ice cream for breakfast, ice cream for lunch, ice cream for dinner. We made only three flavors at most. Vanilla and chocolate or strawberry. Me, I was quickly sick of all of them.

Rhinebeck, Poughkeepsie. Albany. Churchyards and picnic grounds. Esso stations. As we drove upstate, I found myself looking not only for dairies but for sanitariums. We came across two. As we pulled up to the gates, my heart pounded furiously; I made Bert wait in the car. *Would she really be there after all this time? What would she look like? What would I say?*

Yet neither asylum had any record of my mother. "Tillie Bialystoker? No, I'm sorry. No one by that name here that I can see." The disappointment I felt was girdled by a peculiar sense of relief.

Come autumn, we headed south. Somehow Bert maneuvered that Divco bakery truck all the way down to Virginia, through the Carolinas, the roads barely paved. We were in rural America now, and in our hunger and fatigue it materialized before us like a hallucination. Who'd ever seen tobacco fields before? Shanties crammed with families who looked as parched and eroded as the land. Stained tents flapping in the hot wind. Desiccated trees. Bone-jutting children in the road. Weary men who'd walked from as far away as the Allegheny Mountains looking for work. Our voices and even our gestures set us apart. Still, the dairymen and grocers were grateful for our business. And everyone likes ice cream. Only three cents a cone we charged.

Bert and I, we did not starve. Our truck, with the ice cream freezer that Bert had hooked up to the engine—miraculously, it continued to work. Each day we had just enough power. Each day we manufactured just enough ice cream. Sometimes only vanilla. Yet always enough to keep us fed during the worst of the Great Depression.

That is, until the morning we careened into the fire hydrant in Bellmore, Long Island.

∞

By the time Bert figured out a way to jerry-rig extension cords from the freezers to the generator to the main electrical outlet in the Corwins' shop, the other drivers had returned to their cars. They started their engines and slowly moved out from Bellmore in a solemn procession. The yellow Nash roadster. The Hudson. Two Model-T's. A few of the children waved as they passed, dust kicking up in their wake.

A sense of desolation set in. We were stranded in a hamlet on the edge of a marshland. A lone car would appear on the road and wobble past without stopping. It was well after one o'clock in the afternoon. Only the generator chugged on the sidewalk, making a racket. Donald stabbed a large beach umbrella into the grass beside it to keep off the sun.

"Got some tools and junk in the back," he told Bert, pointing to a crawl space under the porch. "Might as well have a look."

While the men poked around for something for repairs, Doris and I cleaned up the inside of the truck.

"Anything in here you can salvage?" she said.

The gallons in our freezer shimmered in liquidy circles like tubs of pastel paints. All of our ice cream had melted. The freezer, it had simply been turned back on too late.

"It's going to take awhile for the ice cream to recongeal. *If* it freezes again," I said with despair. "It's likely all ruined."

"Well?" Doris glanced around helplessly. "Can't you just put it back in this ice cream maker of yours?" She rapped on the casing of the vertical batch freezer. "Now that you've got electricity. Can't you just pour in all the melted stuff and refreeze it?"

It seemed dubious, yet I supposed we could try. "Why not?" I gave a bitter laugh. "We have nothing left to lose. You don't mind?"

Bending over the storage freezer, Doris lifted out the tub of melted strawberry with a grunt. "Heck, anything not to spend another minute staring at Donald's doodads." She laughed. "I'd drive off in this contraption myself if I could."

After we ran the melted ice cream through the machine again, I dipped a spoon in. This twice-frozen strawberry ice cream was not only still edible but unusually silky, closer to the gelato the Dinellos and I used to make back on Mulberry Street with the hand crank. "Tell me what you think." I gave a spoonful to Doris.

"Mmm." She nodded agreeably. "I don't think anyone will be the wiser."

We had salvaged the ice cream somehow—yet now there were no more customers to be had. Bellmore was deserted. The farm stand selling strawberries and the general store had shut down for the rest of the weekend. It was the Fourth of July, after all. A hot breeze ruffled through the empty fields around us. Nothing but seagulls. The throb of insects.

Just then, however, a lone car passed our truck, slowed, pulled over to the side of the road, and jerked to a stop. A middle-aged woman climbed out and hurried over, her pocketbook jiggling from her forearm, sweat jeweling her hairline.

"I'm so sorry to bother you," she said, "but would you happen to have an extra pint I could buy? My husband left our picnic back in the pantry. And I've got two hungry children—"

"Will cones do?" I said. "I've got a fresh batch of strawberry, made right here."

"You're making ice cream?" she said. "Inside the truck? How funny. Cones would be fine. Cones would be better. Do you have four?"

Doris scooped out two and stepped down onto the road. "I'll bring these over for you, ma'am."

"Oh, my word. What do I owe you?"

The woman's car was a voluptuous new Pierce-Arrow, gleaming in the sun like claret.

"They're seven cents apiece," I said.

Without blinking, the woman counted out the coins and thanked me profusely. I handed her the second pair of cones. One of them was already starting to drip; she licked it hungrily. She paused, holding the ice cream in her mouth without swallowing, her eyes half closed. She seemed to be considering it. For an instant my heart kicked. Perhaps it was spoiled after all. Yet the woman swallowed and came back to life. "Mm!" she exhaled. "Pure heaven. And so creamy!"

As she hurried back to her car, I heard her exclaim as she handed over the cones, "Right here on the roadside!"

I exhaled, puddled with relief. Then, as if it had been choreographed, another car trundled down Merrick Road. After seeing the giant Neapolitan brick of our truck, this driver stopped, too.

"Excuse me. Would you happen to be selling ice cream?" his date called out from the passenger seat.

As I was pocketing another fourteen cents, another car slowed to a halt. And another. Each car on its way to the beach slowed at the bright spectacle of our truck, the other cars parked haphazardly along the roadside, the families sitting at the shaded picnic tables with their pale pink ice cream cones. They all pulled over, too.

You have to understand, darlings. Back then you could drive for miles without seeing a single place to eat. Highways were new,

empty ribbons of asphalt running through pastures and wood-
lands. Perhaps there would be a gas station at a junction, or a juke
joint, or a luncheonette near a railroad station. Yet a roadside ice
cream stand? It was a novelty.

"Isn't this a hoot?" Doris giggled as we struggled to fill all the
orders. Soon we had to holler for Bert to get a garden hose and
clean out the freezer so that we could run the other melting flavors through it, too.

That Fourth of July, Bert and I sold the rest of our inventory
at seven cents a cone. The Corwins, however? All day long
customers wandered aimlessly through their shop. They pressed
Donald Corwin's seashells to their ears and fondled his ashtrays,
then set them back down indifferently. In the end, all the Corwins
sold was a deck of playing cards and three books of matches.

That evening, when it became clear that our truck would not
be fixed until Monday, Doris prepared us supper and insisted we
spend the night on their back porch. The Corwins lived in a
single room behind their store with a small kitchen on one end
and a lumpy, iron-framed bed pushed against the wall. Everything
smelled of mildew, of the distant, salty sea. "Please. It's no bother
at all," Doris said with an intense smile at Bert. "Heck. I can't remember the last time we had such excitement around here."

After eating a dinner of fried potatoes, we all sat outside. Donald leaned in the doorway, chewing on his pipe. Doris sat on the
steps in her gingham apron, staring out at the darkening marshes.
Bert and I sat side by side on their little wooden porch swing,
gently rocking, our hands clasped on my good thigh. Far in the
distance, a few fireworks exploded over the bay, starbursts of red
and silver. We watched them bloom, then rain glitter down over
the black water. All of us were quiet. Yet everyone was thinking.

By the end of that weekend, we had a deal. As soon as Bert repaired the Divco truck, he painted it silver and handed over the keys to the Corwins. As they set off for Fresno—where Doris had a sister—they stopped to post some signs along the roadside outside Bellmore: DUNKLE'S FAMOUS ICE CREAM STRAIGHT AHEAD! . . . GETTING HUNGRY? DUNKLE'S FAMOUS ICE CREAM IN 5 MIN-UTES! . . . DUNKLE'S FAMOUS ICE CREAM: YOU'RE ALMOST THERE!

The fates had finally begun to smile on us. For what Bert and I had not realized—as we busied ourselves painting the outside of the Corwins' former shack with thick bands of pink, cream, and beige and installing our ice cream maker inside the old souvenir stand—was that not one full week later the Triborough Bridge would open. Spanning both the East and the Harlem Rivers, it linked Manhattan, Queens, and the Bronx for the very first time. And it funneled all their drivers directly onto parkways leading to the beaches of Long Island.

President Roosevelt himself inaugurated the bridge with a mo-torcade. Overnight, sleepy Bellmore was inundated with traffic. Coming from as far away as New Rochelle and Croton, scores of Model-T Fords, Packards, and Hudsons pulled over to gawk at our whimsical shack painted to look like a giant Neapolitan ice cream brick. In the roasting heat, hundreds of families climbed out onto the roadside, stretching and fanning themselves, clamor-ing for our ice cream.

The first Dunkle's Ice Cream shop was born.

Recently, on my television show, I asked the children how ice cream was made. They sat there in their absurd kiddie bell-bottoms and explosive flowered minidresses—with those irritating Lender's Bagel necklaces that our co-sponsor gave them roped around their necks—and answered, "You mix ice with cream?"

How this country put a man on the moon, I'll never know.

"Wrong," I said. "There is no 'ice' in ice cream at all. It's called 'ice cream' because it's *cream* that's frozen."

In fact, the last goddamn thing you ever want in ice cream is *ice* itself. We manufacturers constantly struggle to keep our product from crystallizing. The worst thing in the world is when ice cream develops that rash of frost that makes it gummy and stale.

Here's what we *do* want in ice cream, though, which nobody ever seems to grasp:

Air.

Whenever you make ice cream, you have to freeze the ingredients while whipping them full of air at the very same time. Air is the secret ingredient—just as it is in meringue or chocolate mousse. Air is what gives ice cream its butter-cloud consistency, its magical texture.

It's also—why be coy?—what creates our profit margin. The more air you can whip into ice cream, the more you can stretch your other ingredients. We manufacturers call this final, whipped-up ratio of ingredients-to-air "overrun." Too little overrun and your ice cream is dense and gluey. Too much and it's as insubstantial as a soufflé. The challenge is to pump as much air into your ice cream as you can without sacrificing its texture, flavor, or richness.

Air. For weeks after we'd arrived in Bellmore, Bert and I, we were haunted by the taste of that wonderfully rich, airy confection we had manufactured by accident when our truck crashed into the fire hydrant. Alone out there in the marshes—without any newspapers or books—my husband, he became fairly obsessed with it. "Lil, there has got to be some way to replicate that ice cream without having to melt it first, then refreeze it," he said.

Using the Corwins' '27 Ford, Bert made several forays to junkyards in Queens and transformed the back porch of our shack

into a machinist's shop. He bought an old, smaller freezer, a set
of bellows, vacuum tubes, motor parts. My husband got so en-
grossed some evenings that he never came to bed. I could hear
him thumping around on the floorboards on his knees, grunt-
ing as he pried apart casings. Fuses blew. Tubing burst. Ice cream
clogged or came out runny. Every minute change that Bert made
to his design, he had me record in a notebook for him like a scientist.

"Almost," he kept saying. "I think with just a few more
adjustments..."

One morning he woke me up at dawn, holding out a small dish
of shiny vanilla and a teaspoon. "Lil." He smiled. "Try it."

Bert's prototype was a thing of beauty, darlings, though it was
unlovely to look at. No bigger than an icebox, it sprouted tubes
and an accordion compressor and had dials strapped to it with
wiring. Yet its small hydraulic pump could swirl out buttery,
heavenly ribbons of soft ice cream directly into a cup or a cone.
It pumped so much air into our ice cream that our profit margin,
I realized quickly, would likely more than double.

Although the ice cream formula itself had to be recalibrated—it
required more stabilizers and corn syrup in place of cane sugar,
I discovered—it ultimately saved us so much time and hassle. It
could be stored in bottles in our icebox, then poured directly into
the machine as needed. Bert's invention: Oh, it was miraculous!
All weekend long we tried it out on our customers. "Here," we
said, handing them first a spoonful of vanilla ice cream made from
our traditional freezer, then one from Bert's. "Why, that second
one's even better," they agreed.

"It's like frozen velvet," one woman proclaimed. "It doesn't
burn your mouth with cold."

Yet, having watched the Cannolettis steal my ice cream flavor ideas for years, I knew better by then. As soon as Bert

and I had streamlined his machine and perfected its "secret soft ice cream formula," we drove to Manhattan and hired a patent lawyer.

Dunkle's Famous Soft Ice Cream. In chocolate and vanilla. Word spread from car to car, town to town. People drove for miles to taste it.

After we closed up for the evening, I poured all the change from our cash register into a milk pail. Scooping up handfuls of coins, I let the copper and nickel rain through my fingers in a triumphant, metallic clatter. Giggling like a child, I pressed two dimes to my forehead and let them stick to my damp skin like jewelry. "Bert! Look!" *If those Dinellos could see me now. And Mama,* I thought. Married. To a dashing, inventive man no less. With our very own ice cream business. And two patents pending. Me. The useless little *meeskite* with the limp.

Before we went to sleep, I tiptoed over to the curtain that separated our bed from the storefront and peeked like a naughty, excited child at my own darkened shop—*our* shop—with its cold cabinet and the little bell over the door and the brand-new drive-up window Bert had cut into the side wall so we could serve customers directly in their cars. The fresh paint filling the air with a chemical tang. I ran my hands over the cool metal chassis of Bert's soft ice cream machine just as I had the continuous-batch freezer at the Dinellos'. I opened the icebox and peeked at the little white ceramic dish of butter cooling inside, and the sliced chicken left over from supper: Food to spare, we had! And on the bottom shelf? A dozen milk bottles filled with our "secret" ice cream formula. Six brown, six white, lined up like rows of toy soldiers.

A delicate sea breeze washed through the rooms. For the first time in my life, I slept in a real bed in perfect quiet and solitude. No neighbors or rude, galumphing boarders, no relentless street noise and clatter. Why, for the first time in my life, I even had a private toilet!

Yet I suppose that such peace, it never lasts for long.

Drawing me to him one night, cupping my breasts beneath my nightgown, Bert whispered, "Lil? What do you think? Should we finally make a baby?"

I twisted around to face him. We were so close it felt as if our eyelashes were touching. Blinking rapidly, I ran my finger along the fine mantel of his cheek. "A baby?" I said. I arranged my face into my most adoring and supplicating smile, but my heart, darlings, grew instantly sick. For years I had been using the pessary I had gotten at the Mother's Clinic after our wedding. A baby? How on earth could I handle a baby? Why, a pregnancy alone could tear you to pieces. Babies split you open like a fruit, sent your innards gushing out of you. My mother had nearly bled to death giving birth to me. As a child in Vishnev, I had seen for myself the muddy stains burned into the mattress. And Mr. Lefkowitz's wife, she *had* died in childbirth. Plenty did. It was not uncommon then. And even if you survived bearing it, a baby could suck all the life out of you; every day on Mulberry Street, I saw women decimated with exhaustion and worry, their shoulders, faces, and bosoms collapsing from the never-ending burdens of diapers and colic and wailing and *need*. Children pummeled you, wore you out like fabric. Many of the women on the Lower East Side—unless they were Catholics—they were as relieved and grateful for a pessary as I was. Besides, how could I possibly run our business with both a child and my leg? I was not like other women, after all. Some days, when my joints ached, I needed Bert's help simply to fasten my shoes.

Delicately, Bert's fingertips traced my hip bones, then slowly made their way down. "Wouldn't it be so nice to have a little one?" he whispered. He placed his hand between my legs. "Did you take care already?"

A husband, he could divorce his wife for refusing him children. Had I not gotten down on my knees before the altar at the Most Precious Blood Church and prayed for Bert Dunkle to love me? What sort of a monster was I? Why did I not desire what every woman was born and destined to do? Bringing Bert's palm to my lips, I kissed it miserably. "No," I lied. *God forgive me,* I thought. "I didn't put my pessary in."

But the worst, it was yet to come. In the spring of 1937, Bert and I drove to the city for an appointment at the Niff-Tee Arctic Freezer Company. Bert's patented Prest-O Soft Serve ice cream machine was wondrous, yet too expensive to manufacture ourselves. And so we'd brokered a deal.

While the president of Niff-Tee ushered Bert into his office, I was shown to a seat on the edge of the sales floor and handed an old copy of *Collier's.* All around me were posters for the newest models of Niff-Tee Arctic ice cream freezers. They looked like fantastical rocket ships. Chrome submarines. Weaponry.

When you are crippled, nobody engages you in chitchat, darlings. Nobody says, "Nice weather we're having," or "How about those Yankees?" Their eyes flit over your twisted leg, your mangled arm, your wheelchair. Then they stop seeing you at all. The salesmen at Niff-Tee went about their business without so much as a nod. One of them, seated directly in front of me, lit up a cigarette and sorted through a stack of catalogs as if I weren't even three feet away.

"You could be polite and offer me a cigarette," I said loudly. "It's only my leg that's damaged, you know. Not my brain or my personality."

His face reddened. "Oh, I'm so sorry," he said awkwardly. "I simply didn't see you there, Miss—"

"Missus. Dunkle. My husband is meeting with your boss."

"Oh! I'm so sorry. Forgive me." Scrambling to his feet, he came around his desk and proffered a slim brass cigarette case.

"No. No, thank you." I waved him away. "I don't smoke. It ruins your taste buds."

"Well." He forced a smile. "If your husband is considering purchasing a Niff-Tee Arctic freezer, I can tell you that they are top of the line. No doubt about it. Sold five of them already this week alone. Two to Schrafft's, one to Muldoon's, two to Candie. So you're in good company."

I suddenly felt as if I'd been slapped. "Excuse me?" I said. "Candie?"

"Over on Flushing Avenue?"

"Oh, no. No," I said. "The Candie Ice Cream Company went out of business three or four years ago."

"Where did you hear that?" The salesman waved away a milky plume of smoke and stared after a secretary, her backside twitching as she rolled a file cart past his desk. "They've been one of our steadiest customers for ages."

When we got to the address that the salesman had scribbled out for me, I ordered Bert to stop. Sitting on a wide lot right there on the waterfront was a large brick loaf of a building with CANDIE ICE CREAM CO. painted across the top in red block letters. Its trademark peppermint swirl seemed to spin like a pinwheel. Rows of casement windows glinted in the sun. Gulls from the river circled lazily above it in a halo. Bert and I sat side by side in our little dented truck, staring up at it. The Candie Company's factory had the heft and monumentality of an institution. As if in response to our presence, one of the metal garage doors rumbled up just then and a large white refrigerator truck thundered past, kicking up dust, the peppermint-swirl logo bright on its side.

"Well." Bert let out a long, hapless breath. His hands were limp at his sides. "I guess they've done okay for themselves after all."

Me, I felt as if I'd been kicked. The Dinellos' physical presence was palpable; it was as if their greedy heartbeats inside were radiating out through the building and synchronizing with my own, their breath as warm and moist and audible as Rocco's had been those nights when he'd curled up beside me and cried as a boy. Beyond the frosted panes, I imagined Vittorio sitting smugly behind his desk in his shirtsleeves and a pin-striped vest, Rocco grinning beside him, mentholated with aftershave, telling his crude jokes, the two of them passing around a box of cigars to the Cannolettis in their slick, manly, thuggish way.

Bert turned to me. "Do you ever miss them?"

"What?" The violence of my cry surprised us both. "How can you even ask that?"

He shrugged. "They were your brothers." He added, "In a way."

Twisting the key in the ignition, he started the engine.

As Bert steered the Ford down Sunrise Highway that afternoon—it was now clogged with cars and bulldozers and dump trucks belching exhaust fumes—I stared out the window and felt my wrath and humiliation spread over the landscape like tentacles. How naïve and foolish I had been! Taking the word of a single soda jerk on Sixth Avenue. All this time Bert and I had been crisscrossing the country, breaking our backs, barely getting by, living on ice cream dregs, and serving up two flavors in a road-side shack in a backwater, the Dinellos and the Cannolettis had been thriving in Brooklyn. Building an empire, it seemed.

One day Bert and I, why, we would run their horrid Candie

Ice Cream Company right into the ground, I vowed. Suddenly I could not imagine ever wanting anything else but this: our triumph, their utter destruction.

The problem, however, was *how*. Bellmore was a town of less than a hundred. We had only a few local boys willing to work the drive-up window in the summer. Most evenings, Bert and I, we were so exhausted, we just flopped into the Corwins' old armchairs and drank a cocktail and ate bread and butter for dinner, listening to the radio in a stupor.

I stared miserably out at the highway. After crossing the Triborough, our truck had come to a standstill. Dozens of workers to one side of us were slathering molten tar over lanes of gravel with long-handled brooms. *Bert should have gone into construction instead*, I thought. Building bridges and parkways: That was where all the money was now.

Then it dawned on me.

Roads.

In a few years, according to the newspapers, Long Island would be striated with highways. The government, it had big plans. Well, what better place to sell ice cream than on routes leading directly to the beaches? The smartest pushcart peddlers on the Lower East Side had always gotten to Orchard Street before dawn—to claim the best locations for themselves before anyone else snapped them up. Bert and I, why, we could do the same.

If we could secure plots of land along the parkways before they were even completed, we could put a Dunkle's Famous Soft Ice Cream stand on every major road on Long Island. And we would not have to run all these shops ourselves. Just as Mr. Dinello had done with his Italian ices as a *padrone*, we could have other people sell our product for us. "Dunkle's," after all, was becoming synonymous with "soft ice cream" in our part of Long Island. It was popular. And unique.

We could "license" other people to sell Dunkle's from stands bearing our name. Since it had already proved so arresting, each of these stands could sport our distinctive look—with three "flavor" stripes. Each store owner would buy Bert's exclusive, patented Prest-O Soft Serve ice cream freezer and our secret ice cream formula directly from us. Making the ice cream would be so easy for them—they would never have to fuss with gathering or mixing any ingredients themselves—and the quality of our ice cream would be uniform and ensured. No matter where they stopped, Dunkle's customers would always get the same, delicious-tasting soft ice cream. And Bert and I, of course, would make a profit on every machine and every bottle of ice cream mix sold. It was a win-win proposition for everyone. And with all the immigrants scrambling to flee the turmoil in Europe right now? Surely they would jump at a chance to own their own American ice cream stand. Perhaps Bert could meet them himself, right off the boat.

No one, darlings, had ever thought of franchising like this before.

I finally saw how we could trump the Dinellos. The more ice cream stores that were a part of our system, using our patented machines and our patented recipes—the fewer venues there would be for the Candie Company to sell to. Our ice cream could spread across the entire state of New York simply by following the roads. One day Rocco, Pasquale, and Vittorio would go for a drive and all they would see along every parkway, at every junction, on every billboard would be DUNKLE'S, DUNKLE'S, DUNKLE'S. Our name. Our ice cream. Our inventions. We would be everywhere.

Terrible things were happening in the world by then, of course. So sue me: I became too preoccupied to pay much attention.

While Hitler was banning Jews from universities and swimming pools and Mussolini was ranting about how the proletariat "deserved a bath of blood," I sat up nights wondering, *How could we secure a bank loan to buy plots of land along a roadway that had yet to be built? How could we entice people to become Dunkle's owners?*

The desire for vengeance, darlings, it is like venom in your bloodstream. One drop can quickly take over your entire being. Yet while I dreamed and strategized and plotted tirelessly against the Dinellos, Bert seemed strangely listless. His thoughts, it turned out, were elsewhere, too.

"Oh, Lil," he said one evening, staring down into his glass of rye, "do you ever think that maybe, I should be in Andalusia?"

"Excuse me?"

"Americans are going over, you know."

I gave a sour, hiccuppy laugh. "Are you being a wisenheimer? You're thirty-six years old. You're an ice cream man. What are you going to do? Hurl sundaes at Franco?"

"You read Robeson's speech. 'The artist must elect to fight for freedom or slavery.' Well, why not us, too? I'm still strong. How can we stand by in the face of fascism?"

I stared at my husband; his face was suddenly like one of those Picassos with two eyes on one side of the nose, the mouths bizarrely askew. Sometimes, it seemed as if Bert had dropped into his armchair straight through the roof. His alienness arrived like a meteor. I had not understood this about marriage: how your spouse could invert with a shifting of light and present to you as a complete stranger. Just like that.

"Stop talking crazy," I said. "You want to fight somebody else's war halfway around the world?"

"Not alone, of course, doll. With you." But as soon as he

said this, we both looked at my right foot, soaking in Epsom salts.

I set my drink down. "For God's sake, Bert. We have a business. Two patents pending."

Bert looked about the little room in distress, as if he hoped some ready-made answer might present itself to him. He picked up his drink, then set it back down, then scooted his chair closer to mine and took up my hands in his.

"You remember Jay, from the *Daily Worker*? When I was in the city getting supplies last week, I heard that he's in Barcelona, training with the troops. Yet what I am doing? Just sitting here like some *shmendrik* serving ice cream."

A shiver ran through me.

"You're not a *shmendrik*," I said, as gently as I could. Reaching up, I brushed back the forelock of his hair. "All this nonsense going on—Franco, Hitler, Schmitler. You think we can control that? The best we can hope to do is survive, Bert. And we're doing that. Without anyone's help. And we're building a business. A business you love, that makes people happy. This is something to be proud of. We can't just pack our valises and go fight somebody else's civil war."

"No, no, you're right, doll." Bert shook his head as if to dislodge the thought. He squeezed my hand. "Of course not."

Yet a few weeks later, the postman appeared at our door.

"Got a package for your husband, Mrs. Dunkle," he said. When I unlaced the twine, there, rolled in plain brown paper, was the latest issue of the *Daily Worker*. And a few days after that, an airmail letter followed. From Jay. In Spain.

My grandson thinks that because I've contributed to President Reagan's reelection campaign, I am some sort of right-wing lunatic. "'Ronald Wilson Reagan' is just an anagram for 'Insane Anglo Warlord,' Grandma," he says. "'Trickle-down economics' is just a handout for rich people."

"Oh, really? I've got news for you, *tateleh*. We *are* rich people," I say. "Reagan hates taxes, hates the Soviets, and likes Israel. So what's not to love?"

"I can't believe you're not even pro-choice," Jason says peevishly. "I mean, like, what if I ever get a girl pregnant by accident?"

I slap him playfully on the knee. "Then hurray for me. I'll be a great-grandmother!"

Yet the truth of it is, darlings, I donate to Planned Parenthood and the National Abortion Rights Action League, as well as to the Republican National Committee, thank you very much. Find a politician who thinks exactly the way you do, I tell Jason, and you might as well chop your head off right then and there—because it means you don't have a single original thought left in it.

I am all for women planning their pregnancies. Certainly, if you are in the ice cream industry, you want to avoid having a baby anytime during the high season between April and September. Ideally, you want to conceive around March, give birth around Christmas.

And if you can throw away your pessary and manage to get pregnant just when your husband is thinking of joining the Lincoln Brigade?

Well then.

So much the better.

The night after I burned Jay's letter, my hands became vines, climbing over the muscular wall of Bert's back, creeping over the smooth plates of his chest, sliding along the fine bones of his hips, as hard and sculpted as handles. Slowly, I guided him toward me and found his mouth hungrily with mine. As he pushed up my nightgown, my heart thumped frantically—not from excitement, but from secrecy. And terror. And dread.

Yet I whispered hotly in his ear, "Oh. Bert."

I had scores to settle. And franchises to build. Something simply had to be done.

Chapter 9

I MAGINE A SINGLE REGIMENT of beleaguered men, landing on a tiny island in the middle of the South Pacific. As they stumble onto an empty white scythe of beach, a lone Japanese warplane rips overhead. Yet just as quickly it disappears. The horizon seems to absorb it. Slowly, the U.S. soldiers of the 81st Infantry realize they are alone. Bits of coral crunch beneath them as they trudge up the shore trying to figure out exactly where they are.

When their military surveyors arrive two days later, rowing across a wide turquoise lagoon protected by miles of reef, they realize they have struck gold.

The Japanese have believed that the sheer size of the Pacific will hobble America's war efforts; the distances to refuel are simply too cumbersome. Yet the islet of Ulithi is perfectly situated between Hawaii, Japan, and the Philippines in a tiny archipelago. Its volcanic crags barely poke above the ocean. And the Japanese have relinquished it.

Within a single month in the autumn of 1944, the United States converts this blip into the largest secret naval base in the world.

A port is constructed holding seven hundred vessels. An airstrip is cleared. Floating dry docks repair enormous battleships. An entire water-distillation plant is anchored beside a bakery large enough to grind out thousands of loaves of bread, cakes, and pies daily.

Every day, Ulithi gushes out bullets, boots, K-rations, bayonets, compasses, radio equipment, explosives, helmets, parachutes, industrial lubricants, playing cards, antiaircraft rockets, flashlights, gasoline, chocolate, mosquito repellent, batteries, grenades, and syrettes of morphine tartrate.

And in 1945, still another vessel pulls into the port. It is called simply the "Ice Cream Barge."

The Second World War. You want to know about Kristallnacht and Iwo Jima and the Battle of the Hedgerows? Well, there are books and movies for that. Go take yourself to a library. What *I* can tell you, darlings, is that, with the start of World War II, nearly every nation on earth stopped producing ice cream. Sugar was too scarce. Equipment had to be redirected to the war effort. In Italy, Mussolini banned ice cream simply because he woke up one morning and decided it was "decadent."

Only the United States of America deemed ice cream "an essential item for troop morale." And so it alone continued producing, ordering ice cream freezers on submarines, ice cream freezers on tankers, ice cream freezers on cargo ships. Over the course of the war, the United States military became the largest ice cream manufacturer in history.

This Ice Cream Barge in Ulithi was commissioned to be the world's biggest "floating ice cream parlor." Made of concrete, it did not even have an engine. It was a refrigerated leviathan that had to be towed across the Pacific.

And among its crew of twenty-three soldiers was one civilian who had been given a special dispensation from the Army Corps of Engineers. He alone was in charge of overseeing the enormous ice cream freezer that churned out fifteen thousand gallons of ice cream per day. For the duration of the war, he toiled inside the concrete hull, personally ensuring that the machinery he himself helped to design remained in perfect working order.

This man, of course, was my Bert.

The telephone call came in those frigid first months of 1942. We had twelve Dunkle's franchises by then, though most had shuttered for the winter. That March the sky seemed perpetually shrouded in twilight. Air-raid sirens droned across the city. As soon as the wailing began, New Yorkers were instructed to click off our lights and yank down our window shades, plunging our neighborhoods into darkness, bracing for the evening when German bombers finally succeeded in flying across the Atlantic. Our secretary at the Dunkle's plant, a prim, prune-faced woman named Mrs. Preminger, kept a flask in her drawer for just such occasions.

Now she stood in the doorway in her boxy wool suit. "Mrs. Dunkle," she announced, "there's a man on the line from the War Department."

Bert happened to be out that afternoon training with the Civil Defense Authority. As an air warden, he would have the responsibility during the drills of scrambling up onto the roof and watching for enemy planes.

I took the call at his desk. The man on the phone identified himself as a Mr. Orson Maytree Jr., deputy secretary of the War Procurement Board. "Ma'am, I'm sorry to bother you," he said, "but I was wondering if you might take a few minutes to answer some questions we have about your husband's ice cream formula?"

Isaac was crawling around on the carpet by my chair, revving a toy locomotive along its legs. I signaled to Mrs. Preminger to take my son out into the hallway and shut the door. Cradling the receiver with my right shoulder, I pulled off my pearl clip-on.

Through Bert's office window, I could see out across the East River to the smokestacks of Manhattan. We lived only a few blocks away from our plant in Hunters Point now, yet it felt like we spent our whole lives in the factory.

"What exactly do you need to know?" I tossed my earring onto the desk. "We use only corn syrup as a sweetener, so there should be no problem with exceeding our sugar rations." This man, I assumed, was an inspector of sorts.

"Oh, I'm well aware of that, ma'am," he said. "I happen to have your file from the Patent Office right here in front of me. Frankly, it's impressive. I don't imagine we could have come up with a better set of ingredients ourselves if we tried." He had a deep southern drawl, this Orson Maytree, like warm butterscotch poured over custard. When he spoke, he sounded as if he were leaning back on a veranda with an iced drink in his hand. His sweetness, however, teetered on insincerity; I wondered if he was mocking me.

"To be honest, ma'am, none of us here had ever heard of your ice cream until last Thursday. I was driving back from a ship-yard when I saw one of those big, fancy Dunkle's signs you've got posted on Route One."

Our new billboards were adorned with the Dunkle's logo I had designed myself, thank you very much—of the Statue of Liberty lifting a red-white-and-blue, star-spangled ice cream cone in place of her torch. I had insisted Bert place one on every major high-way in the area.

"Very eye-catching, those billboards, I must say. Very patri-otic," Orson Maytree said. "And they must have worked their magic on me, ma'am, because wouldn't you know? I stopped at the very next Dunkle's I saw, that one up in Stamford, and ordered myself a vanilla cone. The little gal behind the counter, she showed me that system you have, where you just pour the ice cream mix right into the machine. I have to say, I was mightily impressed."

"I see."

"She said, 'It's so simple even a girl can do it.'"

"Well, yes. That's the whole point. You can serve it soft or freeze it again overnight for traditional hard," I said with a tinge of irritation. It was unclear to me exactly where this Mr. Maytree was going with all this. From the reception area, I heard Isaac holler, "No, no! I want it there!" If he threw a tantrum, I'd have to call our domestic and cajole her to come fetch him again, even though it was her day off. Often, it seemed my son was ill-behaved just to spite me.

"We manufacture the machines and the ice cream mixes ourselves, Mr. Maytree," I said brusquely. "All anyone ever has to do is push a button."

"And this magic formula of yours—just how many quarts do you produce a day, Mrs. Dunkle?"

"Excuse me?" Twirling the phone cord around my finger, I stopped. I was about to tell this Mr. Orson Maytree that our production numbers were none of his goddamn business when it hit me: why the deputy secretary of the War Procurement Board was calling, sniffing around like this. *Oh, Lillian*, I thought. *You imbecile.*

"Mr. Maytree. However much ice cream mix our troops need right now," I said quickly, "*that's* how much we can produce."

"Well, well." He chuckled. "Aren't you the clever little saleslady?" Then he exhaled. "Here's the thing, Mrs. Dunkle. Right now we've got 1.5 million troops to feed, and that number is only going to grow exponentially. The Nazis are a vicious foe. The Japs are hardly even human. And the Commies may be our allies now, but not for long, I expect. We have to work quickly."

A million and a half troops. Already I was doing the math. If

Dunkle's provided them with our ice cream formula, why, we'd likely have to supply them with our machines as well. A government contract was almost too marvelous to contemplate.

"My husband and I would be deeply honored to serve our country in any way that we can, Mr. Maytree," I said. "Our ice cream formula is at your disposal for however long you need it. And perhaps you should know, too, that my husband still retains the patents on all his soft serve machines as well."

"Well, that's certainly good to know. Good to know indeed." I heard a light scratching; he wrote something down.

"But here's the thing of it, ma'am," he said, his attention returning. "No one ice cream company in America is large enough to supply us with everything we need. So we're contacting all the biggest we can find. Up in your region, I see, there's Muldoon's. Louis Sherry. Candie. High-Ho. Schrafft's. Yourselves, of course. A few others. The boys here have put together a list. My team and I, we'd like to pay you a visit. Take a look around the facilities. See exactly what we have to work with and who all we might get on board. Maybe invite the others over to see your factory, in fact, if you don't mind."

A sickening feeling took hold within me like dye seeping into fabric. "Other companies," I said.

"Ma'am, it's wartime. It's what I call an all-hands-on-deck situation. From what I hear, High-Ho Ice Cream has a plant right near the shipyards in New Jersey, which could be enormously beneficial. The Candie Ice Cream Company has a big factory right on the waterfront in Brooklyn. Schrafft's has a big outfit up in Boston. I'm telling all of them same as I'm telling you, Mrs. Dunkle. We have to consider every option. We've asked the auto industry to work together, and we certainly hope you folks can do the same."

"I see," I said faintly. "Of course."

"One thing I can assure you, though. Your husband's ice cream formula could prove a godsend. Not having to ship ice cream frozen? Or transport all the ingredients separately?" He let out a low, admiring whistle. "Your husband, Mrs. Dunkle, why, he might be able to do more for the U.S. military than any other ice cream man in history."

The night before the meeting, I sat in our kitchen. I picked up my fork, jabbed a boiled potato, and set it back down. Glenn Miller's "Moonlight Cocktail" played softly on the radio, an antidote to all the bad news broadcast earlier. "I should have known there would be a catch," I said to Bert bitterly. "The thought of those *mamzers* in our factory. In the place that *we* built—"

Try as I might, the Candie Ice Cream Company was still thriving, belching out its ten flavors at its fortress over in Brooklyn. Occasionally I saw grainy photographs of the Dinellos in the *Ice Cream Manufacturers' Gazette*. Or in the business pages of the newspapers. Bert himself had run into Pasquale several times at the Associated Dairies.

"Did that bastard say anything to you?" I pressed afterward.

"It happened too quickly, Lil. Pasquale was coming in, I was going out. He tipped his hat at me. I tipped mine at him. That was all."

I, however, had studiously managed to avoid all of them. Industry events were easy enough to bypass. Often, as just a wife and a cripple, I was not even invited.

Now, however, we'd be ushering the Dinello brothers right into our very own offices, sitting them down at our very own table, showing them our very own machinery. The men who betrayed me, who had cast me out onto the street. Oh, how desperately I wanted to beg the war board to exclude them! Yet what reason could I possibly give? Just that day, thirteen U.S. warships had been sunk off the coast of Indonesia. The first trainload of French Jews had been deported to Germany. Nobody cared a whit about my little personal vendetta. Even I knew: It seemed petty.

"Lil, the way I see this, it's simply wonderful news." Reaching across the tablecloth, Bert stroked the back of my hand. "Uncle Sam wants *us*. Our ice cream. And why shouldn't we join forces with the others? We're at war."

"We certainly are," I said petulantly. I sounded like Isaac. That was the difficulty I had with my son: Too often I looked at him and saw not Bert but my own unlovely, unvarnished self reflected right back at me.

"Lil, the Dinellos are coming to *us*. To our plant, to see our ice cream. Isn't that a victory in and of itself? We're the ones the government is most interested in."

"*You*," I grumbled. "You're the ice cream man."

Bert tilted his head at me with indulgent affection. "Me, you. You, me. What's the difference, doll? *We're* Dunkle's. And we're as big as the Candie Company. I think it's time to lay the past to rest, Lil. There are so many bigger battles now." Bert stroked my forearm. "The Dinellos, Candie—they're not the enemy."

I frowned, got up brusquely, dropped a napkin over my plate, and set it in the icebox with a clatter. But as I stood gripping the sides of the sink, I suspected, in my heart, that my husband was right. We had a child now, and a real business, and the world was on the brink of cataclysm. I should know better, be better. Furthermore, the drive to compete with the Candie Company, it was becoming exhausting. Perhaps the Dinello brothers had grown softer and more generous with age, too, just as their grandparents had. Perhaps a whole new set of possibilities—of alliances—could be born.

Staring at a smudge of rust by the drain, I could not tell, darlings, whether I felt furious or thwarted—or relieved. Or even something strangely akin to hope: All of us, finally, banded together. I took a deep breath, brushed my damp wrist across my forehead, and turned back toward my husband.

When Orson Maytree Jr. and his men arrived, Bert and I had been at the factory two straight days. Bert had meticulously oiled and cleaned every bit of machinery until the entire plant gleamed like a metropolis. While Isaac slept with his stuffed dog and his locomotive on the little couch, we transformed the main office into a conference room. I hung a large American flag across the back wall beside an article we had framed from the *Ice Cream Manufacturers' Gazette*: "DUNKLE'S NEW FORMULA HITS A SWEET SPOT." I even brought in from home a photograph of Isaac dressed as Uncle Sam for Halloween. The Bible that Mrs. Dinello had given me for my confirmation. Bert's new white AIR WARDEN hat and his binoculars. A collection box for the war effort. I positioned all of these props as casually as I could atop our desks, where the war board would be sure to see them. One could never appear too patriotic, too all-American.

As I stood in the doorway smoothing my new dress, I felt as flushed as I had back on Mulberry Street, waiting for Bert to arrive for his tutoring.

"Well, Mrs. Dunkle. Thank you very much indeed for your hospitality," Orson Maytree Jr. said, shaking my hand. He was a large oak tree of a man with the most magnificent dollop of white hair. Although he was dressed in a civilian jacket and tie, the military was evident in his bearing—in his pinned-back shoulders, in the gleam of his belt buckle. His masculine assurance filled our little conference room like aftershave.

He seemed to take no notice of my leg or my cane. "Let me introduce you around. Gentlemen." I smoothed my new dress again and shook hands nervously with each member of the war board, one after the other after the other. "Welcome to Dunkle's." I attempted to smile like Rita Hayworth. "So glad you could come."

Dewey Muldoon arrived, the owner of Muldoon's Ice Cream, dressed foppishly in a bow tie, his forehead glistening with sweat. A representative from Schrafft's had made the trip—I overheard him boast—all the way from Boston. The president of High-Ho Ice Cream shook Bert's hand and tucked a red paper daisy—High-Ho's trademark—crisply into his buttonhole. All the bigwigs of the Northeast's ice cream industry were gathering right there inside our factory with their bluster and gimmicks. I had plucked our prettiest worker, Sonia, off the assembly line and paid her an extra dollar to put on some nylons and Tangee lipstick and circulate among the men with a coffeepot and a tray. Yet none of them helped themselves. The mood in the room was peculiar. We were an elite group summoned together by the War Department like the Knights of the Templar. There was the frisson of having been selected, anointed. Yet also: unease. Were we all compatriots now—or still one another's competition? A lot of money was at stake. The men stood coughing into their fists and smiling uncomfortably, groping for conversation.

Can you believe those Yankees? Trading Holmes for Hassett and Moore?

Well, at least they're letting the soldiers in for free. Five thousand seats is a lotta tickets. That's gotta hurt.

As the room filled, Bert sidled up to me and placed his hand in the small of my back. "Doll," he murmured.

There, in the doorway, stood Rocco Dinello handing his coat and hat over to Sonia. I had seen him, of course, in those blurry newsprint photographs over the years, yet the reality of him was jarring. He was dressed superbly, I saw, in an expensive three-piece suit with a silk pocket square. His thatch of slick hair was nearly pewter now, and the feral boniness of his face had vanished: Both his chin and stomach were girdled with fat. He was not merely stocky but gelatinous. Yet his smug, boyish grin was still intact, glinting out from the bloat of his face, and although he had aged, he carried himself with expansive agility, slapping the other men on the back as he moved through the room, pantomiming brotherly punches and feints, his gold cuff links winking in the light.

My spine went cold. I stood among our guests, feigning attentiveness, a dumb smile glazed on my face. Yet I was aware only of Rocco's animal presence behind me and the friendly commotion he was creating as he made his way through the conference room like a slow-moving tornado. *Dewey! Richard! How's business up in Boston, fellas? Hey, Archibald. Congratulations on the new grandson.* As always, he seemed to know everyone. I felt a strange bolt of anguish and panic and nostalgia all mixed together. What would I possibly say to him? I could not help it. Despite whatever I had told myself back in the kitchen with Bert, my reaction to Rocco, it was chemical.

I swallowed and patted my lips. Perhaps Rocco and I could simply manage to politely ignore each other for the duration of the meeting, conducting an elaborate sort of do-si-do. Perhaps that would be best.

Yet in a flash he was towering before me. "Well, look who we have here. Albert Dunkle. Compadre. Great to see you. Great to see you." He slapped Bert on the shoulder. Stepping back theatrically, he feigned surprise at seeing me, too. "And who is this? Could it possibly be?"

His outsize warmth: I was wholly unprepared for it.

"Rocco Dinello. How do you do?" Gingerly, I held out my hand.

"Please, Horsey." Scowling, he aimed both his thumbs at his chest. "Who do you think you're talking to here?" Spreading his arms wide, he enveloped me in a crushing bear hug. "Been a long time, eh?" As he patted me heartily on the back, he smelled of brilliantine, cotton sheets washed in brown soap mixed with sweet vinegar and onions. It was so familiar, such an intimate scent, so utterly Rocco, that for a moment I felt a stab of heartbreak.

Finally he released me. I wobbled backward. "Uh-uh. Wait. Not so fast." Pulling me toward him again, he planted a fat, wet kiss on each of my cheeks. "That's from the family." I jerked my head, and he got me on the jaw by my ear.

"Ywhahahaha." He laughed his old staccato laugh and shook his head. "Still the same old Horsey, I see."

Righting the front of my dress, I felt myself reddening. "Please, Rocco."

He threw up his hands in mock contrition. "Oh, excuse me," he chortled to the room.

"*Lillian.* I forgot. She doesn't like being called Horsey. She's touchy, this one, eh? Be careful, or she's likely to haul off and break all your windows. Ain't that right, Bert?"

Yet my husband had been roped into shaking hands with a representative from Louis Sherry. Rocco slapped his meaty hand on the nape of my neck and kneaded it. "Ah. I'm just playing here. Just breaking the ice. All in good fun, right?"

Taking a step back, he regarded me as if I were a shipment of goods.

"Well, you're looking no worse for the wear and tear. So where you living these days? You ever get back to the old neighborhood?"

"Just a few blocks from here." I motioned with my chin. I felt almost whiplashed. "Over on Forty-Ninth Avenue. So I can walk to work." My eyes fixed on Rocco's face. I could see the remnants of the boy I'd once known darting just beneath the surface like a silvery fish. Rocco and I were here in my Hunters Point factory all right, yet at the very same instant we were standing on tiptoe in the corner of the schoolyard tossing pebbles through the chain-link fence. Poking each other on the dusty velvet settee in his grandmother's parlor on Easter Sunday. Making paper fans in the kitchen of Dinello & Sons and scrunching them between our lips and our noses like mustaches and giggling.

"Really? People live over here? I thought it was all industrial." Leaning back on his heels, Rocco glanced around the office. "We're out in Dyker Heights ourselves. Big house, of course. Very swanky. Lots of room for the kids. Four sons, I've got. A complete set. My oldest, Sal? Oh, Horsey, you should see this kid with a baseball. I'm telling you. He's going to be the next Babe Ruth. Looks just like my pop, too. The spitting image." He blinked down at his shoes. "May he rest in peace."

I thought of Luigi all those years ago, with his heavy boots and his mud-caked pickax. A shudder ran through me like a wire. *Rocco.* Perhaps we were lucky. We had both been given second chances.

"You?" he said. "You got kids?"

"Just one." We were standing near my desk. I handed him the framed photograph of Isaac. "He just turned four. He wants to be a railroad conductor, he tells me."

"Mm. Looks like you." Rocco nodded. Compared to his, my family suddenly seemed paltry. Rocco set the picture back down and sauntered over to the window overlooking the production floor. He rapped on the glass with his knuckles as if testing its strength. From below came the rapid-fire *thug-thug-thug* of the mixers and the *clack-clack-clack* of the conveyor belt, muted through the glass. Rocco watched as our bottling machine filled each quart with ice cream formula, then capped it with a twist and slapped a label on it before shuttling it down the belt.

"Impressive. Very impressive indeed. I see you've done quite well for yourselves," he said, turning. "Looks like we taught you well, eh?"

"Excuse me?"

Rocco grinned, yet only the corners of his mouth went up; his eyes remained narrow and pinned on me. "Looks like we ended up doing you one big fat favor, *capisce?*"

Orson Maytree clinked his water glass with a spoon. "Gentlemen?"

As the men installed themselves noisily around the table, Maytree leaned forward with his palms splayed out on the knees of his serge slacks. "Now, I'm from Texas, and we like our niceties down there. But as you know, there's a war on. So I hope you won't mind if I dispense with the pleasantries and get right down to the business of defeating the Nazis, the Japs, Mussolini, and making sure those Commies understand we're a force to be reckoned with."

With military efficiency Orson Maytree launched into his spiel, repeating what he had told me over the phone but this time revising the number of troops, the estimated orders, time frames, logistics. "I've had us all meet here today because it's our belief," he said, "that Mr. Dunkle's formula here could save everyone an enormous amount of time, money, and effort."

On cue, my husband poured a quart of vanilla mix into the Prest-O Soft Serve ice cream machine he'd brought up to demonstrate. With the flick of a switch, the freezer started, shuddered, then blurped out a beautiful curlicue of white into a little bowl. Bert filled up one dish, then another. Sonia distributed them around the table to all the men, many of whom eyed her as wolfishly as they did the ice cream.

I was certain that the other manufacturers had tasted Dunkle's before, much as I had made it my business to sample all of theirs. Still, the men bobbed their heads as they ate, nodding with approval. Our ice cream was delicious; they could appreciate the quality. I felt a bolt of pride. However, Rocco, I noticed, did not finish his. He pushed his dish pointedly to the side and sat back in his chair with his arms crossed, staring at Bert's machine.

"As I see it, we can do one of two things," Orson Maytree Jr. concluded as everyone began wiping their mouths and lighting up cigarettes. "We can contract with some of you to supply thousands of gallons to the military each month yourselves. Or—if you're willing instead to manufacture Dunkle's ice cream formula and your factories can be modified to make it—Albert Dunkle here has agreed to license his patent to anyone else contracted as a supplier to the military."

At this, a murmur went around the room. I noticed a bitter little smile flicker in the corners of Rocco's mouth. "Well, that's very generous of you, Bert," he said loudly.

My husband, he simply shrugged. "We're all on the same side now. Anything to defeat our enemies."

"Exactly, my friend. Couldn't agree more," Rocco said, grinning. A sickening feeling came over me.

As the men gathered to collect their coats, Rocco brushed up beside me and said in a low voice, "So your husband is going to let us in on his trade secrets, now, is he?" He shrugged on his heavy wool overcoat, then squinted at me, all pleasantness draining from his face. "You know, some of the fellas here, they're really impressed by that. They think your Bert is quite the altruist." He tugged on one cuff of his overcoat, then another, adjusting them. "But me personally? Frankly, I think it's the least he can do, Horsey. Because I don't know who the hell you think you're kidding." He fixed his gaze on me. "Everything you learned, you learned from us. So now it only seems fair." He slapped me vigorously on the shoulder. "We're going to learn a few things back from you, eh?"

I shot him a vicious look.

"Aw, come now." He grinned. "What's wrong? You lose your sense of humor? Don't you know when I'm teasing? Besides, your husband said it himself. We're all on the same side now."

Grabbing his hat, he pivoted dramatically. "I'd like to thank everybody for coming. Always a pleasure, fellas." Tipping his hat with exaggerated deference toward Bert, he said unctuously, "And I'm particularly looking forward to doing business with you, *Mr. Dunkle*. Very much indeed."

His shoes *slonked* against the metal staircase. In a blur of dark wool, he was gone.

As soon as the room emptied, I felt behind me for my desk chair and sank down onto it. The machines on the production floor had been shut off for lunchtime. The silence of the factory felt sonic. My pulse pounded so hard in my head that my vision began to jiggle. When Bert returned from seeing the men off downstairs, he fairly skipped up the steps two at a time to the office, whistling "A-Tisket, A-Tasket."

"Oh, Lil, I think that went very well. Don't you?" Striding across the room, he ducked beneath the trolley, unplugged the Prest-O machine, and began spooling the cord around his knuckles. "The war board. Everyone. They were very impressed with our facilities, they told me. Even Schrafft's. I think they loved our ice cream, too."

"I believe so," was all I could manage to say.

"Mr. Maytree says we should expect to hear from him imminently. That was the word he used, doll. 'Imminently.'" Bert beamed as he enunciated each syllable clearly. "He advised we speak to our lawyers." As he wheeled the ice cream machine toward the little elevator, he stopped by the desk and planted a generous kiss on the top of my forehead. "Have Mrs. Preminger put this in the book," he said happily, placing Mr. Maytree's card on the desk blotter in front of me. A little gold-embossed eagle glinted in the corner. "He's at the Hotel Pennsylvania until Friday, and it's his hope, he said, to get something approved for us before he even leaves town. I think we should put in a call to Aaron, just in case."

Bert vanished behind the doors of the little elevator. A moment later I could hear the squeak and clatter as he pushed the cart out onto the concrete floor below me. He was so pleased, my husband. I had not seen him so joyous since Isaac was born. It made my heart hurt.

I picked up Orson Maytree's card by its edges, then tossed it carelessly back down onto the blotter. Aaron was our lawyer. I did not want to put in a call to him at all. Though legal safeguards and stipulations and restrictions could of course be written into any contract, in the end what was a piece of paper? Perhaps the other ice cream manufacturers would honor it; perhaps they would prove to be men of valor and decency, guarding our trade secrets even as they employed them. Not Rocco Dinello, though. This much I knew. Why, he himself had said it outright: *Everything you learned, you learned from us. So we're going to learn a few things back from you.* It could not have been any clearer.

As soon as they got their hands on our recipe, the Candie Ice Cream Company, they would concoct their own copycat version of our soft ice cream, tweaking the formula just enough to avoid a lawsuit, offering up their own swirly cones and sundaes and malted milk shakes, branching out into our territory with their own roadside shops and franchises. I was sure of it.

Yet a midsize business like ours, it could not survive the war without supplying the military. Rationing was only going to get worse. Already, Americans were being urged to forgo using rubber and car parts; rumor had it that there would soon be restrictions placed on gasoline, raw materials, metal. Regardless of whether we cut a deal to share our formula with the War Department, the Candie Ice Cream Company would still happily sign on the dotted line. Either way they would win—and we would lose.

Bert and I, we were going to become destitute all over again. And our little boy?

I picked up the framed photo of Isaac dressed as Uncle Sam. His star-spangled top hat was lopsided, made from a cardboard cutout he'd colored in himself with crayons. Mrs. Preminger had attached a tuft of cotton batting to his chin with spirit gum. He was standing solemnly, gazing directly into the camera. It had been his first Halloween.

My son.

From the very first day, everyone else had cooed over Isaac. *Oh, those tiny fingers and toes! That delicious baby smell! Couldn't you just eat him up? Mrs. Dunkle, don't you want to hold him some more?* Bert, he arrived at the hospital cradling a ridiculous bouquet of red roses fattened with baby's breath for me. A box of Prince Hamlet cigars for the doctors. Whitman's chocolates for the nurses. "Congratulations, Mr. Dunkle," the nurses chimed when they saw him, converging suddenly from all areas of the hospital, arraying themselves before him like a row of glossy show ponies. "Your son is so beautiful." They beamed, tucking one foot behind the other, leaning across the reception desk. "He looks just like you, you know. The very spitting image."

I don't know who they thought they were kidding. One look at my son, even as a baby, and you knew: He was mostly his mother's stock.

So sue me. Other mothers will never confess to this—and indeed perhaps I have never been a typical mother at all. Yet that tsunami of ecstatic, obliterating love a mother is supposed to feel for her baby the instant he's placed in her arms? I felt none of it. Oh, darlings. All I experienced was panic. And a terrible, drowning sensation. I tried as best I could to paste a smile across my face as I lay like a gutted whale on the iron-framed hospital bed, incoherent with the twilight sleep of scopolamine, my privates gashed and stitched up like a ripped, throbbing cushion. My whole pregnancy had been a misery; each day felt like I was reliving that voyage I'd made as a child aboard the SS *Amerika*, queasy and dizzy and dread-filled. I was carrying low, and I had my limp and my cane to contend with. All my helplessness, my pregnancy increased it tenfold. I was ungainly and fumbling. My unborn son—how I resented him.

By the time he finally emerged from me and had been placed in the crook of my arm, a tiny, squalling loaf, he knew. My ambivalence. My monstrousness. Even then, in those very first days of his life, he gazed at me with indictment. In all his miniature sinews and synapses, in his fragile fontanel and unformed muscles, he knew instinctively that I had borne him not out of love but desperation—that I had wanted not a baby but a tether for my husband. And so he set about punishing me. Wailing for hours. Refusing my breast. Shrinking from me when I reached out for him as a toddler.

And yet.

Studying the little sepia photo of Isaac now, with his cheeks puffed out and his stuffed dog clutched in his hand, the love I felt was fierce, combative. My difficult, unsmiling little boy: I would be damned if he grew up in the same poverty as I had, if Rocco Dinello in any way torpedoed his future the same way he had mine. My son: *He* would finish college. *He* would not be driven out of a family business. *He* would rightly inherit what Bert and I had wrought.

I glanced frantically around the office for some sort of solution, as if it might appear like our ice cream mix, perfectly formulated, awaiting in a bottle. *Think, Lillian, think.* Yet I could not. I hoisted myself up and paced around the office. Bert was down on the production floor now, talking to our foreman over by the industrial mixers—no doubt telling him how beautifully the visit from the war board had gone, how our future gleamed like polished steel. Mrs. Preminger was on her lunch break. Though I'd never done so before, I opened her bottom drawer, unscrewed the little flask she kept hidden beneath the payroll tablet, and took a quick swig. The whiskey had been watered down; it offered only a sting. Yet the transgression itself brought a sudden bite of clarity: For there, on Bert's desk, where I'd positioned it for the benefit of the war board, I spied the Bible that Mrs. Dinello had given me for my confirmation all those years ago.

A few ruffles peeked out from the edges. In my haste I had not bothered to remove the cherished pressed pansy from the little bouquet at our wedding. Our marriage license. Souvenirs from our first dates.

The idea hit me like a shock wave. Pulling out the paper, I scanned it quickly, my heart thudding. And it was there, just as I had hoped, smack in the middle of the page.

The audacity of what I was about to do made my hands tremble so furiously I almost could not slot my finger into the brass dial of the telephone to connect to the operator and have her put me through to the Hotel Pennsylvania in Manhattan.

When he called me back, Orson Maytree Jr. sounded less surprised than I had imagined. With a war on, I supposed, more and more wives were taking on command roles in their husbands' businesses. After we arranged to meet, I told Bert that I was going to go to Manhattan to pay my dressmaker, then took a streetcar and a subway to Thirty-Fourth Street.

The coffee shop at the Hotel Pennsylvania was overrun with new recruits in khaki pants and military caps creased as crisply as envelopes. The sleek chrome-and-Formica tables gave it the feel of an ocean liner. Except for two ladies seated by the window eating toasted liverwurst sandwiches, I was the only woman in the restaurant. All the other tables had been taken over by soldiers drinking milk and wolfing down pieces of pie. Indeed, there was no place at all to sit. This only increased my nervousness. Then I spied Orson Maytree flagging me across the dining room. He had already installed himself at one of the booths in the corner. In front of him was a plate with a half-finished slice of Boston cream pie. Across from him a slice of apple pie also awaited with a sweating wedge of cheddar cheese and a second glass of milk.

"I hope you do forgive me, Miss Lillian." Rising to his feet, he shook my hand vigorously. "The waitress over there, she told me that there were only a few items left on the whole menu. If I didn't order right away, why, there would be nothing left but toast and marmalade by the time you arrived."

Gallantly, he pulled out my chair for me. He seemed to know instinctively that banquettes were difficult for me to navigate—I always preferred a chair—and the apple pie and the cheese and the milk, I realized, he had ordered not for himself but for me.

"I daresay I took a gamble." Orson Maytree Jr. smiled, working away at his own pie with the side of his fork. "You struck me as more of an apple-pie gal than a Boston-cream-pie one. Am I right?"

"Oh, my. Yes," I said quietly, though the truth was, I had no appetite whatsoever. Orson Maytree's kindness made me feel teary.

My heart was thudding away frantically. At least, I thought, no one would notice me amid this hubbub of soldiers. No one would overhear what I was about to say. I looked at Orson Maytree Jr.

"Pie before business, am I right? I hope you don't mind, Miss Lillian, but all this traveling from plant to plant, meeting with one group of leaders, then another. It's got me tuckered out." He patted his stomach as if it were a pet. "I know I have to be careful. Yet it seems I'm always hungry long before suppertime."

With a few twists of his wrist, he made fast work of the rest of his pie, even scraping the last streaks of custard from the plate, and dabbed at his mouth with his napkin. "Now, then." He looked at me pleasantly. The custardy treat had sated him, infused him with goodwill. He sat back heavily in the banquette.

For a moment I was unsure of how to proceed.

"Mr. Maytree, there's something I think I need to share with you." I looked at him cautiously. "This is delicate. Not even my husband knows. Nor should he *ever*."

I gave Mr. Maytree a concentrated, vehement look. I had his attention now, I saw.

"Normally I wouldn't have said anything. America is a free country, after all. And we're all entitled to believe as we please. But given that we are a nation at war..."

Taking a deep breath, I unsnapped my pocketbook and carefully removed the old, cracked Bible. The binding flaked as I opened it and drew out the petition from the workers' meeting that Bert and I had attended so many years ago in that basement off Delancey Street. Its edges had aged to a biscuit color. Gingerly, I unfolded it and passed it to Orson Maytree.

"What is this?" he said.

With some difficulty I brought my chair around so that I was adjacent to him. I pointed to the *Daily Worker* letterhead with its hammer-and-sickle logo, then to the paragraph typed beneath it, beginning, "Comrades, we, the undersigned, unite," demanding the release of Sacco and Vanzetti.

"A petition," I said. "Issued by the Communist Party of America a few years ago in support of two known Italian anarchist murderers."

As soon as I said this, I could see Orson Maytree's back stiffen. "Oh?" He pushed his empty pie plate across the table with a clatter and unfolded his reading glasses from his breast pocket. As the waitress approached, he waved her away.

"It's not mine," I added quickly. "Back when Bert and I were first courting—" I swallowed. I could feel my face flush. I smiled at Orson Maytree as best I could.

"I had heard a rumor that a new girl in the neighborhood was sweet on my Bert. I did not know her name, only that the boys called her 'Red.' I thought this was on account of her hair. One night when I saw her stepping out, I followed her. I couldn't help it. I was sure she'd be meeting him."

As this story I'd invented unspooled on my tongue, I felt like myself yet not myself. The words felt spontaneous, each one coming to me like one of the little songs I used to invent as a child.

"Instead I tracked her to a basement. She wasn't having a tryst with my Bert, I discovered, but conducting a political meeting," I continued. "She and a young man were addressing everybody as 'comrade' and circulating this petition for the members to sign. As soon as it came around, I tucked it in my coat and ran out. I had no idea what it was. I just wanted to learn the girl's name."

I pointed at the sheet of paper, to a random name. "Violet Bromberger. There. 'Red.' But it honestly wasn't until much later, Mr. Maytree, when I was going through some old papers of mine, that I came across this again. Only then did I see who the young man leading the meeting had been. The one calling everyone 'comrade' and demanding the release of the anarchists."

With my finger I directed Orson Maytree's attention midway down the page to a signature.

"*Rocco Dinello?*" he read aloud.

"The co-owner of the Candie Ice Cream Company," I said grimly. "Who was at the table this morning." As I said this, it felt as if a Roman candle had gone off inside me. "He was the other chief organizer, you see." And in that moment I became so dedicated to my lie that I actually believed it. I remembered Rocco not as he had been all those years ago, leaning disinterestedly against the wall of that awful, mildewed basement off Delancey Street, but standing before the benches of activists, boldly, a prime Communist agitator in dungarees and a work shirt, scorching the walls with his calls for revolutionary justice.

A look of alarm came over Orson Maytree's face. Clicking open the briefcase that sat beside him on the banquette, he riffled through his folder for his list of ice cream manufacturers in the Northeast. He carefully checked the name there against the one on the petition. He had the sign-in sheet from the meeting at our factory that morning, too. He placed the petition I'd given him beside it. The signatures must have proved one and the same, because he looked stricken.

"Now, Mr. Maytree," I said quickly, "when you first mentioned the Candie Company to me, why, I was not even sure Rocco Dinello still owned it. And I believe it is only right that you know that, as fellow ice cream makers, the Candie Ice Cream Company makes a decent enough product, I must say, even if they do cut corners, perhaps, in ways that I myself might not consider ethical. But with all the talk these days about spies and 'the enemies within' and the Red Menace—and with what you said this morning about the Russians not really being our allies—well, I just could not in good conscience let you risk enlisting a Communist—"

"Indeed, ma'am," Orson Maytree declared, "you should not."

"Truth be told, I wasn't even sure if I should give this to you," I said, making a great show of reluctance. "After all, as you yourself said, we Americans are supposed to set our personal differences aside right now and—"

"Oh, no. Ma'am," Orson Maytree said with adamancy, "you did exactly the right thing. This is war, not a garden party." His hands trembled as he continued studying the petition. "You know, out there in California right now, they've got them under curfew."

"The Communists?"

"No. The Italians. I have to tell you, ma'am, when I see things like this—" He shook his head. His face reddened. "If you don't mind," he said, opening his folder, "I'd like to bring this to the attention of Francis Biddle."

"The attorney general?"

"And the War Relocation Authority. And the Dies Committee. You know, Martin—excuse me, Congressman Dies—he's an old, personal friend of mine. Grew up in Beaumont, same as I did. Even went to the same elementary school."

"You don't say?"

"And he knows, as I do, that Commies, anarchists, Italian radicals—they pose a grave threat to us, Mrs. Dunkle. They need to be weeded out and dealt with. They're enemy insurgents."

I looked at Orson Maytree Jr. The violence of his reaction surprised me. Certainly it had not occurred to me that he might take the petition all the way to authorities in Washington. While I did not know what the War Relocation Authority was, I had certainly heard of the Dies Committee before. It was the congressional commission dedicated to hunting down Communists. Would they actually investigate Rocco? I felt an odd mixture of shock and queasiness and glee. My own cleverness astounded me.

Was it really that easy? I had half expected Mr. Maytree to see right through my little ruse—to dismiss it as the desperate gambit that it was. Surely a man like him would not be duped so easily by fear and stereotypes—would he? But I knew the answer already. I'd been born into a town decimated by pogroms, after all. And frankly, while I was surprised by the potency of my own lie, it felt unexpectedly marvelous to be on the other side of the manipulation for once—to be the one fomenting the prejudice instead of its victim.

Struggling to conceal my delight, I said contritely, "Oh, Mr. Maytree. It would have been so easy for us to work with the Candie Ice Cream Company, seeing as they're practically our neighbors."

Then, just as I had on Orchard Street, I made my eyes tear up on cue. "Yet as you said, this is war. And I just want to do what's best for America."

"That's absolutely right, ma'am," Mr. Maytree said, nodding. "I greatly appreciate your honesty." As I dabbed away my tears, he sat back and studied me, seeming to assess me anew. "We need more citizens like you in this country," he said, removing his reading glasses and slipping them into his pocket. "Mrs. Dunkle, I cannot thank you enough for your honesty. And your vigilance."

That Friday, as promised, Bert received a phone call from Orson Maytree. Ten days later he was to come down to Washington to finalize and sign the contracts that Dunkle's was being awarded by the United States government.

"Did he happen to mention if the Dinellos got a contract, too?" I asked as nonchalantly as I could.

Bert shrugged. "All he said was to bring our lawyers."

The morning of Bert's meeting in Washington, I dropped Isaac off at his nursery school and headed over to the factory. I was dressed in my very best green gabardine suit and a hat with a black silk rose pinned to the brim. The wind off the river made everything smell watery. Rising light glinted off the chrome refrigerator trucks. Gulls circled overhead, cawing, heralding the promise of spring.

As I crossed the parking lot, one of our truck drivers called out to me. "Hey, Mrs. Dunkle. Can I ask you something?"

I stopped.

"You wouldn't be looking to hire any more drivers now, would you, ma'am?"

"Excuse me?"

"My buddy over in Brooklyn," he said sheepishly. "A 4-F like me? And with the shutdown?"

I looked at him curiously and hobbled on. No sooner had I switched on the overhead fixture in the office and hung my coat and hat on the hook, however, than the telephone rang.

"Mrs. Dunkle," a familiar voice said over the line. "Artie Flent over at Durkee." Durkee supplied us with over half a dozen flavorings. "I don't suppose you folks have any interest in purchasing an extra eighty-case shipment of vanilla flavoring, do you?"

"Vanilla?"

"Guess you didn't hear the news yet. The Candie Ice Cream Company just went bust. No warning at all. And I'll be damned if their latest order isn't sitting on one of our trucks already halfway up the turnpike. For two days now I've been calling, but no one's answered the phone."

When I hung up, I sat back, stunned. For a moment I did not know what to do with myself. Was it true? Quickly, I dialed our wholesalers, our dairies, even the Chamber of Commerce to see what anyone had heard. All I learned was that the Candie Ice Cream Company had shut down abruptly over the weekend.

"Oddest thing. One week they're producing like gangbusters, the next, suddenly, ka-pow," our paper-cup supplier said. "But I guess if you're not making bullets these days, it's tough going."

Finally, our accounts man over at Niff-Tee told me he'd heard a rumor. "According to my guy at the docks, a bunch of feds just came in and seized the place overnight. Confiscated everything. The entire factory. No real reason at all. Just something about the waterfront being 'strategic.'"

The phone went leaden in my hand. Had that really happened? But it was all so fast. It couldn't possibly be right. I realized I was trembling. I could not tell what I felt: Delight? Nausea? I looked down from the window at our production floor. The workers had not yet arrived in their crisp white kerchiefs and aprons; our assembly line gleamed beneath me like an enormous silver serpent, the industrial refrigerators, ventilators, and compressors hissing and throbbing in unison.

In the parking lot, our last delivery truck was about to depart. Hurriedly, I knocked on the side of the cab. "Drive me to Red Hook," I ordered. This time, I was not going to take anybody else's word for it.

What I would do once I got there—providing the rumors were right—was unclear. Would I stand gloating? Offer my condolences? Tell them in a sugary voice how sorry I was, how much Bert and I had truly been looking forward to working with them? I felt in my pocketbook. I had brought Dunkle's checkbook with me. Why, perhaps I could offer to buy some of their equipment; perhaps that would seem the noble, charitable thing to do. Suddenly, I imagined the workers. Scores of them with their kerchiefs and caps and aprons and lunch pails, with bull's-eyes worn away into the soles of their shoes. Would they be gathered there weeping? Clamoring for their pay? Saying, *Now, how in the world am I going to feed my family?* What the hell would

I do then? What *could* I do then? I simply could not bear to think about this.

When our truck arrived at the waterfront, however, it became clear that I would not need to contemplate any action at all. The gate in front of Candie's lot was padlocked shut. Beyond it, the brick building stood silent, absolutely dark. The garage doors were chained. Wind whipped in from the river, sending a single brown paper bag tumbling end over end across the lot before catching in the swirl of dead leaves and debris from the gutter. The red-and-white peppermint-swirl trademark presided over the abandoned facility like a single rheumy eye.

"Wait," I told the delivery-truck driver.

We sat there in the frigid cab, staring out at the bleak tableau of brick through the windshield. I kept expecting someone to come along eventually—a delivery truck rumbling in, perhaps. Or the Dinellos themselves alighting from a car with brooms and cartons to clean out their offices. For an instant, at the far end of the parking lot, I saw a solitary man in a tattered coat, keeled over on the pavement. I rolled down the window. "Sir?" I called out. But the wind blew violently, and he disintegrated; indeed, he appeared to have been only a trick of the shadows. After nearly an hour, nothing more stirred.

Was it all a big coincidence, or had I myself done this—just as I swore I would thirteen years before as a young bride, barely twenty-one, cast off and humiliated in the streets of New York?

Regardless, it was over. It was done. Yet, blinking out at the dark factory, I found I felt no satisfaction at all. Only a sensation of something needling. And turbulent. And horrible.

Word traveled, of course. All afternoon while Bert was in Washington, people in the industry called. The consensus was that the

Candie Ice Cream Company had simply gone bankrupt. Me, I was all too happy to perpetuate this rumor. "Well, you know," I said to our dairyman as I sat at my office desk with my shoes kicked off, "Bert and I could easily be in the same boat if we hadn't switched to corn sugars awhile back. Candie just didn't have good business sense, I guess. If you followed what was happening in Europe, you saw the writing on the wall clearly enough."

When Bert arrived home from Washington the next evening, I had a bottle of Great Western chilling in an ice bucket. I had no reason to feel bad at all, I kept telling myself.

"Oh, doll, it's been a very big day." Bert loosened his tie and raised his glass jubilantly.

"To our brand-new customer. To Uncle Sam and the War Department!" I chimed. The bubbles tingled and burned in my throat. I raised my glass again. "And to them choosing us but not Candie."

"Oh," Bert said abruptly, shaking his head. "We shouldn't toast to that."

"Why? Why not?" I twirled the stem of my champagne glass and tried to appear nonchalant. "Was something the matter?"

"Well, apparently, our government is not keen on doing business with Italians right now," Bert said grimly.

"Oh?"

For a moment Bert's gaze remained fastened on the dark street beyond our living-room window. Because of the war, all the streetlamps had been dimmed. It was like living with gaslight again.

"Lil." He turned to me suddenly. "Did you know that a law has been passed requiring all Italians who don't have U.S. citizenship to register at the post office as enemy aliens?"

"Excuse me?" I gave a little laugh. "Bert, that's absurd."

"That's what I thought, too. But apparently it's true. And if Italians own shortwave radios, or flashlights, or any property near the ports or along the water, it can be confiscated?"

"No. That can't be right. That can't be right at all, Bert. Here." Nervously, I picked up his glass and refilled it.

"Some guys at the barbershop, they were talking a few weeks ago. They say that if you're an enemy alien and the government thinks you're up to no good, they can ship you off to a camp somewhere or send you back to Italy. They've got something here now called the War Relocation Authority."

The War Relocation Authority. What Orson Maytree had mentioned to me. I felt my chest constrict.

"Please," I said quickly. "This is America, for God's sake, Bert. Not Germany."

"That's what I said, too." From somewhere outside, a siren screamed past, throwing manic, bloodred light across the living-room wall for a moment. One little piece of paper, I had handed over. That was it.

Avoiding Bert's eyes, I took a sip of champagne and forced a bright, airy laugh. "You don't honestly think Candie was declared to be an enemy of the state or some such nonsense just because they're Italians? Please, Bert." I waved at the air. "I've known those *shmendriks* a long time." Reaching for the bottle, I refilled my glass again. "Trust me. I bet the war board took one look at how badly they run their operations and simply realized it would be a boondoggle."

"I suppose," Bert said haplessly.

"Tonight it's about us."

"Absolutely, doll. You're right. It's good to be home." Squeezing my thigh, Bert raised his glass and touched it lightly to mine. "To our good news."

I took one more sip of my champagne, then another, and closed my eyes. All day long I had been waiting for a sense of relief and exaltation—clouds in the heavens parting, a great beam of triumph shining down like sunlight. Yet instead I kept thinking of my visit to Red Hook. I kept seeing that lone shadow of a man, keening in the shadows. I *had* imagined him, hadn't I? Flashes of Mr. and Mrs. Dinello appeared in my mind's eye—him with his sad white mustache and his modest cart rattling over the cobblestones, mournfully singing his arias—she in her hairnet with her hawkish gaze, sweating and smelling of rose water as she cranked the old ice cream maker with me in the dank tenement kitchen. *We make you strong, Ninella,* capisce? And then, for some reason, I thought of Rocco, small and bony, sob-riddled as he curled in my arms after his mother had died—and how he'd leaned back on his heels in my factory just a week before, boasting about how good his little boy was at baseball. Certainly the U.S. government had not deported him. I remembered the day well when we had all become American citizens—all of us together at the clerk's office downtown, standing solemnly beneath the flag with our hands raised. Afterward we had gorged on sfogliatelli and rhumbaba to celebrate. But the Cannolettis? And the factory workers? Had they been herded onto steamers bound for Naples and Palermo?

I shook my head violently to dislodge the very thought. Pressing my hand to my heart, I recited what I kept telling myself like the prayers of a rosary: I had simply done what I'd had to do. I had protected our livelihood. I had protected our business. I had protected my *son.* Anybody else in my position would have done exactly the same.

After a moment the fibrillation subsided. I reached over to pour myself another glass of Great Western. But the bottle, I found, was now empty.

∞

By 1945, Dunkle's ice cream was being eaten by troops at Fort Bragg and Fort Dix. On tankers in the Pacific. In PXs in the

British Midlands and evac hospitals in France. Yet at home I was feeding Isaac suppers of scrambled eggs or chicken broth in order to economize. For Bert, you see, had happily agreed to fulfill our government contracts for mere pennies on the dollar. When he'd shown me the numbers he'd negotiated with the War Department, I almost had a coronary.

"Bert, how could you possibly settle for so little? We'll earn practically nothing! *Bupkis!*" I cried, pressing my fingertips to my temples. "Companies spend their lives trying to land a government contract! We should be getting rich now!"

"That's just it, Lil," Bert said quietly. "I thought you'd be proud of me. I don't want us to get rich like this. Certainly not off our boys, fighting and dying to defeat Hitler. Certainly not off a war."

So now, even though my husband owned a prestigious ice cream company—with what should have been a big, fat, lucrative government contract—I found myself no better off than the girls in our neighborhood who worked as telegraph operators. Welders. Assembly-line laborers at Premco Industrial Tool & Die.

A city of women. That's what Dunkle's had become. And our apartment building on Forty-Ninth Avenue as well. With so many men away at war, mothers, sisters, sisters-in-law, and daughters all moved in together to share expenses, child rearing, ration coupons. The building took on the perfumy, gossipy feel of a girls' dormitory. Every afternoon muffled broadcasts of *Amanda of Honeymoon Hill* and Frank Sinatra records could be heard echoing throughout the hallways, along with feminine shrieks of *I told you so!* and, huffily, *I've just about had it*. Rows and rows of pale pink bloomers, putty-colored girdles, and cheap lemon yellow nighties snapped in the wind from the clotheslines like the flags of a nation of women.

Since I occupied the ground-floor apartment overlooking the building's victory garden, I soon grew accustomed to seeing my neighbors tromping back and forth with their tomato plants and pruning shears. Eventually, as they came to regard me as just another neighbor, they began rapping on my kitchen window and inviting themselves in. Henrietta Mueller, who lived directly upstairs, often plunked down at my table and helped herself to coffee and cake. "So how's tricks, Ice Cream Lady?" she'd say in her husky voice before lighting a cigarette and yelling at her son, "Otto! Stop hitting your sister and go play with Isaac!" Henrietta was sharing a bed with her mother-in-law in Apartment 2C, which is why, I suspect, she lingered at my place any chance she got. Her husband, Walter, had first been stationed aboard a frigate off the coast of Labrador, intercepting cables from the Germans. Now he was serving in the Philippines.

Oddly, there was something comforting about all the traffic and chitchat and hubbub; it reminded me of the tenements. Yet when the postman turned on to Forty-Ninth Avenue each day, you could hear the collective intake of breath. Everyone congregated around the front stoop in a hush, watching anxiously as any woman who received a letter read it first to herself, then shared the most crucial parts aloud.

—*My Herbert, he's in a field hospital in Liège. He writes, "Thank you so much for the playing cards, Estelle. I'm making us a bundle playing the other guys at poker, and the nurses are teaching me to speak French!"*

—*Oh, listen to this, listen to this. "Dear Betty, I miss you so much, I have created my own constellation of you in the sky, so when I look up every night, I can see your face shining down on me."*

—*"Dear Marj. My leg is on the mend. Please don't worry. Kiss the girls for me, and thank them for the picture. Tell Tommy not to hold the bat too high when he takes a swing. . . ."*

Bert was not off fighting. He was in coveralls on an air base brandishing a socket wrench. In the end he'd gotten to fight his war against the fascists after all, in his own particular way. Under contract to the military, he traveled from one manufacturing plant to another in Michigan, Florida, Texas—retrofitting and adapting his ice cream machines—then to naval yards and army bases to instruct men how to operate them. When the shortage of army mechanics grew severe, he was given a special dispensation and trained to repair tanks, jeeps, even airplanes. Long before the Ice Cream Barge was commissioned, he was in demand, my husband, moving from one base to another as an ice cream man and a mechanic.

When Orson Maytree Jr. had approached us in early 1942, there were 1.5 million troops to feed. By 1945 there were close to 16 million. Supplying them with our share of ice cream now largely fell to me. It was I who oversaw all of Dunkle's operations, coordinating the production, the shipments, the suppliers. Some days I felt as mechanized and worn as our assembly lines. The closest thing I had to an ally was Mrs. Preminger. She was exactly what one could ever want in a secretary: Efficient. Unsentimental. Every day she donned the same worsted skirt and sensible shoes. Whenever our domestic dropped Isaac off after school, Mrs. Preminger kept him out of my hair by feeding him Chuckles and giving him her prized cat paperweights to play with. Like me, she kept a little notebook squirreled away with a running tally of every penny she ever spent. *Daily News 5 cents. Ball of yarn 12 cents. Bank deposit $4*—which I greatly respected. Her one transgression seemed to be that she secretly played the horses. On her lunch hour, I often found her hunched over the pay phone in the stockroom whispering, "Three on Tallulah Bankhead. Five on Planter's Punch and one on Okey Dokey to show." Hanging up, she looked at me mawkishly. "My nephew, Mrs. Dunkle. Poor child has dropsy again."

Mrs. Preminger also smoked tiny, stinky cigars wrapped in dark paper that she purchased on the black market through her estranged husband, a man whom she called simply "the Relic." He brought her bouquets of red carnations and seemed to be in and out of the picture. Since she was older than me by at least fifteen years, I had less trouble seeing Mrs. Preminger as an equal. Together we began to have an extra cocktail or two in the evenings after work, mixing them with top-notch whiskey that the Relic managed to procure.

I was as well-off as a woman could be during wartime, I supposed, yet listening to my neighbors pore over their precious letters from their husbands made me hideously heartsick. Because Bert, of course, never sent more than postcards—little rectangles with serrated edges and dreamy pastel photos of Galveston, Tallahassee, Garden City. All he ever wrote on the back were smiley faces, hearts, X's and O's and "BERT" in his schoolboy scratch. Seeing them filled me with doubt. Frustration. And longing. Oh, he tried, my husband. Occasionally he did manage to telephone. Yet these long-distance calls were just as unsatisfying. "I only have a few minutes, doll!" he'd shout over a line plagued by whistles and static. "Please, tell Isaac I love him."

Even though I knew that my husband could not write, I found myself growing resentful. How convenient Bert's illiteracy happened to be! Where I'd once seen it as merely heartbreaking, it now seemed like a tool he could wield like one of his mechanics' wrenches. He could enjoy the war unencumbered by any responsibility to report back to me—and unhindered by the specter of his adoring wife and child waiting for him at home. Though, of course, as soon as I had such thoughts, I felt monstrously guilty—*he was at war, after all.* Yet in my most panicked moments, blinking up at the darkened ceiling in our bedroom, my wildest wifely fears took root: I saw Bert in his jaunty uniform, his fingers dispensing with a cocktail waitress's featherlight slip, undoing her garters with their intricate hooks. Women in port-side honky-tonks running their index fingers seductively around the rims of their martini glasses as he winked at them. *Really?* A chorus girl from the USO giggled coyly, *You've got a cripple for a wife?* Her face just a breath apart from his as he ran the back of his hand along her creamy, glistening legs.

"Your Bert doesn't write you much, does he?" Henrietta remarked one afternoon as we were all convening on the steps.

I felt my back stiffen. "Of course he does," I said tartly. Suddenly I was aware of my neighbors' eyes on me, glittering, everyone but me holding a tissuey aerogram. "He sends his letters to our office, is all."

The next evening, as soon as Mrs. Preminger left, I sat down at her Underwood. *"My darling Lil,"* I typed. *"I love you so. Everywhere I go, I carry you with me. I know you are a good woman, so smart and clever. And you are beautiful, doll, in your very own way. I miss you terribly."* As I pulled the finished sheet from the carriage, I realized I was weeping.

When my own airmail letter arrived for me at Forty-Ninth Avenue, I waved it above my head before the rest of the women congregating in the lobby, my thumb carefully obscuring the postmark. "Look!" I cried, tearing it open. "'Dear Lil,'" I read aloud, and my voice cracked. "'In Texas today, it's 102 degrees in the shade. Yet in the smell of the heat and the magnolia blossoms, I can only think of you.'"

For the duration of the war, my husband sent me exquisitely detailed, tender letters that I generously shared with my neighbors. Often, as I read them aloud, I cried.

One Saturday, however, Bert telephoned from Delaware.

"Lil, I'm so glad I've reached you!" he shouted over the seashore sound of the connection. "Doll, I'm shipping out."

"Shipping out? What do you mean, 'shipping out'?"

"They're putting me on a special barge. One of the machines I designed is on it. The biggest ever built. The guy I trained, who was supposed to go? The last night of his furlough, he got into a bar fight. He's now in the hospital with a concussion and a punctured spleen. So they have to send me in his place."

"A barge? They're putting you on a barge? Bert, are they even allowed to do that?"

"It's called the Ice Cream Barge, Lil. At 0500 I start out for California."

"Then where?"

"I wish I could say, Lil. It's an 'undisclosed location.' Top secret." He sounded so proud. Yet I felt my panic rising: *What about me? And Isaac? And the company?* He couldn't just leave the country like that.

"But how will I know where you are? How will I know if you're okay?"

"Please, Lil. Don't you worry. This barge, it's more like a pier. It has to be towed. So I can't imagine we'll be going very far at all."

"I should hope not." Piers, by definition, were anchored somewhere. "Will you be able to call at least?"

There was a pause. "I—I don't know."

"You can't simply sit on a pier somewhere and not be able to contact me, Bert! What if something happens to you? Or our business? Or our son? If you can't call, then you have to write me. Henrietta, she gets letters all the time. All the women here do. And at the factory, it's all the girls talk about—"

"L-L-L-Lil, please. You know me," he said miserably. "It's bad enough—some of the men here, they call me 'the ice cream hebe.' And they have me doing all sorts of mechanics. Not just the ice cream. I have to keep up, Lil. Everything has to be done so quickly. I've got so many people here doing me little favors already. I just can't—"

"Please, Bert! Enough with your *meshuggeneh* pride already!"

"L-L-L-L-Lil—"

"It's not fair. Do you hear me? You leave me with all this responsibility—these terrible contracts—and a son whining for his papa day and night. But you cannot be bothered to find one person to help you write one goddamn letter?" I was trembling. "Fine. So go, then. Just go. Leave me all alone in this world while you sail off and do hell-knows-what on some goddamn ice cream barge."

After I slammed down the receiver, I picked up the coffeepot, then dropped it into the sink with a clatter. I opened the icebox and slammed it shut.

"Mama?" Isaac called plaintively from the parlor.

I turned on the faucet and rinsed off the breakfast plates furiously, jamming them, still soapy, onto the drying rack. I did not know what to do with myself.

"He can't pay a guy a quarter—just once—to write me one goddamn letter?" I cried aloud to no one. "Do I have to do every goddamn thing here myself?"

And this "undisclosed location." An undisclosed location—what on earth could that possibly mean? Then I recalled. That past spring, Mrs. Tilden, on the third floor. Her son had been sent to an undisclosed location. He was a radio operator. On June 8 he was killed during the invasion of Normandy.

The metal basket of the coffee percolator went heavy in my hand. If a place wasn't dangerous, then why was it "top secret"?

A terrible feeling overtook me. A barge capsizing, a roiling ocean swallowing Bert. I saw it clearly. The fates, they would be taking my husband from me—as payment—as punishment for all my sins.

I had to do something.

Snatching up the receiver, I tried telephoning Dover Airfield, but the call rang and rang relentlessly, unanswered. Depositing Isaac at Henrietta's, I hurried to the factory. I stuffed all the cash we had on hand—four hundred dollars—into my pocketbook. Dover was almost two hundred miles away. It was now past noon. The only Greyhound bus of the day had already departed, I discovered, as had the train. Finally, I telephoned Mrs. Preminger. "I need a car and driver," I said breathlessly. "Can the Relic call any of his people?"

Cars. Taxis. Drivers. It's hard to imagine now, darlings, but during the war they were contraband. In Europe the black market was for things like nylons. Chocolates. French wine. In the United States, it was mostly for "black gasoline," as they called it. Pleasure driving was outlawed, and a speed limit was imposed of no more than thirty-five miles an hour. People were allotted fuel depending on their jobs, the level of their necessity. Even if I asked one of Dunkle's truck drivers to take me to Dover, we still wouldn't have enough gas to get us any farther than New Jersey. Those refrigeration trucks, they gobbled up fuel.

Yet a friend of a friend of the Relic's, it turned out, knew of an outfit in Williamsburg run out of a bakery. "Gas chiselers" who hoarded gas coupons—real and counterfeit—and had a small fleet of cars and trucks at their disposal whose gas gauges they'd rigged. They loaned these vehicles out or employed them as a private livery service—but at an exorbitant price, Mrs. Preminger warned me. Yet it was chiselers like these who could assemble gasoline, a car, and a driver—good for two hundred miles of travel—with only a few hours' notice over a weekend.

Exiting the streetcar on Flushing Avenue, I followed the directions she'd given me to a place called the Starlite Bakery. Its neon sign was switched off, the metal grates rolled down. The air smelled like an incinerator. Around the back a dented metal door stood propped open. I could hear the husky, sandy voices of men laughing inside, a radio playing. Louis Jordan's "G.I. Jive"—a hit from the year before. With my cane thunking, the men heard me before they saw me.

"Can I help you?" A man in an undershirt and suspenders planted himself in the doorway. Behind him in the shadows, I could make out a table, a card game in progress, beer bottles on the floor. His thick, smudged eyeglasses sat halfway down the bridge of his nose.

"Mr. Preminger sent me," I said. "He told me I should ask for Milton, Ezra, or Hank."

The man eyed my cane, my dress. "Right. Right. You're the lady that needs a ride to Delaware. Watch your step." He motioned for us to cross over a slat into the little entranceway between the kitchen and the back door. Then he stopped. Clearly we were to go no farther. I could feel the other men's eyes slide over me from the kitchen; they continued playing cards. Nobody stopped or stood up to greet me—I supposed I was not pretty enough for that. Inside, it was hot and dark and seedy, and the men had that sour smell of old age and cigarettes about them. It reminded me of the tenements again, the old childhood dangers. It was no place I wanted to be.

"You say it's an emergency?" The man pushed his glasses up the bridge of his nose with a greasy finger and squinted.

I nodded.

"Did he tell you the price?"

I considered lowering the amount the Relic had quoted. Yet if you're going to bargain, you have to be prepared to walk away, darlings. You have to have options.

"One hundred and fifty," I said faintly.

The man nodded "Plus twenty for the gasoline."

"Plus twenty." I patted my pocketbook.

He ushered me into the kitchen. "Hank, Ezra," he called out. "Your date's here, fellas. Which one of you lowlifes owes me more?"

The men chuckled grimly. "Bailey's almost down to his shorts," one of them hooted.

"Just give me another minute, damn it."

"Listen to him. Already seventy in the hole."

In the dim light, someone was tapping his fingernails against a beer bottle in time to the radio. I drew my pocketbook against my chest.

"Gentlemen. The lady here has an emergency."

"All right. All right, Milt. Lemme take a leak first."

One of the men pushed back his chair with a scrape. "*Oy gevalt!* I know you!" he cried. "I know you from somewhere."

The man was on his feet, pointing at me accusatorily. "I know you!" he shouted.

My mind slammed into itself, and then I realized. E. Ezra. *E. Lazarre.* The pawnbroker whom Bert and I had hustled back when we were starting out. The one we'd sold the fake watches to. It was him—it had to be. Though aged and diminished, he was still in the black market. Of course. I was a fool. He recognized me instantly. The ugly girl with the bad leg. There were not too many like me around. I was entirely, wholly conspicuous.

"I know you!" he cried.

I sucked in my cheeks and glanced away from him. "No you don't," I said, my heart pounding. "That's not possible." I tried to come up with some plausible lie, some way to extricate myself as quickly as possible. "Please. I can pay double." I fumbled to open my purse. "Can we just go? I'm in a terrible hurry. My husband is shipping out tomorrow, you see."

By presenting myself as a soldier's wife, I hoped to cast myself in a softer, more sympathetic light. Yet the man bore down on me, circling me, studying my face. "Your husband?" he yelped. He was so close I could feel his hot breath on me, his animal presence. When he reached out to grab my chin, I jerked my head away.

"You're right. I can't possibly know you. You're far too young," he said with astonishment. "But I do. Tillie?"

And that's when I looked at the ghostly, familiar face, fleshier and grizzled in the half-light, the now-rheumy gray eyes. The old gangster circling me. He knew me, all right.

He wasn't E. Lazarre at all.

He was my father.

Chapter 10

To this day, darlings, I have no actual memory of Salvatore Dinello's horse colliding with me and crushing my legs, ribs, and pelvis on the cobblestone streets of the Lower East Side. The trauma, the sheer shock of it, from what I understand, can wipe your mind clean like a blackboard. And so, similarly, I have no memory of how I wound up in a brown DeSoto seated beside my father as he gunned the engine—such as one could with the speed limit at thirty-five miles per hour—down Canal Street toward the Holland Tunnel.

"Well." He exhaled. "I guess it's been awhile, hasn't it?" He steered with one hand, his arm slung casually over the back of the seat. But he kept glancing at me, checking if I was really still there. He was more compact and jowlier than I remembered, and his thinned hair had only a faint sheen of copper left to it. He wore it combed back with pomade, the way older men did. He also appeared to have false teeth. Yet even in his sixties, he was still handsome in a vaguely canine way.

"My God." He shook his head. "You're the spitting image of her. It's *bashert*, I suppose."

Bashert is the Yiddish word for "fate." Yet he was speaking English to me. We had each been speaking English for nearly thirty years, in fact—though this was the first time, of course, that we had conversed in it to each other.

"Look at you, Malka." He let out a long, disbelieving whistle. "All grown up." It was hard to tell if he was pleased or not.

"I'm Lillian now," I said faintly. "*Mrs.* Lillian Dunkle."

"Well, well. How do you do, Mrs. Lillian Dunkle? I go by Hank Bailey myself these days." We were stopped at a red light. He offered his hand awkwardly. Dumbly, I shook it. I was not sure how to proceed at all. Part of me wanted to demand he stop the car. I wanted him to hold still and let me catch my breath and think.

For so many years, oh, how I had imagined this moment in such extravagant detail! Back in the Beth Israel Dispensary, I had even believed that once I was reunited with Papa, my leg would grow anew like the fresh green shoot of a flower. I envisioned elaborate scenarios where I raced into his arms and apologized to him—for singing at the dinner table, for having a big mouth that caused nothing but *tsuris*, for begging to go to America. And Papa, he would see my goodness—and my sincerity, and my damaged leg—and take me back with tears in his eyes, saying, "I forgive you, Malka. I promise I'll stay." *Where did you go?* I would ask. And in my dreams his answer was always, *I was simply out searching for you.*

Until, of course, I had concluded he was dead.

Yet now, as Papa maneuvered the car down into the Holland Tunnel, it felt as if a butterfly had alighted on my palm. Any sudden movement, I feared, would scare it off for good. Better to breathe quietly and remain stock-still. To take my cue from Papa and behave as if this were the most natural and unremarkable thing in the world—a father and daughter simply going for a Saturday-afternoon drive together—as if we hadn't been separated for more than thirty years.

"Just drove her back from Saratoga." Papa laughed glibly, like a salesman. "Milt changed her oil. I've driven this route several times since I came back east. There's the speed limit, all right, but I know a few tricks." Yet nothing he said registered. I was too disconcerted by his face, by his all-American clothes—a sharp, almost preposterously tailored jacket and hat—and, of course, by the very fact of him. I absorbed only the cadences of what he was saying, like a song in a foreign language—even though there was no Russian or Yiddish inflection at all to his English. At some point he must have taken great pains to get rid of his accent. He wore a small gold ring on his right pinkie finger with a seed pearl set inside a gouged starburst. A few liver spots salted the backs of his hands. Two tan lines marked where a wristwatch had been. He smelled of vinegary cologne and cigarettes.

He cleared his throat. "So," he said, trying to sound offhand, "you're married? Your husband's in Dover?"

After the oppressive darkness of the tunnel, the hazy marshlands of New Jersey came as a bright shock. Between sneaking glances at Papa, I watched the landscape unspool. Little shields along the roadside read U.S. 1. I had first been on this highway on the bus with Bert going to Atlantic City on our honeymoon. Thinking about how hopeful and unknowing we had been—it made me feel like weeping.

"You don't say very much, do you?" Papa said. Was I imagining it, or did a look of displeasure cross his face? I grew suddenly aware of the fact that I had not had time to don my best dress. Nor had I been to the beauty parlor all week.

Papa regarded my leg. "Polio?"

I did not know how to begin to reply to this.

He lit a cigarette as he steered. In an afterthought, he offered me one. I shook my head, waved it away.

"I seem to remember you were a very talkative little girl. A regular chatterbox," Papa remarked.

"You remember?" My voice, when it finally came out, sounded more reproachful than I intended.

"Well, of course," he said irritably, sucking deeply on the cigarette. "As I recall, your mama always complained that you asked too many questions."

The word "mama," as soon as he said it, hung in the air. We both grew quiet, as if waiting for a bomb to explode. Finally I said, softly, "She's gone, you know. From what I understand."

"Oh," said Papa, staring at the road. "You don't say."

"And Flora and Bella, too. I don't know where. Rose, she died of diphtheria."

"Oh," Papa said again, somberly. His eyes remained fixed on the horizon. "I am truly sorry to hear that."

"Papa," I said carefully, "what happened?"

"What happened?"

"Where did you go?"

He let out a long, beleaguered sigh. "That was another lifetime ago, Malka."

"I'm just curious, is all." I tried to sound as offhand as possible. "Did I do something wrong?" I smiled intensely. "Did you leave because of me?"

"Christ," he groaned, turning the steering wheel sharply. "Here we go with the questions."

"No, Papa. I just—"

A trapped look came into his eyes. Yet then he seemed to calm down. "Listen," he said. "I just needed to try my luck. Score big somewhere. But a man can't do that with a family in tow. You understand?"

"Were you ever planning to come back?" I said quietly. For all my difficulties with Isaac, I could never imagine abandoning him.

Papa looked at me as if he were greatly offended. "How can you even ask me that, Malka? What kind of person do you think I am?"

He fixed his gaze on me long and hard. For a moment I thought he was going to drive right off the road.

"It got complicated, okay? Some deals fell through. I had a sort of accident." He motioned to his thigh.

With a sudden jerk, he slid the car across both lanes, brought it to a halt on the shoulder of the road, and got out. "You see?" He paraded grandly back and forth along the gravel, then nodded at my cane. "Just like you."

I squinted. Frankly, I couldn't see anything at all. "Your right leg or your left?"

"My right," he said with exasperation. He walked more slowly now, with an exaggerated drag, then got back into the car and started up the engine.

"Broken ribs I had, too." He maneuvered the DeSoto back onto the turnpike. "A concussion. For a while, in fact, they thought I was blind. That's right. And the shysters who did this to me, they took everything I had."

"You didn't go to the police?" Though, having grown up in Little Italy, I knew better. No immigrant with any brains ever went to the police.

Before Papa could reply, a billboard appeared. The Statue of Liberty came into focus, lifting her star-spangled red-white-and-blue ice cream cone instead of her torch.

I could not help it. "Papa, look." I pointed.

"What? The Statue of Liberty?"

"No. Dunkle's Ice Cream. Dunkle. That's me. Lillian Dunkle."

Papa glanced at me, then up at the passing billboard, then back at me. "You own an ice cream store?"

I nodded. "My husband and I. You've never eaten at a Dunkle's?"

"Can't say I have."

"There's one right here in New Jersey."

"So you must be doing pretty well for yourselves if you can afford a big, fancy billboard like that," he said. "Well, good for you, Malka. Good for you."

"We could make a quick stop," I suggested. "It's got a drive-up window, even. Just ahead in Edison. You could try anything you'd like. A sundae. A soda."

Papa shook his head. "I prefer to keep moving, if you don't mind. Milt will be pacing like a cat until I get this car back. Besides, ice cream has never been my cup of tea."

For a moment we drove on in silence. Though I didn't want them to, my eyes started to tear. I was not even sure exactly why. I felt foolish.

Papa jerked the DeSoto to a halt on the side of the highway again.

"I can't drive if you start blubbering. It's distracting," he said. "Look, I'm sorry," he said, more gently, rubbing his hands on his thighs. "I don't mean for us to get off on the wrong foot here. I just have a lot on my mind, okay?"

He took out a handkerchief and offered it to me. "I understand. It's been a long time. If you want to share a treat together," he said, "let's share a treat. It's probably a good idea, in fact."

Reaching into his jacket, he pulled out a small brown bottle and unscrewed it. He took two furious gulps, then passed it to me.

I stared at him.

"This is a treat, too." He winked. "Tell me you only eat ice cream."

I took the flask from him and swigged it in a big, defiant swallow. The whiskey was cheap, a hot wire scorching my throat. Yet it felt good to drink. In fact, I realized, it was exactly what the moment demanded.

"Attagirl." Papa grinned. "Isn't that better?"

I took another swig.

He chuckled. "I guess you are my daughter, all right."

I handed it back to him, my insides aflame. But something had shifted between us. He was smiling at me slyly now, knowingly, in that same conspiratorial way he'd had when I was a little girl. Suddenly we were a team again. "I seem to remember," Papa said nostalgically, taking another swig, "you and I, we always did have a special connection, didn't we, Malka?"

I felt a peculiar shudder of delight. "Remember in Hamburg?" I said. "When you bought me that chocolate?"

"Oh, yes. Of course," Papa said. "Chocolate. Yes. Well." He wiped his mouth on the back of his hand. He screwed the cap back onto the flask. I felt a little sorry to see him tuck it away.

"Why don't we continue this in a classier joint?" Papa said. "I know a place not too far from here. What do you say, you and I, we stop and get some fortification for the road? Have a little nosh. Get reacquainted properly, someplace where I can concentrate?"

I looked at him, torn. "Papa," I said pleadingly. "My husband. He's shipping out."

Already it was nearly four o'clock in the afternoon; the sun was sliding in through the windshield, glazing us with bronzed, winter light. Dover was at least four hours away.

My father made a face. "Surely you can spare one measly hour for your long-lost papa?"

Oh, I wanted to cry, suddenly *now* you have the time for me? And yet, my years of waiting, they tugged at me as insistently as a child. I thought fleetingly of Bert, of my hideous parting shot on the telephone. That "undisclosed location" looming with all its promise of catastrophe. The factory. Isaac's whining. Yet who could possibly have anticipated this? Papa, he was right here. Right now.

"One hour," I said cautiously. Bert, I reminded myself, he *did* have until 5:00 A.M.

Reaching over, Papa squeezed my shoulder. "That's my girl," he said. "Let's do this up right."

Rickie's Round-Up sat on a barren patch near the railroad tracks just off of Route 1 in Rahway, New Jersey. BREAKFAST, STEAKS, COCKTAILS was stenciled on the windows. Inside, padded red banquettes and heavy red drapes gave the place the feel of an old Pullman train car. The restaurant was empty, yet several old men sat clustered around the long, dark bar in the back, drinking and listening to the radio. An opened newspaper and a couple of stacks of coupons sat on the counter before them. As soon as my father walked in, the bartender waved. "Hiya, Hank. Long time no see." All the men turned around on their barstools at once, as if we had caught them at something. "Hoo-hoo-hoo," one of them joked. "If it ain't Beetle Bailey."

"Hey, hey. At ease, fellas." Papa grinned. "Just passing through." He moved in quickly among them, slapping their backs and shaking hands like a politician. "Is Rickie around?" Papa climbed up onto a stool beside them.

Suddenly I got a sinking feeling.

I stood there in the doorway in my hat and coat. As the bartender wiped down his station with a rag, he glanced up and saw me. "Excuse me, ma'am, may I help you?"

"Oh, she's with me." Papa waved me over to the bar and tapped the red stool beside him. "This is, uh—"

"I'm his daughter. Lillian. Papa, I changed my mind," I said. "My husband is waiting. Let's just go."

All the men stared at me. Nobody moved.

"Papa, please." Those words in my mouth, they felt so strange.

A man with white tufts of hair sprouting out of his ears like pillow stuffing said, "Hank, you never told me you had a daughter." He turned to me. "Hiya, Lillian. I'm Sid." He offered his hand.

Call me Pickles, said another. *Charlie. Irving.* The men had regional accents, but like my father they did not dress or carry themselves like immigrants. It was hard to tell where they were from beyond New Jersey.

"What's everybody drinking?" Papa announced, rubbing his hands together. "I'm buying."

"Whoo-hoo. Beetle Bailey's buying? What is it?" Irving snorted. "Christmas?"

Papa shot me a wink. It was clear that we would be staying for a cocktail. Resignedly, I unbuttoned my coat and set my hat, cane, and pocketbook down on the stool beside me. Papa put his hand on the small of my back and guided me over to his friends.

"Today, gentlemen"—he exhaled—"today is the day that I happened to be reunited with my long-lost daughter here. That's right, fellas. My daughter from the old country. And guess what? It's her birthday."

The men chortled. "Is it, now?" Sid said dryly.

"Which means, of course, that drinks are on the house for us, right, Julius?" Papa winked at the bartender. "I'll take a bourbon on the rocks. Malka, what'll you have?"

"The same, I suppose," I said dispiritedly.

"Ah," Papa said approvingly. "I see the lady likes her liquor."

"I'm not fussy, is all."

"Wait a minute, birthday girl," said Julius. "Are you Malka or Lillian? If you two are gonna hoodwink me, you better get your stories straight."

"My name is Lillian," I said sharply, more for Papa's benefit than the bartender's. "Lillian Dunkle. Malka was just a nickname. From childhood."

Julius set two highballs down in front of us. They bled wet rings onto the polished bar.

"What's this?" Papa chuckled. "No coaster?"

"You get a coaster when you pay for a coaster," said Julius.

Papa held his drink out by the rim and dried off the bottom with his handkerchief. Then he reached over and wiped the condensation off mine. He was being extremely gentlemanly now. "Happy birthday," he said, raising his glass. We clinked and took a sip in unison. Our movements were effortlessly synchronized. Father and daughter. The bourbon was surprisingly sweetish and strong.

"Dunkle, Dunkle," said Sid, studying me. "Is that like the ice cream?"

"It's exactly like the ice cream," I said. "That's our company. Dunkle's Ice Cream."

"Hey, Julius," Papa called out. "You ever hear of Dunkle's Ice Cream?"

Julius shrugged. "I never hear anything," he said. "That's why I'm a good bartender."

My father laughed. "And a great husband, I bet."

"Ain't that the truth."

"Wait a minute," Charlie said to me. "We're talking about the Dunkle's on the roadsides? With those pink-and-brown stripes? And those specials, those—what do you call them? Where you buy one, get one free?"

"Two-for-One Sundae Mondays," I said. We'd had an advertisement for these on the radio recently. I was pleased to see that someone had heard them.

"Those stores are really yours?" Charlie said.

Even Papa was listening now.

"Well, we franchise them out," I explained. "But yes. We had twelve before the war, but a few closed because of the gas rationing. So now there are eight." Our owners, we'd given them all jobs in our factories instead.

"Ha!" Charlie pounded his fist down on the bar. "I'll be damned! I stop there all the time. I get chocolate with chocolate jimmies. Or the Yankee Doodle Parfait. My wife, she loves your butter pecan. At least twice a month, we go. You've got a place over in Edison, right?"

I nodded. "A Greek couple owns that one. The Papadakises."

"*Zaftig,* good-looking broad? And the husband with the mustache?"

"I guess," I said vaguely.

My father stared at me, astounded.

"Malka," he declared.

The man called "Pickles" pounded him on the shoulder. "Your little girl here is rich, Bailey! Did you know that?"

"Please," I said. "Hardly."

"Did you see her billboard?" Charlie said excitedly. "Your kid's got a billboard. Right out there on the highway."

"I did," Papa said proudly. "The Statue of Liberty no less."

"I'd say this calls for a celebration," said Irving. "Next round's on you, Bailey. Drinks for everyone."

There were six of us at the bar, plus Julius. Papa ordered a round for all of us, then gave my shoulder a little squeeze.

"You weren't kidding back there when you told Milton you could pay double." He pressed his palm to my cheek. "*Kindeleh,*" he marveled. "Look at you. This really is *bashert.* Really, Malka. You and I? Meeting like this? What are the chances? Dunkle's Ice Cream." He shook his head and exhaled.

"To my daughter!" He raised his highball.

"To your daughter!" the men chorused. We drank one round, then another. They toasted me again. "To Lillian! To ice cream!"

When I tugged at Papa's sleeve and reminded him that Bert

was indeed waiting, the men insisted on drinking a toast to him as well. "To Captain Albert Dunkle!" they cheered. "To crushing the Japs and the Hun!" Clinking their glasses, they smiled at me. Quite frankly, I had never had so much male attention—or quite so many drinks in such rapid succession—before. The inside of the restaurant took on a wavering quality, like a dry riverbed rippling in the heat.

A waitress appeared clutching menus. Suddenly we were all moving to a table by the window and Papa was gallantly pulling out a padded red chair for me. The sky was awash with melancholy pink and violet, and a lone streetlight near the railroad station came on dimly. The other men ordered tongue sandwiches or plates of meat loaf, but Papa insisted that he and I have a proper steak dinner on account of it being my birthday.

"But I planned to eat dinner with my husband," I slurred. Suddenly I was having trouble feeling my teeth.

"So you'll eat a second one later, when you arrive," Papa said magnanimously. Signaling for the waitress, he ordered fruit cups for us both, followed by the sirloin special with mashed potatoes and peas. Plus another round of bourbons for everyone.

"Malka," he kept saying adoringly, shaking his head. "All grown up."

My insides, they were blooming. Yet it was hard to make the cognitive leap between the restless, red-haired man in the dark coat who had sat beside me on the floor of the Hilfsverein's detention center so many years ago in Hamburg and the assured, glinty old man seated beside me now, entertaining the table with stories about a friend who was building a grand hotel out in the desert of Nevada. Papa spoke with great gusto and humor, re-creating the dialogue theatrically. The more elaborate he got, the more the men hooted and applauded. My father, I realized proudly. He was beloved. Still. He was the star of the entire restaurant.

"I'm telling you fellas, the potential is huge. A pleasure resort like no one has ever seen. Malka." He turned to me. "Your husband is going to want to get in on this, too."

Watching him, it occurred to me that we had become exactly what we had dreamed of all those years ago, Papa and I. We were like the actors in the moving pictures. In the first scene, we had been Malka and Herschel Bialystoker, two poor, ratty Russians speaking Yiddish, arriving on the Lower East Side in the stinking heat. Yet now here we were, transformed into Lillian Dunkle and Hank Bailey, two scrubbed, enterprising Americans dressed in clean, department-store clothing, driving in a DeSoto across the farmlands of New Jersey with a pocketbook full of money. We were as malleable as actors, my father and I. We could be anybody.

Papa signaled the waitress again. A pretty brunette with an overbite.

"Hey, gorgeous, I'm just curious." He leaned back in his chair. "What's your name? Tell me it's Betty. Or Lana. Tell me you weren't named after a movie star."

"Uh-oh." Sid elbowed Irving beside him. "Here he goes. On your mark, get set—"

The waitress blushed. After some cajoling she allowed that her name was Sally. Watching her, I felt the back of my neck prickle.

"Sally. Sally," my father said rapturously, letting the word roll off his tongue. "Sally, this is my long-lost daughter. Malk—I mean Lillian. And today is her birthday. And she is a great success. Her husband, he is a rich ice cream magnate."

Charlie leaned over and whispered something to Papa that made him laugh. "Okay, okay," Papa conceded. He waved Sally off dismissively and quickly turned back to me.

"*Kindeleh*, this ice cream business," Papa said, gesturing with his glass. "How much does your husband share with you about it? Because, you see, I know some very interested parties who might be very partial to opening some Dunkle's franchises themselves. In fact, some of them"—he gestured expansively around him—"might even be seated right here at this table."

I had not expected to be asked for a sales pitch. Yet I heard myself saying, "Why, I know everything, Papa."

"Well, well." He sat back. "You don't say."

"Bert and I, we built Dunkle's together. From scratch. Most of it was my idea."

"You hear that, fellas?" Papa boomed. *"From scratch."*

The men leaned in attentively. I found myself telling them about all the innovations Bert and I had come up with, the ice cream machine and our special patented formula. I explained to them our franchise model. I even estimated our gross, net, and overhead—which I did not usually do. My own candor surprised me. Yet the liquor had made me expansive, and this was my father, after all. My urge to please him was suddenly overwhelming. The way he gazed at me, encouragingly, with rapt admiration, it felt like stars raining down. Champagne uncorking.

"So those are the nuts and bolts of it," I said finally, feeling flushed with the effort. "Are you really interested in all this?"

"Are you kidding?" Irving said, more to Papa than to me. "Out there in the desert? With that heat? It's genius. And who doesn't love ice cream? Meyer himself, I've seen that guy polish off a quart of fudge ripple in an hour."

"Even gamblers gotta eat," Sid agreed.

"Malka." Papa leaned forward, tenting his fingers. "If we wanted to open, say, three or four of these places out in Nevada, you think we could?"

"I don't see why not," I said, even though, in the back of my mind, I had the vague idea that perhaps it was actually not quite so simple. Different states had different laws regarding shipping and agriculture, after all, and I knew of no dairies in the area.

Suddenly I was sopping up the last of my gravy with a dinner roll. I'd had no idea how hungry I'd been. Outside, it had grown dark. The bright reflections from inside the dining room shone against the plate-glass window, mirroring images of what was transpiring inside. The whole world seemed to be contained within the blazing, curtained box of Rickie's Round-Up. I had the terrible feeling that there was something urgent I was supposed to be attending to, yet anytime I tried to concentrate, my thoughts became like fistfuls of confetti tossed into the wind. I was cognizant only of this: I was advancing our business!

Sally arrived bearing plates of apple pie à la mode. Mine had a little candle in it for my birthday. As Papa, his friends, and Sally all sang to me, I heard myself laughing with pleasure.

"Happy birthday, *kindeleh*." Across the table Papa squeezed my hand. I was so caught off guard—I felt so giddy—that I neglected to make a wish or to ask the waitress if the ice cream was homemade, as was my custom. Indeed, I had trouble feeling the vanilla sliding onto my tongue when I finally took a bite.

Papa shoveled a great forkful of pie into his mouth, his pinkie ring glinting. He took another sip of his drink. "To getting rich in America with my long-lost daughter," he saluted. "To ice cream in Las Vegas."

"Here, here," the men toasted.

I laughed, raising my glass. "To gold rings on everyone's fingers!" I cried, gesturing toward Papa's hand.

Pickles teased, "Since when did you start wearing jewelry, Hank?"

Papa glanced down. "Ah, that's just Enid's."

"Who's Enid?" I said.

"His second wife," Charlie brayed. "May she rest in peace. Or was she your third, Hank? I can never keep up."

"Bridget. I thought Bridget was his third." Irving made an hourglass shape in the air with his hands.

"No. Bridget was the common-law gal," said Charlie.

"Wait. So who's the one he's with now? Whatsername?"

I sat back heavily in my chair. Papa continued eating as if nothing were amiss. "Josie," he said, chewing.

I picked up my spoon and threw it on the floor. All the men looked at me.

"You've had three other wives?" Suddenly I felt sick.

The restaurant grew quiet. Other diners were eating now. They glanced over at us.

"Malka." Papa glared at me. "We're just kibitzing. Just making conversation."

"You think this is a joke?"

"I thought we were having a good time here. Finish your pie."

"My pie? MY PIE?"

"You know, fellas, I think I'm going to head over to the bar," Sid announced, standing. "Me, too," said the others, nearly in unison. In a flurry they rose, taking their drinks. Papa and I, we were abandoned at the table.

"Well, thanks a helluva lot. Now you've embarrassed me," Papa hissed.

Suddenly, there were two of him before me, blurring around the edges. I tried to fuse the double images back into one. "You *mamzer.*"

"Excuse me?"

"You men."

"Christ. Listen to you." Papa gestured. "You really are exactly like your mother."

His words were a slap. "I am not!" I shouted, struggling to stand. I swayed like a metronome. A glass of water spilled, drenching the tablecloth. Papa's friends at the bar glanced over at us. Sid, I noticed, was pulling his coat on.

"Sit down, would you?" Papa whispered furiously. "You're making a spectacle of yourself."

He yanked me back down into my chair.

"If we're going to go into business together, you had better learn to hold your liquor," he said in a low voice. "An ugly woman only makes an uglier drunk."

I put my face in my hands. My lovely birthday pie sat only half-eaten on my plate, the ice cream melting and pooling around it. The little candle nub had somehow rolled onto the floor. Though I hated myself for it, I started to cry.

"Ach." My father stood up again, then sat back down in his own chair and raked his hands through his hair. "I'm sorry, okay?" he said finally, in a voice that did not sound very sorry at all. "I didn't mean it. You're not ugly."

I sniffled and swallowed, even as the restaurant seemed to rotate around me. "Papa," I rasped, taking a deep breath, "please? Tell me something. Tell me just one, single, solitary goddamn thing."

He glanced around uncomfortably. "The truth is, all right, I'm very impressed with you, Malka. You've grown up into quite a dame. You really have. You've got moxie. You've got money—"

"Papa—" My voice caught like a bone in my throat. "Why? Please tell me. Why are men unfaithful?" This was not the question I had intended—indeed, there were a thousand more I had longed to ask him for years—yet there it was. The one that came out.

Papa sat back, his chest rising and falling, regarding me.

"Papa, I know that I've never been pretty. And I have this horrible leg." Suddenly I began to weep all over again. I was humiliating myself, I knew, yet I could not stop. "Bert—he seems to love me anyway. But sometimes? And especially now, since he's with the military, he's in a different port all the time, and I don't hear from him for months— Why, Papa? Why do men always need a Violet *and* a Doris *and* a Frieda?"

My father shook his head and glanced bleakly around the restaurant. "I don't know why, *kindeleh.*" He sighed. He sounded as if the question made him weary. "Why do your stores offer twelve different flavors of ice cream?"

For a while I just sat across from him with my head bowed, sobbing quietly into my napkin. I felt so ashamed.

"This husband of yours." Papa massaged the bridge of his nose. "He's in Delaware?"

Blowing my nose into my napkin, I nodded. "He's leaving in the morning. For an undisclosed location."

"Well then." Papa stood up unsteadily. "We should hit the road." He pointed to the ladies' room. "Go take a powder. He'll appreciate it if you look nice."

He signaled to the waitress for the bill. As I made my way toward the back of the restaurant, I heard the *ding* of the cash register and Papa smirking to Julius. "Women. It's always an opera with them."

The floor of the ladies' room pitched and rolled like a ship. I had never been this drunk before. It was a struggle for me to unpeel my panty girdle. Studying myself in the mirror, I was astounded by how disheveled I looked. I was in need of my comb, my compact of powder and rouge. My Rose Red lipstick. Fumbling around, I realized I had left my pocketbook with my scarf at the table. I swayed and belched. Papa was right. I was exactly like Mama. Hawk-faced. Shrewish. But he had kept calling me his business partner. Why, we had just agreed to become a team, he and I—here, on this very night, in Rahway, New Jersey! Together we were going to open multiple Dunkle's franchises way out west, in this city his friends were building in Nevada. Nobody was even there yet, Papa had bragged. To grab some land—just as Bert and I had done once in Long Island—why, it would give Dunkle's the perfect leg up over our competition after the war. Certainly it would offset the losses Bert had negotiated in his dealings with the military. I might be drunk, I said aloud to the mirror, but I was not stupid.

And Isaac, he would finally have a grandfather. "A real character," as Mrs. Preminger might say. Yet a bona fide relative nonetheless. It was almost too marvelous to contemplate. In an instant, the future had turned so much sweeter and richer and more peopled than I had ever imagined. I could not wait to bring Bert this great bouquet of good news.

Bert. Oh, God. My sweet, sweet Bert. It was so late. I had yelled at him. I had been horrid. I had to go to him immediately. I glanced frantically around the tiny bathroom. Why did bathrooms never have clocks? There should be big, beautiful ones, in cast iron and gold leaf. Like they had at Penn Station and the Biltmore.

Suddenly, I felt a wave of vertigo. If I could just sit down for a minute and catch my breath, perhaps I could get the walls to stop revolving. Stumbling back into the toilet stall, I keeled over before it and vomited. Once. Then twice. Violently. Peas and steak and pie. My entire life seemed to pour out of my throat.

Whether I awoke minutes or hours later, I do not know. I only recall that I found myself collapsed on the yellow tile floor beside the toilet, Sally hovering over me, shaking me by the arm. "Lillian. Wake up. Your father's waiting. Lillian. Are you okay? Are you sick?" Helping me to my feet, she wet a towel and helped me to clean myself up a bit. "Those fellas can lead a gal astray," she said, not unkindly.

Back inside the dining room, only the reddish stained-glass lamp above the bar remained switched on. All the chairs had been overturned and stacked on the tables. Julius was mopping the floor.

"Your father went outside to warm up the car," Sally said gently, handing me my coat and hat. "I gave him your scarf and your pocketbook." Did I imagine it, or was Julius eyeing me with trepidation? There was no hiding it, darlings. I looked and smelled terrible—of bourbon and rose soap and bile. My own odor almost made me sick again. It was so late. I wondered if Bert would ever forgive me.

"I think she's too drunk to walk," Julius said. He took one of my elbows, and Sally took the other. My back, my armpits, my forehead—everything felt sopping wet and sour-smelling, even though I also did not quite feel as if I were inhabiting my own body. I heard myself apologizing over and over—for some reason in Italian: *"Mi dispiace. Mi dispiace."*

Together they helped me into the parking lot. My head pounded furiously, my heels scraped along the pavement. Yet more than anything else, I felt ashamed.

The parking lot was empty. "That's queer," Sally said.

The night air was frigid and quiet. We kept listening and listening, looking back and forth at the deserted road in front of us. But Rahway, New Jersey, remained utterly still. Confronting us was only a vacuum of starless black. Silent houses. Dark fields. Miles of empty railroad tracks. We waited and waited for the DeSoto to materialize, but it never did.

Papa had vanished, taking my purse.

Chapter 11

THERE ARE BOOKKEEPERS nowadays known as "forensic accountants." Such a fancy-schmancy name for people who
essentially sort through your trash. Old bank statements, tax
records. Sales receipts. Canceled checks. The minute my lawyers
recommended a firm, Isaac paid them a retainer without so much
as a phone call to me. Now they have meticulously pieced together my finances like a jigsaw puzzle, and I am scheduled to go
into the city to meet with them. I suspect that their prognosis
will not be good. When a grand jury has already indicted you for
tax evasion, chances are the IRS has some fairly damning
evidence.

My appointment is on Lexington Avenue in the new Citicorp
Building. Modern, white, striated with black windows, it looks to
me, from a distance, like a cartoon prison uniform. I order Hector to drive me down to the Garment District first.

The address on West Twenty-Second Street is not what I expect. A shabby brick low-rise with a cheap new glass door and
a landslide of Chinese takeout menus littering the vestibule. Beneath a buzzer labeled H. BALLENTINE, the letters GMHC have been
added on a piece of masking tape.

Harvey is already awaiting me on the landing, leaning against
his doorframe, a pearl gray cat slinking in figure eights around

his ankles. I have had trepidations about telephoning him—about coming here in person. Yet here I am.

It is odd. I am his former boss. Although Harvey worked for me for seventeen years, I have never once been to his apartment. And several years have passed. Without his clown makeup, Harvey looks strangely denuded and gaunt. Thinner than I recall. Instead of his satin balloon pants and goofy bow tie, he is dressed simply in a faded T-shirt that clings to his chest like plating. Shredded blue jeans hang from the struts of his hip bones. His pale feet are clad in silk Chinese slippers. Though his grizzled face glints with boyishness, it is sunken. He must be close to fifty now.

"Well, color me indicted," he says tartly, one hand on his hip. "How are you, Lillian?" His voice still has its snide, musical quality. Though it is more subdued than I remember, something in his tone, just as it did decades ago, tickles me.

"I believe that's 'the Mussolini of Ice Cream' to you, is it not?"

Harvey clamps a hand over his mouth. "Oh, my God. You read that? You actually read that? I am so sorry. I was totally misquoted."

"Were you, now?"

"Well, no. It's actually *exactly* what I said. I just never dreamed you'd *read* it, is all," Harvey says flippantly. "You know. At your *highly advanced* age." I assume he is teasing me as always, yet his smile is icy, short-lived. "Come," he says abruptly, swiveling. "Let's get this little melodrama over with, shall we?"

He waves me into his living room. A small desk is pushed up against an exposed brick wall. An electric typewriter sits purring amid stacks of manila folders. Propped above it is a bulletin board covered with newspaper articles, press releases, mimeographed lists. On the other side of the room, a pair of plum-colored velvet curtains have been drawn back to reveal a voluptuous bed sitting on a sleeping platform. A doll-size kitchenette runs along the wall by the door, half concealed by another velvet curtain, this one a dull harlequin gold. But this, I realize, is it. Harvey's entire apartment. A single room. Overlooking the street.

He rummages through a cabinet above his tiny stove. "May I offer you some tea? You know I don't drink anymore. And judging from that latest performance of yours, honey"—he looks me up and down—"you probably shouldn't either."

I draw myself up. "Well, aren't you Mister Rogers all of a sudden? No tea, thank you. I'm perfectly fine."

"Oh, thank God." Harvey tosses a tin back into the cabinet with a clatter. "That tea is actually dreadful. Like drinking potpourri. Besides"—he crosses his arms and looks at me squarely—"I'd prefer not to draw this out, Lillian, if you don't mind. Just say your piece and go, all right?"

I lean heavily on my cane. "Excuse me?"

"I don't know why you've insisted on coming here. You're not my boss anymore, you know?"

"*Harvey*," I say, "you've got a lot of goddamn nerve."

He gives a little, incredulous yelp. "Me? Me? *I've* got a lot of nerve? Already this week I've been chewed out by your publicist, Lillian. And your lawyers? Faxing me over a cease-and-desist order. Twice?" Suddenly he is animated, his hands fluttering like birds. "You know, I'm not going to fight it, Lillian—not because I agree with it—I absolutely do not—it's horrible, and it's a travesty—but because, frankly, I simply don't give a shit anymore, do you understand? You want me to stop saying I was Spreckles the Clown for seventeen years? Fine. You got it. It's erased. It's done. It's expunged from my résumé." Harvey slaps himself theatrically on the forehead. "Whoops. See? I just hit myself on the head. Just gave myself total amnesia. Spreckles the Clown? Who on earth is that? It's like it never happened at all."

I glare at him indignantly. Finally I say in a low voice, "What the hell did I ever do to you?"

He blinks at me. "Excuse me. Was everything I just said somehow not enough?"

"All I ever did was put you on television. On billboards. Drink with you during every ghastly, goddamn show we did together. The Christmas when your mother died? Did I not give you an extra week off? And take you to that party with Andy Warhol that you couldn't stop blabbering about? Why, I paid you severance—severance, Harvey!—when it was you—you, you whiny little ingrate—who walked off my show in a tantrum!"

For a moment we stand there, panting at each other across his miniature table.

"What the hell did I ever do to you," I say, "except give you a job and put up with your nonsense for seventeen goddamn years? *Wait, I have to wash my hands again! Don't get any chocolate syrup on me!* And this is the thanks I get? You call me a dictator in *New York* magazine? 'The Mussolini of Ice Cream'? Persecuting me in the press along with everyone else?"

Harvey's face suddenly grows livid. "I'm persecuting you? I'm persecuting you, Lillian?" He clutches his temples, then flings open his hands. "Is that all you can think about? Oh my God. Your fucking reputation? Men across this city are dying like flies, Lillian. Do you not get this? Young, beautiful men in their prime—their entire lives ahead of them—they're falling sick and dying horrible, torturous deaths. And is anybody doing anything? Certainly not our mayor—who's so deep in the closet he'd rather let every last gay man drop dead before he utters a word! Certainly not our public health department. Certainly not our president. The *New York Times* devoted more ink to that Tylenol scandal than to the fact that hundreds of people are dying within a mile of their office!"

Harvey stands before me, wild-eyed. "Three men in this building alone, Lillian. Right here. On the floors around us. A math teacher on two. An opera singer, with a voice like an angel, in 4B. And a nineteen-year-old kid—a nineteen-year-old—whose parents in Utica disowned him, kicked him out into the street like a dog—they're all dying. Right here. Right now. And yet you, Lillian Dunkle—just one or two wisecracks to the press—God forbid some little smart-ass like me sometimes chooses to frost his cakes a little when he speaks—and boom! Suddenly you've got your lawyers and your publicist all calling me up, night and day, threatening to sue, because you're worried I'm making your ice cream company look bad? 'We don't want this gay plague and homosexuality associated with Dunkle's and children's television,' your publicist told me. That's right. Don't give me that look, Lillian. Those were her exact words. Here? See. I wrote it down on a notepad. Yet even this apparently is not enough for you. You've got to come down here yourself, in person, the big Ice Cream Queen of America, just to berate me like you do everybody else. Just to make sure that, ooh, I'm not going to embarrass you and your ice cream!"

His face becomes a landslide then. He bends over the sink in his kitchenette, clutching his abdomen. A ragged sob rises from his throat.

Spreckles the Clown.

I watch his knobby shoulders heave up and down, up and down. From outside, a car alarm begins whooping insanely, then stops. Harvey's cat slides soundlessly past us and disappears through a narrow door; a moment later I hear scratching in a litter box. The clock on the stove ticks off the seconds. The minutes. A faint rumbling of the subway deep beneath the street becomes audible, then fades.

I clear my throat.

"Harvey, I want to know," I say quietly. "Are you sick?"

He continues standing with his back to me. He draws in a long sniffle, then jerks on the faucet and runs his hands quickly under the water before pressing them to his eyes.

When he turns around, he looks as if he might cry again. "I don't know, Lil," he whispers, his voice cracking like plaster. "There's no way to tell if you're sick with this thing. Until, of course, you are."

Blinking up at the ceiling, he struggles to contain himself. "They say, 'How can we even test for something when we don't know what it is?' But then they look at me, Lillian. And I see it. In that invisible cartoon bubble floating above their heads: *It's your own damn fault, you sick little faggot. A plague on all your houses.*"

I stand there, still in my coat, regarding him. Slowly, I unsnap my pocketbook and take out my checkbook. "May I?" I point to his little desk in the corner. I go over and pluck a ballpoint pen from a glazed ceramic mug by his phone.

Rose's name printed in white chalk on the side of the school. My mother, going crazy from the grief, unable to contact me because of the quarantine. Me, waking up from that hallucinatory fever in Beatrice's room, only to find her gone, half the tenement empty.

"You know, there have always been plagues, Harvey." I sigh, ripping the check from its fibrous spine. "And nobody ever has a goddamn clue. They blame and they blame, those idiots. The Black Plague on the Jews. The Spanish flu on the Spanish. Polio on ice cream."

Limping over, I hand Harvey the checks—one to him, one to his organization.

Harvey looks at me, then down at the slips of paper. He tries to feign indifference, though the amounts are extraordinarily generous, thank you.

"So." With difficulty he swallows. Waving the checks in the air with a little flourish, he tries to sound flirtatious and acerbic and diffident again. "Hush money?"

I pick up my pocketbook and turn away stiffly. I cannot bear to look at him any longer. "I will be damned if another epidemic threatens my business," I sniff.

Back in the car, I struggle to keep my hand steady as I dutifully record the amounts in the balance section of my checkbook. Staring up at the forlorn brick building one last time, I yell at Hector to start the Cadillac already and drive me uptown, leaving Harvey Ballentine and his fax machine and his soft, pearl gray cat trembling alone in their one little room full of velvet.

⌒⌒

Of course, I never did manage to see Bert before he shipped out. And Papa, after that drunken night in New Jersey, he vanished again.

Yet, following months of anguishing radio silence, with no postcards or phone calls arriving whatsoever—and me with no idea where on earth my husband was stationed—the war finally ended. And when Bert did come home from his "undisclosed location," it turned out that we did not need a string of franchises in a fledgling desert resort called Las Vegas. We did not need Papa and his "friends" investing in our company at all. Dunkle's thrived more *after* the war than during it.

All those returning veterans? Many of them had already eaten our ice cream aboard aircraft carriers and submarines, in mess halls and hospitals. Already they loved our product. Arriving home in Williamsport and Chapel Hill and Sandusky and Beaver Falls, they were only too happy to open their own Dunkle's franchises. What better antithesis to warfare than a bright new candy-colored

ice cream parlor? In honor of their homecoming, I even concocted several special flavors: Welcome Back Walnut. Victory
Vanilla. Armistachio. GI Love Chocolate. A simple gesture. But
the soldiers, oh, they went mad for it.

Like many of them, however, my own husband came home
from the war an enigma. Although he had not seen combat,
spending months and months making fifteen hundred gallons of
ice cream each day in a huge concrete shell bobbing in the middle of the Pacific—all the while listening to war planes tearing
overhead and the incessant hammering of machinery reverberat-
ing through the steel hull—the stress of it had reconfigured his
internal wiring somehow. His hearing in one ear had been damaged. Words and verbal communication had receded from him
even further, making him appear foggy at times—even "simple."
He could sit in his armchair by the window for hours, drinking
a glass of rye while the radio played too loudly, his eyes fixed on
a taxi, perhaps, slowly maneuvering down the wet, leaf-matted
street. I in turn watched him from the kitchen doorway with trepidation. I felt I had to decipher him now the way that Henrietta's
husband, Walter, had once deciphered intercepted cables from the
Germans.

Like so many couples, too, Bert and I had forgotten how to
be together—how our bodies interlocked in bed, how our morning rhythms in the kitchen and bathroom syncopated like musical
instruments. "Oh, excuse me," we said. "Did you want the tooth-
paste? No. Please. You first."

To my great relief, Bert did seem to have lost his appetite for
radicalism. "I don't know, Lil," he said plainly one night as we
were having cocktails, "any extremism just seems dangerous and
oppressive to me now. When people follow any leader—any set
of ideas blindly…" His voice trailed off.

Such an odd thing about servicemen, though: During the war

they spent all their time penning letters to their wives, mothers, and sweethearts, longing for home, rhapsodizing about the smell of fresh-cut lawns and dancing the Lindy hop and eating their wives' famous meat loaf. Yet as soon as they returned, they couldn't bear to stick around their families. Every Thursday, Bert and Walter Mueller and a few other vets went out for dinner at Luchow's, then headed over to Fifty-Second Street to listen to jazz. In loud nightclubs, where little conversation was required, Bert apparently came alive again, tapping his feet to Coleman Hawkins at the Three Deuces. Bobbing along to Louis Prima at Jimmy Ryan's. Musicians I would have loved to hear myself, thank you, with him on my arm.

"I don't understand why you have to go out every single week," I sniffed. "It's expensive, you know."

"We can afford it now, doll," Bert said, sliding on his good jacket. "What's all our money for, if not this?" He tugged at his sleeves, adjusted his cuff links.

Yet it was more than money that bothered me, of course. All the rumors about how army men had behaved: the "comfort women." The cocktail girls. The Tokyo roses and French *femmes fatales*. These stories trailed after veterans like phantoms, swirled around them like clouds of ash and perfume.

I observed my husband hawkishly. The conversation with Papa kept playing over and over in my head: Why did men cheat? *Why do your stores offer twelve different flavors of ice cream?* At the beauty parlor one morning, I ordered my hairdresser to dye my hair blond. It came out coppery instead, but it was still a marvelous improvement; indeed, it infused my face with light, making me look thoughtful and regal instead of sullen. Bert let out a long, slow whistle when he saw me. My hair, he had always said, was my "crowning glory." Thick and satiny. Now it shone like cognac, and he ran his fingers through it, nuzzling it, squeezing me around the waist. "Lil, you only get better-looking with age," he said. "Not too many women can have that said of them."

Yet gold hair, I worried, would simply not be enough.

When Bert went out carousing with his new buddies, I listened in a torturous half sleep to the clock on our bed stand ticking like a metronome. I could not rest until I heard the metallic clack of the lock turning. Often it was two or three in the morning when Bert thudded through the darkened kitchen, tossed his keys cavalierly onto the Formica counter, and negotiated his way around the furniture. When he finally lurched into bed beside me, he smelled of cigars. Acrid, floral cologne. Apricot brandy. Face powder. Sauerkraut. Stale leather. Beer. I was afraid that if I rolled over, he would perhaps admit to something reckless and impetuous that I did not want to hear. Trying not to swallow, I pretended to be asleep, letting him lock his sweaty arms around my waist and press damply against my back. Soon he began snoring. Yet me, I remained awake, blinking at the window sheers fluttering from the curtain rod like ghosts, mushrooming with the fumes from the street.

In the mornings Bert stood before the mirror looping his silk tie over and under, whistling along to Fats Waller on the Victrola as if absolutely nothing were wrong. "Hey, doll," he said mildly. Occasionally he made a playful grab for my buttocks as I maneuvered around him in my slip toward the bathroom. I was not sure how to interpret this. Was it guilt? Residual lust left over from some showgirl? Or was it possible he still cared for me?

Of course I went through his pockets. His slim leather appointment book. Eavesdropped on his phone calls. There was never any definitive proof—but then, I suppose, I was careful never to look too closely. For the day after my father had abandoned me in the parking lot of Rickie's Round-Up, I returned to the apartment on Forty-Ninth Avenue feeling wretched and humiliated.

And standing by the window, nursing my hangover, I had made a vow: No one would ever, ever walk out on me again.

My marriage, I decided, I would treat like our business. I would simply do whatever it took. I would turn a blind eye. I would keep my big mouth shut and not ask my usual torrent of questions. I would chew off my own tongue if I had to.

One morning Bert sat on the edge of the bed, a shoehorn in one hand, a brand-new wing tip in the other. "Lil, I've been thinking. I need to discuss something with you."

My leg went heavy. I slid awkwardly onto the flouncy, quilted stool of my dressing table and gripped its scratchy edge. "Oh?" Adrenaline sizzled through me like a jolt of electricity. I knew already what Bert was going to say. I could imagine the onerous words. I could see his mouth shaping them, in fact, before they rose in the air, like a moving picture that had fallen out of synchronization with the sound reel. *This was finally it.* My heart thudded with misery. *Oh, dear God. Do not let him leave me.*

"Lil," Bert said gently. "What do you say we buy a house?"

"A house?"

"Someplace nice, up in Westchester or out on Long Island. With a pool, maybe, or a garden."

My voice broke in a peal of preposterous, relieved laughter. For this he had nearly given me a heart attack?

"What on earth would we do with a house, Bert? We're barely ever home. I spend all my time at the factory."

"Yes, but why should we, Lil?" He leaned toward me, sandwiching his hands between his knees. "We have the means now. It would be good for Isaac to have some fresh air. Don't you think you deserve it?"

I glanced at him, and when I did, darlings, I saw the real *Bert*, the old Bert, the tender, stuttering man who wanted desperately to please me.

"I want to live in a high-rise, not a house," I said. "All my life I've been stuck in tenements. Ground-floor apartments. That horrible shack in Bellmore. You want us to move? Fine. Marvelous. Then get us a place with an elevator and a view."

By that autumn we were ensconced on the tenth floor of a grand building on East Seventy-Second Street in Manhattan, with seven airy rooms and a brand-new dinette set, a velveteen davenport, and matching silk-upholstered armchairs that sat by the windows like a pair of dowagers. Plus a new, sleek Victrola in a mahogany cabinet. Every evening a gloved doorman ushered us into the elevator, with a brass gate that he pulled shut like the door on an elaborate birdcage. While I went to soak in the voluminous bathtub before supper, Bert walked from room to room with a drink in his hand, surveying all the treasures he'd purchased. For a former Communist, he certainly liked his furniture.

One morning, however, we awoke to a sound like machine guns gunning, hammers clopping, and great plumes of smoke and dust billowing through our windows. What Bert had not anticipated was that a newer high-rise was being built directly across the street.

Floor by floor our expensive view of the skyline was devoured. Soon we faced nothing but a wall of windows and brick; we had scarcely more air or light than we'd had in the tenements. Oh, how I wanted to box Bert's ears! "You saw the lot across the street!" I cried. "Did you never once think to ask?"

"L-L-Lil, I'm so sorry," he stuttered, holding out his hands.

"The one thing I ask you for! The one thing I ask!"

To appease me, he bought an ink-blue 1948 Chevrolet Fleetmaster with sand-colored seats. He rented a garage space for it over in Yorkville and hired a driver named Martin to bring the car around every morning to take us to the factory. One Friday night when Bert and I arrived home, I found a large box on our bed, tied with gold ribbon. Inside was a calf-length black sable coat. It was absurdly heavy and soft. It must have cost nearly two hundred dollars. Of course, I had never had anything so marvelous in all my life. "Oh, no. This is far too expensive," I said. "Where am I going to wear this, you *nudnik?* The refrigeration room in the plant?"

"Why not?" Bert brushed back a lock of my hair. "I want you to have nice things, Lil."

"Bert, money is not for spending."

"Why not?" He shrugged. "We earned it honestly."

A pang shot through me. A rivet of guilt. Yet I said nothing.

The coat was lined with pearl gray satin. Stitched inside was a label: MADE EXPRESSLY FOR BONWIT TELLER AND LILLIAN DUNKLE. Even the buttons were padded with fur. Bert draped it gently over my shoulders like a cape. I turned toward the full-length mirror. Cloaked in black sable, I looked feline. Imperial. Nearly seductive. I slapped Bert giddily on the chest. "This is *meshuggeneh!*"

He produced a slim velvet box from his sleeve. "So if I bought you a string of pearls to go with it, you'd be upset?"

Our life of luxury, darlings. This is how it began. It was Bert's idea first, you see. Never, ever mine.

Perhaps we should have known better.

The very summer after Bert had bought me my fur, a thoughtful, meticulous scientist named Dr. Sandler was working as a nutrition specialist at the Oteen Veterans Administration Hospital in

Asheville, North Carolina. Summer was always "polio season," and the disease struck children disproportionately. Little limbs gnarled and twisted like grapevines. Respiratory systems atrophied, and children had to be encased in iron lungs: medieval-looking machinery performed the mechanics of breathing for them. People believed that the heat and the crowds were to blame—public swimming pools, county fairs, picnics—all that exposed flesh and sweat creating a primordial soup of disease and infection.

That summer of 1948, the worst polio epidemic in North Carolina history broke out. Every family in Asheville that could fled to the country. Yet Dr. Sandler began to suspect that neither crowds nor the heat was the real culprit. In the summer, he observed, children consumed significantly more candy. And soft drinks. And, in particular, ice cream.

As Asheville's devastation from polio grew steadily worse, Dr. Sandler felt compelled to go to the local newspapers and radio stations. *Please, do not eat ice cream or candy*, he urged his fellow citizens. *Do not consume sugar at all.* A desperate and frightened population across North Carolina took notice. *Don't eat ice cream*, people raced to tell each other. *It causes polio!*

By the time the polio season of 1949 approached, much of the South was already on alert. Although Bert had initially refused to allow Dunkle's franchises to open in segregated areas (my husband, he aspired to be the Branch Rickey of ice cream), he could never deny any veteran. And so we had six Dunkle's located in North Carolina by then, and ten other franchises in neighboring states. Our headquarters began receiving panicked phone calls from our owners: *No one's coming into our shops. Folks are saying our ice cream is poisoning their children. I'm not sure I can make my monthly payments.*

It was, of course, a disaster. In June alone, Dunkle's shipped

400,000 gallons less ice cream mix to the South than the previous year. By July 650,000 gallons less. By August our stores from Washington, D.C., to Atlanta were nearly deserted. All six of our franchises in North Carolina were facing bankruptcy.

"Does Bonwit Teller take back purchases?" I asked grimly, though the idea of selling back my sable—or my pearls, or the Chevrolet—was now unthinkable. That's the odd thing about luxury, darlings. The moment you become accustomed to it, it's no longer a luxury at all but a necessity.

People forget this.

"Perhaps we've gotten too big, Lil." Bert raked his hands through his now-silvery hair. "Perhaps we should just close down the shops and cut our losses?"

"But then what?" The problem with Dr. Sandler's dietary claims, unfortunately, was that they appeared to have merit. All over the country, the polio epidemic of 1949 had proved even worse than the epidemic of 1948. Except in North Carolina—where citizens had reduced their ice cream and sugar consumption by almost 90 percent.

Switching out the lights in our factory each evening, I was haunted by the sense that everything we'd built was about to crumble cataclysmically around me. Finally, perhaps, I was being punished. All my unconfessed sins. The lies. The thieving. The Dinellos. Those nameless, faceless Candie employees whom I had likely put out of work. Those Italian immigrants, innocents who had not yet become citizens, whose lives had possibly been— Here I forced myself to stop thinking altogether.

Yet as word spread about Dr. Sandler's theory, I knew it would only be a matter of time. Our franchises would fold, one by one, South to North, East to West. All our postwar innovations— all the frozen novelties and gimmicky flavors we'd been developing—could not save our industry from the threat of this epidemic. And then what?

One night as we were sitting down to dinner, the telephone rang. Isaac, now a knock-kneed twelve-year-old with his first crush on a girl, scrambled to answer.

"Pop, it's for you." Glumly, he set the receiver down on the credenza. "Some woman, Ada? She says it's important."

Bert's face seized and he dropped his napkin. "I'll take this inside." Hurrying into the bedroom, he shut the door.

An alarm went off inside me.

"Go to your room," I told Isaac. "I'll call you back when it's dinner."

Gingerly, I lifted up the receiver and pressed it to my ear like a seashell.

"—I told you," I heard Bert saying, "I'm not meeting with you tomorrow. It's a betrayal—"

I felt woozy, arrhythmic. Yet a voice on the other end interrupted, "For Chrissakes, Dunkle. The whole industry is going to be there." It was male. Clipped. Sonorous. "High-Ho. Muldoon's. All your competition. Even the Rockefellers are sending a lawyer from their milk trust."

Ada. ADA. The Atlantic Dairy Association, that was who was on the line. Not a woman at all. Slowly, I exhaled. I identified the voice. Clark Bauer, the president. I had heard him give a drunken toast at the Christmas party hosted by the *Ice Cream Manufacturers' Gazette* the year before. His secretary had likely put the call through to Bert.

"If we let the sugar people take the lead on this, without enough dairymen and ice cream companies on board, what do you think is likely to happen?" Bauer said. "I'll tell you what. They'll pass Truman's buck. As soon as they're challenged—as soon as they're asked, 'If sugar doesn't cause polio, then how come

Dr. Sandler's diet is working in Asheville?'—do you know what they'll say? 'Why, it's *milk* that causes polio, not sugar.' They'll turn against ice cream in a heartbeat trying to save themselves. You know I'm right, Albert. Those sugar people are spineless—"

"B-but, Clark . . ." I could hear Bert's voice wavering. "None of us *do* know why the diet works."

"Well, I've got news for you. We may never know. But I eat sugar and ice cream. You eat sugar and ice cream. Have we gotten polio? Millions of Americans eat ice cream every day during the summer. And you know what? Millions of them do not get polio. As far as I'm concerned, this Dr. Sandler is a quack. So get on board and fight this thing with the rest of us, will you? We'll go down to North Carolina ourselves next summer if we have to. Hand out free ice cream cones to every man, woman, and child in the goddamn state. Show them they have absolutely nothing to fear but their own stu—"

I was shocked: For at that moment, Bert hung up with a defiant click. Suddenly all I heard was Bauer's disembodied voice groping: "Albert? Albert are you there? Goddamn it!" I barely had time to replace my own receiver in its cradle before my husband returned to the dining room, red-faced, agitated. I had never seen him in such a state.

"Anything the matter?" I said, carefully arranging myself before my dinner plate.

He shook his head violently. "Isaac!" he shouted with unusual force. "Here, doll," he said, motioning to my plate, though he appeared distracted. "Let me serve you."

All night long, Bert was inordinately lovely and solicitous to me. Yet he related nothing at all of his conversation with Clark Bauer. And so I quietly seethed. What was the matter with my husband? Bauer was right. I read science journals. I kept up on the news. Dr. Sandler's claims were pure hypothesis. Nothing scientific had been proved linking sugar to polio at all. But rumor and fear—I knew firsthand how quick and effective these were. Our entire industry was in danger, and its leaders were beseeching Dunkle's to join with them to save it. Why had Bert opposed this? He wanted *certainty*? Since when was there ever certainty in this life? Oh, I could have given him such a thump!

The next afternoon I slipped out of the factory and had Martin drive me into Manhattan to pay a visit to Clark Bauer myself. I thought he would be pleased to see me, to learn that I was committed to getting my husband on board. Yet when his secretary ushered me in, Clark Bauer's lips tightened like a drawstring purse, and his chin elevated slightly. Indeed, he appeared to appraise me not through his eyes but through his nostrils. I could see him take in my leg, my cane, my sable coat in one dismissive sniff. An elaborate cruelty radiated off him like a scent. He did not invite me to sit.

Not knowing quite what to do, I propped my cane against the edge of his desk and clutched my pocketbook. "It's come to my attention that my husband is refusing to attend your meeting," I said crisply. "But I'm in agreement with you, Mr. Bauer, that we all need to act together to save our industry. So I'd like to come in Bert's place tonight, if I may."

"Excuse me?" Mr. Bauer sat up as if he had been stung. He fixed me in an annihilating stare. "With all due respect, Mrs. Dunkle, your husband is the one we deal with here."

"Mr. Bauer," I said, drawing myself up to my full height before him, though admittedly this was not very much. "Bert and I have always worked as a team. I have as much a hand in our company as Bert does, and if he sees that I'm on board with you—"

Bauer held up his hand as if putting a stop to traffic. "Well, if you're such a 'team,' Mrs. Dunkle, did your husband not explain to you why you were not invited to this meeting with him? Did he not tell you that the association agreed unanimously that during this campaign, *you*, of all people, must be kept completely out of sight?"

"Excuse me?" I said. Though I did not mean to, I took a step back. My throat felt filled with broken glass.

"It's nothing personal, Mrs. Dunkle. But surely even you can understand how detrimental it would be to have a cripple seen trying to reassure the public that sugar and ice cream do not cause polio."

"It wasn't polio at all," I said indignantly. "It was a street accident."

Clark Bauer stared at me, incredulous. "Do you think that matters, Mrs. Dunkle? All people need to see right now is a gimp-legged ice cream maker with a cane, and they'll jump to their own conclusions. All their worst fears will be confirmed. Certainly you understand the power of images in advertising. Do I really have to spell this all out for you," he said, reaching for his intercom, "or can you grasp this more quickly than your husband?"

To sit stewing at home after this, in a dark parlor, walled off from the air and light by other, higher, brighter apartments, all the while listening to the insipid clatter of our domestic, Emeraldine, ladling beef stew onto a plate for Isaac's supper—my awkward, finicky son (he didn't like strawberries, because the seeds stuck in his teeth; he refused to wear sweaters, because the collars were itchy), my son, in all his indulged pubescence—with his new royal blue bicycle, and his trumpet lessons after school that Bert and I had paid for, and his store-bought track uniform—I did not work him as hard as I had worked at his age, yet still he shrank from me whenever I pulled him toward me and said, "Give Mama a kiss now"—to sit there listening to him inanely reporting the details

of his school day to Emeraldine in the humid kitchen while the
clock above the icebox ticked relentlessly and I listened for Bert,
out carousing with his goddamn war buddies—Bert, who had
forfeited a chance to join with the biggest men in our industry
in a campaign to promote sugar and ice cream— Why? To protect me. And his precious principles, no doubt—should I box his
ears or kiss him?—to sit at home in a narcotizing armchair after all of this, all the while seething, riddled with animosity and
frustration—why, the prospect of it was simply unbearable!

"Drive me to the office," I barked at Martin.

Back at the factory, I tried reviewing the accounts, yet I could
absorb nothing. Conflicting, unseemly emotions ran rampant inside me like quicksilver. Mrs. Preminger had left early. I poured
myself a scotch from her drawer. I ran my finger along the edge
of her brass letter opener. I pulled apart the jaws of her Swingline
stapler, then snapped them shut. I picked up her newest cat paperweight. It was made of onyx, a gift, she'd said, from her nephew,
though I suspected she'd bought it herself. It felt so cold and heavy
in my hand. Reaching back, I heaved it as hard as I could through
the frosted-glass office partition. The violent shattering was so
immensely satisfying. It had been a long time since I'd done something like this. I hadn't realized how much I craved it.

For a moment I stood panting, surveying my handiwork. Then
I hobbled over and began mashing the shards into the carpet with
the tip of my cane. I ground them down with as much force as
I could muster. The sound was horrible; it ran up my spine like
dry chalk on a blackboard. Finally I saw I had made quite a mess.
I supposed I should leave it—we had janitors for this sort of thing
now. Yet I hated disorder. I picked up the chipped paperweight
and set it back on Mrs. Preminger's desk. The job really required
a vacuum cleaner, but all I found in the supply closet was a broom
and a dustpan.

Suddenly the phone rang. In the silence, the shrillness felt accusatory, as if God or Mrs. Preminger were telephoning down from the sky to reprimand me. I tried to ignore it, but the ringing continued, so finally I answered. It was Silas, our watchman. "Oh, Mrs. Dunkle," he said with surprise. "There's a man here to see you. I told him I thought you'd gone for the day, but he insisted I check. He says it's an emergency."

For a moment my heart leaped. Had something happened to Bert? To Isaac?

"Who is it?" I said.

"He won't give his name. He says he's a friend of your father's."

It was not until Pickles sauntered into the office that I was able to place him from the group of men that night at Rickie's Round-Up. He had a heavy, cumbersome gait, and his name, I saw now, likely came from his nose, a bulbous gherkin dominating his face. His small, dark eyes, in contrast, were like peppercorns. He was wearing a raincoat, though it was not raining. As he entered, he removed his hat and glanced around slowly, appraisingly, as if he were considering buying the factory.

"Wow. Quite a big joint here," he said. "Though I figured for some reason it would be fancier."

He picked up the small wooden file box by Mrs. Preminger's telephone, flipped up the lid with a greasy finger, then set it back down. He seemed to be in no hurry at all. Noticing her little beveled-glass candy dish of sour balls, he helped himself to a lime one, slipped it from its cellophane, and popped it into his mouth. Only men ever took such liberties: They walked into an office behaving as if it were theirs.

"Can I help you?" I said with irritation. "You told my guard it was urgent."

Pickles picked up the Swingline stapler, just as I had. Only once he'd set it down did he notice the broken partition and the bits of glass sparkling in the carpet beneath it. I saw him survey the broom propped against the doorframe and the empty glass of scotch on the corner of her desk.

"Am I interrupting something?" he said with bemusement.

I crossed my arms. "What's wrong with my father?"

"Can we sit?" Pickles motioned to the chairs on either side of Mrs. Preminger's desk.

We sat.

"I'm here on his behalf," Pickles said.

"Where is he?"

"He's . . . um, indisposed at the moment."

"Is he sick? Is he in the hospital?"

"No, no." Pickles shook his head. "Nothing like that. Not yet anyway. I'm not going to mince words, Mrs. Dunkle. Your father—your papa—he owes some very important people a lot of money. And he needs it. Immediately."

"Oh," I said sharply. I leaned back in my chair. Of course he needed money. *Of course he did.* I felt a shiver of bitterness. "Last time I saw my father was five years ago. With you. He took off with my pocketbook, and I haven't heard from him since. Not one letter. Not even a phone call. For years I sat waiting. *Now* he remembers me?"

Pickles looked at me haplessly. "If that's how you feel about it," he said.

"If it's so damn important to him, why doesn't he come here to see me himself?"

"He can't come to see you. He's stuck out in Nevada. His one phone call was to me." His eyes bored into mine.

"Papa's in prison?"

"Let's just say that some of our business associates don't want to let him out of their sight. A deal of his went south, okay? So they're sort of holding him. As collateral."

"What kind of deal?" Though of course I could only imagine. In fact, I had enough of an idea to suspect that it was best not to know. Papa: I could box his ears.

"He needs to pay them this week," Pickles said.

"Five years ago he leaves me in a parking lot. Now suddenly I'm his bank?"

"Look. It's your choice." Pickles shrugged, rising, finally, to leave. "But if your papa can't come up with the money and you can live with yourself knowing—"

My heart began pounding. *Goddamn it.* I pointed to the telephone on Mrs. Preminger's desk. "Call him."

"Call who?"

"Papa. I want to hear for myself."

Pickles shook his head. "I don't think it works like—"

"Call," I commanded, my leg shaking beneath the desk. "They want money? Then let him talk to me."

Reluctantly, Pickles took a slip of paper from his pocket, turned the telephone around toward himself, and dialed. "Yeah, it's Pickles," I heard him say. "Bailey's daughter wants to talk to him. . . . I know, I told her. But she insists she needs to hear it directly. . . ."

As he cradled the receiver between his ear and his chin, he shot me an exasperated look. "What's the phone number here? They'll have him call you back."

After he hung up, he eyed me blankly.

"Who are you in all of this?" I squinted at him. All these men, these goddamn shysters.

"Me?" He shrugged with a self-congratulatory grin. "I'm just Pickles."

I had the urge to slap him. Instead we both sat staring at the telephone for a few minutes, breathing heavily, as if willing it to ring through telepathy.

Lo and behold, it did.

"Papa?" I said into the receiver.

"Malka!" he cried. "*Kindeleh.* I am so pleased to hear from you. So pleased, you do not know."

"You're right," I said. "I don't."

"Really, Malka. Do you think this is the time and the place?"

"Why not?" Though I had not meant to sound threatening or accusatory, I felt a sudden, peculiar rush. He had to answer me. For the first time, Papa needed what I had.

"Explain it to me a little," I said, leaning back. "Humor me. Last time I saw you, you left me stranded. I had to sleep on that waitress's couch and call a delivery truck to get me home, and I never got to see my husband before he shipped out to the Pacific. For months I waited for a word from you. So, please," I said, my pulse thrumming in my ears, "enlighten me."

"I left you? I left you? How can you possibly say that, Malka? How can you accuse me of such a thing? You were drunk, do you remember? You were drunk, and you were sick. And so I went to find you a doctor, you see. That's why I left. And I took your purse to pay him, do you understand? I drove and I drove. I drove all the way to Trenton looking for a doctor for you, in fact, my dear long-lost daughter, but by the time I came back—okay, to be honest, I couldn't find a doctor—but *poof!* You had just disappeared! You were like Harry Houdini, Malka! So what could I do? Why, you just left *me* there. Abandoned by my own daughter. Just like that." For emphasis he snapped his fingers right into the receiver.

I did not say anything. His words were nothing more than a confection of air. Of course they made me angry—at him, but also at myself, for I realized against all reason that I also wanted desperately to believe them—in all their cartoonish implausibility, in their audacity.

Papa continued, "But that's just water under the bridge, okay? It's just your word against mine, Malka, in the end, and that's no way for a father and daughter to be, is it? Let's just let bygones be bygones, all right, *kindeleh*? I won't hold it against you if you won't hold it against me. Just tell me now: How's my favorite girl? My big success story? I did try your ice cream, you know. Not too long ago I had that vanilla of yours, with the cookie crumbs. I'm not much of an ice cream man, as I told you, but I have got to say—"

"Papa," I cut him off. "Exactly how much do you need?"

He paused. "Uh." His voice grew faint. I could picture him, glancing around a boardinghouse in Nevada somewhere. "About four thousand dollars."

"Four thousand dollars?"

"Well, four thousand five hundred, to be exact," he said. "Actually, forty-seven hundred. Forty-seven hundred would be a lifesaver. Wire it. Or, better yet, give it straight to Pickles. Come to think of it, cash—and small bills would be best."

"Ha. You think I'm giving forty-seven hundred dollars in cash to a stranger? I'll write you a check. To you and only you."

There was a pause. "Well, that is truly kind, Malka."

"This is a loan. Not a gift. You understand? You pay me back all five thousand."

"Five thousand? I thought we agreed I only needed four."

"You said four thousand seven hundred. Plus the three hundred you stole from me in New Jersey. That makes five."

I heard him let out a low whistle. "I told you. I took that money just to pay for a doctor. For *you*."

The man's chutzpah: It was impressive.

"Five thousand, Papa. And you pay me back in person. Take it or leave it."

"Of course! Of course," Papa said. "You think I would take charity from my own daughter? In fact, as soon as I sort everything out here, when I get back east again, you and I, we are going to go out for another steak dinner. This time in Manhattan. Someplace really swanky. And I want to meet that husband of yours, too, okay? We'll talk some real business. Your franchises, Malka, I haven't forgotten. I tell everybody here, in fact, about what a big *macher* my daughter is."

Some sort of commotion erupted in the background. I heard Papa's hand clamp over the receiver and muffled voices. When he came back on the line, he was saying, "All right already," though not to me.

His voice grew clear again. "So forty-seven hundred, Malka? You can do that for me? For your old papa? Oh, you are a real lifesaver. A real lifesaver, *kindeleh*. Just like the candy."

When I hung up, I glared at Pickles, took out my checkbook, furiously wrote a check to Hank Bailey, tore it off with a *fwip*, and handed it to him.

"There. Happy?"

His grin, from across the desk, was lupine. "Good girl," he said, folding the paper crisply in half.

Watching him leave, I had the sickening sense that I would not see Papa—nor my money again—anytime soon.

Each day, as I'd suspected, there was no word, no phone call, certainly no letters postmarked Nevada. Yet still, as I limped through the factory each morning and poured bath salts into my tub at night, I found myself reciting the same incantations I had said to myself as a tiny girl on Mulberry Street, defying all reason: *Papa, please. Papa, say something. Papa, come back.*

Three weeks later I did get a telephone call. Yet it was from our bank. "Mrs. Dunkle, we were wondering if you still wanted to keep your personal account with us?"

"Why, of course," I said distractedly, unclipping my earring. "Why wouldn't I?"

"Well, your last check bounced."

Snatching up my checkbook, I thumbed through it. "Five dollars and forty-nine cents to the telephone company?" I said. "How is that possible?"

"No, the most recent one. From last Thursday. For two thousand eight hundred dollars to a Hank Bailey."

"What?"

"Your other checks to him have cleared. But now the account is empty," they said. "So what would you like us to do?"

Chapter 12

A FEW YEARS AGO, when 20th Century Fox was developing some made-for-television movie about my life (those dingbats and time wasters—it never got anywhere), a scene was to be filmed in which Bert and I arrived at the Franklin Sherman Elementary School. First the camera was to pan to a school nurse sitting deject-edly beneath a banner reading FREE POLIO VACCINES TODAY in an empty gymnasium. Then it would cut to our ice cream truck bounc-ing over the hills in the distance like the cavalry, bells a-jingling.

While the sound track swelled, word would spread from child to child, classroom to classroom: "The ice cream lady is coming!" Suddenly the gym would be mobbed with children rolling up their sleeves to be vaccinated. The scene would conclude outside our ice cream truck, with Bert and the school principal hoisting me up onto their shoulders amid a cheering crowd. "Together we will defeat polio!" I'd shout, waving my cane triumphantly.

The Pied Piper of Polio, the film was supposed to be called, or some such nonsense as that. If people think I'm a liar and a thief these days, well then. Clearly, they have never met a screenwriter.

Polio and humiliation. These, I suppose, are as responsible for my success as much as anything else in the end. For if my very own father had not embezzled from me—on the very same day, no less, that Clark Bauer had dismissed me so nastily from his office—perhaps I never would have gotten the gumption or the inspiration to do what I did next.

The day the bank telephoned, I went down to its main branch on Twenty-Third Street. There, stamped in my leathery passbook, in purple-blue typewriter ink, the new balance was confirmed: $00.00. My personal checking account. The only money that was mine outright—that Bert had given me to use at my own discretion. Gone.

"May I see the canceled checks, please?" I asked the teller. The signatures matched mine almost perfectly. "*Lillian Dunkle*," with the cockeyed *L* and the little flourish at the end of the *e*. Those forgers, oh, they were good.

Behind a low partition, I could see the bank manager smoking a cigarette, flicking his ashes into a potted palm. Yet I could not bear to alert him. Papa was still my father, after all. A thin flame of hope, of protective, irrational love, flickered within me like a pilot light. Better to hire a private detective, I resolved miserably. Handle it all myself somehow.

I guarded so many secrets now, darlings. Some were small, like lipsticks I'd pocketed from the display counters at Macy's (it's not as if they could sell the testers anyway!). Others were bigger. I had never told Bert that Papa was alive and had resurfaced during the war. Perhaps I feared that Bert might be more willing to leave me one day if he knew I was not an orphan. Perhaps, hearing how Papa had abandoned and robbed me, Bert might think it was my fault. Perhaps he would begin to see me as I believed Papa saw me: as inherently unlovable. A *meeskite*. A shrew.

There in the bank, my limbs felt like sandbags. My wretchedness saturated me. Oh, what a fool I had been! Twenty thousand dollars. My entire emergency fund. My financial life raft (in case, God forbid, Bert did in fact leave—or the Cossacks returned—or the Dinellos resurfaced). The only money I could access myself, that enabled me to sleep at night. It had been cleaned out precisely when the polio epidemic was threatening our whole business. I sat down hard on the polished bench. The hall echoed with the particle hush of a library. Its marble floor amplified the shuffling of people waiting on line to withdraw money for the weekend. The bell over the door *chinged*. Yet all I could hear was Pickles saying *Attagirl* with that mocking, predatory gleam in his eye. Clark Bauer sneering, *Surely even you can understand how detrimental it would be to have a cripple seen trying to reassure the public.*

A little boy peeked out at me impishly from the folds of his mother's skirt as she stood filling out a deposit slip. A hand clopped him hard on the back of his head. "Jimmy, don't stare at the cripple," his mother barked. "It's not polite."

The whole bank glanced at me.

I dropped my passbook into my purse and stood up straight. "It's only my leg that's bad," I said loudly. "I'm not deaf, you know."

And right there, it hit me. The world, it was always going to stare at my deformity. If people believed I'd had polio, so let them. I was done hiding in the shadows, being mistaken for a weakling. A freak. A pushover.

And I'd be damned if Dunkle's would go bankrupt either.

Let those other ice cream makers travel down to North Carolina like carnival barkers, handing out free Popsicles and sundae cups at swimming pools and county fairs, trying to convince the public that their products were safe. Bert and I would launch our own goddamn anti-polio campaign. Yet we would take the exact opposite tack and beat our competition to the punch.

My husband, he loved my idea as soon as I explained it to him. We agreed that I should meet with the March of Dimes

Campaign personally. "Being crippled myself, I do not want my child—or anyone else's—to suffer the way that I have from this dreadful disease," I told the organizers. "Which is why my husband and I want Dunkle's Ice Cream to partner with your foundation."

Soon every Dunkle's franchise in the country displayed cardboard dime collectors by their cash registers and offered two special ice cream flavors as part of our new "Dips for Dimes" campaign. For every scoop of Fight Polio Peppermint or March of Dimes Marshmallow that customers purchased, Dunkle's donated a penny to the National Foundation for Infantile Paralysis.

Oh, what a publicity coup this proved to be! In a single ingenious stroke, I established Dunkle's as the most "trusted" and "wholesome" ice cream company in America. Even as the polio epidemic worsened, our sales soared. For our ice cream alone was now associated with "finding a cure." We were celebrated in newspaper editorials for our "responsibility and dedication." For our sunshiny, sprinkle-coated campaign on behalf of handicapped children everywhere. So sue me. Even Bert did not know: All of this was simply born from my desire for restitution, of course. And for vengeance.

And, darlings, it turned out to serve another vital purpose as well. For in the news each day came reports of the U.S. Senate investigations into suspected American Communists. People in the arts, government, industry—who had once simply attended a socialist rally or a union meeting—were suddenly being targeted. Blacklisted. Disgraced. Guilt by association was enough. Oh, how I worried! Bert and his *meshuggeneh* politics! What if they came back to ruin us? My husband himself seemed only mildly concerned. "Lil, the last meeting I went to was over twenty years ago. I never once spoke. You know I never signed anything. Why, there's no proof I ever attended at all."

Yet he was utterly unaware, of course, of the petition I'd handed over to Orson Maytree. No doubt it was still sitting in a government file somewhere, just waiting to be rediscovered by some zealous office assistant. Then, signators would be summoned before the committee and compelled to name names. I was certain of it. Somebody in that Delancey Street basement would likely remember my good-looking Bert. What if Rocco Dinello himself were called upon to testify?

At any moment, that single sheet of paper could resurface to destroy us. At night it unfolded and flapped before me in my dreams like an ominous bird. Each time the phone rang or a stranger appeared in Dunkle's reception area, my heart lurched. Had my husband been identified? Was he being *subpoenaed*?

Unable to calm my frantic pulse, I finally telephoned Orson Maytree. "Why, Miss Lillian!" he exclaimed. "Just last night the missus had a taste for your strawberry ice cream."

"Mr. Maytree," I said quietly, glancing around the office, though I'd made sure to lock the door, "I was just wondering. Is there any way you might be able to put me in touch with Senator Joseph McCarthy?"

Now, of course, a huge ruckus is being made about all this in the press. A "rabid McCarthyite," they're calling me. "A collaborator in the Communist witch-hunts." Yet all I ever supplied to the senator, darlings, was ice cream. Vanilla, mostly. Some maple walnut. Each week during the hearings, I secretly paid one of our franchises in Washington to send over a few quarts of the senator's favorite flavors "as a token of Dunkle's appreciation." That was it. And okay, so I once had a tub specially made for him called Better-Dead-Than-Red Raspberry. But Joseph McCarthy was an extremely appreciative man; he always sent over lovely little thank-you notes. (By contrast, Roy Cohn, that cocksucker, once hollered at me, "Is it too much to ask for a few goddamn sprinkles?") So spare me your outrage. All I did was ingratiate my-self. That—along with Dunkle's very public work for the March of Dimes—was the only way I could think of to cement our rep-utation as upstanding, loyal Americans.

For God forbid anyone ever dug up anything on Bert.

Although scientists would eventually conclude that there was no connection between ice cream consumption and polio at all, by the start of 1954 the debate was rendered moot. Jonas Salk's won-drous polio vaccine was ready to be tested nationwide. The goal was to have no fewer than a million American children involved in the trials by the year's end.

Since the vaccines needed to be refrigerated, Bert and I volun-teered Dunkle's fleet of ice cream trucks to help transport them across the country. Our franchise owners themselves got involved recruiting "Polio Pioneers," as they were called (never "guinea pigs"). They taped up posters and handed out leaflets in their shops, at the Elks Clubs, the Rotary, 4-H, the local Boy Scouts. Nobody gives us credit nowadays, but I am telling you: Dunkle's was responsible for encouraging hundreds of thousands of chil-dren to get inoculated against polio.

The first national trials were to be held at the Franklin Sherman Elementary School in McLean, Virginia. Bert and I decided we'd go down personally to hand out free Dunkle's ice cream to all the brave little Polio Pioneers as a reward. Why, it was history in the making! And besides, the publicity, I imagined, would be mar-velous.

Commandeering an ice cream truck from our franchise in Washington, we drove to McLean bearing gallons and gallons of chocolate and vanilla ice cream mix, a huge bouquet of pink and brown helium-filled balloons, and a life-size cardboard cutout of our brand-new mascot, Spreckles the Clown. After each child was inoculated, I would hand them a coupon for a free Dunkle's ice cream, which could be redeemed from our truck parked right outside the school, where Bert would be waiting.

"We've come to celebrate all the brave little Polio Pioneers volunteering here today," I announced over the school's PA system from the principal's office.

Yet the cafeteria, where the vaccinations were to be administered, was thick with the queasy, chemical stench of poster paint and floor cleaner mixing with fumes of overheated alphabet soup. As soon as you inhaled it, you felt instantly anxious. The mothers waiting with their children chain-smoked cigarettes, chipped at their nail polish, gnawed on their cuticles. I couldn't blame them. Their little boys and girls, five, six, seven years old—their most precious possessions in the entire world—were being offered up as human sacrifices to the gods of science—volunteering their tiny arms to be injected with an experimental vaccination. Dr. Salk had assured the nation that the polio virus he was using had been "killed." But nobody really knew for certain. Nothing quite like this had ever been done before. It was an enormous leap of faith. Indeed, some of the parents had dressed their children as if for church, the boys' hair slicked carefully in place, the girls in crinolined dresses and polite hair ribbons.

The only people who seemed to take the scene in stride were the reporters. Local newspapermen. Radio announcers. Two men from NBC, one with a big, heavy camera balanced on his shoulder like a piece of artillery. They milled around smoking cigarettes and wisecracking, waiting for something striking to strike them. I decided it was smart to introduce myself, offer them Dunkle's ice cream coupons.

"Ice cream?" one of them said dryly. "You don't have anything stronger?"

Dr. Richard Mulvaney was administering the vaccines. His very own children were the first to receive them. "We're Polio Pioneers," his daughter announced earnestly, pushing up her puffed sleeve to show the reporters her Band-Aid.

The trials proceeded smoothly enough from then on—though solemnly. They reminded me a little of the lines for taking Communion back at the Most Precious Blood Church—and my stack of coupons thinned. Yet suddenly the doors swung open with a horrible metallic *thwonk!* An exasperated mother charged into the cafeteria, yanking her son along behind her as if he were an obstinate dog. The boy was shrieking, "No! I don't wanna get a shot! No, no! Don't make me!" Dropping to his knees on the linoleum, he became deadweight, howling and writhing as she tugged at him.

"Billy Junior, don't make me whup you. I will not have you get sick and crippled for the rest of your life, do you hear me? You pick yourself up off that floor this instant, or I'll really give you something to cry about."

"No! No! No! You can't! Don't make me! Please, Ma! Don't! Please!" Billy Junior's face was red as raw meat and slick with mucus; his scorching shrieks caused some of the other children to shrink back in panic. The cafeteria had grown humid. Perspiration was sliding down the back of my dress. My leg was beginning to throb. The reporters were exchanging dubious looks. The boy's cries started to ignite everyone else's misgivings. Mothers began murmuring and glancing toward the door. Children tugged at their mothers' hems and began whimpering. In a moment, it seemed, there could be a massive stampede for the exit. The trials would be abandoned—years of hard work and research left in shreds.

"Stop making such a ruckus and listen to your mother," I bellowed, thumping my cane on the linoleum floor. "Look at me," I heard myself say. "Is this how you want to end up?"

The cafeteria grew quiet.

"That's right. You heard the lady," Billy Junior's mother said unsteadily, gesturing at me. "Do you want to end up like that?"

Sniffling, the little boy regarded me with a mixture of timidity and fascination. No one, darlings, ever expects cripples to speak. Certainly they never expect us to be so candid about a condition that they themselves are trying so desperately to ignore. "You had polio?" he asked in a small voice. Sucking on his bottom lip, he inched closer. I could see his gaze trailing up and down my calf, his pupils following the crosshatch of my scars. "Can I touch?"

"Billy Junior," his mother scolded.

No one but Bert or my doctors had ever bothered to look at me, to see me up close, respectfully. I shrugged. "Be my guest." Lifting up the hem of my dress slightly, I extended my bad leg in its clunky black orthopedic shoe. The boy touched my calf hesitantly, gingerly, with only the very tip of his finger, as if he were afraid I might detonate. Some of the other children abandoned their places on line and gathered around, angling for a glimpse.

"You see, kids?" I said in a teacherly voice. "I can't climb a tree. I can't roller-skate. I can't ride a bicycle. Unless you want to have a bad leg like mine your whole life, go get your polio vaccine." I motioned toward the nurse's station with my chin. "And then you can have ice cream."

"We did good today, Lil," Bert said proudly as he steered the truck back toward Washington. Reaching over to the passenger seat, he kneaded my shoulder. We had not worked so hard, been on our feet so long, since the Depression. The momentousness of the day, the historical significance, had devolved into just another ice cream line for us, full of whiny children, sticky hands, and melty ice cream dripping everywhere. Bert and I were so tired we decided to spend the night in Washington instead of catching the train back to New York. He booked us into the Willard. It was the fanciest hotel we had ever stayed in—right down the block from the White House! Dinner we ordered from room service. Gin gimlets. Shrimp cocktail. Steaks. Our room had its own television—far bigger than the console we had at home! As we switched it on and sat down on the couch in a daze with our cocktails, I gave a *geschrei*. For lo and behold, there on the six o'clock news was me—pointing at my cane and telling Billy Junior, "Unless you want to have a bad leg like mine your whole life, go get your polio vaccine." Then Bert appeared in grainy black and white, leaning out of his truck to hand the boy a vanilla ice cream cone.

"Even the folks at Dunkle's Ice Cream came to help out on this historic day," the newscaster intoned. "They offered special encouragement—and plenty of free ice cream—to all of McLean, Virginia's brave young Polio Pioneers."

Grabbing the telephone, I dialed our publicist, Larry Melnick, at home back in New York. I'd wanted Dunkle's to receive plenty of attention, of course. But on television I had looked so homely, so unglamorous. Clark Bauer—everyone who had ever discouraged me against stepping into the limelight—was exactly right.

"I'm not sure I've done Dunkle's any favors today," I told Larry miserably. "I looked terrible. Ugly and old and crippled. And repellent."

But all Larry could say was, "You and Bert were on TV? Lillian, do you know how much Texaco and Colgate have to pay for that sort of publicity?"

And so, on May 21, 1954, I arrived in a small studio on West Fifty-Third Street in Manhattan with the very first actor hired to play Spreckles the Clown. For the occasion I'd had my hair done at the beauty parlor—dyed even blonder, whooshed into a meringue—and I was carrying a cane whimsically painted to look like a peppermint stick. Why not? My "candy cane," I decided to call it. Children, they loved that sort of nonsense. Larry had instructed me to wear only a plain gingham dress and an apron. "You're a mother, a homemaker, an ice cream lady. Which is precisely your appeal, Lillian. Don't try to be a movie star."

"Please. Do I look to you like Betty Grable?"

The idea was to shoot an inexpensive television ad promoting Salk's polio vaccine, *courtesy* of Dunkle's Ice Cream. "If we offer it as a public-service announcement, perhaps a few stations will run it for free," Larry said.

It was our attempt, of course, to get something for nothing—that one extra potato, that handful of rice, tossed into the sack by the pushcart man.

The commercial was shot with a single camera against the felt wall of the studio. I stood on a small platform so that my bad leg and orthopedic shoes were clearly visible. Staring directly into the lens beside Spreckles the Clown, I took a deep breath and recited woodenly:

Hi. I'm Lillian Dunkle of Dunkle's Ice Cream. Spreckles the Clown and I, we are begging you. (Here Spreckles got down on his knees and clasped his hands together in a hammy plea.) *Please, get your children immunized against polio. I may not have a leg to stand on* (and here I pointed to my bum leg and waggled my striped cane), *but your kids should. And once they've been vaccinated, bring them to your local Dunkle's for a free, wholesome ice cream cone as a reward. Try our delicious homemade I Got a Shot Sherbet, our Polio Pioneer Peach, or our yummy Choco-Full-of-Antibodies. Listen to me, darlings. I know what it's like to go through life like this. And you shouldn't have to. Besides, I'm a mother.* (I smiled and shrugged.) *So sue me: I worry.*

A deep male announcer's voice (Larry's) then concluded, *This announcement is brought to you by Dunkle's: America's Freshest Ice Cream.*

What can I say, darlings? We filmed it and handed it over to our advertising guys at Promovox, and that was that. One local CBS network aired it at some dismal time, right after the test patterns shut off before the earliest morning news. Few people saw it. Or so we assumed. But then our franchise owners started telephoning: "Our customers saw Mrs. Dunkle on television and want to meet her." "Some children here in Mamaroneck came in with pictures they drew of Mrs. Dunkle and Spreckles the Clown. They want to know: Is her cane really made of candy?"

Then, as fate would have it, some insomniac bigwig over at NBC saw the commercial. He himself had had polio as a child. Before we knew it, he was on the phone to our admen, offering to air the spot for free if we abandoned his rival at CBS. He placed our commercial smack in the middle of prime time, just before the enormous hit show *This Is Your Life.*

Suddenly there I was, darlings, on national television. Me. Little Malka Treynovsky Bialystoker. *La Ragazza del Cavallo.* Showing off my leg and my cane.

Most of the other "mothers" on the small screen at the time, they were as cheery and prefabricated as Bakelite. Harriet Nelson of *Ozzie and Harriet.* Jane Wyatt in *Father Knows Best.* Barbara Billingsley in *Leave It to Beaver.* Smiling gamely, they sashayed to the front doors of their TV homes in a taffeta skirt and an apron without a hair out of place. Lemon meringue pie for personalities. But me? What can I say? I was plainspoken. I was humble. I was crippled. And I was funny. Not Lucille Ball or Imogene Coca funny: I did not do slapstick or goofball characters. It was just something in my voice, I suppose. That folksy, shrugging Italian-Jewish New York way of speaking. My character, it put people at ease, drew them in, allowed them to relax contentedly in themselves.

Besides which, I had a new, gentler face.

Today, of course, everyone mocks the plastic surgery I've had. The comedians on television, oh, are they having a field day. Please. Is this something I'm supposed to be ashamed of? *You* go back and live with my leg and my looks, darlings, then tell me what *you* would do. Few people have either my money or my guts, however, to have such work done. So as far as I'm concerned, this ruckus is just jealousy.

And what I had corrected back then, it was tasteful. A slight lift, a slight thinning. None of this ski-jump-nose nonsense or those death masks they're giving actresses nowadays. I simply became more refined. While I would never be beautiful, I went from looking intense and hawkish to merely earnest. Endearing.

And the public, they went wild for me. The same mob impulse that causes pogroms and schoolyard teasing? This time, such a frenzy worked in reverse.

Soon, "So sue me: I worry" became a hugely popular catchphrase. Customers, they gleefully parroted it in our stores, mimicking my accent. I heard it cited on the radio and on television's *Your Show of Shows*. Nancy Walker even played me in a sketch with Phil Silvers! (*Listen to me, darlings. Get your polio shot. Wear clean underwear. Pick up your room. Walk the dog already. And stop dating men who work as hairdressers. I'm a mother. So sue me: I worry,* she said in her parody.) Finally it was decided that our Dunkle's billboards themselves should include a picture of me, Yours Truly, waving my candy cane, beside Spreckles the Clown. LILLIAN DUNKLE SAYS, GET YOUR POLIO SHOT AND COME TO DUNKLE'S FOR A FREE ICE CREAM CONE. "LISTEN TO ME, DARLINGS. I'M A MOTHER. SO SUE ME: I WORRY!"

Dunkle's had to hire a clipping service to keep track of all the newspaper articles about "Lillian Dunkle, the Pied Piper of Polio," "Lillian Dunkle, the Queen of Vaccines." "'Don't Be Like Me,' Says Dunkle's Doyenne. 'Immunize Your Kids.'" "Raising Her Cane—and Her Voice—for America's Children." Suddenly there was a photograph in the *New York Times* of Jonas Salk himself standing beside me and Bert at a March of Dimes fund-raiser at the Plaza's Grand Ballroom. As the microphones were thrust before me and the flashbulbs burst, I began to enjoy myself a little. Folksy, heartwarming tales I spun about my colorful immigrant upbringing on the Lower East Side. "I'm half Jewish, half Italian, just like Mayor Fiorello La Guardia!" I told reporters. So what can I say? So I embellished a little. So I edited. I may have invented a few choice details. For Chrissakes, it was showbiz.

By the end of the year, I was on the cover of both *Life* and *Look* magazines. Nowadays every *farkakte* product has some sort of novelty spokesperson. Mr. Whipple, squeezing the Charmin. Goddamn Morris the Cat pulls in six figures a year. But I was the first-ever trademark sales personality, thank you very much. In 1955 I was even a celebrity mystery guest on *What's My Line?* It took Dorothy Kilgallen less than five minutes to identify me because I slipped up and answered her questions in my real voice. "Oh, I know who you are!" she exclaimed gleefully from behind her pearl-trimmed blindfold. "You're what's-her-name? The ice cream lady with the candy cane! 'So sue me: I worry'! That's it! Are you Lillian Dunkle?" To hear the whole audience roar in delight and approval, oh, it was marvelous. Bert, he and Isaac were both waiting for me in the wings afterward, with roses. I introduced them to the host, John Daly, and we went to Sardi's to eat. Beneath the table Bert squeezed my good leg adoringly. Even Isaac said shyly, "Ma, I'm really proud of you. You were really, really boss."

"Lillian," Larry told me, "you're everybody's warm, Italian-

Yiddishe mama. Even in Peoria they love you. You have to make more commercials, and fast."

And so we did. This time with Bert standing beside me, simply waving.

And our company, it grew and grew—more than I had even imagined. Even when the vaccine trials were over and a report came out attesting to its success, customers still flocked to our stores. (Where, upon Bert's insistence, we still kept collection cards for the March of Dimes right beside our cash registers. They remain there to this very day.)

In one year we went from 116 to 157 stores, then 184, then 203. Some of them were built with a newfangled design, Dunkle's Drive-Ups. Each new franchise we ceremoniously marked on a "Dunkle's Locations Across America" map in our headquarters with bright silver thumbtacks. Soon it was glittering up and down the East Coast, as far south as Pensacola, as far west as Kalamazoo. We bought more factories, enlisted as many big dairy and sugar suppliers as we could find. The bank loans, the contracts, the lawyers: Oh, you do not want to know.

Me, I kept inventing fresh flavors and novelties. The Mint Everest. The Nilla Rilla ice cream cake. The lessons of the tenements, they stood me exceedingly well. One day I realized we were losing money on our ice cream sandwiches every time the chocolate wafers got crushed. I ordered our franchises to take the crumbs and fold them into vanilla ice cream. "Call it Chocolate Cookie Crunch," I instructed in our newsletter. "Tout it as a special flavor. Use it as a topping, or a filling in our molds." This is how our Secret Cookie Crunchies came to be—the prime ingredient in our ice cream cakes. Now we're famous for them. I even had them trademarked. But they started out as garbage.

"Nothing is to go to waste, do you understand? Every drop of spilled ice cream formula is a penny down the drain." Every server was trained to make ice cream scoops weighing no more than 3.5 ounces apiece. If they botched up an order, they were to spoon the ice cream into a big tub and mix it up with the other mistakes. The next day this was sold as Pirate's Treasure Ice Cream. Loaded with sprinkles, nuts, cherries, fudge sauce. The kids loved it. A bestseller. We discarded *nothing*. We squeezed out every cent of profit that we could.

More billboards went up. Me and Spreckles the Clown, everywhere. On the radio. On NBC's *Today* show. People asked us to speak at their elementary schools, at their Junior League meetings. The National Chamber of Commerce presented me with a cane coated in gold leaf; the March of Dimes enlisted Bert and me as cohosts for their annual benefit.

For the first time in my life, people stared at me openly—not with repulsed fascination but with respect. Excitement, even. Bert and I went out to dinner at the 21 Club one evening, and a woman in a silk stole approached. "I'm so sorry to disturb you, but are you Lillian Dunkle from the commercials?" she said breathlessly. Behind her, her mortified husband tried to wave her back to their table. With a trembling hand, she held out a dinner napkin and a pen. "It's such an honor, such an honor, Mrs. Dunkle. I'm sorry, but would you very much mind?"

"*Lillian Dunkle,*" I signed across the linen with a flourish. "*The 'Lame Dame' of Ice Cream! So sue me: I worry!*"

"Oh," the woman said, fanning herself. "Aren't you just the best! And that cane of yours—it really is peppermint-striped! Oh, that's just darling."

Autographs. Photographs. Public appearances. And still more television commercials with me doing the talking and Bert smiling and waving as mutely and adorably as Harpo Marx. The highlight, however, was being asked to the White House. Mamie Eisenhower hosted a luncheon honoring Jonas Salk, Dr.

Mulvaney, the March of Dimes—and Bert and me. Again we stayed at the Willard. I felt like a queen. That's when I wore my first Chanel suit, custom-made, the color of strawberry ice cream. Bert, he wore a bespoke suit with a gold tie tack I had specially made for him in the shape of an ice cream cone. Both of us, we were so nervous we could not speak. Bert was afraid he would stutter, of course. Yet me?

As a White House butler ushered us through a portico out into the Rose Garden, I was suddenly no longer aware of the photographers standing discreetly on the periphery—or even of the other guests nervously wobbling about on the lawn, holding delicate, untouched teacups. Instead I was somehow moving through the dim, low-ceilinged front room in Vishnev with its dirt floors and the bloodstain that would not come out of the window sash. I felt Mama hoisting me and my sisters one by one into the rickety wagon full of rotting cabbages, and the handful of rubles stitched into the armpit of my threadbare gray coat, digging into my underarm, and the cold seeping in behind my collar. A color guard announced, "Ladies and gentlemen, the president of the United States," and suddenly a brass band was playing "Hail to the Chief," and an American flag was snapping in the wind, and I was aware of the sun overhead, turning the Washington Monument into an enormous sundial, and the SS *Amerika* was bucking and heaving in the gunmetal sea, and I was vomiting over the grimy edge of the bunk beside Flora, clutching a handmade babushka doll that a woman whose own child had died had given me. President Eisenhower himself was moving toward me, shaking everyone's hands in a half circle, and he was smiling and moon-faced, this man who had landed in Normandy and saved the world, his smile as broad and happy as the nicest vanilla ice cream—and I felt a stab of exquisite grief. I smelled the manure of the cobblestones on the Lower East Side, the mealy rags, the cockroaches, the soupy, miserable stench of the Beth Israel Dispensary. I saw myself jabbing at the vicious black rat in the Dinellos' kitchen with a broom, then Bert sliding the cigar band over my finger, and I saw the Corwins' shack—that banging screen door that never got fixed—and I heard the hammer of the machines in our first factory and saw miles and miles of automobiles flooding the parkways, tubs and tubs of ice cream packaged in our distinctive beige-pink-and-white striped tubs. For a moment, my body seemed to float outside itself, so great was the sense of unrealness and the aching yearning that Mama and Flora and Mr. and Mrs. Dinello could be there beside me as President Eisenhower was right now towering above me in his blue-gray suit, smelling of expensive, lemony aftershave, as he was smiling, leaning down, shaking my hand, and saying jovially, warmly, "Ah, Mrs. Lillian Dunkle. The Ice Cream Queen of America herself. Welcome to Washington." The elation and utter sadness of the moment, darlings! My eyes teared up, and I found myself swallowing and my mouth opening dumbly: "Mr. President." That was it. In an instant he had moved on. Out of the corner of my eye, I saw Mamie, blinking adoringly up at Bert and drawling, "The president and I do so love your butter pecan. And everything you've done for the March of Dimes, of course," shaking one of his hands with both of hers, her knuckles stubby and pink. My mind, it felt like it was disintegrating into particles in the sunlight as I tried desperately, desperately, to absorb the entire moment of me, Malka Treynovsky fusing into Malka Bialystoker fusing into Lillian Maria Dinello fusing into Lillian Dunkle right there in the Rose Garden of the White House, trying to distill the very essence of shaking the president's hand, and then Mamie's, while also trying, somehow, to capture it all in epic color, free of all time, space, and decay, crystallized, so that Bert and I, we could remain in this very moment forever and share it with every generation of our family, before us and after. Albert and Lillian Dunkle.

Drinking tea and nibbling little ham sandwiches with the First Lady and President Dwight D. Eisenhower, cameras whirring and clicking away. Two guests at the White House.

That afternoon when we returned to the Willard, oh, did Bert and I drink! And then, slowly, after our hearts calmed, we made love—like two hesitant virgins—regarding each other with a sort of questioning awe, trying to reassure ourselves that our bodies were still there—that we were rooted together and that this wondrous event had in fact really happened. Those rich, glamorous people photographed shaking hands with the president of the United States of America as his guests at the White House.

They had really been us.

"Lil, this is all your doing," Bert said quietly, his hand softly touching my hip. "You're a star now, you know that? All this." He gestured around the grand hotel suite, with its sumptuous brocaded bedding, its ornate furniture, its sweating silver ice bucket of champagne sent up compliments of the management. "I always knew we could do it, doll. People everywhere, they love us. They love our ice cream. And they especially love you."

"They do, don't they?" I laughed.

Yet, though I reached for Bert's hand and pressed it to my heart, deep inside I felt only this: a hot, fierce explosion of panic.

PART THREE

Chapter 13

THE PRESS ALWAYS GIVES ME GRIEF for wearing large sunglasses. But you try getting out of a goddamn Cadillac with flashbulbs exploding in your face and see how you fare—especially with a cane.

The New York Supreme Court hadn't been built yet when my family walked up toward Orchard Street that very first day in America. Now it rises above Centre Street like the Parthenon. It's elegant, I suppose, but architecture has rarely been about beauty, darlings. Most buildings throughout history have been designed to promote power or fear. Dunkle's helped change this, I like to believe. Certainly the ancient Greeks and Romans never built glass drive-ins with fiberglass ice cream sundaes twirling atop their roofs.

"We could go around toward the back, Mrs. Dunkle," my lawyer says, nodding at the driver. "There's a side entrance for the disabled."

"Please," I say. "Back entrances are for servants or criminals. I have nothing to hide."

"I just thought with all the stairs—"

"You just 'thought'? Well, don't."

My car glides to a stop at the curb. Through the tinted windows, I can see them. All waiting for me. Such a production.

Channels 2, 4, and 7, WNEW, even WPIX, my old station, those pricks, with their satellite trucks and their blazing lights and their wires draped across the sidewalk like black licorice. All those reporters and photographers, primed for action like hunters in a duck blind. Who do they think they're kidding?

Hector, my driver, switches off the radio. Jason has set the dial to some station where everyone screams at you. I don't care for it much, except that it greatly irritates the lawyers.

Miss Slocum glances at me as she reaches for her briefcase. Her white incisors match the string of pearls at her throat. I cannot stop staring at them.

"Are you okay, Lillian?" she says with exaggerated concern.

"It's 'Mrs. Dunkle,'" I say, glancing out the window.

"I'd take that as a yes." Jason grins.

She clears her throat, swings her legs around, and wriggles toward the door with one hand clutching the hem of her skirt so it won't bunch up. Hector helps her out gallantly. Jason pats my knee. "Okay, Grandma." He laughs, unfolding a pair of reflective black sunglasses. "Showtime, huh?"

"Tateleh." I rub his leg. The sunglasses make him look like a young assassin. Underneath the Brooks Brothers jacket his mother made him wear, he's got on a yellow T-shirt with a silk screen of Che Guevara. Such a wisenheimer.

"Whoa. Look at all the reporters outside," he says, cracking his knuckles one by one, working his fingers along his hand like it was a musical instrument. "Okay. Here we go." He slides down the length of the seat in his leather pants and struggles to unfold himself from the back of the Cadillac. Beyond him I can see the rest of my legal team assembling on the street, conferring with Miss Slocum and Mr. Beecham, ignoring the phalanx of reporters.

Hector comes around to help me out. The Cadillac acts as a buffer between me and the press. "Give me my handbag," I say.

"Do you want your cane first?"

"Handbag." As I slide it into the crook of my left elbow, the lightness of my purse is dispiriting. I'd wanted to bring Petunia with me, but dogs are not allowed in the courthouse apparently, unless they're "service animals." My lawyers also insist that carrying a Chanel handbag with a Chihuahua tucked into it will not endear me to the jury. They want me to look "as sympathetic as possible."

"Now give me my walking stick," I tell Hector. My new walking stick is custom-made, with black Chinese lacquer and a filigreed silver head. My lawyers, of course, would have preferred it if I hobbled into court on one of those ghastly aluminum walkers—or, better yet, rolled in in a wheelchair. Ideally, I suppose, they'd love it if I were paraplegic. They seem determined to play up my disability. How little they know. Being a cripple never inspires pity so much as it does repulsion, darlings. And no, I did not refrain from wearing my good jewelry either.

My sunglasses are already in place, and the coiffeur came to the house before breakfast. Sunny fixed my face as she always does, but with extra powder and rouge. I know from being on television all these years what those lights can do. My suit is the color of butter pecan ice cream. Packaging is so important. You never want to wear dark colors to a court appearance. Purple makes a jury think you're mentally unstable. Navy: trying too hard, hiding something. Red or black: might as well hang a sandwich board around your neck reading GUILTY. I do not need a three-hundred-dollar-an-hour lawyer to tell me this. People are not sophisticated. They see dark, they think "bad," "shady," "untrustworthy." They see light, they think "clean," "pure," "fresh." Jason tells me this is racist. So sue me: I'm just saying what I've observed. In the ice cream industry, you always want your chocolate-based flavors to appear creamy, not earthy or bitter. Our Devil's Food Cake, our

Molten Fudge, our Cocoa-Loco. Marvelous flavors, all of them, but most of them sat in the cases for weeks, slowly crystallizing. Vanilla, meanwhile, is the number-one-selling flavor in America. You can't tell me this is simply because of the taste. Not when you have rum raisin available. Or mint chip. Yet Aryanism still carries the day, darlings, even in the ice cream freezer. I don't like this any more than you do. But there it is.

Each time I go to court, I make sure I'm adorned in nothing darker than peach. And my silvery hair is streaked with so much blond now that it looks like lemon ices.

"Lillian! Lillian! Over here!" the reporters shout as soon as they spot me.

I grip Jason's hand tightly in my left. "Stay with me, you hear?" The flashbulbs start exploding, blinding filaments of hot white.

"Gotcha." He grins at the reporters, my grandson, draws back his shoulders, and actually waves like a movie star. "Good morning, Neewww Yoorkk!" he yodels. "And if any of you like what you see here this morning, hey, come by an' check out Alarm Clock at the Pyramid Club on Monday night. Four hours of totally rad performance-art madness." The head lawyer shoots him a vicious look. I beam, however. Thank God someone else in this family understands marketing.

Isaac opposed having Jason accompany me, of course. "The kid's eighteen, Ma. You're not dragging him into any of this."

"Petunia isn't allowed inside the courthouse," I said. "I'm not going in there alone."

"I'm going with you. I'm your son."

"I don't want you. You make me nervous. I want Jason."

"He's not spending his summer vacation embroiled in a scandal, Ma."

"How is this embroiling him in a scandal? He helps me into

the car, he helps me out of the car. He walks with me. He sits on a bench. Afterward maybe we go to the Plaza. Have a little something for the mouth."

"I'll be there at seven and ride down with you."

"You'll do no such thing. You're not on my side, Isaac. Not you, not Rita. Don't think I don't know what you're up to."

"Oh, Ma. Stop it already with the paranoia."

"Don't tell me to stop. For months you're too busy to see me. But all of a sudden, you have time to hire these big-shot lawyers? To go through every last bit of paperwork and watch every piddly thing I do?"

"Edgar was a crook, Ma. I'm protecting your interests and the company's."

I sniffed. "Sunny can accompany me to court."

"C'mon, Ma. Somebody had to step in, and you know it. It was getting way out of hand. And now all *these* charges on top of everything else?"

"It was a mistake!" I shouted. "One tiny, ten-second mistake! The kid is fine! Nobody was even watching at that hour!"

"Oh, yeah? Then why were you arrested, Ma? Why all the lawsuits?"

"Don't you dare treat me like a criminal."

"Who's—I'm not, Ma—I just—"

"Put my grandson on the phone!" I hollered. "I'm finished with you."

The first day Jason came with me was for the hearing on the assault charges. He showed up wearing a black motorcycle jacket with zippers all over it and combat boots and about a pound of Vaseline in his hair. It stood straight up from his scalp. He appeared to have been electrocuted. The lawyers almost had a coronary. "Mrs. Dunkle," they said, "with all due respect, we're not sure this is the image you want to present."

"What image?" I said.

"Your grandson. He looks like a juvenile delinquent."

Jason laughed. "Actually, I'm like fifty percent water," he said, holding up his hands.

"Excuse me?" said the lawyer.

"Please," I said. "My grandson looks like a *meshuggeneh* teenager. What else is he supposed to look like?"

Of course, I myself would have preferred that Jason dressed nicely. But he's eighteen, for Chrissakes. What was I going to do—buy him a suit and tie on the way to court at nine in the morning? In the past perhaps I would have. But I have no patience for that sort of rigmarole anymore. If I'd wanted another adult beside me who looked like a lawyer, I'd have taken my son.

It turned out that the photos—of Jason in all his punk-rock nonsense escorting me to the courthouse—were a public-relations coup. A little old lady with her rebellious but doting grandson: That's what the public saw. Those pictures humanized me more than any cane or walker or lady lawyer ever could.

As for Jason, girls have been showing up outside the Dunkle's on Lexington Avenue where he works, he says, and leaving little notes and gifts for him at home with his doorman. "Going to court with you has been the most awesome thing all summer, Grandma," he laughed this morning as I measured out our cocktails. "Alarm Clock is even going to do a bunch of monologues about it."

Now, still holding my hand, he pivots before the photographers for an instant and grins brazenly. He may be tipsy, but he's not stupid, my grandson. He doesn't utter another word.

"Lillian, do you have anything to say to the Newhouse family before the hearing?" a reporter shouts out from the melee.

"Lillian, what do you say to the charges that the Dunkle Ice Cream Corporation has not paid any taxes since 1978?"

"Lillian, they've been calling you the 'Ice Queen,' the 'I-Scream Queen,' and the 'Ice Cream Scam-Witch.' Do you have any response to this?"

"No comment. My client has no comment," Miss Slocum shouts, waving them away furiously and guiding me by the elbow. For a moment the squadron of microphones jabbing at me—the flashbulbs creating a wall of exploding light—are horrible and disorienting. I lose my footing. I wobble backward. Jason steadies me. "Just keep going, Grandma," he whispers. Beecham steps in front of us and shoos the reporters back.

The granite steps of the courthouse rise before us like a pyramid. "I'm okay now," I murmur, dropping Jason's hand. "I'll take these on my own."

"You sure?"

Waving him off, I step up with my left foot, then drag the right one up behind it. My hands are shaking, yet I refuse to reach for a railing. "One," I say under my breath. *"Uno."*

All these years later, I still count stairs in Italian.

I step up the next step.

"Due." I exhale.

I step up the next.

Tre.

The rhythm, the tune in my head, is building.

Jason hovers by my left elbow, Miss Slocum is behind me on my right.

Quattro.

Slowly, one turgid step after another, I rise. At the base of the courthouse, everyone watches. I am aware of their gaze on me, the judge and jury of them all, their faces tilted upward, their malicious delight focused on my predicament. Beneath my buttery designer suit, I feel myself perspire. A nerve under my left eye begins to spasm. I grip my cane more tightly. All of it could go in an instant. Just one bad turn and I could lose everything. I swallow. I refuse to even entertain the possibility. For a moment, though, my heart feels as if it is fibrillating. I have to stop to catch my breath. Yet I straighten the hem of my jacket and point my chin like a compass needle up toward the door to the courthouse. Doggedly, I resume my climb. I am making it to the top of these goddamn steps on my own. Without anyone helping me. This is the image I want in the press. This is the picture the whole world needs to see.

∞

Everybody thinks that once you reach the top, you can lie back on a divan with a goddamn mai tai. No. Wrong. Success is not a mountain climb. Success is a treadmill.

You should only know such pressures, darlings. At the peak of it all, in those *meshuggeneh* 1960s, twice a week my days started with a 4:30 A.M. wake-up call from NBC. On those mornings I slept in our guestroom so as not to disturb Bert. I placed our antique gilt telephone by the bed so I could hear it even if I took a Nembutal.

Everything I had timed. Like an assembly line at one of our ice cream plants. At exactly 4:35 A.M., Sunny brought me my black-coffee-and-buttered-toast breakfast on a tray. Ten minutes later I bathed. At 5:00 A.M. Sunny helped me into my costume. In keeping with the times, my producers had decided that I should try to look "groovy" and "mod." Cilla, the wardrobe girl, had developed a signature look for me. Whimsical. Cartoonish. Shiny vinyl smocks in rainbow colors. A stiff, quilted sherbet-colored minidress, a Mary Quant knockoff—though to the knee. At age fifty-seven, although I was in perhaps the best shape of my life, there was absolutely no need for gynecological hemlines, I assured everyone.

After Sunny zipped me into my custom-made white orthopedic go-go boots and handed me my rhinestone-encrusted cat glasses, she turned me toward the full-length mirror. "Mrs. Dunkle, you look very nice, yes?" On the set I would don my ice cream crown and cape. But ta-da. Here I was. "The Ice Cream Queen of America." The bona fide TV character of myself. I looked like I'd come from the future.

By 5:30 A.M. I was in NBC's town car, heading west. By the time I arrived at the studio no more than fifteen minutes later, it was usually pandemonium. The lighting crew, the sound crew, the camera crew, the handlers for the guests. Plus ninety-six crazed children who had been chosen by a lottery months before to appear on the show. So you can only imagine. We had the kids arrive early to allow for all the stomachaches, tantrums, pants wettings, and throw-ups that inevitably occurred just before airtime at 6:30. This was something, frankly, that Promovox, NBC, and I had not taken into account when we first conceived of the *Funhouse*. If you wanted to work with real kids instead of insipid child actors or puppets, you had to weather all sorts of nonsense.

While Lanzo teased my hair into a mass of cotton candy, Harvey sashayed into the hair-and-makeup room, already dressed as Spreckles the Clown. "Seeing those brats out there makes me think Marie Antoinette was grossly under-appreciated," he declared, flinging himself into his makeup chair beside mine.

"Morning, Harvey. How's your mother doing?" I said, my eyes closed beneath the dryer.

"The same," he said, reclining so that the makeup girl could work on him. "I keep telling the hospital that she's only suffering from hypochondria, but of course no one ever listens to me."

"Well, do you go there dressed as a clown?"

"Of course not. I wear my Mata Hari outfit. Honey, the only thing St. Vincent's is good for are the magazines in the waiting room. Did you know that Debbie Reynolds is *still* offering Liz advice about Dick? I mean, where do I start with *that*?"

While Harvey, Nilla Rilla, Chocohontas, and I got the finishing touches on our makeup (mine being the easiest, of course, since I was dressed as neither a clown nor an Indian nor an albino gorilla), the assistant producer herded the children into their seats, where they were instructed how to behave and entertained by a magician until the theme music cued. The sixty seconds before we went on the air were always the most nerve-racking. Since we were live, nothing could be edited. During our first season, in 1959, a real orchestra had played the opening music, yet NBC put the kibosh on it because the snare drum scared some of the children; when the camera panned over them, they were crying. Now, as the first taped bars of the *Dunkle's Ice Cream Funhouse* theme song chimed, Harvey and I took a couple of swigs from the flask he kept stashed in his Spreckles the Clown prop box. *Bottoms up!* we said. *Mud in your eye!* On the other side of the set, Don Pardo stepped up to the microphone and boomed, *Boys and girls of America! It's* Dunkle's Ice Cream Funhouse, *live from NBC Studios. Please welcome your hostess, Mrs. Lillian Dunkle, the Ice Cream Queen of America!*

Flame-red signs flashed above the audience: APPLAUSE APPLAUSE. With kids, however, you really didn't need this. As soon as I stepped out into the spotlight, in my pink, fur-trimmed cape and my gold plastic ice cream crown, twirling my candy cane like a baton, they started shrieking. A few of the younger ones jounced up and down in their seats squealing, "Oooh! Look! The Ice Cream Queeenn!"

Their enthusiasm, darlings, it was always rapturous. I'd stand there smiling, letting it pour over me like caramel, even as my heart thumped frantically. Such absolute, uncomplicated adoration of me.

Like a politician, I began shaking hands with those in the front row. "Who wants ice cream?" I cheered. The set behind me was a garish cartoon schoolroom, with ice cream bars for desks and candy-cane window frames.

"WE DO!" the children screeched back.

And now, boys and girls, Don Pardo bellowed, *please welcome your cohost, Spreckles the Clown!*

Harvey Ballentine ran out in a goofy semicircle, waving hugely at the children and, if he'd had another swig or two backstage, shaking his *tuches* at them in his ballooning, strawberry-colored fat pants. More than once, Spreckles the Clown got a warning from management. I myself, in fact, was once called to task for hiring him.

"Where the hell did you find this guy, Lillian? Alcoholics Anonymous?"

"Well, if I did, then he wouldn't be drunk *now*, would he?" I sniffed. So what if Harvey Ballentine tippled a little? As long as he remained lucid. And vertical.

After the ruckus died down, Spreckles kicked off the program by leaning on my shoulder and saying in his galumphing clown voice, "So, Miss Lillian, what kind of wholesome ice cream fun do you have planned for us today?"

"Well, Spreckles, today we have a marvelous show for our youngsters," I announced. "For our special guest, we have the pop-group sensation the McCoys, singing their number-one smash hit 'Hang on Sloopy' (APPLAUSE). We have some of your all-time favorite cartoons, courtesy of Warner Brothers (APPLAUSE). Nilla Rilla the Ice Cream Gorilla and his Indian friend Choco-hontas are going to pay us a special visit later, to talk to all our youngsters here about *good oral hygiene* (APPLAUSE). And of course, Spreckles, I think it's only fair that we host everybody's favorite ice cream–eating contest, too: Dunkle's Name That Flavor (WILD APPLAUSE)."

"Sounds swell, Your Highness. But first"—and here Spreckles the Clown plopped down on the edge of the stage with exaggerated glumness—"can I talk to you and the boys and girls about a little problem a friend of mine has?"

"Well, sure. What is it, Spreckles?" I feigned innocence. "Tell me, and maybe the boys and girls can help."

Since the original idea was to have our program fill the void left by *The Mickey Mouse Club*, NBC insisted that *Dunkle's Ice Cream Funhouse* offer regular moral and ethical "character lessons" to children as a key part of the show. And so each episode began with "Dear Spreckles," a segment where children sent in letters asking Spreckles for help with their daily problems. Today Eugene, age nine, from Syosset, wrote that he'd borrowed his friend's bicycle without asking, then accidentally broken it: *"I know what I did was wrong. Spreckles, what should I do?"*

Spreckles walked among the children in the audience with his microphone, soliciting suggestions. *Maybe Eugene could tell his best friend that he's really sorry*, they offered. *Maybe he should save up his allowance to buy him a new bike.* Afterward Spreckles selected a few volunteers to act out the scenarios onstage so that all the children (including, presumably, Eugene watching back home in Syosset) could see for themselves how to resolve the dilemma.

The studio lights were extremely hot, so during this portion I sat on the sidelines fanning myself. After the first commercial break—for Dunkle's Ice Cream, naturally—came the guest-star segment: Always, for me, the highlight. Because I was persistent and I played up my Jewish-Italian mama persona to great effect in both New York and Hollywood—and because Dunkle's bombarded celebrities with free tubs of ice cream flavors concocted especially for them (Cherry Lewis, Bob Vanillin, Sean Cone-ery)—*Dunkle's Ice Cream Funhouse* landed some truly marvelous guest stars over the years. Cassius Clay was on once. Sandy Koufax. Tippi Hedren and Mary Martin. Often the guests were musical. The Four Seasons performed. Dusty Springfield. Sam Cooke. And I got to interview all of them. *What advice can you give our youngsters today? Whom do you admire most?* And, of course, *What's your favorite Dunkle's ice cream flavor?*

Then came the cartoons. Personal grooming with Nilla Rilla and Chocohontas. And finally the ice cream contest. Big. Messy. Thrilling. Every kid in the audience vied to participate. Ice Cream Relays like egg relays, except with a scoop of ice cream balanced on the end of the spoon. Scooper Troopers, perhaps best described as "Which team can scoop more ice cream out of the tub and transfer it across the set into a bowl without using their hands?" Or Name that Flavor, where blindfolded contestants raced over to a table full of "mystery ice cream" and had to identify each flavor while the clock ticked. Several years later, the game show producers for the revival of *Beat the Clock* stole several of these challenges outright, the pricks.

For this segment the set was always covered in plastic drop cloths, and the lucky contestants were given rain ponchos and galoshes to wear. Oh, what a spectacle it was! As soon as I blew the whistle, the children went slipping and sliding on the slick, ice cream–spattered racecourse. The din of the audience's cheering was deafening. Everything culminated in a terrific, gooey, Jackson Pollock–y mess. It made for marvelous television, I am telling you. This was what children loved to see. Not some guy talking to a goddamn sock puppet and putting on a cardigan.

At the end, as Don Pardo announced that today's grand prize was a special-edition Ross Apollo bicycle, I thanked all our youngsters for playing. Winners or not, I cooed, everyone would receive a complimentary Dunkle's gift bag containing an Imperial yo-yo, Silly Putty, a Lactona toothbrush, a bottle of Mr. Bubble, and a coupon for a free Dunkle's Nilla Rilla ice cream cake. If our special guest happened to be a pop star, everyone got a free copy of their latest 45 as well.

Spreckles and I then waved good-bye into the camera in a rain of pink and brown confetti as the closing theme music kicked in and the dazed children were hustled off the set behind us. As soon as the red light blinked off and the producer shouted, "That's it! All done, guys," Harvey Ballentine yanked off his nose and said, "Thank God those little fuckers are finally gone. Oh, do I need a piss."

Bert was usually still asleep when I arrived back home at Park Avenue. I showered again, donned one of my suits, and called for the car to take me to the office, so that I could get there before 9:00 A.M. to see who arrived late, before putting in a full day's work myself.

Sometimes, as I shuffled about our room fastening my earrings, rummaging through the drawers for my compact and my keys, Bert would call to me sleepily from the bed, patting the empty space on the mattress beside him. "Doll, relax. Come back for a few minutes. Let Isaac handle things this morning."

But how could I possibly relax? I was the Ice Cream Queen of America, for Chrissakes. Sometimes I felt as if a roller coaster were careening inside me, cresting and plummeting, cresting and plummeting. So often I was out there in the spotlight by myself. I never for a minute forgot how cutthroat our business was. Narrowing profit margins. Enormous outlays and loans. Competition nipping at our heels. And although Bert was oblivious to it, we had enemies. Vigilance was imperative.

I could not simply "let Isaac handle things."

Ever since he had gotten his degree from NYU—just as I'd once vowed he would—our son had assumed more and more responsibility at the company. When we first moved Dunkle's headquarters to Manhattan, in fact, Bert had installed him in a spacious, glass-walled office right next door to his own. Though in the past I had experienced my son as standoffish, picky, and fretful, over the years these qualities had coalesced into a meticulous intelligence that I had come to value. My son, he had an eye for structuring deals, for analyzing numbers. He and I began having lunches together. Just the two of us. With our heads bowed together over a conference table—our matching deli sandwiches half eaten beside us on their mayonnaise-y waxed paper—we discussed finances and reviewed contracts that Bert could not absorb. Never had I felt so proud of my child. Nor quite so close to him. Business: It had become our shared secret language.

Bert was in his sixties now. Increasingly he ducked out of the office to play golf and tennis. Physical things—things he still excelled at. He took long lunches at Sammy's Roumanian Steak House with Edgar, our lawyer. Drinks at the Carlyle with men from Mayor Wagner's office. A few times a year, he went on lavish junkets to Washington, D.C., to glad-hand senators and congressmen, taking them out for steak dinners at the Palm with representatives from the dairy lobby, Dow Chemical, Westinghouse. Inordinately good-looking people like Bert can always just sit at a restaurant table, nodding and not saying much. Of course, I understood the need for all his schmoozing, as we called it—big business needs big friends, after all. Yet the bills he ran up! He seemed to have reverted to his pampered childhood back in Vienna. Cigars. Bottles of Bordeaux. Jazz clubs. Junior suites. Receipts, I demanded. Give me the receipts!

To my great amazement, Isaac backed me up. "Pop, Mom's right," he said one afternoon, clicking his pen. "All these little things accumulate. Don't reach for your wallet in a restaurant until you've double-checked the bill, okay?"

Finally, I found, I had an ally. My very own son, no less.

Yet one Sunday morning back in 1962, Bert turned to me in the kitchen as he was cranking the coffee grinder. A puzzled, pre-occupied look came over his face. "Lil," he said vaguely. "Hamburgers. They don't really go well with milk shakes, do they?"

"Excuse me?" I was rummaging through the Frigidaire for a grapefruit.

"People prefer soft drinks with their meals, yes?" His eyebrows pinched together like curtains. "Oh, never mind, doll. I did the right thing. I know I did." But his hand, I noticed, stayed on the crank of the coffee grinder and did not move.

"Bert, what's going on?"

He gazed down into the sink. "A restaurant owner from Illinois came to see me. He took me to lunch. At the Biltmore. H-h-h-he owns some h-h-h-hamburger restaurants. Out in the Midwest. Franchises, like we have." Bert shook his head.

"Oh?"

"Apparently, he used to sell milk-shake machines back in the forties. Now he's considering adding milk shakes to his hamburger menus—or maybe ice cream. He's just 'doing due diligence,' he said, but he wondered if perhaps we'd be open to combining our Dunkle's franchises with his."

I leaned back against the Frigidaire and crossed my arms. "And you did not even think to mention this to me?"

Bert cast about the kitchen helplessly. "You were so busy with the TV show, doll. And the new grocery division."

"When exactly did you meet with this hamburger man?"

Bert's lips folded into each other for a moment until they disappeared entirely. "March," he said quietly.

"March? Bert, that was four months ago!"

"I didn't think it was important enough to bring up, Lil. This man, he didn't want our full menu. Only vanilla and chocolate. Maybe strawberry. With Dunkle's great variety—partnering with him, it just didn't seem to be to our advantage—"

"Did you at least offer to supply him with the flavors he does want?"

"Oh, Lil. I know that was probably the wrong call. But it just seemed like an awful lot of expansion in a direction we didn't think we wanted to go. I mean, we have over two hundred franchises now. And the vending trucks. And the whole new supermarket division. Do we really want to start supplying restaurants as well? What if we spread ourselves too thin?"

"Well, how many restaurants does this guy even have?" I said. "Six? Seven?"

Bert looked down at the new raffia mat that Sunny had placed on the floor by the sink. "Three hundred and twenty-one," he said quietly.

"What?"

"Three hundred and twenty-one. So it wouldn't be so simple, Lil. You see? It would be a lot of work. It could consume us entirely."

"Three hundred and twenty-one? You said no to supplying ice cream to three hundred and twenty-one hamburger franchises?" I thumped my cane so hard against the floor that all the dishes rattled in the cabinets.

My husband shrank from me. He cupped his hands like parentheses around his eyes, clutching his temples, rocking back and forth miserably. He appeared to be in physical pain. "Oh, doll," he whispered. "I know. I know. I made a terrible mistake. And for months I've been carrying this around. The thing is, Lil, Isaac and I, we just had an odd feeling about this guy. His last name, even. Kroc. As in 'a crock.' It seemed like a bad omen—"

"Isaac?" I felt a stab in my gut. "Isaac was with you?"

"Well, of course. And he had the same feeling that I did. The guy's restaurants? They're called McDonald's. Like farms. Neither of us could see them having much appeal, frankly, beyond the heartland—and they'd only use two or three of our flavors at most—and it just didn't seem—"

Storming into the dining room, I poured myself a drink, though my hands were shaking. If the decanter wasn't Baccarat, I'd have hurled it against the wall. "What happened to us being a team?" I shouted. "To us being 'quite a pair'?"

"B-b-b-but, Lil," Bert said forlornly, "I-I-I-I—"

I polished off the drink in a single swallow, then another, though neither made me feel the least bit better. Pressing the intercom, I barked at our doorman to hail me a cab.

Isaac and Rita had just returned from their honeymoon. They were living in a new apartment building off Lexington Avenue.

"How could you do this?" I hollered as I stormed into their parlor. Hundreds of dollars they had spent on furniture, yet the room was chilly and stark. Chairs like tweedy mushrooms. A brick of brown Naugahyde for a couch. "Your father is a bumbling, half-deaf illiterate. *This*, we all know. But *you*?"

"Ma, please—what are you talking about?" Isaac held up his hands in front of him, as if shielding himself. Boxes of wedding gifts sat on an ugly Danish Modern side table: chafing dishes and casseroles still nestled in tufts of paper.

"A man's name is Kroc—so you assume *he* is a crock? Well, guess what, *bubeleh*? Now, someone is going to supply ice cream to this Mr. Kroc and his three hundred and twenty-one McDonald's franchises out there in Illinois. But it's not going to be us. So thank you very much. You've just created a huge window for our competition. Any competition."

A terrible idea came upon me then like a seizure: Was it possible, somehow, that the Dinello family had finally gotten back into the ice cream business? All these years I kept waiting for them to roar back to life like some mythical beast, grown exponentially stronger and hungrier from adversity, accumulating energy like a cyclone. The first detective agency I'd hired to track down Papa, they'd had nothing much to report on the Dinellos either. A frozen-vegetable company out in Mineola. A furniture outlet in Howard Beach. Yet still. I kept waiting, reading the trades. It was only a matter of time. Frozen vegetables could be a stepping-stone. The Dinellos would come back to haunt me yet. I was sure of it. McDonald's was the perfect opportunity.

"What the hell is the matter with you?"

"Ma," Isaac said defensively, "what was I supposed to do?"

"Well, for starters, did it never once occur to you that perhaps I, of all people, should have been there?"

My son blanched. The same guilty pallor spread across his face that he used to get as a little boy whenever I caught him by the ice box, eating U-bet syrup from the jar with his fingers.

"Ma, it was at the Men's Bar at the Biltmore—so even if—I mean, it's not like you could have—"

"Oh? So you couldn't have asked him to change the venue? Hold it someplace that allows women?"

Isaac gave an incredulous little yelp. "Come on, Ma. Nobody does business like that. I mean, what was I supposed to say? 'Excuse me, Mr. Kroc, but my *mommy* wants to come along'?"

Hurrying into the foyer, I yanked my coat from the closet. I heard his footsteps behind me, but I jabbed the elevator button and refused to turn around.

For months afterward, just as my parents had once refused to speak to each other, so I boycotted my son. If I needed to tell him something, I did so pointedly through Rita. Only the trauma of the Cuban Missile Crisis compelled me to begin talking to him again. The one thing Castro, I suppose, has ever been good for.

Yet even after my miraculous grandson was born two years later—on Thanksgiving—and Isaac and I resumed having lunch together on occasion—every morning, as soon as I arrived at the office, I made sure that Mrs. Preminger reported directly to me. Not just everything in my schedule book but in Bert's and Isaac's as well. Every meeting, every dinner invitation. Every goddamn dentist appointment. Nothing, nothing at all, would be allowed to slip past me again.

One particular morning after hosting the *Funhouse*, I arrived at the office to find Mrs. Preminger waiting for me in the reception area with a troubled look on her face. She had aged, I saw suddenly. Her flesh was like stewed chicken. I wondered suddenly if she was about to give notice. For years she had been secretly X-ing out the days on her calendar, writing in tiny, cramped figures at the bottom just how many she had left until her retirement.

"What is it?" As I unknotted my Hermès scarf, I sensed a disturbance, a disruption of molecules in the air.

"There was a young man waiting here for you when I arrived this morning," Mrs. Preminger said, following me back toward my office. "I told him you were still at the television studio, but he refused to leave. He said it was urgent. He said he'd wait all day if he had to. I put him in the conference room to keep him out of the way."

"Let me guess," I said with irritation. I was wearing a new navy blue Chanel suit, and the chain stitched into the back was rubbing against my neck, which was bothersome. "He wants a job. With the foundation."

A few years earlier, Dunkle's had set up a charitable foundation—for tax purposes, of course, but also to build upon our work with the March of Dimes. The Albert J. and Lillian M. Dunkle Foundation funded mobile children's health clinics that regularly made visits to slums and rural areas. Recently, lots of young men had been approaching Dunkle's asking to work for our foundation's clinics as medics or drivers. They didn't seem to understand that the foundation was in a separate office over on Seventh Avenue. They wanted a job yet never did even the most basic homework. Nine times out of ten, it seemed to me, they were not so much looking to help poor children as to avoid the draft. To be classified as a Conscientious Objector. To use capitalism and charity to avoid fighting Communism. Such chutzpah— it was astonishing.

"Why didn't you send him over to Seventh Avenue?" I asked Mrs. Preminger. "They're the ones who should be dealing with this."

"I tried, Mrs. Dunkle. He claims this matter is personal."

"It's always personal." I sighed, wriggling out of my coat.

"Mrs. Dunkle," Mrs. Preminger said carefully, the severe black helmet of her hair—a wig, I realized—shifting subtly on her head. "He says he's your brother. Samuel."

"My brother?" I pivoted as if I'd been slapped. "That's impossible. My brother, Samuel, died sixty years ago in Russia."

Inside my office I poured myself a drink. My hands were trembling, making the rim of the bottle rattle against the glass. Clearly it was a prank. An elaborate practical joke. "Allen Funt," I said out loud. "You cocksucker." The host of *Candid Camera* on CBS—he'd had it in for me ever since I was selected to give the opening remarks instead of him at the North American Broadcasters Association luncheon two years earlier at the Pierre. Now Funt was paying me back, no doubt, setting me up and recording me on a hidden camera to embarrass me for one of his show's "Celebrity Candids." Send in an impostor pretending to be my long-lost brother from Vishnev. Let the high jinks begin. That bastard. *Spare me your idea of wit*, I thought.

One detail perplexed me, though, and made the back of my neck prickle. Who in the world had tipped Allen Funt off about Samuel? My brother had died before I was born. I had barely even mentioned him to Bert.

Mrs. Preminger rapped lightly on my door. "Mrs. Dunkle?"

The young man she ushered into my office could not have been more than eighteen. His sleepy, indolent face had a bee-stung quality to it, with red-rimmed eyes. He was dressed in a cranberry-colored Ban-Lon sweater with a tie peeking out: A boy's idea of dressing like an adult. His hair was slicked severely to one side like a marionette's. I could imagine a production assistant styling it with Brylcreem.

"Okay. Who are you?" I said, standing.

The young man hurried across the office, extending his knobby hand. Even from behind my desk, I could smell the chemical wash of his sweater.

"My name is Samuel, Mrs. Dunkle." His voice was deliberate in its enunciations, and there was a faint false inflection to it, like an amateur aspiring to be a Shakespearean actor, to give himself more gravitas. "I'm afraid I'm your brother."

"The hell you are." I looked him up and down disdainfully. "Tell Allen Funt or whatever wisenheimer sent you over that I don't have time for this nonsense."

"I'm sorry. Your half brother. Just half," he said quickly, correcting himself, his eyelashes fluttering rapidly, like insects. "'Hank,' your father? He's my father, too. My mother is Josie. Wife number three? Well, four if you count the common-law one." He had a rash from shaving, I saw, on the underside of his jaw, merging with the sprinkle of red pimples salting his chin and left cheek. "I'm sorry. She said not to come, but I did anyway."

I sat back down in my chair and glared at him. "If you're my half brother, I'm Marie of Romania."

Samuel pulled out his wallet. "See? I have my driver's license. And my draft card—"

"Of course you do." I glanced at them. "They say 'Samuel Pratt.' Nice try. Mrs. Preminger!" I shouted, not bothering with the intercom. "See this young man out, please?"

"Oh, but Dad, he goes by Pratt now, these days," Samuel said quickly. "When he and my mother got married, he insisted on taking her maiden name instead. Mama said it was his way of proving that she was not just another wife to him. Right before the wedding, she said, Dad told the clerk his last name was Pratt, while she said hers was Bailey. So they both became Pratts afterward. So that's mine and my sisters' name."

He stood before me breathlessly, as if he had just run up a hill.

Unfortunately, something about this story—either the way Samuel related it or the tale itself—sounded disturbingly like Papa. I could in fact see him making up some cockamamie story, rushing his girlfriend down to some clerk's office, and paying off some secretary perhaps, in order to erase one identity and replace it quickly with another. Twenty years ago: That was just around the time he had forged all those checks from my account. It would explain why my detectives had come up with nothing. "Hank Bailey?" they'd said, handing me the folder. "Poof. Gone. No record of him at all."

"I wouldn't have come to you now at all, except that Dad—our dad—he's very, very sick," the boy said.

"Oh?" I said archly. "Is he?"

"Really, truly." In his animated, ham-fisted way, Samuel began pouring forth a great convoluted story. The words "diabetic," "Paterson," "bankruptcy," "amputation," "beef stew," "foreclosure," and "cocktail waitress" whisked by like bits of debris circling a drain.

I stared at the boy, this Samuel Pratt, searching for some inkling, some physical echo of my father in him. He looked like Papa not at all, and yet he didn't *not* look like him either. Was this little *shmendrik* really my half brother?

Then something else struck me. *Sisters,* he had mentioned.

Twenty years ago Papa had already had four wives. He had re-placed Mama and me and my sisters without a backward glance, his whole past life from Russia, with a new, improved version here in America. How had it not occurred to me in all this time that he might have had other children as well? Yet that he had recycled the name of his first, dead son was particularly galling.

"And with the hospital bills, and Dad needing such expensive medications," Samuel continued, his Adam's apple bobbing as he spoke, his hands sandwiched between his knees, his eyes fixed on the wall behind my head. "He's eighty-four and has no insurance. The wheelchair, the X-rays. And that's not counting...well, the car we had, the Pontiac, it died, you see, so we were hoping—my mom, and I—well, I was hoping that since you're a big television star—that maybe you might—"

"Stop," I said. "Your sisters. How many of them are there?"

"Um, two. But they don't have any money either. You see—"

"Do they have names?"

"Peg. Peg and Coralee."

Not Rose or Flora at least. Yet they were out there somewhere, these girls, Peg and Coralee, with their farm-fresh, all-American, Christian names. Girls who no doubt had faces like strawberries and cream. I could see them dressed in freshly ironed skirts and headbands, swishing into a bright yellow breakfast kitchen, calling my father not Papa but Daddy, planting a good-morning kiss sun-nily on his cheek as he winked at them over his plate of bacon and eggs. Two daughters who had grown up with him taking them to the seaside and the circus, buying them gumdrops and birthday cakes and bicycles. I instantly hated these girls with more ferocity than I had ever hated almost anyone.

As if he could sense the thoughts unspooling in my head, Samuel seemed compelled to mention quickly that Coralee had two children and a drunken husband who worked as a janitor, and that Peg's husband was stationed in Chu Lai. As he went on, I saw all too clearly that yes, this young man—the yarn he was spinning, the desperate glitter in his eye, the dogged persuasiveness, the determination to separate me from my money—he was Papa's progeny all right.

And his mother, this Josie Pratt, of course she had fallen on hard times—of course! The American childhood I would never have, clearly that was not enough for her brood. These shysters had their greedy eyes trained on far more. Samuel's little visit here this morning was only a reconnaissance mission. For all I knew, Josie had been keenly aware of what Papa was doing when he'd taken her name. There must be no presumption of innocence here. Soon enough, I suspected, all these Pratts would come knocking on my office door with squalling babies in their arms, eviction notices stuffed in their purses, arms in gauze slings—a parade of long-lost stepmothers and half sisters and aunts and God knows who else, looking for a handout. They would bleed me dry. Just like Papa had.

My heart quickened, punching my chest like a fist. "Get out," I said.

"I'm sorry?"

I pointed to the door. "Go. Vamoose."

"But, Mrs. Dunkle. Our father. He's dying," Samuel said with distress. "Please, I'm trying to explain. He needs your help."

"He's helped himself plenty over the years," I said. "Over

twenty-five thousand dollars by my last count. So *basta*, as we say in Italian. I'm done."

Saying these words, I realized I meant them. Clarity broke over me like a wave. Why, nothing I could do or give to Papa would ever be enough. He had simply never wanted me. For years, I had been waiting for him to reappear somehow, somewhere, so that I might finally redeem myself, resuscitate his love for me. How I clung to this rope! But his love, it had never existed. Some parents never really liked their own children. I knew this too well myself.

Papa chose other wives, other daughters. He took what he could from me, from Mama, from my sisters, then left, discarding us like orange rinds. Broken toys. Unopened books. That was simply that. I could replay the misery and injustice of it over and over, like a broken record. Or I could simply get back to work.

Samuel looked like a roulette wheel sent spinning. He grabbed the back of a chair to steady himself. "Please. I'm asking you. I'm begging you, Mrs. Dunkle. Without your help," he said hoarsely, "Dad is going to die."

"Die? Please. The man has nine lives, nine wives, and a different name for each one. Spare me the melodrama."

He was crying now, this Samuel, tears leaking down the front of his pockmarked cheeks, catching on his pimples. Oh, but he was good. He would not give up. I had to give him credit. Papa had trained him well. "Mrs. Dunkle. Please. I don't know where else to turn. I'm 1-A, my mother is ailing, my sisters are broke. And one of them, Peg, did I mention, she is pregnant again? I know Dad is sometimes difficult. And not the most reliable. And he's caused my mom some heartache over the years. But, Mrs. Dunkle, he's going blind. His kidneys are failing. I don't know what else to do. You're his family."

"Family? Family?" I said acidly. "How do you even know that? Do you have any proof?"

"What? Mrs. Dunkle, Dad talks about you all the time. You're his big successful daughter, he always says. In the hospital he watches you on TV. Every Tuesday and Friday mornings. Six-thirty A.M. sharp. Even though he can barely see anymore, he still points at the screen when he hears your voice. He boasts to all the nurses."

I clamped my hands over my ears. "Shut up. Shut up!"

Samuel's doughy, nubbled face contorted into something belligerent. "I can't believe you. *'Help the children.' 'Stop the polio.'* You have everything in the world—but you won't give our dad a single cent on his deathbed?"

With a furious sweep of my hand, I sent everything on top of my desk clattering violently to the floor. The boy jumped back, stunned. Yanking open my top drawer, I pulled out one of our coupons good for a free Nilla Rilla ice cream cake, then slammed the desk shut so hard the whole office shuddered. "You want something? You want something, you little prick? All of you still haven't gotten enough from me? Fine. Here!" I shouted, thrusting the coupon into his hand. "Go! Throw yourselves a goddamn party!"

Chapter 14

GLENLIVET. CAMPARI. COURVOISIER. With their musical names. Each with a particular, seductive promise. The caramel burn of cognac. Vodka's bracing, metallic bite, like frozen chrome. Dubonnet, the color of melted garnet, a comma of lemon peel bobbing in the tang of it. Such elegant anesthetics. The first sip, always, like a silk glove run lightly across the back of my hand, dispersing in me the way dye diffuses in cotton. Slowly, a rose unclenches. A bandage unfurls.

I held the liquor on my tongue like a lozenge and threw my head back. Closed my eyes. Jiggled the glass, feeling the satisfying heft of it in my hand, the ice cubes rattling like maracas.

Isaac had once criticized me for keeping a little bar in my office on an antique sideboard. "Nobody is doing this anymore, Ma," he said when he first saw the cut-glass decanters assembled on the tray, each with a little silver nameplate hung around its neck like a dog tag. "What did you do to this place anyway?" He glanced around. "It looks like Versailles."

"Exactly," I agreed. When we'd had our Manhattan offices renovated, I'd ordered the walls of my office covered in pink silk brocade the color of strawberry ice cream. I spent more time in there than at home, so why not? "An Ice Cream Queen deserves her own palace, thank you." Petunia leaped onto my lap, and I offered her a sniff of my glass. "Don't give me that look," I said. "Do you know for how many years I slept on a bench in a storefront?"

I did not need to explain myself to anybody. Three hundred and two Dunkle's franchises we had now, plus the supermarket freezer line, plus the latest contract with the U.S. military, again for a hefty profit, thank you. Even after Vietnam, VA hospitals continued to serve our brand. My television show now aired live for three hours, too—albeit once, on Sunday mornings only—rechristened as *Dunkle's Sundae Morning Funhouse*. Several times a month, I also appeared as a guest star on *Hollywood Squares*, sitting in for Karen Valentine, Rose Marie, or Charo. I enjoyed this greatly. Plus the monthly column I "wrote" for *Good Housekeeping*, "Lillian Dunkle's Delectable Frozen Desserts," featuring dozens of imaginative ways to serve ice cream using Jell-O molds, meringues, pastel-coated almonds, canned peaches. Always with my picture in a box to the side. No less than Scribner had compiled my recipes and published them. Two bestselling cookbooks, I had now.

So what if I had an extra cocktail or two during the day back at my office? Sometimes I liked to steady the nerves. A little fortification. Certainly I'd earned it.

For Bert's seventy-fifth-birthday party in Palm Beach, I'd ordered not only top-end scotch, vodka, and gin but cases and cases of Moët Impérial champagne to be passed on silver trays and to be poured freely from fountains by the gazebo.

Now, from the patio, I watched the pool boy ladle the surface of the pool with a long-handled net like a parfait spoon.

"Skim!" I shouted, motioning. "Don't scoop!" I didn't want debris swirling around, getting sucked into the filters. "These guys get paid by the hour," I said to Isaac. "Earlier this morning the nursery delivered topiaries that looked like Easter eggs, those dingbats. How hard is it to trim a bush into a goddamn circle? I've had to order them all reclipped. They botch things up on purpose, you know, to run up overtime."

I picked up my glass and rattled the ice cubes. Isaac leaned forward on the padded lounger beside mine, rubbed his paper-white, hairy ankles, and blinked out at the ocean, the fractured glare of it. His pate shone at the back of his head. How did I suddenly have a middle-aged son? Distantly, I heard the *thwock* of a tennis ball bouncing off the clay; Bert was on our court playing with David Lambert, the new head of accounts at Promovox. Lambert had flown down yesterday with Wife Number Three. "Tre," I called her. The stupid girl did not speak Italian, so she believed this was a term of endearment. Her real name—who the hell could remember?—was something that ended with an *i*. "Mindi"? "Staci"?

The Lamberts were staying in the guesthouse at the northern edge of Bella Flora, the smaller one with the rotunda and the hot tub outside. With all the money we paid their firm, you'd think they could afford a hotel. Yet Bert had insisted. And since he was the birthday boy, who was I to begrudge him?

I shrugged and tilted my glass back to get the last of the Sazerac at the bottom. "Sunny!" I shouted. I had no idea where I'd put my bell. "You want?" I asked Isaac. He shook his head. "And some pistachios," I announced when Sunny arrived with the shaker to refresh my drink.

I turned to Isaac. "Why don't you drink? It's happy hour." I pointed to my little gold Bulova. "See. Eleven A.M."

"Ma," Isaac groaned. He removed his glasses and massaged the bridge of his nose.

"I'm just kidding." I whacked him playfully on the side of his knee.

Why didn't my son ever appreciate me? My humor. The fact

that I was a wisenheimer. Even at thirty-eight years old, he was still so guarded around me, so stingy with his affections. When he was a little boy, my leg and my cane frightened him. Yet even now, at almost six feet tall, he cowered. Certainly he had never been fearful of his father. I could hear them laughing jocularly on the tennis courts sometimes, just whacking a ball around for fun, talking more than playing. I saw their robust, pounding bear hugs whenever Isaac first arrived, Bert tousling Isaac's hair, Isaac grinning, saying, "Hey, Pop, still lookin' good." Their steak lunches back in New York each week. Their little trips now in the sailboat with Jason to Peanut Island. Always without me.

Around me Isaac just acted scalded. As if *he* had been the one wronged? Oh, how I wished he would kid with me, fence with me, push back a little, even. Show some backbone, some goddamn chutzpah for once. Frankly, I didn't know what was worse: that I was often surrounded by thieves and liars and incompetents—or by obsequious, easily intimidated handwringers who tried skirting around me. Even my own son. *Especially* my own son. Was there no one who could simply deal with me normally?

"I'm sorry, Ma. You're right." Isaac took a deep breath and spread his hands out atop his knees. "I'm just worried, is all."

"Please," I said with irritation. "We're not discussing Umlaut this weekend."

"Umlaut" was the nickname I'd given to another ice cream company. I had made it our policy never to dignify our competition by uttering their real names. There was a brand, for example, sold mostly in supermarkets, that promoted itself as being "simple" and "all natural." Since its logo was a mint leaf, I referred to it only as "Leaf."

Umlaut, as I called it, was a company that was making waves lately because it produced a "super-premium," high-fat ice cream with a nearly unpronounceable name—two *a*'s, an umlaut over one of them, and a hyphen, for Chrissakes. It was supposed to be Danish—there was even a map of Scandinavia printed on its containers—yet the goddamn stuff was really manufactured by two Jews in the Bronx. What a bunch of shysters. But people were eating it up, all right—literally. Umlaut had a new Chocolate Chocolate Chip ice cream that a food writer in *New York* magazine had described as "transcendent," if you can believe that. Sure, with 17 percent butterfat, why wouldn't it be? With 17 percent butterfat, you could make ice cream out of dog shit and everyone would think it was heaven.

Until recently, pints of Umlaut ice cream were sold only in health-food stores and gourmet delis. Yet several months ago the company had announced it would be opening franchises across America—just like Dunkle's. Starting right in our own backyard, no less. Brooklyn.

"So I'm just wondering, Ma"—Isaac sighed, leaning forward on his lounger—"if developing our own luxury ice cream might not be the best way to go right now. Beat them at their own game."

"We've got double-digit inflation, and we just came out of an oil crisis. Who the hell's going to pay extra for ice cream?" I said.

Isaac studied the backs of his hands, the smooth tapers of his fingers. His wedding ring was a sheen of scuffed gold. No calluses. No blisters in the half-moon of skin between his thumb and his forefinger from cranking a handle.

"A lot of people seem to be buying it," he said unhappily.

"With seventeen percent butterfat and almost no overrun? No artificial anything? Top-dollar ingredients? Sure, why not?" I threw up my hands. "Let's develop a recipe that costs a small fortune to manufacture and makes your father's patented ice cream machine completely obsolete. What a brilliant idea, *bubeleh*. Let's just flush our entire business model right down the toilet."

"I was thinking we start small. A test, is all. A few premium flavors in targeted markets. That's how Häagen-Dazs manages—"

"Umlaut! Umlaut! That's what we call them in this house, do you understand? Umlaut! Don't roll your eyes at me."

We sat there watching the workers move a ladder from the base of one palm tree to another, winding garlands of lights around the trunks. "Ma, I'm just suggesting," Isaac said after a moment.

"This discussion is over." I stood up defiantly, bumping the glass table as I did. "This Umlaut is nothing but a fad. 'Luxury ice cream'? Boysenberry? Carob? Are those even flavors? Who the hell eats that? In three years, I'm telling you, they'll be bankrupt." I reached for my cane. "Now, excuse me. I've got the caterers."

Yet something else occurred to me, and I could not resist turning around. "You know," I said tartly, "none of this would be a problem now if you'd simply bothered to do that business with McDonald's."

Bert's seventy-fifth birthday. Dunkle's fortieth anniversary. America's Bicentennial. They all coincided beautifully the very same year. I had been planning this gala for ages, right down to the ice cream–scented guest soaps in the bathrooms. Two hundred and fifty-six people were coming—including the Annenbergs, Laurance Rockefeller, Valerie Perrine, Merv Griffin, Bob Hope. As a special surprise for Bert, I secretly hired the Dave Brubeck Ensemble to play during dinner. The singer Barry Manilow, who wrote a new Dunkle's jingle for us a few years back, was coming to perform some of his hits as well. Quite a name, that boy had made for himself recently. Dionne Warwick would be singing, and Neil Diamond, too. Crystal Gayle. All friends I had made through *Dunkle's Funhouse*. Children's entertainment was such an icebreaker; performing for seven-year-olds stripped away stars' egos. Plus, people felt relaxed around me. I pinched their cheeks. I told them to "eat a little. Have a little something for the mouth." I was homey. I was impressed by no one. I was everyone's Italian-Jewish mother that they'd never had before. (Dr. Ruth Westheimer, that bitch. She's begun stealing my act now, in case you haven't noticed.)

I had spared no expense for Bert's party—unusual for me. Peacocks would roam the gardens. Mimes would serve hors d'oeuvres. After the five-course dinner, there would be a fireworks display on the beach heralding the giant Baked Alaska birthday cake. Such a gala must be befitting the Ice Cream King of America and his queen, after all. No one less than Halston himself had designed my dress for me (with a matching little outfit for Petunia, of course). Lanzo was flying down specially to do my hair.

As the day wore on, however, I found myself getting increasingly irritated. Could you blame me? Twenty-one acres along the beachfront we had, yet everywhere was a ruckus. Hammering. Shouting. Drilling. Workers finishing up the installation of the dance floor, rolling tables thunderously down the ramps. It was like a tropical sweatshop. The truck with the extra generators did not show up until noon.

To keep him surprised—and out of my hair—I had banished Bert to the guest villa at the southern edge of the property. To keep Jason from moping about in his special, petulant, twelve-year-old's way, I had Isaac take him out in the motorboat for lunch. Yet even though both Rita and I warned them not to stop at those bayside fish shacks for lunch, my grandson had consumed an entire basket of fried clams. He was now prostrate on the floor of the green marble guest bathroom, vomiting through his braces. Isaac and Rita stood over him yelling at each other. In the middle of all this, Sunny stumbled breathlessly up the stairs holding the telephone again. It was my new publicist, Roxanne. The editor at *People* magazine had apparently just asked if their photographer and reporter could come to Bella Flora earlier than planned. They wanted to photograph the grounds before any guests arrived. "*Now* they ask this?" I snapped.

Amazingly, a photographer from *Women's Wear Daily* was also expected. Bert's seventy-fifth birthday was turning out to be one of the "in" invites of the season, which I found particularly gratifying. After all, Bert and I were considered terribly nouveau riche down here. Nobody said it to my face, of course. Yet I was no dummy, darlings. Our being millionaires, television personalities, philanthropists—these meant nothing in Palm Beach. They wanted you to have sailed in on the *Mayflower* just to sip a gin and tonic at their goddamn B&T Club. But what did I care? I was proud to be "new money." Everything Bert and I had, we built ourselves. Not like some folks, sucking off the teat of their dead ancestors, pretending that it was some great achievement to lie around doing nothing all day but making snide remarks about other people's clothing and bloodlines. As far as I was concerned, I had my own "social register." If you hadn't earned your reputation yourself, frankly, I didn't want to know from you. Laurance Rockefeller being the exception, of course. We'd done business with him on the philanthropy front and supported his brother's run for governor of New York. Besides, given that it was also the Bicentennial, it only seemed fair that we had a few American luminaries represented. President Ford himself had sent down a proclamation declaring both Dunkle's Ice Cream and Bert himself "National Treasures."

Yet my earlier conversation with Isaac kept needling me. *Super-premium ice cream.*

"Where the hell is Sunny?" I barked as I emerged from the elevator back onto the main floor. Florists were fussing over the arrangements in the grand entry hall. The wrought-iron banisters snaking up the marble staircases had been draped with cascades of white roses, dendrobium orchids, white amaryllis, swaths of white silk organza. They looked like dripping lace.

"I want more color in those. Get some pink and violet in there. All this white looks like a goddamn funeral."

"Mrs. Dunkle," Sunny said nervously, motioning to the front salon. "Your husband is looking for you."

Bert was standing over by the grand piano, gazing fondly at a baby picture of Jason in a gilt frame. "Doll, there you are." He smiled expansively, setting the picture back down on the wrong shelf. He was still in his tennis whites and his terry-cloth head-band. Three-quarters of a century old, and still he followed a punishing morning exercise regime that his no-good father had instilled in him back in Vienna. I supposed this was not a bad thing. Bert's skin was looser and leopard-spotted now with age, of course, and he'd shrunk about an inch or so, yet my husband had kept that marvelous basic physique that he'd had almost fifty years ago when I first saw him standing in the lobby of the Henry Street Settlement. An Adonis still. His hair was leonine, white. His face glinted with happiness, with symmetry.

"You're supposed to be under quarantine," I said. "Isaac will come fetch you in the golf cart when it's time." I didn't want Bert ruining his tuxedo by walking across the lawn.

"Come with me to the villa, doll." Bert reached out and ran his papery fingertips down the gooseflesh of my arm. "Let's spend some time together before the party starts and everything gets too busy."

I looked at him with exasperation. What was wrong with this man? Two hundred and fifty-six people we had coming. "I can't. There's too much to supervise."

"Lil. Isn't that what we're paying the party planners for? The caterers? The staff? Come. Let's you and I have a little lunch together."

"I don't want lunch. I have no appetite before social events. You know that."

"So we'll have a little swim." The southern guesthouse, it had its own private pool, overlooking the beach. I thought back to our honeymoon in Atlantic City, all those years ago; we owned a piece of that same oceanfront now, albeit a thousand miles south.

"Bert, please. Parties don't plan themselves."

He gave me such an innocent, wounded look, I felt monstrous. "Fine. I'm only going because it's your birthday." Yet I made little attempt to hide my resentment, my impatience.

He already had the golf cart waiting. When we arrived at the guest villa, I saw that Dimitri, our boy, had prepared a luncheon for us and set it out on the patio table beneath the large yellow umbrella, angled in the direction of the sun. There was Waldorf salad, cold poached tarragon chicken breasts, fresh seeded rolls. A bottle of Soave Bolla sweating in a Lucite ice bucket. Bert liked to drink this after tennis, though I did not care for it. A Sazerac awaited me instead.

"My, this is lovely," I conceded. "You arranged all this?"

Bert helped me into my chair, very gentlemanly. "At all these grand parties," he said, "we never get any time alone together."

"I suppose I could pick a little," I said, eyeing the cold chicken.

The sea breeze tickled us over the low dunes and made the tablecloth flutter. Bert, in between sips of his pale wine, kept reaching over and squeezing my hand. He began to speak about a sailing trip to the Keys he wanted us to take with Isaac and Rita, about the upcoming election—he was not sure, at that point, if he was more partial to Carter or to Ford. Carter was a Democrat, yet Ford we knew personally.

As Bert began to stammer out the pros and cons of both candidates, however, I found I was no longer listening. No matter how much of my Sazerac I drank, I still could not stop thinking about my conversation with Isaac. The whole beauty of ice cream was its democracy. Always, always, it was cold and sweet and affordable for everyone. Suddenly elevating it to a luxury? Why, that went against the very *essence* of ice cream itself. You might as well start charging money for water.

Yet there was a problem, darlings. For you see, I had secretly tasted this "super-premium" ice cream. Both the "transcendent" Chocolate Chocolate Chip and the vanilla. And oh, they were a revelation. Umlaut's ice cream was unctuous. Buttery. With a concentration of flavor that, frankly, put our own product to shame. Eating it, I had the sickening premonition that such a product could revolutionize entirely what people desired—and expected—from ice cream. For once my son was right. There was reason indeed to be worried.

"Bert?" I cut him off midsentence as he was elaborating on how charming he had found Rosalynn Carter. "You've tasted Umlaut by now, haven't you?"

He concentrated on cutting his chicken with the side of his fork and did not look at me. "W-w-w-w-w-w-w-w-w—" he said.

I set down my utensils, sat back, and crossed my arms, the wind fierce in my hair. "Do you think we should be developing our own luxury ice cream brand?"

He chewed thoughtfully. "You mean with higher butterfat?"

"And minimal overrun. Fancy ingredients. No artificial additives."

Bert tilted his head from side to side noncommittally.

"Our son, he seems to think that luxury ice cream is the wave of the future," I said. "That we should start competing with Umlaut the same way they're starting to copy our franchises."

Bert shrugged. "Lots of companies have franchises nowadays, doll. It seems to me there should be room for both kinds of ice cream. Luxury and regular."

"So you don't think we should bother with it? Not even a few limited-edition test flavors?"

Bert reached over and poured himself a second glass of wine. "H-honestly? I don't know, Lil. Frankly, I don't trust my own judgment on these things anymore. You're the expert here, not me. I'm sure whatever you decide, it will be the right choice."

"I don't want to decide this time." I scrunched up my napkin in my lap. "I'm asking for advice, Bert. I need your opinion."

"That is my opinion, doll."

"That is not an opinion, Bert. That is a relinquishing of responsibility. That is a 'passing of the buck,' as Truman said."

"Lil, please." Bert touched the back of my hand, his face arranged in an ingratiating smile. "We're here at the beach. We're supposed to be on vacation. The sun is shining. We have nice wine to drink and a pool right here in front of us. We're having a wonderful party this evening. Isaac is here. Rita and Jason. Can't we just relax for a few minutes, you and I? Have a swim maybe, and not talk about business?"

Instantly I felt my face flush. "No. No, we cannot 'just relax' and 'not talk about business.' Do you have any idea at all, Bert, how vigilant I have to be? How much still has to be done?"

"L-L-L-L-L-L-L—"

"Don't 'L-L-Lil' me." I banged on the table. "While you're

off playing golf and tennis, who do you think is manning our store? Spreckles the goddamn Clown? Your fainthearted son? Do you have any appreciation for what is potentially at risk with these new franchises coming onto the market?" I waved my arm wildly in the air toward the house, the tennis courts, the pool. "But it's all up to me, isn't it? Like it always is. 'Don't worry, Lil'? 'Just relax, Lil'? Meanwhile these *gonifs* up in the Bronx are priming to bury our enterprise with their 'super-premium ice cream'!"

Grabbing my cane, I struggled to get up, yet my iron garden chair was impossible to maneuver. "Jesus Christ!" I hollered. "Do I have to do absolutely goddamn everything around here myself?"

"Lil, p-p-p-p-p-p-please," Bert begged, motioning. "I'm sorry. Sit down. I just want to have a nice lunch with my lovely wife, is all." The pleading look he gave me was heartbreaking. Yet I was having none of it. His weakness, it could be so goddamn manipulative sometimes.

"Sit down?" I bellowed. "Why are people always telling me to sit down? To relax? To take it easy? You think I'm some sort of pathetic invalid?"

"N-n-n-n-," Bert sputtered. Lurching halfway out of his seat, he grasped my hand desperately. His face contorted in pleading.

"L-L-L-L-L-L-L-"

"Bert, what are you doing?"

Almost in slow motion, his mouth went slack, as if he'd been punched in the gut, and he keeled forward over the table, slamming down onto it hard, like a felled tree. His chin smashed flat into the remaining lump of Waldorf salad on his plate. His glasses flew off. Mayonnaise and blood splattered across his forehead, his shoulders. His wineglass slipped from his hand, shattering against the paving stones. His arm, it dangled at his side, swinging gently, indifferently, like a pendulum.

"Bert!" I screamed.

Overhead, the gulls circled lazily in the obliterating sun. The tablecloth continued to snap in the breeze. Everything else went quiet.

Chapter 15

S O SUE ME: I spend a little too much time in the ladies' room.
In the stall on the end, the frosted, graffitied window can be
opened about four inches. Miss Slocum paces outside like a sentry.
"Mrs. Dunkle? Are you all right?" She knocks, even though I told
her I just needed a moment to myself, thank you, and not to let
anyone in. I wave in as much cool air as I can. I unwrap a
Schrafft's peppermint, blow my nose, study myself in my compact
mirror, pushing the flesh on my face back like dough. Somewhere
my youth is buried in there. *Bert*, I think. *How I wish you were still
here.* On the back of the metal stall door, someone has written
MARIO CUOMO IS A HOMO and SUGAR HILL GANG in purple marker
amid a rain of misspellings. Beyond the window is a thin slice of
river, the sound of an ambulance.

"Don't come in!" I holler.

When she finally manages to coax me out, Miss Slocum in-
forms me that we are now late. She hustles me into the courtroom
just as the officer is bellowing, "All rise!" Though the room is
nearly empty, the few people in it get to their feet. For a moment
it appears that they are standing not for His Honor but for me.
The judge, of course, is not pleased by this. I know that judges
are supposed to be impartial, but trust me, darlings. There is a lot

of ego under those black robes. Give any schmuck a gavel and he thinks he's Earl Warren.

"Counsel, are we having trouble telling time this morning?" the judge says dryly, pointing to his watch. From what I can tell, it's a Timex. The remaining threads of his hair have been shellacked across his skull, and the fluorescent lights overhead reflect off his glasses, obscuring his eyes. Not the best look. The name plaque before him reads HON. LESTER KUKLINSKY. I stare straight at him and never once glance in the direction of the plaintiffs. The Newhouse family is all assembled, however, with their little angel in tow, of course. A fresh pillow of gauze is taped ostentatiously over her left eye, even though it's been months. None of us are actually required to appear in person for the pretrial hearing, yet the Newhouses are no dummies. Showing up with their visual aid, decked out in her little puffed-sleeve dress and her Mary Janes, with her pigtails and her woeful lisp—they're banking that the sight of her will score them big points with the judge. And so it's best to counter this with me, my lawyers have decided, the Other Visual: a poor, sweet, crippled little old lady with her cane and her thick, dark glasses (suggesting, erroneously, cataracts). In short, it's Granny versus the Moppet. Why we even bother to file a goddamn motion is beyond me. In the end, no matter what the court claims, we're all going to be judged on gut reactions and appearances. People always are.

Judge Kuklinsky is apparently the only person in the room not to have seen a television lately or to have prepared for our case ahead of time. "So what do we have here?" he says, perusing a piece of paper. The Newhouses' lawyer, a pockmarked man in a double-breasted suit—his name is Mr. Tottle—and apparently, this Mr. Tottle has made quite a name for himself doing this sort of thing, the *gonif*—he clears his throat. I'm pleased to see the judge ignore him. I glance at Jason. He is sitting directly behind me in the visitors' gallery, leaning forward with his chin resting on the rail as if he's taking in a puppet show.

"Sit up straight, please," I tell him. "You're in court."

He grins sheepishly.

"And spit out that chewing gum," I say more loudly, digging around in my purse for a tissue.

"Lillian!" my lawyer shushes me.

"Excuse me, is there a problem over there?" says the judge.

"I'm sorry, Your Honor. I'm just reminding my grandson here to use good manners, is all," I say in my most pearly, grandmotherly voice. I hand Jason a pink tissue. "Stop slouching, *tateleh*," I whisper loudly. "Do you want your spine should stick like that? I'm sorry, Judge." I face forward again and smile at him brightly. "That was for my grandson, of course, not you."

I see a faint smile play around the corners of Miss Slocum's mouth. She's no dummy after all, perhaps. She knows what I'm doing.

"Ah," Judge Kuklinsky says, glancing down at the paper, then over at me. "So. This is the ice cream lady?"

I beam. "Yes I am, Your Honor. Little old me." I smile winningly. "How do you do?"

"I'm fine, thank you. But, Mrs. Dunkle, I'd like to point out that you have a lawyer. From now on, please refrain from speaking to the court directly. Anything you want to address you should communicate through your attorneys. Do you understand? Now." He adjusts his glasses and returns to the paper in front of him. "I see the plaintiffs have filed a complaint and the defense a motion to dismiss?"

I turn to Miss Slocum. "He doesn't like me," I whisper. "I don't want this judge. I want someone else. Get rid of him."

"What?" says Miss Slocum, her leather portfolio going heavy in her hand. "Mrs. Dunkle, you can't choose your own judge."

"Ask him if he's lactose-intolerant. Kuklinsky. That's Polish. Or Jewish. Eastern Europeans have problems digesting dairy. Get him to recuse himself."

"I'm not asking the judge if he's lactose-intolerant," Miss Slocum says. "It's absurd, and it'll only piss him off. We need him to be as predisposed to you as possible."

"But he's not," I say. "Can't you see? He's already got it in for me." Glancing at the judge, darlings, I just know. Behind the lozenges of his eyeglasses, he is calculating, fixing the case, compiling his own evidence and opinions against me. The way he said *So. This is the ice cream lady?*— His voice was like fat dripping off of a roast.

"The judge's diet is not an issue here," Miss Slocum says. "And believe me, we shouldn't make it one."

"What if I were a pig farmer but the judge kept kosher?" I say. "Please. You're saying this wouldn't be relevant? It wouldn't influence him at all, not even unconsciously? What the hell am I paying you for?"

"Excuse me, Counselor," Judge Kuklinsky says, staring in our direction. "I hear a lot of whispering. Do we have a problem here?"

"No," Miss Slocum says, standing.

"Yes," I declare, hoisting myself to my feet with my cane. My whole life—the whole empire that Bert and I have built—whatever's left of it—I will not have it ruined because some judge has an attitude, because some judge gets a stomachache every time he eats a goddamn cheese sandwich. I know what is going on here. You can't tell me otherwise.

"You have to—I want—" I announce. Suddenly the morning sun catches on a soda can that someone has left on the radiator by the window. The glare is like a flashbulb. I feel myself jerk back in reaction to it. Bright nets of light cast across the room, rippling

like the bottom of a swimming pool. My legs, the polished floor
of the courtroom, the judge's bench, his chubby face—they are all
abruptly turning to water. I am the water, and in the water, and
under the water as well. It's like Jason said: All of us are 50 percent
water. Simple molecules of hydrogen and oxygen. Back when
Bert was alive, he would help me into the pool in the summer
and spin me around with my legs wrapped around his waist. I'd
lie back, letting the water buoy me and splay out in glittering
thrashes, and I'd feel like a mermaid in my swimming cap and my
little two-piece with the starfish clasp. Not crippled at all.

"Lillian?" Miss Slocum's voice seems muted, even though it is
laced with panic. "Are you all right?" She is gripping my arm,
shaking it. I feel nothing. I am swirling in our bright turquoise
pool, the sky overhead smeared with treetops. *Oh, Bert.* Somebody yanks off my sunglasses. The other lawyers' faces press in
around mine like grotesque carnival masks, anxious and staring.
"Her pupils are dilated," someone says. I open my mouth to
speak, yet the words, they seem to evaporate. I am having trouble
moving my jaw. "Is she having a stroke?" another says worriedly.
Jason is in front of me now, his hands gripping my shoulders.
"Grandma? Grandma? Are you okay?"

I did not expect it would feel like this.

The crackle of a walkie-talkie. The judge himself on his feet. A
scraping of chairs: I am aware of this, yet only peripherally. The
smell of the chlorine, the baked feel of the summer air, Bert's silhouette above me, eclipsing the sun so that its rays seem to shoot
out from behind him like a halo. Oh, it was all so magnificent!
"STR," someone says. "Isn't that the acronym?"

Then, as if a hypnotist has snapped his fingers, the sensation
stops. The water instantly recedes. I find I can move my jaw again.
"Mmmph," I say, shaking out my waterlogged skull. I realize I am
stifling a laugh. I stare at my hands. The backs of them are mapped

with ropy, purplish veins. Astonishing, darlings. All at once, it seems terribly, terribly funny, though I have the idea that laughing is an unacceptable response right now—that if I do let loose with a cackle, it will negatively affect my case. And yet the laughter breaks over me, and I have to mask it with a fit of coughing, which comes out as a string of peculiar squeaks.

"Mrs. Dunkle? Are you all right?" the judge asks.

Just then a court officer approaches the bench from the side. She is an enormous Negro woman, stuffed into her uniform, with eyebrows that have been plucked off, then inked back in. I am amazed at the girth of her, the rolls of fat coddling her chin and her back, visible through her uniform. There must be a weight requirement for court officers, I decide. Like in boxing. She waddles over to Judge Kuklinsky and whispers something to him. He regards her doubtfully, then sighs.

"Mrs. Dunkle, Counselor, would you both approach the bench, please?" he beckons.

Miss Slocum puts her hand on the small of my back and guides me up.

"Mrs. Dunkle?" Leaning over the bench, Judge Kuklinsky stares into my eyes, observing them, his pupils darting back and forth as if he were studying tiny words printed on the backs of my retinas. "Mrs. Dunkle," he whispers carefully. "Are you by any chance stoned?"

∽

"The Greatest Party That Never Was" made headlines across the nation. Barry Manilow was shown on the news, dressed in a white leisure suit, unfolding himself from a limousine outside the Breakers Hotel. "I was just heading to do a sound check when my manager called with the news," he said, visibly shaken. "It's just tragic. Albert Dunkle was the kindest, nicest man imaginable." Dionne Warwick pushed past the cameras at the West Palm Beach airport, in tears, murmuring, "Please. Not now."

"America lost its favorite ice cream man this evening," Walter Cronkite announced on the *CBS Evening News.* "Albert Dunkle arrived in America a penniless thirteen-year-old boy. After opening the first Dunkle's Ice Cream stand on a roadside during the Great Depression, he went on to invent a soft ice cream machine and a 'secret ice cream formula' that revolutionized the industry. He also devised today's modern franchise model—building a veritable empire of ice cream." A quick montage showed Bert waving from a Dunkle's Ice Cream truck. Bert presenting a laughing President Ford with a special tub of Banana Peel ice cream. A black-and-white still from *Life* of Bert and me arriving at a March of Dimes banquet, him in a tuxedo, me in a sequined gown.

"Although he is perhaps best known as the ice cream genius behind Spreckles the Clown, Nilla Rilla, and Chocohontas, as well as countless ice cream cakes and whimsical trademark flavors," news anchor John Chancellor said on NBC, "Albert Dunkle was also a great philanthropist. During World War II, he insisted on supplying American troops with ice cream for mere pennies on the dollar. And during the fifties—inspired by his polio-stricken wife, Lillian—he personally enlisted his trucks and franchises to distribute the Salk vaccine."

The White House sent condolences. The *New York Times* called. At Bella Flora, the staff got busy with ladders, hastily removing the gigantic gold-and-white banner garlanding the entranceway: HAPPY BIRTHDAY, ALBERT!

For me, nothing registered. All of it was a smear. Bert's friends and associates, in their plaid golf pants and Hawaiian shirts, paced the rooms at Bella Flora well into the night, all of them on the telephone, in the kitchen, our study. Isaac was stony-faced, doubled over beside me on the love seat in my bedroom. Then he was gone. Then he was back with a glass of water. Or was it gin? I glimpsed Edgar, our lawyer, half eclipsed within a hive of men, scribbling frantically on a yellow legal pad. Striding over, his face a mask of concern, he planted his damp palm on my convulsing shoulder. "Don't worry, Lil," he whispered. "I'm taking care of everything."

I was aware only of a horrific, otherworldly animal keening coming from somewhere, *Berrrrrt! Berrrrt!* Obliterating all other sounds, this anguished female howling would not stop; as soon as it seemed to subside, it restarted again, as relentless as the tide thrashing in a storm, until, at some point, my throat felt scorched and a voice from somewhere pleaded, "Will somebody get her a pill already?"

Back in New York, flowers and fruit baskets awaited. Cornucopias of delicacies from Zabar's and Bloomingdale's. What the hell was I supposed to do with two pounds of cheddar-wine cheese spread? Place it on the side of the bed where my Bert used to sleep? (And why did no one but Harvey Ballentine have the good sense to send liquor?) At Riverside Memorial the crowds parted around me. Jason escorted me carefully through the foyer, his young hand firm on my elbow. All those who were supposed to be celebrating Bert's birthday down in Palm Beach were shaking out their umbrellas, stomping their wet feet on the rubber mats laid out by the chapel. Somberly, they signed the guest book, then milled about in their coal-black suits gripping my forearm, telling me how sorry they were, how great Bert was. They fixed me in a gaze of pity and bathos for a moment before checking their watches and ducking out to the pay phones. *Businessmen.* Me, I wore Bert's terry-cloth sports headband wrapped around my wrist like a tourniquet. From the moment the ambulance arrived, I refused to remove it. I was vaguely aware that I was heavily medicated. I kept offering up my quivering arm, showing it to anyone who would look. "This was the last thing he wore," I rasped. "You see this spot? That's him. My Bert. His perspiration. You see that?"

Weeks after the funeral, I limped through the empty apartment every night weeping. *Oh, Bert, where are you?* Every time I heard the scrape of the elevator arriving in the foyer, I turned instinctively, expecting him to be returning from a round of golf, from dinner with the dairy men at Peter Luger's. When I put on a dress, I stood before the mirror with my head bowed, my neck exposed, waiting, until I realized that Bert would never emerge from the bathroom in his robe to help me with my zipper. The loss, over and over, caught me like sniper fire. Like a spooked horse kicking me in the gut. *Oh, Bert.* My knees buckled. I wailed like a child in the hospital.

Bert's jade green eyes, full of awe, glancing nervously around the Henry Street lobby. *Please*, I sobbed, doubling over. Bert pointing out the stone lions from the top deck of the Fifth Avenue bus on a floral summer evening. Bert with his head thrown back, moaning "Lil" as he grasps my shoulders and thrusts into me, the two of us clutching desperately, sparkling with sweat on the narrow mattress beneath the window, believing that we have all the time in the world, that we will never grow old, never die, never be anything but two lovers in that moment, bucking and alive. Bert winking delightedly at a cigarette girl in the foyer of the Ziegfeld. Bert nodding with his eyes closed as I read aloud to him from Hegel's *Dialectic of Reason*. Bert crashing our truck. Bert quickly reaching across the table to add a second pat of butter to his toast when he thinks I'm not looking, his face boyish with mischief. *My love. Come back. Pleasepleaseplease.* Bert teaching Isaac to ride his first two-wheeler, running behind him with his hand on the back fender, cheering "G-g-g-g-go!" before releasing our child pedaling furiously down the sidewalk. Bert sliding his hand down the front of my flowered silk dress, giving my bosom a playful squeeze in a chiming elevator minutes before a business meeting with representatives from DuPont. Bert jiggling the ice cubes in his glass of rye, pleading, *Lil, why won't you believe me?* Bert looking baleful in his powder blue terry-cloth bathrobe as he bends down to pick up the newspaper from the doormat the morning after Robert Kennedy is assassinated. After Nixon resigns. After the fall of Saigon. Bert sprawled across our four-poster bed, his left arm flung over his forehead, snoring with abandon. Bert, setting down the photograph of our grandson, turning to me in his sweaty tennis whites in our vaulted Palm Beach parlor, his weathered face earnest and poignant with love as he smiles and says gently, *Come with me, doll.*

Oh, that last conversation: That horrible last conversation! I could not bear to think of it! All he had wanted, my husband, despite all our money, despite all our success and fame, was simply a lovely lunch with his wife on the patio. Yet look at what I'd done!

Pouring myself a scotch, I swallowed it in one hot, punishing gulp. Then another. For the first time in decades, I longed to go back to a church, to kneel in the little cubby behind a heavy, velvet curtain and whisper my sins through the quatrefoils.

My beloved husband, my dear Bert. I had been hideous. Why could I not let him simply drink his wine and eat in peace? Why had I needed to hector him so? Why had his poignancy, which I'd once loved so fiercely, made me grow so contemptuous?

Everyone I had ever loved, I had repelled.

I was monstrous.

I tore through Bert's dressing room, pulling out his jackets, shirts, cardigans, pressing them to my face, trying to inhale as much of him as I could. From my own, I saw my Blackglama mink, winking from its plastic casing. A gift from him for my sixtieth birthday. Sniffling, I put it on, trying to imagine that Bert's hands were draping it across my shoulders. I tried to get some comfort from it, though I did not deserve it in the least. The sable shrug that he bought me one Christmas—I put that on as well and with a struggle. Pearls, a sapphire brooch I had tossed carelessly into my jewelry box. One by one I began to don everything that Bert had ever given me as a gift over the years. I could not get enough of him close to me. I jammed cocktail rings onto my swollen, arthritic fingers. One brooch I pinned in my hair; I clipped earrings onto the cuffs of my sleeves, until I was positively dripping with Bert's presents.

A pigeon landed on our windowsill, cooing.

I would go to him. To meet my Bert. With his merry eyes. His childlike stammer. The only man who ever loved me at all. The man whom I killed with my petty cruelties and bossiness.

Waddling over to the nightstand, I pulled out Mrs. Dinello's yellowed, cracked Bible—still the repository of all the mementos from Bert's and my early courtship. Clutching it to my bosom, I took a deep breath. I was ready. I was primed.

Yet just as suddenly, as I stood there like that, any sense of a plan deserted me. I was very, very drunk, I realized. Had I meant to climb up onto our roof terrace and perform a swan dive in my furs? Who the hell could even climb in my condition? Miserably, I limped into the bathroom. Inside the medicine chest, I found only a couple of Nembutals and Valiums left in their little amber vials. The impossibly sharp Wusthof knives in the kitchen, they were under Sunny's watch. So now what? We didn't even own so much as a staple gun, a ladder. The apartment building had a maintenance crew. Bert's shaving razor was new. Electric. Preposterous.

I remembered Mr. Lefkowitz, all those years ago on Orchard Street, yelling at his neighbors that he was so poor he did not even have the means to commit suicide properly. Me, I was too rich.

"Put Bella Flora on the market," I ordered Edgar. "The fixtures, the furniture, the fountains. Every goddamn thing."

"Lillian, I understand you're upset, but you may want to hold off for a little while. The market right now—"

"Don't you dare talk to me about the market!" I cried, knocking over a teacup someone had placed beside me on my desk. "You think I give a shit? I want it sold now. I never want to set foot on that property again."

I had my new secretary go through all the condolence cards and telegrams. "Put the ones from anyone famous in a folder. Everything else get rid of."

"But, Mrs. Dunkle, you've gotten bags full of cards from children all over America. Handmade."

"Burn them all." I was not eating. I could not sleep again without a pill. "You think I want to look at a drawing of a crying clown made by some kid in Omaha?

"All four televisions in the apartment are to be kept on at all times," I told Sunny. "And I want all of them turned to the same channel, do you understand? No news. I want *Days of Our Lives*. I want *Match Game* and *$10,000 Pyramid*. I want cartoons."

Every night I fell asleep before the spasming screen with a drink. Until one morning when I awoke unexpectedly. Jerking awake, I screamed. Bert's head flickered before me on the bureau. *Please, I invite you. Come to Dunkle's*, he said carefully, without stuttering, wearing his silly Ice Cream King crown. *Certainly, if it's good enough for my wife*—he smiled at me adoringly—*our famous ice cream is good enough for you.*

The very last commercial Bert and I had ever filmed together. In all the pandemonium, no one had thought to take it off the air.

The Nazis got one thing right, I thought, sipping bourbon in my office one Sunday after the *Funhouse*. If you're already in hell, work offers the only promise of relief.

I called my secretary at her home. "Why are there blank spaces?" I cried. "My calendar should be covered in ink. Send me out to visit our franchises in Duluth. Send me on plant inspections. Every goddamn industry dinner. Fund-raiser. Telethon. I want you to RSVP."

Our competition—as well as some of our very own executives—assumed that now that Bert was gone, Isaac would take over fully, the company would go public, or the Dunkle's Ice Cream Corporation would be sold. They assumed I was merely a figurehead. How they underestimated me. How little they knew. Bert left no instructions when he died; there was no succession plan in writing. But there did not need to be. The company had always been as much mine as his. And whatever I said, of course, went.

I telephoned Isaac. "I'm going to put a plaque reading '*Arbeit Macht Frei*' in my office," I said. "That ought to shore up the work ethic around here."

"Ma," he groaned. "You've been drinking. Where's your driver? Go home. It's Sunday."

"Excuse me, but did you see our sales figures for this quarter? We're hemorrhaging. And why is the entire southeast region paying three cents more per paper napkin than anywhere else?"

"You can't just work all the time, Ma," Isaac said, his voice webbed with fatigue. "Even if the numbers are bad. Take a day off. Go out with a friend to lunch. See a museum."

"I don't have any friends." And it was true. Everyone I'd known socially had been through Bert—his tennis club, the foundation—industry couples. The wives in our business, I never cared for them in the least. They were either decorative scatterbrains or tedious matrons. What could I possibly say to them? And now? Certainly nobody invited widows to anything—even celebrity widows like me. Unless, of course, they wanted money.

"Your father was my only friend," I said quietly.

Isaac exhaled. "Look, Ma. I know it's difficult, but you've got to find something you enjoy outside of the business. You're making yourself crazy."

What he meant, of course, was that I was making *him* crazy. Yet what the hell was I supposed to do? I had been working since I was five years old. My *shmendrik* son, he thought I could just stop?

Besides, going out to the theater—or the moving pictures, or even reading a book—anything Bert and I used to do together, was now too unbearably sad.

In the evenings, loath to go home to our empty apartment, I started ordering our driver to take me to Bert's old haunts—places he used to go without me—so that I could feel his presence. I ate dinner alone at his favorite table at Luchow's, at Sammy's Roumanian Steak House, at Peter Luger's in Brooklyn. "Serve me what you used to serve my husband," I told the worried-looking waiters. Sometimes I sat in the car outside the Russian baths where Bert used to "take a *schvitz*" with Isaac. I watched the men walk in and out. His age. Dressed like him. One evening I told the chauffeur, "Take me where you used to take Bert to buy presents for me." Bonwit's and Saks were now staying open well past 5:00 P.M.

Myself, I'd never had much patience for the rigmarole of shopping. All that schlepping and disrobing—for someone with my leg it was only burdensome, dispiriting. In the past I had my secretaries go to department stores for me or make telephone calls to have items delivered.

Yet suddenly, after all these years, I discovered something: Stepping into Bergdorf Goodman's and being waited on was immensely gratifying! Why had no one ever explained this to me before? A saleswoman ushered me into an exclusive dressing room, seated me on a velvet banquette, offered me ice water with lemon, and brought garments to me for my perusal. Everyone fussed over me grandly, like I was royalty! *Yes, Mrs. Dunkle. Of course, Mrs. Dunkle. Oh, try this one instead. It will look divine on you.* "Give me that in the coral silk," I said imperiously, "not paisley." Never did I feel as beautiful or as powerful, darlings, as when I shopped.

Isaac had wanted me to develop a little hobby.

So sue me: I did.

One Thursday I bought sixteen Chanel suits, ten thousand dollars' worth of sportswear by Geoffrey Beene, a dozen cashmere sweaters in all the latest colors: avocado, burgundy, mauve. Five pairs of Foster Grant sunglasses, three Yves Saint Laurent chiffon evening gowns, four hundred dollars' worth of costume jewelry, and a belted coat with a silver-fox collar. "I refuse to dress like a little old lady," I announced to the salesgirls. "It's bad enough I wear plastic slipcovers on television." I purchased Diamonds by the Yard at Tiffany's and an enormous topaz pendant to wear as "casual" jewelry. A full set of Louis Vuitton luggage. A dozen handbags in assorted colors from Gucci. How marvelous to be the consumer, not the poor schmuck somewhere in the sweatshop, the tannery, the leatherworkers, painstakingly making it all for pennies.

Once you purchased something new—oh, darlings, you just wanted to do it again! The thrill of acquisition gave you the same bloom as the first sip of a cocktail. A pair of Ming-dynasty jade dragons I bought from Christie's to flank the entryway of the house in Bedford. Another Cadillac: wine red. A silver-lacquered grand piano. I went mad for antiques, redecorating our homes completely in Bert's taste. Inlaid credenzas, damask chaise longues. A mahogany bar. Crystal chandeliers for all the bath-rooms. Why not? One weekend I flew all the way to London for Harrods' annual sale. On the Concorde, no less! The harrow-ing journey that had taken my family eighteen days on a rancid, belching steamer I now completed in three and a half hours, glid-ing fifty-six thousand feet above the earth, sipping champagne and nibbling wine-soaked figs above all turbulence and weather, at the edge of outer space itself, the ocular curve of the earth visible through the little convex window like the cerulean eye of God himself. In my little leather seat, I felt almost holy, anointed. I felt like an astronaut. It would've been perfect if it hadn't made me sob. For Bert should have been there with me.

I hired a "personal shopping consultant" from Bergdorf's to ac-company Petunia and me from there on. We went to Paris for the couture collections. Fashion shows, oh, they were the most marvelous theater! Better than church! At Cartier's I ordered a magnificent jewel-encrusted cane for me and matching gold-and-diamond dog tags and collars for Petunia. Other than myself, she was my favorite customer to shop for, of course, as she kvetched about nothing. A pink satin dog bed trimmed with Chantilly lace. A Burberry dog raincoat. A neon light-up water bowl from Fiorucci.

The only problem with shopping, I discovered, was *paying*. Whereas for years I had meticulously kept track of every penny I'd spent—ten cents for the daily newspaper, forty-nine cents for ny-lons, et cetera—now the sums were far too large. Seeing the bills, writing the checks, oh, how it pained me! Why, it nearly took all the joy out of buying altogether. And so, to soften the blow, I started having my items charged to the Dunkle's Ice Cream Corporation instead. This way, when I received the bills at the office, I could pretend that rather than "purchases" they were "expenses." Expenses, darlings, were so much easier to justify. Everything I bought, I expensed to the company, then had gift-wrapped and delivered directly to Park Avenue. So they genuinely seemed like presents. When I arrived home from work each day, there was a cascade of surprises waiting for me to open.

"Ma, what is all this stuff?" Isaac said one morning when he came over with some papers he wanted me to sign. My large front parlor had become my "gift room," filled with my purchases, arranged on coffee tables, shelves, and settees like so many objets d'art in a museum. "What's that pelt doing on the lampshade?"

"It's chinchilla. A dinner jacket."

"It's a fire hazard."

"The lamp is new, too. From Sotheby's. The chair as well. Your father's taste, of course. He would've thought they were marvelous, wouldn't he?"

"Oh, Ma." Isaac sighed. Aimlessly, he picked up a Judith Leiber evening bag—in the shape of a baby penguin covered in crystals—and set it back down dispiritedly beside another shaped like a slice of watermelon. His eyes glossed over a dozen assorted pairs of silver candlesticks arranged atop a tooled leather ottoman. A pile of Hermès scarves. A brass samovar purchased from an antiques dealer on Madison Avenue. An Edwardian secretary desk with a hutch. Fifteen Madame Alexander dolls still in their boxes from FAO Schwarz. The room did look a bit like E. Lazarre's pawnshop. But tasteful, darlings. Tasteful. And certainly clean.

"You're not planning on keeping all this, are you?" Isaac said.

"Of course I am. Why wouldn't I?"

"You have the receipts taped to everything."

"Well, how else will everyone know how expensive they are? Sunny!" I hollered. "Get my son here a cocktail, will you?"

"No thanks, Ma," he said—always unsmiling, my son. "I can't stay long."

"Come." I motioned.

In my study I'd had a business line installed and one of those new Xerox machines, the size of a small meat locker. This way I never had to *not* be working. "What do you think?" I said. I'd had Promovox send over markups for my newest idea, "Mocktail Milkshakes." Several different approaches sat propped up on the easel by Bert's mahogany desk. One ad showed a close-up of a gorgeous young couple straddling bicycles and toasting each other on a country road with Dunkle's milk shakes. Another showed them at a discoteque. "It's Mocktail Hour," the tagline read.

Isaac stared at it. After a minute he chewed on his lip in a way that made his jaw contort to the left. "You sure this is the way you wanna go, Ma?"

Ever since Bert died, I had been developing Mocktails. The idea came to me one afternoon at a party at Merv Griffin's house, when somebody handed me a Brandy Alexander. Oddly, I had never tasted one before. The wonderful, medicinal shock of brandy was blunted by what seemed to be chocolate milk. "What the hell is this?" I blinked, holding the frosted glass at a distance. "Bosco?"

"I thought you'd like it, Lillian." Merv chuckled. "Being the Ice Cream Queen, as you are."

"A cocktail should taste like a cocktail," I grumbled, leaning back on one of his chaise longues in my caftan. "Not a goddamn milk shake." Yet Merv caught me smiling. What can I say? It was delicious.

Drinks like these, I realized, could be our antidote to Umlaut.

After all, it was the seventies. Hosting my television show as I did, I saw how the culture had changed. Nobody wanted to be a good soldier or Horatio Alger anymore. Nobody wanted to knuckle under and build. Parents, when they came to our studio, they were dressed in the same jeans and satin baseball jackets as their children. Adult things had become juvenile. Fruity, ridiculous cocktails. Paint-box-colored cars with cutesy, preschool names like Pinto, Gremlin, and Beetle. Miniature Sony TVs, like for a doll. Everyone wanted to be a child forever, it seemed.

Except high. I hosted the pop singers. I met the artists. So I knew about the drugs. Andy Warhol, the night he brought me to Studio 54, it was like a circus tent. A neon crescent moon descended from the ceiling, inhaling a string of white beads from an illuminated spoon. "Oh, my God, Lillian! Look! Mother Goose for Cokeheads!" Harvey Ballentine squealed.

Alcohol-flavored milk shakes: They were the perfect concoction for the times.

Yet developing these frozen novelties proved challenging. The artificial Brandy Alexander, Kahlúa, amaretto, and vodka had to taste exactly like their real, forty-proof namesakes. But the different chemicals created odd inconsistencies in the ice cream. The hours I spent in the laboratory with our chemists! And the consumer taste tests, oh, such a pain in my ass. It used to be, of course, that Bert and I would just cook up something in our kitchen in Bellmore, serve it to our customers, and watch their faces when they ate it. But now it had become a national industry. Focus groups. Market analysts. Everyone from Tarrytown to Topeka was suddenly a goddamn critic.

It had taken me almost three years to get six Mocktails ready for the market. Yet now, as my son stared at the advertisements sent over from Promovox, his face contorted into a sculpture of unease. Why couldn't he be on my side more? I wondered. The two of us, we were all we had left now.

"After all my work, now you're expressing doubts?"

"I'm just worried, Ma. You've seen the numbers. Most people looking to open an ice cream shop are now going with Häagen—" He caught himself. "Super-premium ice cream is what's 'in.'"

I thumped the poster board. "The public wants richer, more 'sophisticated' ice cream? So this is how we give it to them. These milk shakes *taste* expensive. And *fancy*. But they can still be made with your father's machine. Why do you keep resisting this?"

"It's just— Do you really think that Mocktail Milkshakes are the right product for us? They just seem so . . ." Isaac's voice trailed off as he searched for the words. "So cheap. And racy."

"Cheap and racy is good," I told him. "Cheap and racy is exactly right. Look around you, for Chrissakes. It's 1979."

Just as I predicted, our Mocktail Milkshakes were a great sensation, thank you very much. In the spring of 1980, we offered them "for a limited time only" at our northeastern franchises between D.C. and Boston. Everyone went mad for them; their exclusivity only fueled their cachet. The White Russian, amaretto, and margarita flavors proved particularly popular. *Take that, Umlaut*, I thought as I reviewed our sales figures. Internally, I sent out a company-wide memo, too, extolling our preliminary success— lest anyone still underestimated me.

During my weekly dinner at Isaac and Rita's, I announced that Dunkle's was ready to take Mocktail Milkshakes national. "I want us to launch them from coast to coast with a huge campaign. 'Mocktail parties' everywhere. Billboards on Times Square and Sunset Boulevard reading: 'It's Mocktail Hour.' Advertisements on prime time."

Isaac stared at the half-eaten roast on his plate. Rita got up quietly and went to the sideboard for more wine. Only Jason spoke. "Can I have wine, too?"

When Rita said no, he pushed back his chair. "I don't know why you all have to be such fascists about it. Sixteen is the drinking age in Europe you know."

"We're not in Europe. And you're not sixteen yet."

After Jason stomped off, the glugging of the Bordeaux into my glass was the only sound in the dining room. The silence felt damning.

"Well," I said, dropping my napkin onto my plate. "Don't everyone start cheering at once, darlings. Don't anyone say, 'Nice job, Lillian.' It's only our biggest goddamn product launch in years." I, too, stood up.

Jason was sprawled on the floor in the parlor with his chin in his hands, his silhouette glazed by the iridescence of the television.

"Well, it seems we've both been banished to the rumpus room," I announced, lowering myself onto the sofa behind him. Two police officers with guns were chasing a man down a busy city sidewalk. "Is this your program?"

"Nah," Jason said, still staring at the screen. "I'm just watching. There's nothing good on."

Predictably, the cops knocked over a fruit cart. The only street peddlers I ever saw nowadays were in police dramas.

"*Tateleh*," I said after a moment. "Let me ask you something. What I was talking about before. Our Mocktail Milkshakes. You don't care for them?"

Slowly, Jason rolled over. He sat up and twisted from side to side, cracking his back. Then he stretched out his arms with an "Urrahh" before letting them flop to the carpet. "Well," he said diplomatically, "I like the *taste*, I guess."

"But?" I prompted. "Tell me. Please. You're the only one with any goddamn sense around here."

Jason shrugged, trying to appear nonchalant, though his face brightened. I had anointed him; the privilege of my trust was not lost on him.

"Well," he said carefully, "I just don't understand why you'd, like, sell an alcohol-flavored milk shake with no, like, actual alcohol in it."

From the dining room came a sudden crash of dishes, followed by a volley of bickering. Jason and I exchanged naughty, delighted glances.

"The problem with adding real alcohol, *tateleh*—" I said.

"Grandma?" Jason twisted around to face me. "It's not even that, really. I mean, no offense, but a lot of Dunkle's stuff is just really cheesy. Like, Nilla Rilla? Spreckles the Clown?"

"Oh." I shook my head. "That goddamn clown. Is he ever a pain in my ass—"

Jason gave a whinnying, dopey laugh. "You know what you should have instead? A punk-rock clown. In a leather jacket like the Ramones. With a Mohawk. He could snarl instead of smile, and throw ice cream at the kids, and terrorize people, and smash his guitar."

"Well, thank you," I said, straightening up. "It's nice to get an honest opinion around here for a change."

"Or a kung fu clown. How awesome would that be?" Sensing my unhappiness, however, his expression shifted like clouds. "It's not like your shakes aren't good and all," he said sympathetically. "I just think they *sound* really lame."

His eyes scanned mine, darting back and forth, in a way that suggested he was testing my waters, trusting me with confidential information. For the first time, I saw, my grandson was willing to regard me as more than an old lady with powdery hair, dried fruit for a face. A pact was being forged. "I mean, like, most of the kids at school and stuff?" he said in a low voice. "If they want to get high, they do, like, coke. Or 'ludes. Or 'shrooms. Or we drink vodka and beer. Nobody ever says 'cocktails.' And Mocktails? *Yucch*. That's the stuff they used to serve us at bar mitzvahs."

"So you think they're stodgy," I said plainly.

"Yeah. I guess," Jason said, cracking his knuckles. "Like, if I was going to market them—and okay, I'm just a sophomore, so what do I know?—but I wouldn't try to make them sound tame at all. People actually like stuff a lot more when they think it's kind of bad for them."

I stared at him, astounded. My grandson. My beautiful, impossible grandson.

Two days later, borrowing from his vocabulary, I announced to Promovox that I wanted our new advertising campaign revamped to be "cooler, more happening, and edgy."

"Let's portray our new milk shakes as a sort of an illicit pleasure," I said. "Decadent. Dangerous, even."

"Lillian, I'm not sure that's such a wise move." The head of accounts crossed his arms and leaned back in his leather chair. "It's certainly not in keeping with your brand." His skepticism spread around the table like a contagion. Accounts men began explaining vehemently why such an approach was "a huge misstep" and "entirely wrong for Dunkle's." *Excuse me, Lillian*, one of them clucked. *But has your son signed off on this?*

At the new firm I hired, MKG, there seemed to be nobody over the age of twenty-three. Their offices were in a warehouse on seedy Union Square. Big framed silk screens on the walls. Furniture that looked like TinkerToys. Not a carpet or a piece of upholstery in sight. Jason, I sensed, would approve. And at this agency, they listened to me.

"Absolutely, Mrs. Dunkle," they said, nodding. "Frankly, your company's advertising screams for an overhaul. It looks like it hasn't been dusted off since 1953. You want something slick. Radical. *Provocative.* We're going to come up with a campaign that's totally *cutting-edge.*"

First MKG suggested renaming the Mocktails "Shake-Ups." This was "so much hipper," they insisted—and I agreed. "Why not?" I laughed. "Shake things up." When I ran it by Jason later as a litmus test, he said, "*Those* I would totally drink."

True to their word, MKG came up with advertisements unlike anything Dunkle's had ever done before. No Spreckles. No bucolic American family. No flags or Lady Liberty. Not even me. These ads were elegant. Stark. One of the top fashion photographers in the business did the shoots. All they showed was a close-up of a milk shake in a new, clear take-out cup with "Dunkle's" spelled out on it in sleek, modern letters. The cup was sparkling and sweating with condensation. A straw rose up from the froth invitingly. A pair of glistening red lips parted above it seductively, with the deep pink hint of a tongue. That was it. Foaming, tantalizing milk shake. Erect straw. Shimmering mouth. "Are You Old Enough?" the headlines read. "Controlled Substance." "Highly Addictive." "You'll Want It Again and Again." "Once Is Never Enough." "Do You Dare?" and "Ice-stasy." Along the bottom was always the same tag: *"Dunkle's New Shake-Ups: Ice Cream as You've Never Had It Before."*

So, okay: Subtle they were not.

Yet the advertisements were so adult and sophisticated that I could hardly believe them. Isaac, of course, protested that they were too risqué. Yet Jason declared them "awesome." And Bert, I was sure, would have adored them. They were like works of pop art. Besides, what was wrong with a little sex? I wondered. I was seventy-three goddamn years old. I should be able to sell my product any way I wanted. Have a little fun for a change that did not involve a clown and an albino gorilla.

I placed the blowups around my office like paintings in a gallery, then leaned back in my swivel chair, admiring them.

"Wow!" My secretary whistled when she entered with some letters.

"My son thinks they're too forward. What do you think?" I said.

"Well, they sure are eye-catching," she said uncertainly.

"I think they're marvelous. So very modern, yes?"

For the first time since Bert had died, I woke up each morning feeling energized, expectant. For the first time in my life, the public would finally recognize me for the innovator I had always been. People would see that I, Lillian Dunkle, had been just as integral and as vital to the ice cream industry as my husband had—not just a genial, motherly cripple doing shtick—or a lovable TV personality whose husband financed her kiddie show. I would be given my rightful place in the great pantheon of ice cream makers across the ages who had evolved the confection from mere sugar and snow into the most marvelous and beloved food on earth. Arabs making sherbet. Giambattista della Porta freezing wine. Nancy Johnson inventing the hand-cranked freezer. Christian K. Nelson creating the Eskimo Pie. Ernest Hamwi and Abe Doumar and all those Middle Eastern immigrants cooking up wafer cones at the 1904 World's Fair. Bert with his marvelous soft ice cream machines and formulas. And now, finally. Rightly. Me. Lillian Dunkle. It was I, more than anyone else, who had given ice cream its modern-day whimsy. Its endless variety. And now, oh, darlings, its panache.

As I clipped on my earrings at my dressing table and sprayed myself with Shalimar, I listened to Benny Goodman's "Sing, Sing, Sing" on the hi-fi in my bedroom, then the sound track from *Saturday Night Fever*, which I thought was quite marvelous. Our Shake-Ups were going to breathe fresh life into Dunkle's. They were going to renew the company and put us back on top. They tasted rich yet were cheap to make. We were going to beat our competition at its own game.

If Isaac still had reservations, he wisely kept them to himself. Naysaying has no place in sales, and the new products were delicious. Even he had to admit that.

I introduced Shake-Ups to our franchises at special regional meetings. As I gave the pitch from the podium, attractive young servers in satin vests and sequined bow ties fanned out across the conference room with trays full of miniature Shake-Ups for our franchise owners to sample. "To Shake-Ups," I toasted, lifting my glass. Isaac pulled a cord, and the new promotional posters were revealed. Whistles. Murmurs. Cheers. Gasps. The room erupted in chatter. I was so breathless I could barely register anything: only fragments of smiles, swallows of astonishment, people tugging at my sleeve. No one seemed to be without an opinion. From the corner of my eye, I noticed one of our owners from Chattanooga swigging down the miniature frozen Kamikazes like bar shots, waylaying the servers for more. The entire room seemed animated, a great beast come to life. Never had a new product created such a stir. The heat, the lights, the noise—it was suddenly overwhelming. I had worked so hard, for so long.

"Ma, are you all right?" Isaac asked. My hands and arms, they were quivering.

"Mrs. Dunkle." Someone pushed up to us, waving a tiny empty glass. "Are you sure there's no tequila in this? I've got to tell you, this margarita flavor? It taste like it's eighty proof!"

"Oh, now. Please." I grinned unsteadily, adjusting my eyeglasses.

"There's nothing in these milk shakes that I wouldn't serve to my very own grandson."

"Check the labels," Isaac added quickly, pointing. "We've got printout sheets listing all the ingredients right over there on the tables."

"I don't know." Another franchise owner chuckled warily, in a way that suggested that he *did* know, but was simply unwilling to concede it. "I drink piña coladas all the time on vacation. This certainly tastes like rum to me."

"Then our chemists have simply done their jobs," Isaac said a little hotly.

"You need proof?" I smiled. "Keep drinking them. See how drunk you do not get."

There was a gust of laughter.

"I need some air," I whispered to Isaac.

He handed me my cane—a red lacquered one for the occasion, to match the lips on the posters.

"Stay here," I said. "I'll just be a minute."

Limping into the foyer, I fanned myself rapidly with my hand. Inside the ladies' room, I plunked down on the little cushioned bench. It took me a few minutes to catch my breath. I glanced around. The mirrored lounge, with its fake Oriental vase and satiny orchids and brass Kleenex holder, was perfectly still. A Muzak version of "Have You Never Been Mellow" filtered in softly over a speaker recessed in the ceiling. The air smelled of peach room deodorizer. For a moment, as I sat there, I became aware of the ventilators wheezing in tandem with my breath.

Then I unclasped my pocketbook and removed my little flask. Once I had a few sips, I knew, my hands would be steadier.

Lifting the bottle, I toasted the air. "Bert," I whispered, my eyes filling with tears. "I did it."

Chapter 16

WELL, BY NOW, I SUPPOSE, you all know what happened next, darlings.

The first weeks of our nationwide product launch—when our advertisements hit the newsstands and billboards, when our commercials aired on prime time, when banners flapped across the fronts of our franchises—TRY OUR GREAT NEW SHAKE-UPS!!!—our stores, they couldn't keep up. Indeed, we had to rush extra shipments of the formulas. Our posters instantly became collectors' items as well; people removed them from the sides of bus shelters in New York, Chicago, Boston, trying to "collect the whole set of flavors." *Advertising Age* ran a cover story: "Dunkle's: A Makeover & Milk Shake for the '80s." Supermarkets selling limited-edition pints of our Shake-Up flavors could not keep enough stocked in their freezers either. Everyone, *everyone*, it seemed, loved the unearthly taste of liquor blended into the velvetiness of ice cream. The slight sting contrasting with the cold, milky sweetness. The tease of naughtiness.

It was not until three weeks after our launch that I found a stack of letters on my desk blotter with a note from Isaac: *"Thought you should see these. I'm afraid there are more."*

"Dear Dunkle's," the letter began, *"I have been a faithful franchise*

owner since 1953. If I had wanted to be in the liquor business, however, I'd have opened a roadhouse."

The one beneath it declared, *"I don't care how profitable these things are. These products are WRONG, and I refuse to sell them. Booze and ice cream shouldn't mix."*

"How many more did he bring up?" I said to my secretary. (This one, whom I believe was named Melissa, was a pixieish girl with a wounded look and spidery black eyeliner. I once caught her polishing her nails with Wite-Out. Oh, how I missed Mrs. Preminger.)

Melissa directed her pointed little chin to a large pile of mail atop the file cabinet: manila envelopes, pale pink stationery, a few typed leaves of tissuey onionskin. One was even made of cutout magazine letters, like a ransom note.

"Those idiots!" I cried. All our commercials for Shake-Ups had a disclaimer running across a ribbon at the bottom: CONTAINS NO ACTUAL ALCOHOL. Could it be any clearer? "Do they actually think we're slipping Kahlúa and brandy into our products? At this price point? Don't any of these dingbats read?"

Other franchise owners wrote letters protesting our updated logo and look. *"They're completely out of line with the Dunkle's tradition,"* complained a man in Michigan. *"Our customers don't like it. Why didn't you consult us?"*

"Who the hell is the boss here?" I said aloud. "These people should know better." If a flavor like maple walnut no longer sold well, we retired it. If a typeface or a logo made us look stodgy, we changed it. So what? This sort of triage was necessary in business. It happened all the time. It's what made us our fortune.

Isaac arrived in my office clutching still more letters, including a clip from the *Salt Lake City Tribune* reporting that all our franchises in Utah were refusing to carry Shake-Ups on religious grounds. "Ma, we both know that Mormons are huge ice cream consumers," he said. "If they start to see our brand as incompatible with their—"

"Please." I waved him over to my couch. "Disgruntled Mormons are nothing new. For years they've refused to sell our rum raisin or coffee flavors, either. Why do you think we invented Donny Almond for them?"

I poured myself a scotch and Isaac his now-customary Tab. How I raised a teetotaler, I will never know.

"Trust me. Everyone always kvetches at first." I handed him his soft drink. He set it down on the glass table, untouched. "Back when we first introduced the Fudgie Puppie and the Nilla Rilla? You're too young to remember, but, oh. Everyone was a critic. 'No one will eat anything shaped like a dog or a gorilla,' they said. 'The cake molds are too complicated.'"

I took a sip of my drink. Johnnie Walker Black only gets better with time. "Have you seen the latest earnings reports?" I pressed the button on my intercom.

"Ma, of course I've seen them," Isaac said. Picking up his glass, he realized it was dripping condensation and looked around distractedly for something to wipe it up with. His paper napkin had fallen on the floor. My son, I thought as I watched him reach for the Kleenex box on my desk. He was a mirror: Passive. Impenetrable. Reflecting the qualities of whoever stood before him. With Rita he was acquisitive, striving. In Bert's presence he had been warmhearted and hale. Around me? He was parsimonious. Prickly. So difficult to love. I supposed I deserved it, though it made me unbearably sad. The things I had dreamed for him—for us. For once, couldn't he just acquiesce and remain open to me and my ideas? Why, we were almost there! Could he not see it?

"Within a week or two, all this grumbling will disappear. Trust me," I said. "Everybody will realize just how much goddamn money they're making on these things. And not one customer will have gotten drunk from them." I pointed my glass at him. "I'm telling you. Being a visionary means waiting for the rest of the world to catch up."

Yet a week later my son appeared in my doorway again looking even more frazzled. Recrimination seemed to emanate from him like radio waves.

"Ma, let's take a walk down to my office," he said. "I need you to see something."

Leading me past the particleboard cubicles and clicking typewriters, he ushered me through the frosted-glass wall and nudged his door shut. After Bert died, Isaac had convinced me to move our headquarters to this new building on Sixth Avenue because it afforded us more space for less money. Yet every day I regretted it. New York City was becoming nothing but a forest of ugly, obsidian boxes with polarized windows. Our own offices were like space capsules, hermetically sealed, cut off from everything, floating high above the city. All filled with ghastly modular furniture designed by Swedish depressives. Isaac's "couch": a slab of black leather punctuated with buttons. Scarcely better than the bench back at the Dinellos'. Who the hell could even sit on it?

"Here," he said quickly, pulling up a padded office chair and settling me in. Pictures of him, Rita, and Jason at Disney World smiled down from frames on the walls. "Where's my scotch?" I said. "And would it kill you to put maybe a flag and a house plant in here?"

"Pamela," Isaac ordered, pushing a button on his phone, "would you please bring my mother and me some coffee, please?" He came back around and handed me a letter printed on lemon-colored paper. "We need to discuss this."

It was from an organization called "Defenders of the Family" out in Colorado Springs. It was headed by a minister named Hubert Elkson. Reverend Elkson was one of those newfangled preachers who looked like a department-store mannequin and hosted a syndicated television show. Every Sunday morning he railed against flag burning and called for school prayer while an address flashed on-screen for donations.

Now, it seemed, the Reverend Elkson had issued a press release:

"DEFENDERS OF THE FAMILY" TO LAUNCH NATIONWIDE BOYCOTT OF DUNKLE'S ICE CREAM.
The Reverend Hubert Elkson announced today that "Defenders of the Family" is calling upon its "Flock of the Faithful" to boycott Dunkle's Ice Cream. He told the Baptist Press:

"Dunkle's new Shake-Ups are an obscenity. They are corrupting the children of America by giving them a taste for alcohol in the guise of an 'innocent' milk shake. Yet there is nothing 'innocent' about alcoholic ice cream, particularly when it comes in flavors like White Russian and Kamikaze, which brazenly glorify Communism and our enemies during World War Two."

"Is he insane?" I threw the flyer down on the table.

A crease formed in the center of my son's forehead like a seam. Turning his ballpoint pen end over end between his fingers, he looked at me plainly.

"This is serious, Ma. Elkson's congregation is apparently a very pious bunch."

"Oh, 'pious,' my *tuches*. I met this reverend last year at a fundraiser for Ronald Reagan. All the guy could talk about was how our television shows were competing in the same time slot. He's running a racket, same as everyone else."

Isaac held open his hands helplessly. "Maybe so. But I have to tell you, Ma. For a 'family-friendly' chain like ours to suddenly start running risqué ads for booze-flavored milk shakes? NBC is already concerned that Shake-Ups may not be the best product to have advertised during its top Sunday morning kiddie show. And now churches are threatening to picket us?" Isaac picked up the morning's newspaper and tossed it glumly across his desk. "Prince Charles just got engaged. All we can hope is that nobody will be paying attention to anything other than him and Lady Di all week."

I sat back, astounded. "You actually agree with this prick?"

"All I'm saying is that for a sizable number of Americans, Ma, he may have a point."

"Please. I will not have our company blackmailed into changing our menu because some idiot cannot read a goddamn label. There's not a drop of alcohol in anything. And don't tell me that this has anything to do with Christian morality. I was raised by Christians. The people who took me in were the nicest, kindest people in the world. And they wouldn't for a minute—"

I clamped my hands over my mouth.

"Why, those sons of bitches," I murmured. "Those *stronzi*."

"What? What is it, Ma?"

I struggled to get up, then yanked open Isaac's metal office cabinet, looking for the Yellow Pages. "I need a private investigator. A new one."

"Ma, what are you doing?"

"They must have an in with a Protestant church now. Or they paid off someone in Colorado. Oh, I should have known—"

"What? Who?" Isaac said with confusion.

"People from the past, *bubeleh*. Who have a vendetta. From before you were even born. Those bastards. I knew they would pull something. For years, oh, they've just been waiting."

Isaac's face grew pained. "Ma, you're not making sense. I can't talk to you when you're like this."

I set down my glass. My son's eyes were the same dark brown as mine, yet the right one had a band of yellowish hazel radiating from the pupil like a slice of pie. His cheeks were now covered with gray, velvety stubble. So often, I supposed, he'd had to weather me like a season of storms. I drew in a sharp breath. For some reason the office was wobbling slightly. Perhaps it was because we were on the forty-first floor and there was wind off the Hudson.

Isaac had a novelty game on his desk that he'd inherited from Bert: a rectangular frame with five metal balls suspended from it in a row of matching pendulums. I reached over, pulled one back, and released it, sending it knocking against the others.

"I know who's behind all of this," I said.

For a bunch of devout Christians, Reverend Hubert Elkson's flock certainly had a lot of idle time on its hands. The very next morning, our franchise owners in Cleveland and Denver, in Mobile and Atlanta, in Dallas and Pittsburgh, arrived at their shops to find protesters camped out in beach chairs, waving crucifixes and signs reading STOP CORRUPTING KIDS WITH VICE CREAM! "BOOZE" IS NOT A FLAVOR! And, simply, DRUNKLE'S. Reverend Elkson appeared on the evening news on all three networks: "Dunkle's Shake-Ups exemplify the moral decay of America," he told reporters. "What's next? Selling children french fries flavored with tobacco? Pizza that tastes like marijuana?"

Unfortunately, it seemed that the only person in America who *did* bother to familiarize himself with the ingredients of our Shake-Ups was some lunatic vitamin guru out in Berkeley, California. "Dunkle's ice cream *is* dangerous and immoral," he announced on his health-food program, syndicated to no fewer than fifty-seven public radio stations across the country. "Have you read the ingredients, people? When you hear all the chemicals you're eating, you're going to boycott Dunkle's ice cream, too—as a confection of the military-industrial complex."

That weekend, on *Saturday Night Live*, a fat comedian dressed up as me in a wig and a housecoat. "Hi, I'm Lillian Dunkle, the Ice Cream Queen of America," he said in a chirpy falsetto. "Trust me, boys and girls. There's no alcohol in our Shake-Ups whatsoever." Opening a Dunkle's milk-shake cup, he poured a large mound of white powder out onto a mirror and began snorting it up with the straw. "See? Only a hundred percent medicinal-grade Peruvian cocaine!"

"Oh, Lillian," my publicist said, massaging the bridge of her nose when she reviewed the tape on Monday. "This is not good."

Our sales, they began to plummet.

Over the Fourth of July weekend, the very pinnacle of our season, nearly half our franchises reported heavy losses. Grocery-store sales went way down as well. For the first time in twenty-three years, we had trouble getting co-sponsors for the children's goodie bags on *Dunkle's Sundae Morning Funhouse*. "I'm sorry," said the account man at Mr. Bubble, "but, Lillian, if I may be blunt, your product is literally considered poison right now."

"Ma, let's pull the product," Isaac pleaded.

"No," I cried. "I will not let those bastards win. Not Rocco, not Vittorio—"

"What? Who are you even talking about?"

"Just you wait. I'm not taking anything off the market. I'm getting to the bottom of this."

Two, three times a day, I began telephoning my newest private investigator, an incessant gum chewer named Nick, who lisped slightly. "Look, Mrs. Dunkle, I told you. I've been combing through everything I can find. So far? Nada. No charitable donations to Elkson. No connection to any other ice cream companies, dairies, or the vitamin guy either. I'm sorry, but there doesn't seem to be any link between these two families and this boycott at all," he said. "Unless they're some of those Jesus freaks sitting out there in the parking lots themselves."

"Keep looking," I ordered. "This is them. I know they're doing this to me. D-I-N-E-L-L-O. Make sure you've got it spelled right."

The headlines continued. And on the TV: reports of the spreading boycott. A local Little League coach in Tennessee led a "Dumping Dunkle's Day," in which an entire town emptied Shake-Ups down a sewer.

One after another, our franchises started to close.

Now even my pills would not let me sleep. Every night around 3:00 A.M., I lurched awake in terror, glistening with sweat: Isaac had been a small boy again; crowds were stringing him from a tree, chanting "Kill the Jew" in Russian. I was a little girl running desperately through the cobblestone streets, when my leg suddenly came off and rolled past me like a wheel.

"Goddamn it," I said aloud, stumbling into the incubator of my kitchen. As I sat drinking a scotch, trying to calm myself, my chiffon nightgown plastered to my armpits, I wondered: How had it all come to this?

The shining land I fell so deliriously in love with so many years ago in a movie house in Hamburg. *Ah-MEH-rih-kah.* With all its abundance and ingenuity. We'd won two world wars and put a man on the moon, for Chrissakes. Yet now people were becoming unhinged by a milk shake? When had this country gotten so small-minded and ingrown and frightened?

What the hell had happened to us?

I finished one drink, then another. Squinting through my

empty glass, I turned it like a kaleidoscope. The overhead light in my kitchen blurred through the lead crystal. I spied my newest rhinestone-encrusted cane propped against the counter, its sparkles smearing and refracting in the light. My cane. It had been with me longer than anything else in my entire life, I realized. So what if I had begun treating it like jewelry? At least no one could accuse me of not making the best of my handicap.

With a jerk, I set down the glass and struggled to my feet. I did not know why the idea had not occurred to me earlier. Hobbling into my study, I grabbed the receiver off my antique telephone and called MKG. Of course, since it was three o'clock in the morning, their service took a message. Then I telephoned Isaac at home. "Wake up! Wake up!" I hollered into his new answering machine. "I am having such a brilliant idea, I think I may have a heart attack." I hiccupped. "You call me back."

I arrived at the office at daybreak positively carbonated with excitement. Admittedly, most of the notes I had scribbled down on my personal stationery at 3:00 A.M. were now illegible. Yet my vision was crystalline of what needed to be done, of the brand-new publicity campaign that Dunkle's was going to launch, of how we were going to turn our predicament around into a trump card.

Since no one, it seemed, ever arrived at the goddamn office before 10:00 A.M. now, I started in on the work myself. Oh, I was brimming with inspiration! My heart beat so frantically, in fact, it seemed only sensible to quell it with a bit more scotch. After pouring myself a tumbler, I got busy sketching on a legal pad. The possibilities came to me so quickly my hands and fingers seemed to tangle. I kept dropping my pencil. Goddamn arthritis. Writing was suddenly like embroidering lace.

"*Sinfully delicious,*" I wrote. Beneath this I sketched a mischievous-looking devil. So sue me: I'm no artist. Yet the idea itself was brilliant. *Mae West,* I thought suddenly as I staggered over to my sideboard for a refill. Where the hell was the pencil sharpener? Mae West: Hadn't she once said something along the lines of, "When I'm good, I'm very, very good, but when I'm bad, I'm terrific"? *That* would be our new tagline. Was such a line even copyrighted? Where could I find out precisely what she'd said? I should call my lawyers, I decided. Yet as I was reaching for the receiver, I knocked over my Rolodex. Little cards every-where. Then I stopped. *Mae West.* Why not actually *use* her? Or, better yet—oh, darlings, I was a genius—why not feature all the famous bad girls and renegades throughout history? Lady Godiva. Galileo. Oscar Wilde. Rosa Parks. Elvis, when he first appeared on television—oh, the outrage he sparked! People said he was the devil! These could be Dunkle's new poster children! Surely there existed a way to doctor up famous portraits to make it look as if scandalous and rebellious people throughout the ages were eating our ice cream. Why, Eve herself could be shown in the Garden of Eden eating a Dunkle's ice cream cone instead of an apple! And the Marquis de Sade—why the hell not?—with a chocolate milk shake! And who was that tedious Scandinavian filmmaker, the one accused of pornography? Oh! And that kidnapped girl—Patty Hearst. Would she be willing to pose with a Fudgie Puppie? A singer. Orange hair. Moon boots...his name was eluding me. Suffragettes, of course! Evel Knievel...My thoughts were a tor-rent. No matter. Graphic designers could do so much nowadays with Xeroxes and silk-screening. I could envision it perfectly. Black-and-white pictures, with only our ice cream cones, sun-daes, and Shake-Ups colored in bright relief.

My God: It was lunchtime! Why had no one—not even my own son—bothered to return my calls? Collapsing into my swivel chair, I dialed Isaac again, though I found I was having trouble hitting the correct buttons. I kept punching them, over and over.

"Where have you been?" I bellowed. "Come down here this

minute. Your mother is a genius, darling. I've figured it all out. A whole new campaign. It'll redeem Shake-Ups and the whole goddamn company. Already I've put in calls to MKG. Oh, and the Bettmann Archive. Do you know how marvelous they are over there? The assistant, he sounds exactly like Ernest Borgnine—"

"Ma, listen." Sometimes, when he stammered, my son sounded exactly like his father.

"You'll be so proud of me. They're assembling a portfolio. The most magnificent photographs for us. I've arranged it personally. Oh, darling. Wait until you see—"

"Ma. Stop." Isaac's voice was suddenly like a gavel. "Just stop. Please. Sit. Wait for me."

A moment later he appeared breathlessly in my doorway. With his hands on his middle-aged hips, in his plaid tie and mustard-colored sports coat, he surveyed the piles of drawings strewn about, the notes scribbled on pads and napkins, the discarded lunch tray, the empty bottle of Glenlivet atop the bar, the wastebasket that had somehow been overturned, spewing clumps of balled-up paper across my carpet. I must admit that despite all its fine antiques my office did look ransacked. It was because of the goddamn move to this ugly new building. In our old headquarters, pink silk walls I'd had. A palace.

"Ma?"

A wave of vertigo came over me. I stepped back unsteadily. My eyeglasses shifted on my nose.

Gently, Isaac lifted the tumbler out of my hand. "Stop, Ma." He clasped both my hands firmly in his, staying me. "It's over. I've pulled them. It's done."

After that, whenever I appeared in the office, a peculiar hush settled over it like a snowfall. The delivery boys, the account managers, the secretaries swishing past me in the corridor murmured, "Hello, Mrs. Dunkle," with eerie deference. I suppose the image of me sweeping all the desktops clear with my cane that afternoon was embossed in their memories. So sue me: I had been very upset.

The southern corner of the office, where my traitorous son had installed himself, I refused to set foot in now. The new advisory board he appointed in secret while Rita had lured me away to all those beauty-parlor appointments. The new lawyers he'd hired. The way he'd fired Edgar and MKG behind my back. His radical "restructuring."

"This is a coup d'état!" I hollered. "I built this empire. Not you!"

"Ma. You're still the president. Nobody can take this away from you. But how much longer can you keep doing this? You're seventy-four now. It's nuts. It's taking its toll. And let's be honest. You're drinking too much." He tried to look sympathetic. "It's time to pass along the torch."

"Pass along the torch?" The wallop felt sonic. The company had been mine to give him. My legacy. Why couldn't he have let me *bequeath* it? Why couldn't he have afforded me that one parental pleasure? For once in my life, I could have been noble, a munificent mother. But he'd begrudged me even this, Isaac. Charging ahead and helping himself. "Do you know how hard I've worked to preserve and protect this for you?" I cried. "And you just go ahead and steal it?"

"Ma, please. I didn't steal anything. You know Pop never put anything in writing. There was no formal agreement. But the setup we had? Surely you could see it wasn't working. Those Milk Shake-Ups were a disaster."

"Because you never listen to me! You ignore me, steal from me, then toss me out in the trash!"

Isaac stood up. "No one's discarding you, Ma," he said with fatigue. "You're still the Ice Cream Queen of America. And now that we've pulled Shake-Ups off the market, it's going to be you, in fact, who can convince America to come back to Dunkle's." He attempted a weak smile. "After all. Who can say no to you?"

All the viewers saw was me, Lillian Dunkle, in my wretched signature housedress. I brought a milk shake to my lips, took a sip, made a face, and dumped it out. Spreckles—some generic actor the director had cast—appeared beside me, holding two classic Dunkle's ice cream cones. Vanilla and chocolate swirl. Wordlessly, Spreckles handed one to me, and we began to eat. Slowly, we started to smile. Only then did I look directly into the camera and say, "Mm. That's so much better, isn't it?"

I leaned in. *Recently Dunkle's tried something a little different.* (I shrugged.) *So sue us: it didn't work. But I'm a mother. So I know from experience. Everyone makes a mistake sometimes. But life—and ice cream—goes on, darlings. So please, come back to Dunkle's. Our famous soft-serve ice cream is still the same delicious frozen treat America has known for over forty-five years. And to welcome you back, we're offering our legendary, two-for-the-price-of-one ice cream sundaes all month.* (I took another big bite of my ice cream cone.) *Because forgiveness, darlings . . .* (I smiled) *. . . should always taste sweet.*

Oh, how I hated this hideous public debasement! Every word in my mouth was a knot of barbed wire. And somewhere, somewhere out in Brooklyn and Mineola, I was certain the Dinello brothers and their cronies were toasting each other with Spumante. Grinning. Throwing balled-up tinfoil at the television screen and hooting derisively. I would have refused to do the commercial entirely if I hadn't unwittingly signed a contract agreeing to it the year before—a contract that Isaac had designed to ostensibly "protect and secure" my position as "spokeswoman and president" of the company.

Forgiveness? What the hell did I have to apologize for, I wanted to know?

"Prodigal Dunkle's," the Reverend Elkson called us in the media. "Lillian," he said when he telephoned me personally, "I cannot tell you how glad it makes my heart and how much it pleases our Lord and Savior Jesus Christ that you have seen the error of your ways. 'I was blind, but now I see,' eh? What can I say, Lillian, except that your apology on national television has taught America's children a valuable lesson in humility and redemption—and about what happens when you turn away from sin toward the light of God's love. Any Sunday at all, I invite you to come down to my church in Colorado Springs as our special, honored guest—"

I slammed down the receiver. Sundays I had my own TV show, thank you very much. And he knew it. Oh, the audacity!

Yes, the protesters packed up their signs and their lawn chairs and their Styrofoam picnic coolers and their JESUS LOVES YOU beach balls and stuffed them back into the trunks of their Ford Fiestas. Yes, the rumors subsided, customers began to return. A sprinkle-covered "Dunkle's Kiddie Kone" was even introduced, which helped our sales for the first quarter in a year. Yet only modestly. And I was not surprised. Contrition and spinelessness are never good business strategies. Nobody likes weakness. "We're sorry" is not a marketing tool.

Isaac, from what I heard through my grandson, was sweating to develop a "Deluxe Premium Dunkle's" ice cream to compete directly with Umlaut. It would apparently be made without the use of Bert's patented machines at all, in "exclusive" small batches in flavors such as Chocolate Truffle, Madagascar Vanilla, Java with Cream—whatever the hell that was. Sixteen percent butterfat. Little overrun. Well, good luck to him.

But I knew: The damage had already been done.

Chapter 17

M Y PULMONARY CARDIOLOGIST SAID fresh air and greenery would do me some good. That's what they always say when they don't know what the hell else to tell you. "You're in excellent shape for someone your age," he said, glancing furtively at my leg. "Frankly, I can't find anything the matter with you."

"Then why is my heart always racing? Why do I feel breathless and shaky for no good, goddamn reason at all?"

"You just need to relax," my doctor said, clipping his pen back into his pocket.

"I 'need to relax'? What kind of *meshuggeneh* advice is that? Obviously, if I could goddamn relax, I would relax already."

Besides, I was barely even working! Each month, all I did was endure an elaborate charade in the office orchestrated by Isaac: I arrived at Dunkle's headquarters like some grand dowager. Isaac gallantly pulled out a chair for me at the head of a conference table shaped like a tongue depressor. "Mrs. Dunkle, would you like some tea?" his secretary said, hovering with a tin of Danish butter cookies that nobody bothered to open. The ostensible point of this ritual was to keep me "apprised." Everyone—the accountants, the marketing division, and so forth—spoke to me in overly loud, solicitous tones, as if I were some sort of deaf, idiot child. Whenever I cleared my throat to speak—to question certain expenditures or marketing decisions—the room went deathly quiet and everyone's glances careened off each other like billiard balls. *Of course, Mrs. Dunkle*, they said, nodding and smiling indulgently. *Well, absolutely. We'll consider that.*

I don't know who the hell they thought they were kidding.

Oh, there were foundation meetings and charity luncheons to occupy me. Museum galas where all the guests left their salads untouched and sipped uriney chardonnay while security guards stood discreetly on the peripheries and Mayor Koch moved from table to table like a gadfly. Whenever I could, I brought Petunia in my handbag and fed her bits of the seeded rolls during the speeches. ("Oh, aren't you clever," Brooke Astor once whispered to me across the table. "Next time I'm bringing my parakeet.")

Besides the odd, dutiful visit from my grandson, mostly all I looked forward to was hosting *Dunkle's Sundae Morning Funhouse*. My show had been on the air for twenty-three years now, though for the 1982 fall season it had been reduced to two hours instead of three. That *mamzer* Reverend Elkson and his *New Christian Old-Time Gospel Club* had gobbled up most of the Sunday-morning time slots across the nation. *Dunkle's Sundae Morning Funhouse* was airing on only eleven local stations outside New York City now. Come 1983 we would also stop airing live entirely, I was informed. The show would be videotaped like most other programs. "No one will have to be up at the crack of dawn on Sundays anymore," my producer enthused. But I knew a money saver when I saw it.

I love live television, darlings, which is why I insisted on it for so long. A live television show frees you of all self-consciousness. You simply have to perform on the spot—and that is that. And it has all the energy of the streets!

Until we made the switch to tape, however, I arrived at the studio on Sundays at 6:00 A.M. as always, with my hair and makeup already fixed the way I liked them, my wardrobe pressed (I'd switched to colorful Bill Blass pantsuits to keep up with the times), and hair spray, arthritis medicine, and an empty Geritol bottle filled with vodka tucked neatly into my pocketbook. Vodka has never been my drink of choice, yet it is odorless. And I am nothing, darlings, if not professional.

Yet before the children started filing in from the green room one Sunday, Elliot Paulson, my producer, summoned me to his office upstairs. This was highly unusual, and I knew it could not be good. I took several quick sips from my Geritol bottle, tapped two drops of Binaca Gold onto my tongue, and tugged at the hem of my jacket to right it. I kept Elliot waiting an extra ten minutes, however. People should always be reminded of who the star is.

"Lillian," Elliot said with oversize magnanimity. His office felt like a bunker. All the furniture was half collapsed, cluttered with folders, scripts, newspapers. A large bulletin board extended the chaos onto the wall. Fifty-seven years old my producer was, yet he had souvenir shot glasses, snow globes, and all of those new *Star Wars* figurines little boys are so mad about arrayed on his desk. Who the hell could work like that?

A Styrofoam cup of ice water had already been poured for me and a big, padded swivel chair rolled in from another office. This was ominous. I wished I had brought my pocketbook. Elliot smiled nervously. His assistant, some foppish boy with a skinny satin necktie, hovered, clutching a manila folder.

"Can I get you something other than water, Lillian? Coffee? Perrier?"

"Please. Spare me the chitchat." I set aside the glass of water decisively. The vodka was not doing its job. "What is the trouble, Elliot?"

"Trouble?" Elliot picked up a miniature model of a triangular spacecraft and fidgeted with it absentmindedly. Jason, I recalled, used to have one just like it. That friend of his, that kid Bod-hisattva Rosenblatt, he'd had a *Star Wars*–themed bar mitzvah.

"I just figured that since the holidays are coming up, we could take a few minutes to discuss the revamp. For the switch to video-tape."

I reached for the glass of water and took a large gulp. It went down poorly, and I had to pound myself on the base of my throat. "All right," I said, not disagreeably. Certainly I, of all people, appreciated the need to innovate. "I've had several ideas myself, you know." Which was true, darlings. Now that I'd had more time on my hands. "For example, I'd like to change the name from *Funhouse* to *Clubhouse*. That strikes me as so much more modern."

Elliot jutted his lip. "Not bad," he said with equanimity. Grabbing a pad from beneath the pile on his desk, he scribbled it down.

"Speaking of 'more modern,' Lillian." He exhaled. "We're thinking— Well, the higher-ups are saying, actually—it wasn't my idea at all, I can assure you—but the decision has been made that the host of the *Funhouse*, she should have a fresher look, too."

I stared at him. Something inside me clicked. It only took a second. I supposed I had been anticipating this. "Oh, you little bastards," I said. "I have a contract, you know."

"Of course you do. Of course you do, Lillian. And we get that. You're still the Ice Cream Queen. Nobody can replace you." Elliot held up both his hands as if to stop traffic. "It's for precisely this reason that the suits upstairs want you to have a new *cohost*. The Ice Cream Princess. Someone young. A professional actress. Cool, upbeat—who the kids can relate to more. This way when you retire, the children will already know and love her. We won't lose any more market share."

"Who the hell said anything about retiring?"

"C'mon, Lillian. You're what now? Seventy-four? Five? How much longer can you keep doing this?"

"Oh, and you think some little teenage dingbat is going to have an easier time than me?" I thumped my cane hard on the floor. "I am a workhorse."

"Of course you are, Lillian. Hell, I don't have half the energy you do. But the plain truth is, in this industry?" Elliot pointed to himself helplessly. "Hell, *I'm* a dinosaur! Especially now, with this new MTV? And cable? An old lady doing some Catskills shtick is just not what nine-year-olds want to watch on Sunday mornings anymore. We've done the research." Digging a report out of the landslide of paper on his desk, he tossed it toward me. "See for yourself."

I jerked my head to one side. "We still have ninety-eight franchises nationwide! The revenue we bring NBC— Since 1954—"

Elliot nodded emphatically. "Which is why you get to help choose your successor. Build your legacy. Look, we've put out some casting calls. There are some really bright, mediagenic girls out there."

His assistant leaned over silkily with a stack of head shots. "We've got Heather here. And Samantha. Aimee—"

I knocked them out of his hands. A dozen eight-by-ten glossy photos fluttered to the carpet around me, all of them beautiful teenage girls with long, shiny hair and whitewashed smiles gazing brightly toward some fixed point in the future. And you could bet: Not one of them had a limp.

Back in my dressing room, I poured myself one capful of vodka, then another. My entire central nervous system felt dilated. We were on the air in thirty minutes. Elliot was no dummy. He was a weak, childish man. As such he was extremely adept at evasive maneuvers. For all I knew, he had been sitting on this news for months, dillydallying, screen-testing beautiful young girls, patting his mouth with a handkerchief as they glided in and out of the audition studio smelling of baby powder and strawberry lip gloss. Elliot, playing with his *Star Wars* toys, letting his idiot snow globes rain chemical flakes on tiny plastic Key Wests and Las Vegases, all the while rationalizing that the time simply wasn't right yet to inform me. If I knew Elliot—and I did, darlings—the "right time," of course, meant precisely this—thirty minutes before we went on the air live—when I would be unwilling to raise a ruckus. Elliot was banking on my professionalism, even as he treated me like a child. His gutlessness was appalling. Idiots, idiots everywhere! I was so goddamn sick and tired of it! I swallowed another capful of vodka.

Oh, how I wished Bert were here! I suddenly missed him with such force that my grief felt violent. Mama. Papa. Flora. Rose. Bella. Mr. and Mrs. Dinello. Orson Maytree Jr. Mrs. Preminger. Edgar. Harvey Ballentine, who had quit so abruptly, with barely a good-bye, and not even so much as a Christmas card since. And *Bert*. My Bert. Thinking of him lying beside me with his chest pressed against my back, his right hand curved around my bosoms, his scratchy chin propped on my neck as he looked at the book I was reading aloud to him, his eyes following the words he could not decipher, the two of us breathing in unison on the narrow bed on Thompson Street beneath the hissing electric light, the speckled blue enamel teakettle heating slowly on the little stove across from us—the two of us so young, so full of wonder.

A strangled sound came from deep within me. My heart, it felt as if it were a sponge that Bert himself was wringing dry of all its blood. I clutched my abdomen. Petunia leaped up onto my lap from her little satin pillow in the corner. Drawing her to me, my own craggy hands were unrecognizable to me. My skin looked like runny chocolate-chip ice cream dripping from my bones. As soon as my fingers stopped shaking, I drank another capful of vodka.

From the corridor the PA knocked on my door. "Five minutes!" she shouted.

In the wings just beyond the set, the wardrobe assistant draped my fake fur cape around my shoulders and fastened it with its oversize chain. She righted my plastic ice cream crown with its plastic sundae on top. The soon-to-be-retired theme song, with its cheerful calliope music, had already begun to play, grinding through the studio at a deafening volume. It was Spreckles who opened the show now, singing:

Children across America—
Come to our Funhouse 'n' play!
Ice cream, you scream—
Who's screaming here today?

This newest Spreckles had been hired by Personnel at NBC—without their consulting me at all, of course, thank you. Yet another snub. A "professional clown," this one was. Some actor named Jared. A Buddhist. So you could only imagine. As he sang, he pogoed along the edge of the stage, waving at the children with grotesque enthusiasm, his arms scissoring the air back and forth, as if he were attempting to flag down a helicopter. "C'mon, boys and girls!" he prompted. The whole audience began waving in unison. "Do you like ice cream! Do you want to have fun and win prizes this morning?"

"YES!" the children chorused.

"Then wave!"

That's it. Wave, you pampered little bastards, I thought as I wobbled toward the curtain. Why, this is probably how the Hitler Youth started. *Here, have a treat. Now, march.* Look at them, these tiny puppets, dressed in their miniature Levi's. Plaid shirts. Corduroy dresses. Their shellacked Lender's Bagel necklaces hung proudly from their slender necks, all of them groomed for the camera by frantic mothers kneeling before them, spitting into a Kleenex to rub jelly crust off their cheeks at the very last minute. These small, privileged moppets, who had never had to lug a pail of coal or stitch lace in a dimly lit, tubercular factory or bathe in frigid water in a zinc tub in a kitchen plagued by rats. These "youngsters," with their plastic pencil cases and their crayon-colored backpacks, who ate processed supermarket foods molded especially for them into alphabet letters and precious animal shapes. They had received more doting love and attention from their parents this morning in the green room than I had ever received in my entire goddamn seventy-four years.

Finally the theme song gave way to a drum roll. All the lights went off as DUNKLE'S FUNHOUSE was illuminated above the stage, glittering crazily in large flashing pink, white, and gold bulbs, and a spotlight landed on the satin curtain, and Don Pardo announced as he had for twenty-three years, *Good morning, boys and girls! Welcome to the* Dunkle's Sundae Morning Funhouse, *live from NBC Studios in New York City. Please welcome your hostess, Mrs. Lillian Dunkle, the Ice Cream Queen of America!* As the applause sign flashed insanely overhead, the children became crazed with excitement, shrieking, jumping up and down, waving, hooting with anticipation and fanatical glee, and for one moment I might as well have been Benny Goodman and Frank Sinatra, darlings. I might as well have been Elvis and the Beatles. *Take that, Elliot, you cocksucker,* I thought. *Don't you dare tell me children are not interested in watching me.*

Yet the lights burst back on and the music stopped abruptly. Now that our time slot had been compressed, we had only forty-five seconds to launch the show. The PA beside the camera leaned forward beside the big oaktag cue card and made a rolling gesture with her index finger: *Now. Start. Go!*

"Hello, youngsters! Who wants ice cream?" I shouted.

"WE DO!"

"Good morning, Missus Lillian," Spreckles said in a goofy voice that was not the least bit funny.

"Good morning, Spreckles. Boys and girls! Are you ready to have some fun today?"

"YEAH!" the crowd roared.

"Of course you are," I said. "After all, you don't have to go to work in a factory tomorrow, now, do you? No child labor here."

The cue-card girl flinched. Please: My one goddamn ad-lib in twenty-three years. Yet I smiled broadly, and the children were with me. My minions. My little, uncomprehending pet twits. Even without the applause sign, they cheered.

"It's so marvelous to have all our youngsters here," I contin-ued, reverting to script. The studio lights felt like ghastly heat lamps at a cafeteria buffet. The air stank of floor cleaner. I felt vertiginous. "Spreckles and I, we have lots of goodies in store for you here this morning. Why don't you tell everyone about it, Spreckles?"

Rubbing his hands together with exaggerated relish, Spreckles announced "Dunkle's Disco Dance-off." (Yay!) Cartoons. (Yay!) And the grand-finale competition: the ice cream sundae eating contest. (Double yay!) There was no longer a special musical guest, however. Between the show's diminishing viewership and the rise of this new MTV, it seemed that fewer and fewer record-ing artists were inclined to wake up at 5:00 A.M. on a Sunday to sing live to a hundred elementary-school children.

Another love of mine. Gone.

As we cut for a commercial, I shuffled off into the wings. "Lillian?" the AD called after me. Rifling through my pocketbook, I unscrewed the cap from my Geritol bottle, took a swig, pounded on my chest. "Just need my vitamins." I hurried back to my mark in time for the makeup girl to attack my face with her powder puff. "Lillian. You okay up there? What's going on?" the AD said, stepping toward me over the tangle of cables. Yet the director started counting down, "Five ... four ..."

A flood of warmth came over me. The lights. The liquor. I felt like sugar dissolving. A pillowy, strawberry pink glove suddenly gripped my forearm. Someone, I realized, was addressing me. Spreckles the Clown.

"I said, ahem, Missus Lillian, would you like to read the first letter today from one of our youngsters?" he repeated. Blinking around, I realized we were already back on the air and introducing the first segment of our show. "Dear Spreckles" still remained enormously popular. Children, after all, crave guidance. Authority. Moral instruction. All of which, I'd noticed, were in short supply these days. Parents: They were all too busy now "finding themselves." Getting divorced. Going jogging.

Meanwhile the problems that children wrote to us about had grown increasingly complex. Whereas their letters used to concern banning girls from tree houses, now, darlings, the children of America were asking Spreckles what to do when they were pressured into taking drugs. Shoplifting. Smoking. How to cope with moving to a new city. Which parent they should choose to live with during a custody battle. Even, occasionally, whether to engage in sex. In a few cases, in fact, the producers felt compelled to contact social services.

Today's first dilemma, however, which I read aloud to the children, was benign. *"Dear Spreckles. Last week I stole my best friend's*

Rubik's Cube. What should I do? I know it was wrong. Signed, Jeffrey in New Jersey."

This letter, I suspected, had been doctored by our staff. Rubik's Cube, after all, was now a sponsor of *Dunkle's Sundae Morning Funhouse.* Nevertheless, the letter provided the children with a typical ethical quandary. Spreckles dove right in, asking the audience, "Hey, kids, what do you think we should advise Jeffrey to do?"

I sat on my stool in the wings and massaged my leg. It had started aching again. Taking another discreet sip from my Geritol bottle, I waited for my cue.

The second letter, at least, proved meatier: *"Dear Spreckles, Every day when I ride the school bus, this girl tells all the other kids not to let me sit next to them because I'm 'contaminated.' She sticks gum in my hair. She calls me 'Four Eyes' and pulls up my skirt. She says that if I tattle to anyone, she and all her friends will 'get me.' Now I am scared to go to school. What can I do? Signed, Lila in Connecticut."*

"Hm." Spreckles made an outsize frown and plopped down on the edge of the stage with his chin in his hands. "That sure sounds like a problem, doesn't it, boys and girls? What do you think we should tell Lila to do?"

Several hands sprang up.

Maybe she should tell her teacher, a little girl offered.

She should wear contact lenses so the kids won't tease her about her glasses anymore, said a boy.

I think she should call the mean girl names right back, another boy suggested. This, to me, was the first bright idea I'd heard all god-damn morning. Yet Spreckles looked at him dubiously. "Hm. Well, that's not very nice, now, is it?" he said. "Two wrongs don't make a right, you know."

He regarded the audience bathetically. "You know, sometimes

when people act like bullies, it's just because deep inside they feel really bad about themselves. Maybe Lila should try to talk to this girl in private and ask her why she acts so mean. What do you think, youngsters?"

The children considered this. Sensing this was the answer Spreckles was most likely to reward, they began to nod.

"Do you think that's the best solution?" he encouraged. The applause sign must have flashed on overhead then, because the children suddenly clapped riotously. "Well, okay!" Spreckles leaped up. "Who's going to help show Lila in Connecticut how she might talk to this girl?"

My legs, darlings, they felt rubbery by now. I took another sip from my drink as Spreckles selected a little girl named Tara from the audience to play Lila. She was a tiny slip of a child with a small, trembling mouth and dark, black, doe eyes that seemed to consume half her face.

"Here," Spreckles said. Taking her by the wrist, he positioned Tara front and center, across from Kaitlyn, an older, bigger girl with ponytails, whom he had selected to play the bully. "Can you be mean?" he said to Kaitlyn. She shrugged.

"Just call her 'Four Eyes,'" he instructed.

"Hey, Four Eyes," Kaitlyn parroted.

"Good, good." Spreckles crouched before the two girls. "Now—"

"Four Eyes. Brace Face," Kaitlyn added, clearly warming to her role. She looked over to Spreckles for approval.

"Okay," said Spreckles. "Good. Now, Tara, what should you, as Lila, say to this girl who is being mean to you?"

Tara shrugged shyly, miserably, twisting one little leg behind the other. She was wearing a brown-and-orange dress with an orange bow at the neckline and tiny red Keds sneakers. She glanced over at the audience. She seemed to be deliberating whether to dash back to her seat. Beneath me, my stool seemed to undulate. My neck lolled and cracked.

"You're Four Eyes and you're stupid!" Kaitlyn goaded.

"Stop it!" Tara cried, whirling to face her. And suddenly Tara did look as if she were truly about to cry.

"Okay. Okay, now, Tara. Remember, this is just a game," Spreckles said quickly, giving her shoulder a reassuring squeeze. "We're trying to show a little girl at home how to talk to this other child. Why don't you ask her why she is teasing you?"

Tara looked at him uncertainly, then at Kaitlyn. "Why are you teasing me?" she said in a soft voice.

Kaitlyn placed her hands on her hips. "Because you're Four Eyes and you're ugly." The kid was clearly a natural. No surprise there. From overhead the buzz of the gel lights was relentless.

"Now, Tara," Spreckles guided, "maybe you want to tell her how hurtful it is to say something like that, right? And ask her why she has to be so mean—"

"Oh, for Chrissakes!" I hollered. My pulse was pounding so furiously, it echoed like a backbeat. I was in my body yet hovering outside it. I felt myself rising from the sidelines and heaving my leg as quickly as I could across the stage. "What kind of nonsense is this? You think that's any way to deal with a bully, you *shmendrik?*" I barked at Spreckles. "What on earth is the matter with you?"

From somewhere, children giggled. Perhaps some panicked looks darted across the studio—no doubt the producer and the control room were suddenly on alert. *What on earth?* I heard somebody murmur. Tossing aside my peppermint-striped cane, I knelt beside little Tara with great difficulty and shooed Kaitlyn away.

"Well, hello, Missus Lillian," Spreckles said in an artificially cheerful voice as he stood up, flustered, and looked over the children's heads toward the director with alarm. "I see you'd like to join in our discussion today?"

"You want to know how to deal with a bully?" I said to Tara. "Like this." To demonstrate I positioned myself, one knee forward for balance, bracing. I clamped my own hand over hers and molded them into tiny fists. "Bring your arm in. No, not at your side. Close to your chest, guarding yourself. And the other at chin level. Farther up. Like this. See?"

Lifting her tiny, rubbery arms, I cocked them just so, modeling them after my own. "Now I want you to thrust from here, not the elbow, so that when you punch, you get the whole, big force of your shoulder behind it, you see?"

Suddenly the *Sundae Funhouse* theme music blasted on—an attempt, I supposed, to terminate the segment. Yet just as abruptly, it was yanked off. I thumped around on my knees to face Tara, frozen in her position. Around me the garish spray-paint colors of our new stage set—cobalt blue, egg-yolk yellow, mandarin orange, delineated in thick black lines, comic book style—began to throb and pulse like a migraine. The stage pinwheeled around me.

What the hell was I doing here, cloaked in this ridiculous cape with a plastic crown digging into my temples? The racks of lights overhead, the barricades of the audience, they formed an elaborate cage. Cameras were trained on me like guns from a watchtower. Look at me with this trembling little girl here, the two of us served up to the television viewing audience like trained monkeys. The nurses back at the Beth Israel Dispensary all those years ago, their snide speculations about my future. They were prophecies, darlings. They were exactly right. I had become a freak in a sideshow.

"Draw your arm back, draw your arm back!" I hollered at Tara, holding up my hands before her like two punching bags. Suddenly I was no longer on a sound stage at NBC studios in New

York City at all, but in the men's dormitory at the Hilfsverein's refugee detention center back in Hamburg, Germany, with its tobacco-and-boiled-cabbage stench, surrounded by émigré men in soiled undershirts and black felt hats, smoking, jeering, hooting encouragement in the sickly yellow light, passing a flask as Papa grinned and crouched before me, circling me like a panther, coaching and barking, "Right, left! Right, left, *kindeleh!*"

Hesitantly, Tara punched my open palm as I instructed. "That's it!" I cried. "That's it. Again. Harder!" From the audience a few plaintive cheers went up. "Harder!" some of the children began to shout.

From somewhere I heard my director shouting, "Cut to a commercial! Cut to a commercial, damn it!" Yet the cameramen were glued to the spot. None of them, it seemed, could tear themselves away. This, darlings, was *real. This* was live television. "Hit me harder!" I barked. "Don't just stand there. Fight that bully. Fight back hard! Show 'em who's boss! Right! Left!" Unprompted by any applause sign, the children in the audience began to cheer Tara on. Buoyed by their encouragement—and mine—she began to punch my hands more confidently, more rhythmically, right, then left, just as I had once punched Papa's so many years ago. I knew exactly what she was experiencing in this very moment, that flush of unexpected strength, that awakening sense of power and dominion. "That's it! More!" I cried. "Punch! Punch that bully!" In their excitement the children in the audience began to chant along with me, "Right! Left! Right! Left!"

"Lillian, please! Stop!" Spreckles cried hoarsely behind me. "Children, this is no way to solve a problem."

"That's it! Harder!" I cried. "You've got it. Right! Left! Right! Punch that bully square in the mouth!"

Tara was a tiny child, yet by now she had committed her whole little body. Her eyes were wide, her legs braced in their little red sneakers, her face burning with concentration as she swung. *Right, left. Right, left.* She punched my hands harder and harder, until you could actually hear the soft thwacking sounds against my palms—the satisfying kiss of the blows, and perhaps if my hands were not so icy and numb, I might even have felt some pain—as the children chanted gleefully "Right! Left! Right! Left!" and a few even began jumping up and down now, waving their hands, pleading, "Can I try next? Can I go, please?"

"You see? You see, you Buddhist nincompoop," I growled over my shoulder. "*This* is how you fight." As I glanced back at Spreckles defiantly, however, I lowered my hands slightly. Just for an instant. Just as Papa had all those years ago back in the dormitory in Hamburg. And now, as then, with my guard down, Tara's next blow hit me square on my jaw, just as mine had hit Papa. For a split second, the riot of noxious colors all around me exploded into searing white. I lurched backward on my knees, and a bolt of pain shot up my right leg. There was no breath, no noise, only stillness. From somewhere at the end of a long wind tunnel, I heard a collective gasp. A man shouted, "Oh, Jesus Christ!" Yet then I steadied myself, regaining my balance. Blinking, my jaw throbbing, I gulped down a huge mouthful of air and gave out an ungainly howl.

Then, reflexively, without a moment's thought, I threw a punch back.

Chapter 18

O VER FIFTY YEARS OF MY LIFE I have dedicated to ice cream. And truly, darlings, to the United States of America. With the cartoon characters and "fun flavors" I've created, I have injected joy, whimsy, and sweetness into a brutal and treacherous world. I contributed to our efforts in World War II, brought the comforts of home to boys fighting in Korea and Vietnam, and helped countless veterans start their own businesses. And need I remind you, it was me, Lillian Dunkle, who helped advance the cure for polio. Who promoted popular music. Who was instrumental, too, in the rise of car culture, television, and that great, democratic institution: the fast-food franchise. Oh, people turn up their noses at McDonald's and suchlike now. Suddenly affordable, mass-produced food is "junky," suddenly, it's "cheap." Yet thanks to Yours Truly, average Americans today can now purchase their own ready-made businesses, knowing that the model is tried and tested. And where else in the world can people rest assured that they can stop on a roadside anywhere, anytime, and buy something for the mouth at a reasonable price that will taste just as good whether they are in San Diego or Toledo or Atlanta? When I was a starving child on Orchard Street, I could not have imagined such possibilities! It is no small accomplishment, darlings. I have helped feed and transform America. And for twenty-three

years, I have even baby-sat the nation's children for three goddamn hours every Sunday morning so that their parents can sleep
late. Don't tell me this isn't something!

Yet just once, just once, I accidentally punch a small child on
live television. And suddenly, that is all people care to know.

And so I believe this is why, on June 22, 1983, a jury finds me
guilty on three counts of tax evasion. The federal case against me
is not at all related to the accident on my television show. The
charges are separate. And yet. And yet.

So sue me: It is deeply disturbing. The injustice of it all! The
ingratitude! And so, just moments before my appearance in the
state supreme court for my civil case with Tara Newhouse, I perhaps deign to take a little extra time for myself in the ladies' room.

The court officer, the enormous Negro lady with the painted-on
eyebrows—she claims she smells marijuana moments after I limp
out. She finds a scorched little flake of cigarette still burning on
the windowsill. Dipping the end in water, she places it on a torn
piece of paper towel to present to the court. Everybody in the
building is such a goddamned goody-goody. Now, they all look
from this little browned bit of ash to me: Judge Kuklinsky. Mr.
Beecham and Miss Slocum in their taut gray suits. The Newhouses' lawyer, pockmarked Mr. Tottle. (What is it about pitted
skin that makes you want to file it down with sandpaper?) Jason
takes my elbow, steadying me before the judge. I suddenly notice my grandson is wearing a metal padlock around his neck on
a chain. Another one of his "statements," no doubt.

"Well." Judge Kuklinsky exhales, not to me or the lawyers but
to the court officer. "This is certainly a first."

"But my grandmother isn't stoned," Jason blurts. "She's just, like, old."

In unison Miss Slocum and Mr. Beecham say admonishingly, "Jason."

"Excuse me?" says the judge.

I suppose I do not help my case, because at that very instant, darlings, I stifle a giggle. I cannot help it. Really, it is so absurd. All of it. I feel so overwhelmingly giddy and tickled all of a sudden— as I have not felt in years, if ever in my entire life. Giggles are rising up in me, threatening to spray out like water constricted in a garden hose.

The court officer raises her eyebrows and crosses her arms smugly. "Mm-hm," she says in a cadence that translates distinctly into, *I told you so.*

Turning away, I put my fist to my mouth and harrumph as if I am trying to cover a cough. My eyes catch the Newhouses sitting at the plaintiffs' table. The father with his Germanic, clipped beard, eyes like two bullets; the harried mother deliberately scrubbed of makeup, her lips pinched tight. Little Tara Newhouse sits between them with the enormous rectangle of gauze taped over her left eye. She swings her legs shyly and glances around with bewilderment, as if she is not quite sure where she is. Yet when I fix my gaze on her, her face clouds with recognition and her uncovered eye blinks furiously. She knows who I am, all right. That child is not blind at all. Do they have any idea whom they are dealing with?

"I'm so sorry, Judge," I say in my frailest, most biscuity voice. "It must be my new blood-pressure medication that makes me so woozy."

Mr. Tottle practically spits when he hears this. "Oh, please! C'mon, Your Honor. Look at her! Her pupils alone—"

"Mr. Tottle," the judge admonishes, raising his hand. "Mrs. Dunkle?"

Yet Mr. Tottle cannot help himself. "Your Honor, please. You cannot possibly trust a single word the defendant says." Holding up a manila folder, he flips through it as if it were a magazine, displaying the contents to the judge. Clippings from the *New York Post*, *Newsweek*, the *Times*. "It's documented everywhere that Mrs. Dunkle has been lying to the public about virtually everything."

"Your Honor!" my lawyers object.

Ever since my arrest at NBC and my conviction for tax evasion, it has become open season on Lillian Dunkle. Never mind that the U.S. embassy was bombed in Beirut. Or that President Reagan has announced he's deploying a missile shield in outer space. Some weasel-faced journalists have nothing more important to do, it seems, than to dig up dirt about *me*.

Oh, the headlines! The outrageous misrepresentations they print:

Newsday: Declassified files show that Lillian Dunkle secretly supported Senator Joseph McCarthy's witch-hunts.

The *Daily News:* Lillian Dunkle lived in splendor in a Palm Beach mansion while her elderly, diabetic father died alone and penniless in an old-age home in Paterson, New Jersey! (This accompanied by a photo that looks like security footage of a wizened old man on a respirator and an "exclusive" interview with one Samuel Pratt)

The *National Enquirer:* For years Lillian Dunkle has lied to the American public about being Italian! A priest, one Father Anthony Dinello, of St. Francis Church in Bay Ridge, Brooklyn recently told the *Enquirer* that his great-grandparents, two emigrants from Naples, took Lillian in and raised her as their own after she was abandoned in a street accident in the Jewish area of New York's Lower East Side.

The *New York Times:* Archived records from the former

Beth Israel Dispensary confirm that Dunkle's birth name was Malka Bialystoker and that she never, in fact, suffered from polio. Dunkle apparently faked the disease to generate sympathy for herself and nationwide publicity for her husband's ice cream company.

The *New York Post* runs a picture of me entering the courthouse with MALKA! printed above it in huge block letters. As if changing your name is a crime? It is the schoolyard on the Lower East Side all over again.

Its reporters have even tracked down several disgruntled former secretaries. "The worst boss ever," these piddling women call me. "A total nightmare to work for." The myriad of "abuses" I am apparently guilty of? Yelling. Not giving Christmas bonuses. Banning everyone from wearing Charlie perfume in the office. Well, excuse me, darlings, but the only reason I yell is if people are not listening to me. So whose fault is that? And why the hell should I have to play Santa?

There is that dreadful interview with Harvey Ballentine, of course. And in the newly revived version of *Vanity Fair* magazine, one of my domestics reveals how every time I returned from a business trip, my pocketbooks were filled with silverware and miniature saltshakers from the airlines. How, when I used to swim laps in Bedford in the mornings, I made her run from one end of the pool to the other with a silver tray of herring snacks. Each time I finished one length, she said, I barked "Feed the fishie!" and opened my mouth, waiting for her to bend down and pop a treat into it.

For Chrissakes, it was a game! Besides, I was probably drunk.

Then, just last week, that famous, ghastly Joan Crawford–like photograph of me appeared splashed across the cover of *Time* magazine above the headline I'M MELTING!

Suddenly everybody—everybody, darlings—is tucking napkins into their collars, sharpening their knives, bellying up to the carving board.

Here in court, Mr. Tottle is doing the same.

Yet Judge Kuklinsky waves away the articles. "Mr. Tottle," he says dryly, "if stories in the *New York Post* were admissible as evidence here in this courtroom, half of the Tri-State Area would be under indictment."

Turning back to me, he demands, "So, the truth, Mrs. Dunkle. Please. Right now. Are you high, or in any manner mentally impaired?"

The way his eyes pin me, I know better than to try to be a wisenheimer. "Well," I say apologetically, "this new medicine I'm taking for my blood pressure *has* made me feel awfully dizzy, Your Honor."

"And do you have this prescription here with you?"

Before I can respond, a piteous little voice calls out, "Mommy?"

We all turn to glance at the plaintiffs' table.

Little Tara Newhouse is pressing her hands together between her legs and bouncing anxiously in her chair in her fluffy party dress. "I have to make," she announces.

"Uh, Your Honor?" says Mr. Tottle. "May we—"

Judge Kuklinsky motions wearily to the court officer. "Officer Kendriks, do you mind?"

"I can take her myself, Your Honor." Mrs. Newhouse smiles nervously.

"I think it's best if the officer—"

"I can go by myself," Tara declares, nodding vigorously. "I'm seven now." Pushing herself down off her chair, she slithers under the table before her mother can stop her, crab-walks beneath it in her fancy little patent-leather shoes, then stands up triumphantly on the other side and tugs at the hem of her party dress, righting it. "Mommy?" She turns back to the table. "Can I bring my book with me?"

"Tara? That's your name?" Judge Kuklinsky says gently, glancing down at the deposition before him.

Tara nods shyly.

The judge smiles. "Well, Tara, we all know that you are old enough to go to the bathroom by yourself. But Officer Kendriks here is going to escort you so you don't get lost, okay?"

"Okay!" Tara nods. Turning with a little twirl, she suddenly dashes ahead to the door. Officer Kendriks, who waddles along behind her, shoots Judge Kuklinsky a look.

"Blind in one eye and permanently disabled, hm?" Judge Kuklinsky says to Mr. Tottle, thumbing through the deposition.

There is an uneasy silence. Finally the judge sighs, sets aside the papers, and folds his hands. "Look, folks," he says with exasperation. "From the behavior I'm already seeing on display here, this case strikes me as a likely waste of this court's time and resources. This is not Madison Square Garden. I have half a mind to dismiss this lawsuit altogether as being frivolous and in bad faith, except, Mrs. Dunkle, that even *I* have seen the tapes on the news of you striking this little girl on your television program. Though it may have been unintentional, you created an atmosphere of recklessness, and you endangered a child in the process. I believe that this little girl deserves to see justice served. So here's what I'm going to do. I'm setting a status hearing for three days from now. That's fast-track. Either both parties settle out of court by then, which I strongly urge you to do—and I assume, Mrs. Dunkle, you will be sufficiently sobered up and able to think clearly by then?—or, if not, then come Thursday I'll be assigning you a trial date. Believe me, this is in nobody's best interests. If you are all hankering to put on a show—and it seems to me that you are—be forewarned, a trial will come at great cost to each and every one of you, and with little indulgence from this court. Understood?"

With a bang of the gavel, we are dismissed for the day.

All the lawyers are furious. "The possibility of going to prison for one crime isn't enough for you? When we come back here, you need to be completely lucid, do you understand?" Beecham whispers as he hustles me out of the building. "The only lucky break we caught this morning is that the judge was equally pissed at the plaintiffs."

Yet me, I feel like liquid. I feel like a chiffon scarf tossed in the air. As I slide into the backseat of my car with Jason, I close my eyes and say, "Mm, doesn't a big corned beef sandwich at the Carnegie Deli sound marvelous right now?"

"Oh, my God!" Jason laughs. "Grandma, you are so baked."

I blink at him over the rims of my glasses. "I was nervous, *tateleh*."

"Yeah." He exhales. "Me, too."

I slap him playfully on the knee. "Don't you go telling anyone, you hear?"

Grinning, he cracks his knuckles. "Of course not."

The rain-slicked streets jiggle by in a riot of speckled colors. After Hector picks up our Reubens and cream sodas, I have him drop off Jason and continue on with me to Park Avenue. Since the lawyers are trying to settle, I have been instructed to remain nearby. I have not lived in our Park Avenue apartment for several months now. Not even Petunia is with me. As I open the door, the jangle of my keys echoes over the parquet. It feels like an abandoned church. Whatever giddiness I had felt at the courthouse ebbs.

Hanging up my coat, I pick up the package of mail that Isaac has sent over from the office. The correspondences I receive have shrunk in the past year. I fix myself a drink. Except for the muffled bleating of car horns from the avenue below, the house is unnervingly quiet. As I go to put the hi-fi on, the phone rings. Almost nobody ever calls me at home.

"Hello, is this Mrs. Lillian Dunkle?" a man's voice says when I answer.

"Who is speaking?"

"This is Trevor Marks with Page Six of the *New York Post*—"

"Excuse me? How did you get this number? This is a private—"

"I was just wondering if you cared to comment, Mrs. Dunkle? A source at the courthouse today says that you were high when you appeared before the judge and appeared to have been smoking marijuana—"

I slam down the receiver, yet my hands are shaking. Who the hell would have told the press about what transpired in the courtroom? That Officer Kendriks. She had it in for me. Then I realize: the Newhouses' lawyer, that prick Tottle, is trying to further discredit me in the press.

After leaving a message at Beecham, Mather & Greene, I sit down on my settee and finish my scotch. Frankly, I don't know what the hell to do with myself. I refuse to think of all the ruckus I've caused, of how badly Dunkle's is now doing. All the money we've lost. Everything coming apart in my fingers like wet cardboard.

Perhaps in the wake of Bert's death I acted rashly. Perhaps I did not pay the taxes I was supposed to on the sale of Bella Flora. And yes, I perhaps charged some of my extravagant shopping trips to London and Paris directly to the Dunkle's Ice Cream Corporation. Is it my fault that I believed these were legitimate business expenses? In my capacity as the public face of

Dunkle's, was it not my job to remain well groomed? As for all the renovations and redecorating of my "private" residences that I might also have charged to the company—so okay, Edgar may have fudged a few invoices for me here and there simply to help with the bookkeeping. Yet what difference did that really make, darlings, when I was the president and founder of the whole goddamn operation to begin with? What line is there to blur? Sue me: I fail to see it.

Slowly, I sift through the mail. Junk, all of it. All sorts of organizations soliciting me for money. Yet as I'm tossing one envelope aside, I notice something odd. It has been addressed by hand.

To "Malka Treynovsky."

Inside, on a single piece of stationery beneath a green insignia reading PERFORMING ARTISTS HOME & HOSPITAL FOR THE AGED. RYE BROOK, NEW YORK is a letter in careful, loopy script.

Dear Malka (Mrs. Lillian Dunkle),

I am a nurse's aide here at the PAHHA. Last week I was reading aloud an article about you to one of our residents, a lovely retired dancer named Florence Halloway. When the article mentioned that your name used to be Malka Bialystoker, she gave a little cry. She said that was the name of her sister whom she had lost many years ago. Florence Halloway is her stage name. She said she was originally born "Flora Treynovsky" in Russia.

I have taken it upon myself to reach out to you on her behalf. Miss Halloway has recently suffered a stroke. While she is unable to read or write anymore, she is often lucid and in good spirits. She is afraid that you do not remember her and says that she does not want to be any bother. However, I believe it would mean a lot to her to hear from you, if you are so inclined.

*Please do not hesitate to contact me regarding this matter. We
would welcome you here at the home for a visit at any time.*

Yours truly,
Tricia Knox

For a long time, I sit staring at the letter. *Flora?* Three private
detective agencies I had employed over the years. That last one,
Nick, had located state records for a "Millie Bialy," age "approx.
45," who had died in a mental asylum in Rochester, New York,
in 1921. This was the closest to anyone with my mother's name,
and I had resigned myself to the fact that it had, in all probability,
been Mama. Yet my two sisters?

"I found their names on the ship manifest for the SS *Amerika*
arriving out of Hamburg," he had said, "but nothing else. No
school records. No marriage licenses. No death certificates. Nada.
But back then, though? People just vanished."

Of course I had assumed Flora had died. She had been starving.
Tubercular.

I reread the letter. "Is this some sort of joke?" I say aloud.
In the emptiness of my apartment, my voice echoes. For all I
know, some wisenheimer read *New York* magazine and conjured
up long-lost sister "Florence Halloway" as a way to con me—to
set me up for further humiliation. Someone shrewd enough, with
enough chutzpah and malice. The Dinellos perhaps? My alleged
stepsiblings?

I picture a greasy-faced young woman in hospital scrubs, eating ravioli from a can in an apartment by the railroad tracks.
On the sagging couch beside her, her out-of-work boyfriend
watches pirated cable and cooks up mail-fraud schemes with
friends who are not that dissimilar to the crowd Papa used to run

with. The PAHHA letterhead is a fake. As soon as I telephone, there will be some sob story. *Oh, Florence has just died, and there's no money for the funeral.* This "Tricia Knox," she will ask for a check.

I pour myself another drink and wander around the apartment. Yet I cannot stop my thoughts from spinning like a centrifuge. If Flora had changed her name, that would explain why I had never been able to find her. And, of course, why she had never been able to find me either. I had grown up, after all, as Lillian. And had all my little cosmetic surgeries, of course. And my peroxided hair. Even before going on television. How I had transformed myself, all across America!

With trembling hands, I dial the number on the letterhead. When the operator puts me through to Florence Halloway's room—which I am not quite expecting—the phone rings and rings. *Well, this is all a waste of time,* I think. I am surprised how dejected I feel. Just before I hang up, however, someone answers. I hear only fumbling, a knocking of plastic on plastic, a dull, cochlear roar.

"Hello?" I call out.

After a moment, over a rasp of labored breathing, a creaky voice says, "Yes?"

"Hello? Is this Florence Halloway?"

"Yes?"

I feel a sharp whoosh of vertigo. "Are you also Flora Treynovsky?" I say.

There is nothing on the other end but wheezing.

"Malka?" the bewildered voice finally rasps. "Is that you?" She adds with astonishment, "You remember me?"

A shudder ripples through me. "Is this a joke?" I cry. "Please, please don't be a smart aleck. Is that really you?"

"Of c-c-course," the voice stammers.

I cannot help myself. "Then prove it," I say.

For a time, there is only silence. Then the voice begins in slow, crinkly Yiddish: *"Oh, is this not the most delicious chicken we have ever eaten in our lives? And these potatoes. With the parsley."*

Just as I am struggling into my coat, my lawyer, Mr. Beecham, calls.

"I've got good news and bad," he says. "The Newhouses are willing to settle."

"Let me guess. Those shysters want more money than God."

"They refuse to accept anything under seven figures. They keep insisting their daughter will have to go to 'special' schools now and can never be gainfully employed and how there's a possibility no one will ever marry her when she grows up because she's 'half blind' and 'disabled' and blah-blahblah."

"Oh, they think that, now, do they?" I say acidly. Those dimwits. How little they know. "Well. Guess what, darling? I don't settle either. That's it. Tell them we're going to court."

Mr. Beecham swallows, as if he has perhaps been sipping a glass of water and it has gone down the wrong pipe. "Mrs. Dunkle, I have to tell you. I really do not advise this," he says. "We're lucky enough to have gotten all the criminal charges in *this* case dropped—"

"I want my day in court," I say. "I've had enough of this non-sense. It's my turn to speak."

I hang up the phone. I am finished, darlings. Now all of you, everyone in the whole world, will finally hear from me. My side of the story.

I take a legal pad and begin to compose these thoughts on the drive up. Everything that I am confessing to you right here and now. All that I have to say.

The Performing Artists Home & Hospital for the Aged is housed in a redbrick Colonial plantation-style house; according to the sign, it was established by SAG and Actors' Equity as a retirement community for forgotten actors, actresses, dancers, singers, old vaudevillians. Its gracious lawn is dotted with oak trees and flaking white Adirondack chairs. An oval drive leads up from the access road. In the distance you can hear the constant *thwick-thwick-thwick* of cars speeding by on the expressway beyond a thatch of woods. A little grove to the left camouflages a strip mall with an A&P, a notions shop, a dog groomer, and a Sub Hub, but not—to my dismay—a Dunkle's. Eighty-two franchises we have left now across the country.

As Hector guides the car up between the trees to the front, I can see newer, uglier buildings in the back with prefabricated panels the color of orange sherbet. "Oh, Mrs. Dunkle," Hector calls back from the driver's seat. "Are you thinking of moving here?"

"I should fire you for that," I say.

If she recognizes me from television, the nurse on duty does not let on. I simply sign in like anyone else. *"Malka Treynovsky."* It is the first time in my entire life I have written my birth name.

"Your sister's in a wheelchair now, so we've moved her to the ground floor for better mobility." The nurse motions for me to follow, then halts. "Oh, I'm sorry. Would you like a wheelchair, too?" I shake my head. *Your sister*, she has said. *Your. Sister. Yoursister.*

Flora's room is at the end of the east wing in the main building. The long corridors have the mushroomy, tweedy, sour smell of old age, cafeteria food, and dusty carpeting. Signs stapled to bulletin boards announce "Cabaret Tuesdays" and "Sing Along with Simon Night." When the nurse raps on the door and says "Florence? Florence, are you there? You've got a visitor. Your sister Malka is here," my heart seizes.

I hear a thumping, a clack. "Judy," a brittle, patrician voice calls out. "Could you please help me here?"

For a moment my pulse beats so furiously I think I might faint. Imagine this: coming all this way, after all these years, only to collapse on my sister's threshold? Yet the door clicks open and a fat nurse's aide in white Dacron with the nameplate JUDY bellows, "WHY, HERE YOU ARE. YOU MUST BE FLORENCE'S SISTER. WE HAVE BEEN WAITING FOR YOU. I'VE JUST SET UP SOME TEA FOR FLORENCE. THERE IS A BUZZER HERE." She points to a button mounted low on the wall beneath the light switch. "I'LL JUST BE DOWN THE HALLWAY IF YOU LADIES NEED ANYTHING ELSE."

Then she wheels Flora forward, as if presenting me with a prize.

My sister.

Her skin is translucent parchment pulled tight over the fine bones of her skull, crinkling around her eyes and trembling mouth as she smiles at me. Her eyes, still marble blue, are astonishingly bright in contrast to the deadly white of her skin. "Malka?" she says softly. She is dressed in a bubblegum pink sweatshirt with RE-DONDO BEACH spelled out on it in plaid fabric letters, and a fluffy pale blue blanket is tucked in around her legs. Her white hair is like a baby's. Corn silk. Flyaway. "Oh, my," she rasps, rolling her chair up closer to me to get a better look.

She is not immediately recognizable to me at all. This Flora is an old, tiny, ghostly woman. It is extremely unnerving. Surely,

I imagined, I would glimpse at least a remnant of her old self in her face. Yet no. Nothing except for the color of the eyes. Studying her, however, it is apparent that she was once extremely beautiful. In fact, her cheekbones are still high, her eyes bright. Her deportment, despite her tremors, is regal. My sister is a magnificent, faded flower. But her entire body is twitching and quaking slightly, as if being shot through with electrical impulses. With two trembling hands, she reaches out to clasp one of mine. A sickly smell emanates from her: Industrial disinfectant. Sharp, overly floral perfume. And, perhaps, a hint of urine.

For a second, I feel a bolt of panic. Yes, I, too, am old, darlings. Yet not this old. I have an urge to bat this decay away from me like a swarm of flies, to take a step back. Yet impishly, my sister waggles her finger at me.

"I know what you look like already. I've seen you on TV," she says in a wry, palsied voice. "But me? Oh, it must be a shock. You'll have to excuse my appearance. But I decided to give up on vanity during the Nixon administration."

Oh. I see suddenly. *There she is.*

"My," I chuckle, limping farther into her room. A small kitchenette and dining alcove are separated from the sitting room by a gentle archway. Everything—the sink, the light switches, the seats—has been slightly lowered to accommodate someone in a wheelchair. With its butterscotch paneling and the green netted light fixture suspended from a chain above the dining table, her "residence" is cozy enough. A hand-crocheted afghan that looks like it's made of pot holders is draped across an overstuffed sofa. Beyond it a large window looks out on the back lawn and an un-used therapy pool flecked with the first yellowed, curling leaves of autumn. Glancing around, however, I feel a flutter of despair. After everything we fled in Russia, and the tenements, this is where my sister ends up? In a cheap efficiency with plastic roses stuffed into a souvenir vase from St. Louis and guardrails on her bed? Nurses tromping in and out? There is scarcely more space or privacy than on Orchard Street.

"So this is home now?" I say, glancing at the fake potted plant. A little knickknack shelf in the corner. The bathroom with its horrid railings and medicinal stench, lest you forget for a moment that you are in a facility.

Flora taps on the side of her wheelchair. "Where else am I going to go? Skiing in St. Moritz? Sailing on the *QE2*?" Motioning over my shoulder with her chin, she says, "At least here I'm with other showbiz folks. For a bunch of old fogies, we're lively."

I look behind me. The entire wall is covered with faded play-bills and posters in colorful frames. My sister, I see, was a tap dancer in vaudeville. And a Ziegfeld Girl! Why, she has even been in the movies! *Broadway Melody of 1929.* Busby Berkeley's *42nd Street* and *Gold Diggers of 1933.* ("Oh, I was just in the cho-rus. And was that DP ever a skirt chaser," she says. "To keep us on schedule, they fed us amphetamines.") Having learned the jazz clarinet, she also traveled for a while across America with Rayleen Dupree and Her Red-Hot Swinging Sweethearts' All-Girl Orchestra.

"That's how I met my first husband," Flora says, pointing to the poster for the band appearing at the King's Café outside Davenport, Iowa. "He was a trombonist. He played with Bix Beiderbecke for a little while, in fact. My, he could play." Flora frowns. "Almost as well as he could drink, unfortunately."

"Your first husband was a lush?"

"No. Bix. My first husband... well, he was just a bore. As soon as we got married, he expected me to stop performing. So that didn't last." Flora looks at me with disbelief. "For almost forty years, I was in showbiz, Malka. And you know, I always thought of you, because you were the one who got me started. Do you remember that little act of ours, out on the landings on Orchard Street?"

"Of course." I chuckle. "One penny to sing and dance, another penny to make us be quiet." The Little Cleaning, Singing Bialystoker Sisters.

"Well, I tap-danced my way out of the Lefkowitzes' as soon as I could. We were out in Brooklyn, real slums. Watching the colored kids, I taught myself. For years and years, I was running around the playhouse circuit in gardenias and satin, sequins and bugle beads right up to my bubbies. I think my blood itself turned into cold cream." Flora's face melts into a faraway nostalgia. "Then one day I woke up and said, 'What on earth am I killing myself for in these high heels? I am far too old for this.' So I stopped dyeing my hair and got a job as a telephone operator. Nobody looks at you, and all day long you can sit." She points to her terry-cloth slippers, peeking out from the foot pads beneath her blanket. "And I have been wearing sensible shoes ever since. Makeup. Brassieres. Girdles. I finished with all of it."

Steering us over to the wall by the kitchenette, Flora points with obvious pleasure to photographs of babies, children, a young man in a uniform. I know nothing of her life, though she knows plenty about mine. Thanks to the media, she is already aware of all the disastrous decisions I made. The laws I broke. The money I owe. The tchotchkes I stole. How I have mistreated my maids.

I hobble along the wall, perusing the museum of Florence Halloway. A black-and-white print of a man with horn-rimmed glasses standing stiffly in a white tuxedo beside a fountain where bronze fish spit water into the air outside a villa. Snapshots of a gorgeous blonde, whom I surmise is Flora in her twenties, posing at Mount Rushmore. The Grand Canyon. Niagara Falls. A girl in white lace hot pants, a man with a handlebar mustache and plaid bell-bottoms. Babies in bonnets in a triptych of oval frames. People all holding cocktails squeezing in together in front of a plastic Christmas tree. Seeing them, this bundle of exuberant love, I feel a pang.

"Are all of these your family?"

"Mm." She nods. "Husband Number Two was an Irish Catholic, so we had nieces and nephews coming out of our ears. But they never really approved of me." Gingerly, she unfolds the glasses hanging around her neck on a chain and struggles to hook them over her ears. I help her. She draws closer to one of the photographs and touches it gently. "Not the Jewish part. But the showbiz part. His mother thought I was a tramp. After Joe died, I never did see much of them." With a shaking finger, she points to the girl getting married in hot pants. "Molly, my oldest, she is in New Mexico now, working on a reservation with the Pueblo Indians. Can you imagine? Henry . . . well." She stares, devastated, at the portrait of the young man in uniform. "I don't know how Mama could bear losing four."

"She didn't," I say quietly.

For a moment we are both silent. I am luckier than I realize.

"Well." Flora dabs her eyes. "This," she says with forced cheeriness, wheeling her chair over to a snapshot of a jaunty man in a fringed jacket and a Stetson, "this is Angus. Husband Number Three."

"Flora! You married a cowboy?"

"Oh, heavens no. That was for a Halloween party. Angus sold medical equipment. Autoclaves. Sterilizers."

"I assume he passed?"

"Nah. I divorced him for Husband Number Four, I'm afraid. Allen. You know"—she wheezes—"you have to keep life interesting."

My sister, I realize proudly, is quite the wisenheimer herself.

"Allen was the best of the worst," she recalls with a chuckle.

"Though I'm not much good as a wife either, in case you were wondering. He passed away in '76."

"Oh, the same year as my Bert."

"Your Bert," Flora says fondly. "You know..." She motions to me and wheels herself over to the little table in the kitchenette, covered with plastic gingham. The nurse's aide has already poured the water for the tea, which has been steeping too long and is now cold. A few cream wafers are arranged on a chipped plate. "If it weren't for Bert, I might never have found you again."

"Excuse me?" I am settling myself down into the chair, with its cracked vinyl cushion.

"Years ago," Flora says, "back when I was performing with a Yiddish theater troupe on Second Avenue, this dashing young man came backstage and introduced himself to me one night after the show. Oh, he looked exactly like Errol Flynn. And he told me his name was—"

"Albert Dunkle," I say stiffly. And the teacup goes heavy in my hands. *Frieda.* "At least I think that's her name," Bert had said. "You know how *fartootst* I get." She had been the beautiful blond actress he'd been head over heels about. A sickening feeling washes over me.

"That's right. Albert Dunkle." Flora smiles delightedly. "I never forgot it. He was so handsome we told him that he should consider a career in the theater. But when he came to audition for our troupe? Oh, he had the most terrible stutter! It was almost comical. The entire bunch of us fell about laughing."

"He was humiliated," I say icily.

"Oh, as I recall, he was a wonderful sport about it. Though I never saw him again after that. Not until he began appearing on those ice cream commercials," she says offhandedly. Her tone eases my distress. Bert had simply been a bit of trivia in her life, one of many commuters standing on a train platform as she shot past. That was it. A side note. My sister has no idea that Bert had been so thoroughly besotted with her—nor that I had already met him by the time he had called on her backstage at the Second Avenue theater. She has no idea that I had been racked by jealousy back then—sickened to death at the thought of him loving her and choosing her over me—and that I'm feeling this same fierce stab of possessiveness and anxiety all over again right here, right now, more than half a century later, in the Performing Artists Home & Hospital for the Aged, even though Bert has been dead and gone for over seven years.

"Isn't that a coincidence?" says Flora, struggling to pinch up a cream wafer with her thumb and forefinger. "That I had run into him, way back when?"

What if I had accompanied Bert to his audition that day? I think suddenly. Flora and I, we would likely have recognized each other, would we not? My whole life, I would have had my sister with me. Yet perhaps, with me there, Bert might not have stuttered through his audition either. He might have won her heart yet. What would have happened then?

"How could I possibly have known that Lillian Dunkle, Bert's Ice Cream Queen, was no one other than my sister?" Flora says with amazement, dropping her cookie back down on her plate. "If I had not met Bert all those years ago, I probably would not have been interested in that article about you at all. But Tricia was in here asking what I would like her to read to me. And she was holding up all these magazines. And there was the one with you on the cover. And I thought, why not? It might be interesting to hear about the woman who that charming goofball Albert Dunkle married. And when I heard 'Lillian Dunkle was originally named Malka Bialystoker'? Oh, heavens. I nearly fell out of my wheelchair." Flora beams. "Which is not easy, you understand."

I look at my sister, the radiant, milkweed slip of her.

"To think I could have asked her to read *National Geographic* to me instead." She grins.

Ladies and gentlemen. Readers. My fellow Americans. Members of the press. The jury. I have told you all so much already. Some things, just a few, I will keep for myself. Flora and I have almost seventy years to catch up on. Her career, her four promising yet incompetent husbands. Mr. Lefkowitz. Mama, Bella, and Papa (and oh, my residual shame). We tell each other as much as we can, as much as we can absorb in a single afternoon. The light begins to slant across the lawn in great parabolas. Eager, no doubt, to clock out, the nurses on duty grow impatient, interrupting us with greater frequency.

As the late-summer sun begins to set, Flora herself begins to dim. She grows less coherent, wearier. She starts to repeat herself, then stops, addled, in midsentence, until an uneasy silence comes over us, as if we are a young couple on an awkward blind date. I stare into her glassy, startlingly blue eyes. Her bony palm trembles in mine like a baby bird.

Finally I say softly, "Oh, Flora. It looks like I'm going to prison."

This is the first time I have ever said this aloud to anyone. It is the first time I have even admitted it to myself.

"Over that little girl?" she rasps. Then her eyes close, and she doesn't say anything for a little while. Just when I think she has perhaps dropped off to sleep, she sits upright and announces, "But anyone could see it was an accident, Malka. You hit her as a reflex."

"No," I say plainly. "For taxes. They found me guilty in June. Three counts of tax evasion. My sentencing hearing is next week."

"Do you owe a lot?" Flora has shifted about in her wheelchair and is studying me with her head cocked.

I sigh. "More than a lot. So sue me: I was grieving. I got careless. I was missing Bert, and so I started going shopping. And oh, hell. I suppose I misrepresented a few purchases. I suppose I helped myself to a few things. I got cute with the truth."

Flora nods sympathetically. "Can't you just pay it all back?"

I shrug. "I don't think it's simply about the money at this point."

"But you're an old woman. With a bad leg. It's not as if you're going to run away somewhere, Malka. They can't really lock you up, can they?"

"The judge on this case? He's tough. He may want to make an example out of me." I smile haplessly. "In case you haven't read the papers lately, I am not America's favorite flavor right now."

I look plainly at my sister, the wisp of her. She is the true ice cream princess, I think suddenly. So elegant, even in her decrepitude, with hair like spun sugar. Those blue-glass marble eyes.

"How long would they send you to jail for?" she asks.

"I don't know. Maybe eighteen months. Three years, even? My lawyers say they'll petition to get it waived for 'good behavior.' Though I don't think I've been exhibiting much of that lately, I'm afraid."

Flora gives me a wicked little smile. "I saw on the news last night. They say you might have been smoking drugs in the courthouse bathroom?" Shaking her head, she chuckles, not unkindly. "Oh, Malka. Mama was right. That big, fresh mouth of yours."

Slipping her palsied hand into mine, she squeezes it and grins. "You always were scrappy."

"Flora. *Mia sorella*," I say gently. Oh, how I yearn to add, *Flora, I am afraid. Flora, I am alone. Flora, I've made such a mess of things.* Instead I simply shrug. "Okay. So I'm a little difficult."

"I'll come visit you in prison," she says brightly.

"Oh, will you, now?" I laugh, glancing at her wheelchair.

"Of course." She grins again. "We'll put on a little show."

"Let's do," I say.

"I'll sing," Flora says. "You dance."

The following Monday another judge bangs his gavel. Like a gun-shot it sounds. I am aware of the gleam of handcuffs on the court officer's belt, someone shouting in the corridor. My sentence is one year plus one day at the women's federal minimum-security "facility" in Alderson, West Virginia. With credit for good be-havior, I can be out in eight months, my lawyer whispers. We approach the bench to determine a time and date for my "vol-untary surrender." My family, standing behind me in the gallery, is stunned. Yet I am not. Those stockades they used to set up in public squares? Everybody loves a pariah, darlings. Who can resist sending me, the Ice Cream Queen of America, to prison?

At seventy-five years old, I, Lillian Dunkle, am a convicted felon. I can appeal, of course—though it's likely I'll have finished serving my sentence before the new trial can even be set. I will fight, I suppose, if only to restore my good name. Yet part of me, darlings, simply wants it to be done with. Frankly, I am getting so tired of battling.

I agree to begin my incarceration just after Labor Day. West Virginia, I tell myself, is pretty in the autumn. During the Depres-sion, Bert and I slept there in our truck beneath auburn-leaved trees, wreathed in mist, in the sweet, fragrant wood smoke of morning.

I have journeyed from Russia to the United States. From poor to rich. And now I will be given a number and a uniform. Jason, he looks as if he might break down right there in the courtroom. Rita grips my hand so hard I think she will crush my metacarpals. "Oh, Lillian," she keens. Isaac, he hugs me and hugs me as he has never hugged me in his life. I smell his soapy antiperspirant, the musky fibers of his Pierre Cardin jacket. His arms are like baked bread. It is still surprising to me how substantial he has become. All my life, I have longed for my son to embrace me like this, to call me Mama and draw me to him. Yet now it is too much to bear. "Please," I say, disengaging. "Shoo. All of you. I'll meet you in the lobby." Unable to look at their devastated faces, I get busy collecting my scarf, my pocketbook. Yet as soon as their footsteps retreat, I am stricken. Why did I push them away? My God, I can't help it, I realize: It is like a terrible tic. A reflex. Despite the court officers standing by, hoping to hurry me along—the loneliness I feel is gut-wrenching. I glance around miserably. Only one spectator remains in the gallery.

Harvey Ballentine stands in the last row of pewlike benches. He is dressed in a crisp blue linen jacket, though beneath it he looks cadaverous. He is clutching a crinkled brown paper grocery bag from Gristede's. As I make my way toward the door, he steps out into the aisle. "Lillian," he says in a soldierly fashion.

"Well, look who's here." I swallow. "You came to gloat? To make sure they're really locking me up?"

"Why, however did you guess? In fact, I've got all the munchkins queued up, right outside. Really, Lillian." He rolls his eyes theatrically. "I only gloat when *I've* had a triumph."

The corners of his eyes crinkle like crepe paper. I still have trouble getting used to Harvey's face without its clown makeup, without its florid youth. The deflated, grayish jowls, those veiny cords of his neck.

"Well then. Walk me out." I am surprised how my legs are trembling. Leaning into each other, the two of us are as rickety as chopsticks. I struggle not to smile, not to betray my extravagant gratitude. "So, now you decide to show up?" I say.

"I know. I know. Ambushing is so déclassé. But I kept calling your apartment, and no one ever—"

I stop. "You better not have come here to pity me, Harvey." I thump my cane on the floor. "Because if you did, I am going to box your ears."

"Oh, honey. Puh-lease." Harvey holds the door for me. "I'm only here to antagonize you. I promise.

"Although," he adds coyly, coming to a standstill in the corridor, "with all those marauding hordes out there—those dreadful, tacky reporters—I did figure—well—." Rummaging through his brown paper bag, he pulls out a red plastic clown's nose and a child's insipid birthday crown—the type they sell at dime stores, made out of glossy gold cardboard with a string of elastic like a garrote. "I thought maybe we could face them down together, if you wanted. But now I don't know. What do you think?" He puts his hand on his hip and twists his mouth into a sideways comma. "Too cutesy? Too camp?"

I look at him wickedly. Harvey Ballentine. My Spreckles the Clown. "To hell with 'em," I say, motioning for the crown. "They want a 'media circus'? So we'll give them one."

When we finally make it past the great spanking machine of the press, my lawyers and family are amassed by the curb. A line of town cars is waiting, but I wave Harvey over to my Cadillac. "That was marvelous," I say. "Come. I'll give you a lift."

"You sure?" He clutches his bag in front of him like a pillow. Already he has pulled off his toy clown nose. The photos of the two of us that will appear in the papers and on the evening news: I can only imagine.

"Jason, darling." I turn to my grandson and nudge him out of the backseat. "Go ride up ahead with your parents. Harvey and I have business to discuss."

As Hector maneuvers the car away from the courthouse, I tap Harvey on his kneecap.

"You're too skinny," I say. "We're getting you a knish."

"Ugh, Lillian. You know I hate those things."

"Okay, a cannoli, then. Something. I feel like a drive."

I have the urge to go to Whitehall Street and the South Ferry terminal, to the final, wind-battered tip of Manhattan, to overlook the glittering harbor, the Statue of Liberty, to stand on the very spot where my parents and sisters and I first disembarked and blinked out into the dissipating American sunshine seventy years ago. The pull of all those ghosts, the last gasp of comfort, of nostalgia, of delirious freedom, is magnetic. But the whole area is a mess now. Construction everywhere. Landfill is being shipped in from New Jersey and packed along the Hudson. A brand-new neighborhood is rising along the waterfront in the shadow of the World Trade Center, a complex of buildings with the inelegant name of Battery Park City. A winter garden, supposedly, there will be, and a marina, and a fancy-schmancy promenade. One of Hector's brothers-in-law, from El Salvador, he tells me, is on the construction crew.

So instead I order him to thread the Cadillac north. "Come." I nudge Harvey. "Let me show you."

Orchard Street smells of dry-cleaning fluids and sizzling Chinese food. The low, ugly tenements are still there, I discover, but many of them have dented metal fire doors now, doughnuts of fluorescent lights buzzing spastically in the vestibules. Music like Jason's pulsates from a window; the entire block seems to throb with it. Discount stores sell lurid polyester clothing made in Taiwan. A few woebegone signs in Hebrew letters still swing rustily above the windows, but most are in Chinese. "I thought it was right here," I say as Harvey and I disembark from the backseat. Suddenly I cannot be sure. Everything has been repainted, some walls obscured by graffiti. "I think it was here. We lived upstairs, on the top floor. Six of us in one room. Chickens squawking in the courtyard. Shared privies in the hallways."

Harvey squints up and nods dutifully, though I am growing flustered. Old age is so humiliating, darlings. After a while, there is simply no camouflaging your deterioration, and no one ever sees all the strengths you've acquired along the way. I point shakily to a façade. *This was the tenement, was it not?*

Over on Mulberry Street, we scarcely fare better. Little Italy has shrunk to a few blocks that seem to have become a parody of themselves. Red-white-and-green striped signs boast AUTHENTIC ITALIAN CUISINE JUST LIKE MAMA'S! Shops everywhere sell chains of livid pepperonis, murky bottles of olive oil. A man in a porkpie hat with a portable Hammond organ plays "That's Amore" for a gaggle of tourists. The ground floor of the Dinellos' tenement is now an expensive-looking "cappuccino bar." Beside it: a Laundromat with a flashing, chiming pinball machine. I keep waiting to feel something monumental, yet all I feel is foolish and frail.

Anything that has survived the wrecking ball, it seems, has done so by being reinvented. Renovated. Reborn somehow.

Back in the car, Harvey and I eat our cannolis in silence, the bubbled gold shells shattering as we bite down on them. Swallowing, I glance out the window at the passing buildings, trying to recall the world as it once was, myself as who I had once been. Oh, I had wanted—and gotten—so much! And yet. How unprepared I'd been for the myriad of ways life deformed you, the way grief and rage and bitterness and heartbreak kicked you repeatedly in the gut, sent you sprawling on the pavement. The little girl who had sung her plaintive little songs on the landings on Orchard Street, she wavers and flickers before me like a mirage.

"Harvey," I say quietly. "Am I a terrible person?"

Harvey takes a big, gooey bite of his pastry. "Mm. How, exactly, are we defining 'terrible'?" When I don't respond, he says diplomatically, "Well, honey, you've certainly had your moments." He licks a dab of ricotta cream from the crescent of flesh between his thumb and forefinger. Folding his slip of translucent bakery paper neatly into quarters, he drops it back into the box. "But bad, good. Good, bad. I mean, isn't that everyone?"

I give his hand a little squeeze, even though he is a germophobe.

"One thing, though?" He swivels around on the leather seat to face me. "This 'facility' you're going to, Lil? Well, I was thinking. You should probably approach it like sort of a spa."

"Excuse me?"

"Okay, like rehab. Think 'Betty Ford with a prison motiff.' I mean, they have meetings in those places, Lil, same as everywhere else. And they *are* anonymous—"

"You're saying I have a problem, Harvey? You actually think *I* drink too much? Ha. Excuse me, but that's *you*. Don't you go confusing me with all of your craziness," I snap. Yet as soon as these words are out of my mouth, I know the falsity of them. Of course I have a problem. For Chrissakes, darlings. I hit a small child on live television. Certainly, certainly, this sort of behavior—well, for starters, it is not good for business.

"I'm just saying, Lillian," Harvey says delicately, "that if one day you decide maybe you *do* want to change? Well, where you're going could help."

The night before my lawyers escort me down to prison in Alderson, West Virginia, Isaac and Rita propose going out someplace special for dinner. "La Grenouille? La Côte Basque? You name it, Ma."

"And have everybody in the dining room sit staring at me while I eat foie gras?" I sniff. "No thank you. I prefer we just gather at my apartment. Send out for Chinese."

Jason arrives early with his records, a small Styrofoam cooler balanced on his shoulder. His muscles flexed showily. Sunglasses gleaming. "Mom and Dad'll be over in a few," he announces, dropping the carton with a thud on the kitchen floor. "They sent this ahead. Ta-da. Fresh from the freezer."

Inside is a selection of Dunkle's newest Deluxe Premium Ice Cream. The pints have fancy gold swirls on the lids. Just looking at them makes me dizzy.

"This one is awesome." Jason tosses a container in the air, then catches it. "Madagascar Vanilla. Ka-cha!"

"Well, aren't you in fine spirits?"

"I'm trying to be," he says winsomely, removing his sunglasses, setting them carefully on the counter. He bends over the cooler. "I think you'll like this one, too, Grandma. Java with Cream, though it's really just coffee. Oh, and Chocolate Truffle." He looks around distractedly. "Where do you keep your spoons? You got a tray?"

"Oh." I chuckle. "Are you waiting on me now?"

"I thought before Mom and Dad get here, the two of us could have a special little going-away party of our own." Wiggling his eyebrows, he draws a twisted cigarette from the pocket of his black jeans.

"Oh, _tateleh._" I touch my hand to his cheek. It burns like dry ice. "Thank you. But I think it's best I keep my wits about me now."

He nods solemnly, tucks it away. For a moment we just regard each other, breathing. "Grandma," he says quietly, "are you scared?"

"Oh, I haven't given it much thought," I say breezily. Though, darlings, I am lying. My heart, it is a furious bird. God only knows what sort of thuggishness, violence, or squalor awaits me. Already I have received death threats in the mail. *"I hope you choke. The inmates should cut you. Die, bitch. Die."* Crazies, of course, and my lawyers have assured me that this minimum-security facility has a high degree of civility. Still. Perhaps it is good that most of America has seen my right hook on television. Papa, he may have given me something useful after all.

I am old now. Certainly, this is not how I ever planned to live out my last days, and I cannot bear to think about it for too long. Yet the prison guidelines have informed me that there are mandatory jobs to be performed—in the kitchen. The library. This comes as an enormous relief. In addition, I have been getting ideas. The problem with this fancy-schmancy premium ice cream that my son is now struggling to hawk is that it simply replicates our competition. Dunkle's needs to do something bolder, wittier. With MTV and these portable Walkmans kids are listening to—why not make premium ice cream named after pop musicians? From the records Jason has played for me, I have taken notes: Grandmaster Fudge. Bananarama Split. U2ootie Frutti. I cannot imagine that a prison can be much worse than a tenement to work in. So no doubt, I will stay occupied. There is always, always something more to invent, darlings.

"Why don't you go out on the patio, and I'll set us up the snacks," Jason says magnanimously.

A glass casement door leads from the kitchen. Sunny has not been here much over the summer, so the window boxes and small potted trees have grown dry in their enormous terra-cotta planters, giving the terrace the feel of an overgrown Roman ruin. A faint, warm, late-summer breeze ruffles across the sky. Bert and I bought this penthouse precisely for the view. Looking west, you can see the billows of Central Park, the reservoir set in it like a lozenge of blue topaz. Beyond it, the skyline of the Upper West Side stands sentry, sun radiating from behind the water towers and spires. I lower myself into a wrought-iron patio chair. It really is so lovely out here, even with the fine coating of powdery black soot, the incipient roar from the city.

Jason steps carefully outside with a tray balanced in his hands. He has brought out all five pints of ice cream, along with spoons and two of my Murano glass dishes from Venice that are supposed to be purely decorative. No matter. My grandson, he is clearly trying.

"Well, isn't this lovely, *tateleh*."

He grins. "We aim to please."

My poor grandson. He appears genuinely upset that I am going to prison. He is so solicitous—and such marvelous fun! It is a shame, perhaps, that I will not be leaving him any of my fortune.

Just today, when I met with my lawyers to finalize my affairs, I amended my will. Jason, he will be getting my record collection and thirty-five thousand dollars. Just enough to launch himself in this world—as a kung fu clown, or a performance artist, or any other *meshuggeneh* thing he aspires to if he decides to eschew the family business. Yet no more. I am doing him an enormous favor, darlings. It's always best, in the end, to earn your own money. With nothing to work for, you simply don't work. My grandson is clever, and my grandson is creative. I want to keep him that way. My share of the Dunkle's Ice Cream Corporation—still worth several million, even now—will go to my domestic, Sunny. God knows she's earned it. And so not everybody will be able to say that I'm "the world's worst boss" in the end, thank you very much.

Isaac, as the president of Dunkle's, has seized more than his share already, of course. But Flora's care is provided for, until the end of her days. As will hospital costs and legal bills—God forbid it comes to that—for Harvey Ballentine. A chunk, I've decided, too, will go to his GMHC as well, if only to rankle my publicist.

But otherwise, the rest of my fortune? Whatever the government doesn't seize, I'm leaving to my dog.

Jason finishes arranging the dishes on the table. "Before we dig in, why don't I go inside and put on some tunes, Grandma?"

"Splendid," I say. Petunia leaps onto my lap. "Prop the door open and turn the hi-fi all the way up so we can hear it."

As he saunters back toward the kitchen, his shoulder blades press through his T-shirt like small, fine wings.

Across the gulf of Park Avenue, the city rises, the whole jumble of windows and rooftops aflame with gold light from the late afternoon sun, lives upon lives crammed into compartments of plaster and steel, nestled inside high-rises and tenements and great monoliths of glass. Families borne here on the water, transported through the air, in terror or hope, pulsating with yearning. Well, good luck to them all. A swoop of pigeons scatters like glitter in the air, fluttering down onto ledges and cornices, alighting on the heads of disintegrating angels carved into the limestone.

Jason ducks out the kitchen door. "Grams, what do you want to listen to?" Gamely, he holds up a few of my albums. "You want Benny Goodman? Some Billie Holiday? Some Johnny Cash?"

I close my eyes and tilt my face toward the sun, catching the last warm kiss of it on my face. "Nah, play something different. Play something new, *tateleh*," I tell him.

Surprise me.

ACKNOWLEDGMENTS

This book would not exist without the vision, patience, and brilliant stewardship of my editor, Helen Atsma. Nor would it exist without my agent, Irene Skolnick, who has guided me sagely for years. Nor would it exist without Jamie Raab, Allyson Rudolph, Tareth Mitch, Caitlin Mulrooney-Lyski, and the staff of Grand Central Publishing, who continue to champion me.

Doing my research, I had the great good fortune to be taken in by the generous, warmhearted Zaya Givargidze, owner of the Carvel ice cream store in Massapequa, New York. He not only showed me the ropes of his business but allowed me to work behind the counter and in the kitchen. A huge New York shout-out goes to him and to his staff: Vincenza Pisa, Samantha Spinnato, and Keri Strejlau.

My cousin Susan Dalsimer has been invaluable as an editor and adviser when I was lost in the wilderness—as have my friends and fellow writers Marc Acito, Elizabeth Coleman, Carla Drysdale, Anne Korkeakivi, and Maureen McSherry.

The glorious Lisa Campisi, Emanuel Campisi (a.k.a. Big Manny), and Frank DeSanto assisted with All Things Neapolitan, as did the sainted Luigi Cosentino (a.k.a. Louie)—co-owner of

Gemelli Fine Foods in Babylon, Long Island. A major *grazie mille* to all—and to my beloved Franco Beneduce, in memoriam—for his inspiration and life force.

John C. Crow, Mark Bradford, "Esq.", David Gilman, and Fred Schneider provided me with clarity on numerous legal issues; a special bow of appreciation goes to attorney Laurence Lebowitz.

It seems I cannot write a book unless I begin it at the home of Susie Walker, nor without encouragement from my cousin Joan Stern, nor without my brother, John Seeger Gilman, vital reader, brainstormer, and anchor.

A glass must also be raised multiple times... To the rest of the Most Amazing Book Club that cheered me on: Brigette De Lay, Margot Hendry, Anne Kerr, Suzanne Muskin, Cristina Negrie, Mary Pecaut, and Jean Swanson... To Michael Cannan and Hannah Serota for crucial inspiration... To Stephane Gehringer, Anke Lock, and the staff of the Cambrian Adelboden. To my teachers and mentors, writers Charles Baxter, Rosellen Brown, Nicholas Delbanco, and Al Young, whose lessons continue to resonate throughout my life and work... And to novelist Richard Bausch for sustaining me with his posts of wisdom.

The New-York Historical Society and the Tenement Museum provided crucial resources, as did Avvo.com. Among numerous books and articles that proved vital were Jeri Quinzio's *Of Sugar and Snow: A History of Ice Cream Making*; Linda Stradley's "History of Ice Cream Cones" and the Web site What's Cooking America; *Una Storia Segreta: The Secret History of Italian American Evacuation and Internment During World War II* by Lawrence DiStasi; *97 Orchard: An Edible History of Five Immigrant Families in One Tenement* by Jane Ziegelman; *The Emperor of Ice Cream: The True Story of Häagen-Dazs* by Rose Vesel Mattus; and *Streets: A Memoir of the Lower East Side* by Bella Spewack.

Last but not least: I swoon with gratitude before my husband, Bob Stefanski, who read, edited, and discussed this novel with me endlessly. My Love, I cannot thank you enough for your wisdom, humor, faith, passion, friendship, patience, exquisite judgment, and kindness. You make everything possible. *Je t'aime.*

ABOUT THE AUTHOR

Susan Jane Gilman is the bestselling author of *Hypocrite in a Pouffy White Dress*, *Kiss My Tiara*, and *Undress Me in the Temple of Heaven*. She provides commentary for NPR and has written for the *New York Times*, *Los Angeles Times*, and *Ms.* magazine, among others. She earned an MFA in creative writing from the University of Michigan and has won several literary awards. She divides her time between Geneva, Switzerland, and her hometown of New York. You can visit her at www.SusanJaneGilman.com.

READING GROUP GUIDE

Questions for Discussion

1. Lillian frequently attributes moments in her life to fate: her accident, her arrival in New York City the same year that continuous freezing was invented, et cetera. Do you believe it *was* fate? How does Lillian's assertion about fate "shaping" her destiny square with her story?

2. Do you like Lillian? Do you understand her? How do these two judgments differ? Would you say she's in any way the hero of the book?

3. Lillian's world broadens in almost unimaginable ways, from her fleeing the pogroms to heading an ice cream empire. Do you think this is a specifically American story—or could such radical change take place in another country?

4. At what point does Malka really become Lillian? Is it the baptism, when she changes her name? Earlier? Later? If you had the opportunity to take on a new name and identity, would you?

5. Rocco Dinello is Lillian's nemesis. Do you think he's the main villain in this story? Could you make a case for his actions? Do you sympathize with him at all?

6. How would you characterize Lillian's reactions to the surprises in her life—to Bert's lateness returning from gambling in Atlantic City, for example, or the shock of returning from her honeymoon to find herself out of a job thanks to the Cannoletti and Dinello merger? How are her reactions similar or dissimilar to her mother's responses to disappointment? Would you argue that Lillian is more like her mother or her father?

7. After Lillian sees that the Candie Ice Cream Company has been shut down, she expects to feel elated—but instead finds herself feeling "no satisfaction at all." Did you expect this?

8. How does Lillian's handicap affect her day-to-day life? Her overall story? Do you think it was a major obstacle—or a blessing in disguise?

9. Lillian is the driving force behind Dunkle's Ice Cream Company, but Bert is given the credit for starting, running, and expanding the company. The word "feminist" never crosses Lillian's lips, but do you think she'd call herself one? Why or why not?

10. Many of the characters in this book are tricksters at best, con artists at worst. Lillian and Bert begin their ice cream business by knowingly selling fake watches; Lillian's father kites checks and possibly recruits his children to perpetuate a scam. Is this trickery a family trait? Is there anything likable about it? Why do you think Lillian's schemes tend to work out and her father's tend not to?

11. Do you think Jason spends time with Lillian only because he's eyeing his inheritance, as Lillian once claims? How much do his motives matter?

12. Several points of conflict in the novel are ambiguous. For example, it is not made clear whether Bert is actually cheating on Lillian during their marriage—or whether the Dinello brothers are in fact helping to orchestrate the boycott against Dunkle's. What did you assume? Is it important to know one way or the other?

13. Toward the end of the book, Harvey Ballentine says, "Bad, good. Good, bad...Isn't that everyone?" Do you agree? Are all the characters in this novel both good and bad, or are they largely defined by one or the other?

14. Do you feel sorry for Lillian's son, Isaac? Why or why not?

15. By the end of the book, Lillian is wondering how the great, powerful nation she loved has become "small-minded and ingrown and frightened." Do you think her indictment of America rings true? Or is it her perceptions that have changed?

16. Lillian and Bert both arrive in America through Ellis Island, providing, as Lillian exclaims, less information and documentation than today's children are required to provide to enter preschool. How do you think Lillian's experience compares to the immigration experience today? What is the same? What is different? Have you ever moved to a new country? What difficulties did you experience? What opportunities did you find?

17. *The Ice Cream Queen of Orchard Street* spans seventy years. Did it illuminate any points in American history for you? What surprised you the most?

18. Author Susan Jane Gilman has often been celebrated for her humor. Did you find this to be a predominantly comic novel? Why or why not?

A Conversation with Susan Jane Gilman

Your last book, Undress Me in the Temple of Heaven, *is a nonfiction account of your travels in the People's Republic of China in the eighties.* Hypocrite in a Pouffy White Dress *is a coming-of-age memoir. And* Kiss My Tiara *is an advice book for the "SmartMouth Goddess." All are very different from a sweeping historical novel. Why did you decide to jump to fiction?*

It's always been my plan to write a novel, actually—ever since I was eight years old, when I fell in love with reading and started to write my own short stories in little notebooks I bought from Woolworth's, illustrating them with Magic Markers. From then on I always assumed that one day I'd write some sort of wonderful, fictional opus. Yet as I grew up, I kept getting sidetracked. Although I got an M.F.A. in creative writing and published short stories and even won literary prizes, things in our culture kept pissing me off so much that I felt compelled to respond with books.

In the late nineties, for example, as I was working on a novel, someone handed me a bestselling dating guide that essentially advised women to act like diet soda: be artificially sweet and bubbly for the rest of your life, the authors insisted, and you could trick a man into marrying you. Ugh. It was despicable on so many levels—insulting to women, insulting to men. "What about blueprints for catching a *life*, not a husband?" I cried. That's how *Kiss My Tiara: How to Rule the World as a SmartMouth Goddess* was born. I had a book of short stories and a half-finished novel that my agent was shopping around, but I landed a publishing contract overnight for this guide to power and attitude. It became my first published book.

Although readers always tell me that *Hypocrite in a Pouffy White*

Dress makes them laugh out loud, it actually grew out of the tragedy of September 11. Again, I was struggling to write The Novel. Yet for months after the attacks, I was simply a basket case. All I wanted to read were funny memoirs. However, the ones written by women all seemed to be about (a) being single or (b) going shopping. *Oh, puh-lease*, I thought. *There is so much more to our lives than that.*

That's how *Hypocrite in a Pouffy White Dress* took shape. Tales of growing up groovy and clueless—all the misadventures of coming of age, right up through adulthood—are in it. It debuted on the *New York Times* bestseller list, and I was dubbed "the female David Sedaris." Praise and excitement rained down on me like gold confetti. But it was nothing I'd set out to be.

So finally, again, I turned back to The Novel. I was writing one based on a real, harrowing backpacking trip I made through China in 1986 with a classmate. She and I had decided we wanted to be the female equivalents of the Kerouac and Cassady characters in *On the Road*—except internationally. We planned out this huge, around-the-world trip on a placemat at the International House of Pancakes after—need I say?—a night of copious collegiate drinking. "Let's start our trip by going to China!" we said. No one we knew had ever been there before. It was crazy and ambitious and completely misguided—the equivalent of backpacking through North Korea today. But off we went! We landed in Hong Kong without knowing a single word of Cantonese or Mandarin or anything about the People's Republic of China at all. And so, perhaps unsurprisingly to anyone but us, we quickly found ourselves in completely over our heads. Soon our adventure deteriorated into a modern *Heart of Darkness*. It was so unbelievable, in fact, that I assumed it was best used as the basis for fiction.

Yet then, alas, in 2003, I heard President G. W. Bush say that invading Iraq would be a "cakewalk." "He has got to be kidding," I said to my husband. "That sounds like something stupid I would've said as a drunk twenty-one-year-old back at the IHOP." Soon after, a number of travel memoirs began captivating the public as well—tales of women traveling to another country and renovating a house in Tuscany or going to an ashram in India in order to get over a heartbreak. We Americans seemed to view other cultures simply as arenas for our own personal makeovers or national enrichment. And so it became imperative to me to write my story from China as *nonfiction* instead—to tell the truth in all its messy, naked, improbable humiliation. I felt that it was important to counteract the American assumption that travel is about "conquering." Hence my third book was, again, a memoir: *Undress Me in the Temple of Heaven*.

I never expected to be a nonfiction author at all. It was an accident! *The Ice Cream Queen of Orchard Street* may seem like a departure to my readers, but it doesn't feel like one to me at all. Finally I'm coming home—back to my first love, to what I intended to do all along.

Does The Ice Cream Queen of Orchard Street *have anything in common with your previous nonfiction works?*

Well, all my books, it seems, are notorious for their humor. Certainly there's a bit of a smart-ass in Lillian Dunkle. And the concept itself—of an ice cream lady who hates kids and would rather drink a martini—initially appealed to me because of its absurdity, its great comic potential.

Also, *The Ice Cream Queen of Orchard Street* does attempt to expand upon the way women are so often portrayed in our culture. At least *I* don't see a lot of female antiheroes in literature who are seventy-five, handicapped, and under indictment.

Whether I'm writing fiction or nonfiction, I've always had an impulse to push back against the boundaries of "acceptability," to pop the balloons of presumption—particularly about women.

It's clear that a great amount of research went into the writing of this book and that some scenes are inspired by real-life events—the invention of soft-serve, for example, is credited to Tom Carvel, who began selling melted ice cream after a tire on his truck went flat. How much of this book was inspired by real history? Did you learn anything surprising while you were researching the story?

Tom Carvel's story was a key inspiration. I bow before him and his fabulous ice cream cakes! I initially got the idea for *The Ice Cream Queen of Orchard Street* when a friend and I were reminiscing about these cakes and the wonderfully croaky, homespun Carvel ice cream commercials we used to see on TV when we were kids; Tom Carvel himself would rasp, "Please, buy my Carvel ice cream?" He sounded so grandfatherly, so woebegone and choked, that you wanted to run right out and buy a Brown Bonnet ice cream cone—if only to keep the poor guy from having a heart attack!

Googling "Tom Carvel" on a whim, I learned that his story was a classic American-immigrant rags-to-riches saga. This struck me as a wonderful basis for a novel. However, as I began reading the biographies of Tom Carvel—and then of the Mattuses, the founders of Häagen-Dazs, who were also immigrants—it appeared that ice cream makers are generally phenomenally nice people, with a great love for children and ice cream and charity work.

Writing about good people making a delicious confection, however, held *zero* appeal to me as a writer.

For some time I had been yearning to create a modern female antihero—a sort of combination of Scarlett O'Hara and Leona

Helmsley—who was supremely difficult, amoral, and conniving (yet not a murderer or mentally ill). My two ideas fused. Why not write about a businesswoman who sells ice cream to the public in the guise of a sweet, motherly ice cream lady—but who in real life is a mean-spirited, difficult, kleptomaniacal drunk? That tension and contradiction appealed to me immensely.

Yet at the same time, I knew, such a protagonist had to be compelling, if not sympathetic. So I asked myself: What would make someone become so difficult? Again I looked to the story of the American immigrant for answers. Slowly, an epic developed—especially as I began to research the history of ice cream. I realized how much the ice cream industry was directly affected by the greatest events of the twentieth century. I began to see how these events could parallel and shape Lillian's own life beautifully, and how she would become motivated to lie and cheat over time.

I also needed to understand the nuts-and-bolts of ice cream making. So I contacted my inspiration—the Carvel Ice Cream Company itself—and arranged to work at a Carvel ice cream franchise out in Massapequa, Long Island. The guy who owns that Carvel franchise, Zaya Givargidze—it turns out he had inherited the store from his parents, who were Greek immigrants themselves. They had known Tom Carvel personally! Zaya knew all the history, all the ins and outs of business. It was like hitting the mother lode. It was like a visit to Lourdes. I was beside myself. I'm amazed he didn't throw me out of his shop. I kept running over to the freezers and pointing ecstatically at the ice cream cakes I had loved as a child and shouting, "Look! It's Cookie Puss!"

For two days he let me go behind the scenes, learn the ropes, don a Carvel T-shirt and paper hat, and work as an ice cream maker serving customers. I loved every minute of it—though I have to confess I was slightly disappointed that I got to do a lot less...ahem, "personal quality control" than I'd expected. I'd secretly imagined, I suppose, that "research" would really mean being allowed to lean my head back beneath the soft-serve ice cream dispenser and let it swirl endless amounts of chocolate ice cream directly into my mouth. Yeah, well, no such luck. Zaya was bighearted, but no dummy. He wouldn't let me near that ice cream machine unsupervised.

Everything during my research seemed like a revelation! All the inventions around ice cream, the chemistry of ice cream, and, of course, the way in which the evolution of ice cream paralleled so many historic events in twentieth-century America. The more I researched, the bigger the book became. At one point it ran almost seven hundred pages. It was like the *Moby-Dick* of ice cream. That's what I even wanted to call it: *The Moby-Dick of Ice Cream*. But cooler heads prevailed.

Lillian Dunkle is a colorful but troubled protagonist, in many ways an antiheroine. Was she a challenging character to write?

Actually, Lillian was the easiest part of this novel to write; her voice came to me in the proverbial flash. As I sat down to hammer out the beginning, I heard her speaking, and that was it—I just had her. Yet making her truly real was the tricky part.

While the idea of this mean, manipulative ice cream lady who hates kids and would rather have a martini is funny—and her shtick is amusing—she could too easily become a punch line, and that's the last thing I wanted. Irony is not enough, and a colloquial voice often risks sounding cartoonish. To hold my interest as a writer, and certainly to hold readers' attention, Lillian, as a character, had to have depth, texture, complications, contradictions—all those things that make someone real. And so, once I had her voice—and the book's premise—I worked backward. I had to ask myself: What would make Lillian become so difficult? What would make a woman like her human? Compelling? While I did not want to make her likable, I wanted readers to feel empathy for her—to root for her some of the time.

The Ice Cream Queen of Orchard Street *is arguably a love letter to New York City and to the American dream. What compelled you to write about twentieth-century New York?*

In my daily life, I'm generally obsessed with three things: sex, New York City, and ice cream. Since I'm no good at soft-core pornography, I figured I'd better write about the other two.

Seriously, embarking on a book—be it fiction or nonfiction—is like asking someone to move in with you. You'd better be prepared to want to look at that person for years, even if you're not feeling particularly aroused or inspired at any given moment. There's a myth about us writers, of course, that we just sit down to write and ta-da! Once we're seized by the muse, we're off typing like maniacs. But more often than not, we're awake at 3:00 a.m. worrying the same goddamn sentence or paragraph or scene over and over and over. At those moments, when you're hating yourself and second-guessing everything you're writing—you want to make sure there is still some eternal flame of love there to sustain you through the struggle to the other side. You need that emotional basis, that engine. That's why you have to write about something that turns you on, that fascinates you, that you love.

Me, I'm a made, born, and raised Noo Yawkuh—a cliché in a big, fat, I ♥ NY T-shirt. The city's grimy fingerprints, rhythms, and sensibilities are all threaded through my DNA. I live abroad right now, in a blessed and beautiful country, yet I miss my hometown every day. So I had to make my first novel a valentine to it.

Do you believe that the rags-to-riches story Lillian tells would be possible in today's big cities?

"Rags to riches" has always been a long shot. In the past few decades, we've conflated it with the American dream—which it is not. It's the American fantasy.

The American dream, as I understand it, at least used to be more modest. It was not rags to riches so much as rags to store-bought clothes. Rags to a house and a car. Rags to my children doing better than me. It was the hope that each generation would step up a rung on the socioeconomic ladder.

Whenever I'm back in New York, or Chicago, or Washington, D.C., or San Francisco, I am always encountering new immigrants who are working their butts off—in small businesses, driving taxis, cleaning hotel rooms, taking college classes—and they have big dreams. They tell me they've got a kid graduating from high school, or that they're saving up for a house, or that they have an idea for starting their own company one day. Even in today's lousy economy, they hope and strive. They certainly know that times are bad, but their drive is still fierce. And they seem to make some inroads.

So maybe our original, more human-scale American dream is still possible in our cities, though it's getting tougher and tougher. But rags to riches? That's more on the scale of winning the lottery. Because I'm an American, part of me wants—or even needs—to believe that such a spectacular rise is still possible. And it is, I suppose. But so is winning the lottery. The odds are long. I refuse to speculate.

What are your favorite novels set in New York City?

A few classics, naturally: *The Catcher in the Rye* by J. D. Salinger. Ralph Ellison's *Invisible Man*. *The Collected Short Stories of Dorothy Parker. Manchild in the Promised Land* by Claude Brown.

Otherwise, *The Mambo Kings Play Songs of Love* by Oscar Hijuelos is one of my all-time favorites; reading it made me swoon. Jonathan Lethem's *The Fortress of Solitude* was the first contemporary novel about New York that captured the essence of my own childhood. Although his book is set in Brooklyn, the dicey neighborhood where I grew up in Manhattan had the same vibe, the same street dynamics, the same frisson of excitement, anxiety, racial tensions, danger, possibility, and poetry. He really nailed it.

Richard Price's *Lush Life* is up there, too, along with *What I Loved* by Suri Hustvedt and Mary Gordon's *Spending*—a very sexy novel.

And I'm also a huge sucker for Jack Finney's sentimental time-travel novel, *Time and Again*. I did a radio piece about it for NPR's "My Guilty Pleasure" series a while back. It's a delicious, almost comic book–like read. I go back to it every few years when I'm feeling particularly homesick for New York.